Advance praise for Marilyn Brant and *According to Jane*

"Marilyn Brant's debut novel is proof that Jane Austen never goes out of style. This is a warm, witty and charmingly original story of a woman coming of age and finding her own happy ending—with a little help from the ultimate authority, Jane Austen herself."
—Susan Wiggs, *New York Times* bestselling author

"Entertaining, sincere, real . . . well, okay, that the acclaimed author, Jane Austen, speaks across the centuries to beleaguered romantic Ellie Barnett is not quite *real*, but it is fun. An engaging read for all who have been through the long, dark, dating wars and still believe there's sunshine, and a Mr. Darcy, at the end of the tunnel."
—Cathy Lamb, author of *Henry's Sisters*

" 'Where were the true Darcys?' That's the burning question bookish Ellie Barnett has been asking herself since high school when handsome, charismatic Sam Blaine first captured her heart—and then broke it. In this lively, clever novel by Marilyn Brant, Ellie is accompanied along the perilous path of romance by none other than famed novelist and formidable woman Jane Austen, who, for reasons of her own, has taken up residence in Ellie's head. Ms. Brant wittily parallels the two women's difficult journey to the understanding that love has the power to transform even the most selfish of men into a 'true Darcy.' This is a must-read for Austen lovers as well as for all who believe in the possibility of a happily-ever-after ending."
—Holly Chamberlin, author of *Tuscan Holiday*

According to Jane

MARILYN BRANT

KENSINGTON BOOKS
www.kensingtonbooks.com

KENSINGTON BOOKS are published by

Kensington Publishing Corp.
119 West 40th Street
New York, NY 10018

ISBN-13: 978-0-7582-3461-2
ISBN-10: 0-7582-3461-9

First Kensington Trade Paperback Printing: October 2009
10 9 8 7 6 5 4 3 2 1

Printed in the United States of America

For Jeff, Joe and Andrew
~Incredibly Good Guys~
&
In memory of
Margaret Weigel (1921–2007) and Kim Hintz (1967–2004)
~Inspirations~

ACKNOWLEDGMENTS

Since the road to publication is usually so arduous, meandering and fraught with unexpected twists, writers have ample time to compose (in their heads or on fettuccini-stained restaurant napkins) dissertation-length monologues befitting that of a Shakespearean lead character, during which they describe—in complex, paragraph-long sentences—how exceedingly indebted they are to everyone they've ever met, read a book by or chatted about "Motivation" with online (in their entire lives) for the help given in the writing, acquisition, printing and distribution of their debut novels.

I was *so* not going to be one of those people with the endless lists. Seriously. I was going to do a "brevity is the soul of wit" thing. Heartfelt, but short. Until I started to actually jot down the names of the family members, writing mentors, friends, publishing professionals, librarians and occasional random grocery-store shoppers who've helped me at turning-point moments on this journey and I realized what tremendous teamwork it took to pull this off.

I originally had nine and a half pages. This is the condensed version. So, anyone I may have inadvertently omitted in this draft, please email me and I'll send you the longer edition. (Trust me. Your name is *definitely* on that one. As is the name of every resident in the entire state of Wisconsin.)

First, my infinite thanks to Jane Austen. No, I don't really talk to her, so I'm not sure if she's aware of my gratitude and lifelong admiration. Nevertheless, it's overflowing.

I had the incredible good fortune to join the Chicago-North chapter of RWA, through which I met exceptional authors who also became some of my best friends. Erica O'Rourke, Simone Elkeles, Karen Dale Harris, Laura Moore, Lisa Laing and Jennifer Stevenson—thank you all for reading and critiquing the complete novel and for being so encouraging during every single step toward publication. Erika Danou-Hassan, Sara Daniel, Pamala Knight Duffy,

Ruth Kaufman, Liz Evans, Martha Whitehead and all of my terrific C-N chapter mates—thanks to you, too, for your supportiveness and for sharing in the adventure.

On the National RWA level, I benefited greatly by being a part of the online PRO and PAN loops, by getting to know the Cherries, by being a "Bond Girl" and celebrating milestones with my fellow 007 Golden Heart Finalists and by lucking my way into a blog community full of talented writers, astute readers and enthusiastic Austen fans. I'm also grateful to the *Romantic Times* staff for all I learned as a reviewer, to JASNA for the fun of being surrounded by Janeites, and to the Z-Authors, the Sisters of the Pen and the Girlfriends Cyber Circuit for their guidance and for helping spread the word.

Professionally, I've been so fortunate to have Nephele Tempest as my agent. She believed in this story from the beginning, helped me polish it and worked hard to see it published. The Knight Agency's amazing staff and clients have been behind me at every stage, and I truly appreciate their efforts. As for Kensington Books, I don't think I could've dreamed up an editor more insightful, experienced or supportive than John Scognamiglio. He and the entire publishing team have been ceaseless in their work on this project, from copyediting and publicity to cover art and infinite behind-the-scenes details. Thanks to all of you—we did it!

Here at home, I'm unbelievably lucky to have Sarah Pressly-James, Joyce Twardock, Karen Karris and Pam Russell in my corner. Thanks for your friendship and for your many kindnesses. My dear friend Edna, you've shared your wisdom and your love of literature with me since I was nineteen—I send hugs of love and gratitude from here to Australia for you! My neighbors Jennifer and Heather, I appreciate not only your helpful feedback on my writing but your genuineness and humor. Josh and all our friends from the Y, thanks so much for answering my endless questions. Dorothy Enloe and Raymond Schoen—my writing mentors when I was young and impressionable—you may no longer be with us, but your messages from decades ago are still with me.

Hugs, kisses and colossal thanks to my wonderful family: Mom, for your unwavering encouragement; Dad, for those amazing cliffhanger story endings; Bro, for being the coolest brother imaginable and for helping me build the sound track to every book; Brad, Beth and Dave, for your excitement and interest; my grandparents and extended family for cheering me on (with extra-special thanks to Michelle and Stephanie for your enthusiastic emails); and Joanne, for being as caring as a relative. The love you've all given me through the years is such a gift. The downside? I've been forced to look elsewhere to find prototypes for my most antagonistic characters. (And I can't thank you enough for that!)

Finally, my extraordinarily supportive, loving and generous husband and son—you two made it possible for me to pursue this dream, and you're why I always say "Yes!" when people ask if I'm an optimist. I love you both—even more than ice cream, music, sunshine. . . . Thank you.

Next to being married, a girl likes to be crossed in love a little now and then.

—Jane Austen, *Pride and Prejudice* (1813)

According to Jane

PROLOGUE

In a country neighbourhood you move in a
very confined and unvarying society.

—*Pride and Prejudice*

I always thought Homer painted his character Odysseus as a real
slow learner with that whole twenty-year-journey thing. I mean,
what kind of an idiot needs *two decades* to understand a simple lesson like "Don't be arrogant in the eyes of the gods"? Pretty basic,
once you take out all the hard-to-pronounce Greek names, the
weird epic-poem structure and everything that smacks of immor-
tals playing with magic.

But who am I to talk? For so many years, I, too, *thought* I was
clever. I, too, *thought* I was courageous. I, too, *thought* I'd figured out
all my lessons but, as Jane would say, "I fear this is not so."

See, until this moment, at my wise old age of thirty-four, I had a
long-held theory about my own personal power. An erroneous belief that I had more control over my destiny than I actually have.

But, to prove my point, I can't start explaining from where I am
now. It wouldn't make sense.

Journeys begin where journeys begin . . . and mine began with
big hair, leg warmers and the musty smell of Mrs. Leverson's English class, way back in the mid-1980s when I was all of fifteen.

I was in sophomore lit then—midweek, early November, daydreaming of life after high school—when Sam Blaine made his first
move and Jane Austen made her first comment.

"Ellieeee," the sinfully cute but annoying-as-hell Sam Blaine chanted softly from his seat behind me. "Elllllieee." He walked two of his fingers up the imaginary ladder between my shoulder blades until I shivered.

"Stop it," I hissed. "You're going to get us in trouble."

I scooched forward, trying to focus on Mrs. Leverson's nasal-toned wrap-up lecture of the novel we'd just finished, *Childhood's End*. Although I was pretty sure my childhood had long ended, I resigned myself to acting polite and studious in class if it killed me. I had a reputation to uphold.

Sam, however, had no intention of allowing me to brush him off. Managing to keep his hand out of Mrs. Leverson's line of vision, he snagged my shirt and bra strap with a pinch grip and pulled me back toward him.

"C'mon, Ellie. You know you're as bored as I am." Sam skimmed his fingertips over the spot where my bra's back clasp bulged beneath the cotton fabric. "Tell me your fantasy."

As our teacher gestured with her chubby arms up in front of our suburban Chicago classroom and performed other antics to entice student participation, I thought of my fantasy: Surviving adolescence. Maybe kissing Sam someday. Being a totally cool, in control, woman of the world.

Yeah, right. But I was an optimist in the '80s.

I did not, however, divulge these imaginings to the precocious dark-haired boy who, thanks to the eternal delights of alphabetical order, sat near me in five out of seven classes.

No.

I might lust after Sam. A lot. But I hadn't yet become self-destructive. I knew S-A-M was shorthand for D-A-N-G-E-R.

"In your fantasy, are you groping a guy in the dark, passionately, maybe under the bleachers?" Sam suggested, his voice low. His fingers massaged my spine, channeling toward me all the vigor of a testosterone-driven teen male.

I felt chills—equal parts anxiety and longing—at his touch. I tried to lean away from him again, but he drew me back with one swift motion.

"And are you feeling that guy's hands rubbing *your* body, too?

First, over your clothes, and then"—he paused to stroke his thumb down my bare neck—"underneath them?"

"Cut it *out,* Sam," I whispered over my shoulder, finally breaking away despite my absurd desire for more. Since kindergarten he'd poked me in the back with his pencil tip and badgered me with pesky comments, but this was the first time he'd ever really touched my skin. I didn't know what to make of it.

See, with anyone else I might've thought some tiny crush thing was going on, but I wasn't dealing with a typical, gawky sixteen-year-old boy. This was *Sam Blaine,* a guy who exuded experience even then. A guy who'd morphed into a rare combination of good-looking, athletic, brainy and popular. Versus me, who was, well . . . just brainy. Or, at least, intelligent enough to know I wouldn't rate high on Mr. Cool's "To Date" list.

I sighed, wishing Sam's attentions were sincere, and watched as our teacher wrote the title of our new novel on the chalkboard. *Pride and Prejudice.* Then out came the big box of paperbacks, distributed to us like the slap of breaded chicken patties on our hot-lunch trays.

I picked up my copy. A second later I felt Sam trace a pattern on my arm with his pinky, and I rolled my eyes. Guess he was more bored than usual. Just as I was about to tell him to knock it off yet again, I heard the first *tsk.*

In a panic of self-consciousness, I dropped the book back on my desk and glanced at our classmates. No one seemed to be paying any attention to us in the far-right row. Everyone looked lost in their own daydreams or make-out fantasies or whatever.

But I heard more *tsking.*

"Who said that?" I asked Sam, shooting a look behind me.

"Who said what?"

"The *tsk, tsk* noises."

Sam's forehead crinkled. He motioned me closer and I bent back toward him, a mere three inches away from his mocking blue eyes and those ever-smirking lips. I tried hard to keep my view of him peripheral. Gazing head-on at Sam's striking features always made me sweat.

Another *tsk* came from somewhere in the room.

"That! Did you hear it?" I asked, swiveling around in my seat until I faced him. My eyes darted around in hopes of spotting the *tsker*.

But Sam didn't seem to have heard it. Instead he simply grinned, his hand nudging my left shoulder until I made full eye contact with him. "Must be your subconscious speaking. It's saying—" He tilted his head to the side and squinted as if in deep concentration. "'Ellie Barnett needs more sexual experience or she'll die a virgin.'"

Then his hand slipped lower.

He covertly grazed the side of my left breast with his palm, his fingers daring to dance along the bra's underwire before breaking the connection between us.

I stifled a gasp and stared at him, my mouth agape. For a split second I thought, Did he mean to do that? Was he seriously making a move on me? Then common sense took over, and I knew this had to be one of his little jokes. Sam loved games.

He sent me a smug, defiant look. His hand, an inch away, was still poised for grasping.

Before he could try that trick again, I seized his wrist with my long, strong, meticulously polished fingernails, and I used them as pink claws to dig four crescent-shaped notches into his hairless inner arm. Deep, darkening imprints against that pale skin.

Sam grunted and pulled away. Unfortunately, his moan elicited the attention of our teacher.

"Miss *Barnett*. Mr. *Blaine*." She elongated her syllables with believable menace. "Please flirt on your own time."

The class snickered and my face burned, making me wish I could bolt out the door and hide in the girls' bathroom. I stole a glance at Sam. He didn't quite have the decency to blush, but he slunk down in his seat, obviously displeased at getting caught.

With her reprimand delivered, Mrs. Leverson busied herself locating the handouts for our next novel.

The second she turned her back, Sam hissed in my ear, "Shit, Ellie. Are you trying to scar me for life?" He pointed to the marks on his inner wrist and had the nerve to look indignant.

I fought for a retort that wouldn't get me in trouble. All I could come up with, though, was the really bitchy glare my sister had perfected on my parents, my brother and me.

"Leave me alone, Sam," I managed to say, attempting to replicate the glare. "I mean it."

Of course, I didn't mean it. And Sam knew this.

He was too bright not to have noticed the way I'd studied him all semester, how I sparkled like a mirrored disco ball whenever he paid attention to me. Even getting to second base might've been okay if his interest in me were genuine. And if we were somewhere private.

But Sam did not exude earnestness of any kind, and his motives were nothing if not a complete mystery. He had what the adults called "an attitude," and he was copping it big-time that day.

"You . . . don't . . . want me . . . to . . . touch you?" Sam said, his tone indicating disbelief. He knew I knew that virtually every other girl in our grade would've gladly agreed to be manhandled by him.

But I whispered, "No."

As if guessing the hypocrisy of my words, he narrowed his eyes and opened his mouth. I turned away before he could speak.

Why? Because even then I craved this silly romantic thing. Craved it despite knowing it was stupid. I wanted my first real boyfriend to write me love notes that I could hide in my pocket and reread later. Or hold my hand and dance with me to the latest Journey ballads. Or refuse to tell his friends the exciting things we might do in the back row of a dimly lit movie theater.

I didn't want some guy playing with my emotions for in-school entertainment, especially not the very guy I'd had a secret crush on for eons. No. I wanted pure romantic fantasy. And I got it.

But not from Sam Blaine.

"Our next novel is Jane Austen's *Pride and Prejudice*," Mrs. Leverson informed us, waving her handouts in the air before plopping them on Tanya Hammersley's desk and motioning for her to distribute them. "While Tanya passes these out, take a moment to look at your new novel."

I picked up the book again, flipped to the back cover and scanned it doubtfully: *The sparring of an opinionated young couple in nineteenth-century England creates the classic and enduring romantic theme of* Pride and Prejudice.

Oh, ugh. This hardly sounded like high conflict, but I forced myself to keep reading: *Clever and vivacious Elizabeth Bennet is both drawn to the aloof Mr. Darcy and repulsed by his arrogance, acrid tongue and condescending behavior toward everyone in the neighborhood.*

I imagined using the word "acrid" in a sentence. Like: Sam Blaine deserved to be locked up in a dank dungeon until his groping fingers and his *acrid* tongue disintegrated. Nice, huh?

The passage continued: *Darcy and Elizabeth's lively and unlikely courtship is played out on a genteel stage, with parlor flirtations, assembly-ball intrigues* . . . And blah, blah, blah.

I decided to go ahead, against all clichéd warnings, and judge a book by its cover. It was written too long ago to be any good, despite boasting a *vivacious* heroine who had a name similar to mine. And, anyway, between dealing with the rest of my schoolwork and just making it through the day, my attention span was limited.

Our teacher droned on about the setting and the political climate of Regency England and how dear old Jane spent her days confined to doing dull things like strolling in the park and writing letters, because that was what fine women did back then.

I listened, more or less. But then Mrs. Leverson began telling us about the principal characters in Austen's novel, and the weirdest thing happened.

"Along with Darcy and Elizabeth, George Wickham is an important character to study," she said. "He's a militia officer and his regiment is stationed near the Bennets' family home. As you read your first assignment tonight, pay special attention to the way Austen introduces him and describes his actions."

I was seized by a curiosity I didn't understand about a character I'd never heard of before.

As Mrs. Leverson moved on to secondary players in the story, I flipped through the novel, reading random paragraphs until I saw the first mention of the Wickham guy on page sixty-three. I skimmed the section, getting the flavor of this man who, since he didn't wind up with the heroine at the book's conclusion, couldn't really be as admirable as he seemed, when I heard a lady's voice in my ear.

Beware, Ellie, the voice said before following this up with a decided *tsk* or two. *Sam Blaine is your Mr. Wickham.*

Fear seized my throat and all-out panic gripped my stomach. Okay. Who said that?

I blinked, then glanced wildly in every direction. Even Sam was keeping his distance, for once.

"What?" I said aloud to the unidentified voice. A few students nearby turned their heads to shoot me an odd look.

Sam, sounding sulky, muttered, "Don't look at me. I didn't do anything."

I squinted at him, suspicious.

You would do well to heed my advice, friend, said the voice, and I could've sworn I heard an ironic little laugh right along with an unmistakably British accent. *I am well acquainted with men of his ilk, and they are disinclined to be honourable. You had best keep your distance.*

Not that I doubted her words or anything—she'd nailed Sam's character in a sentence—but this whole hearing voices thing seriously freaked me out. I considered the possibilities:

Maybe I'd been whacked in the head one too many times with a volleyball that week. Gym class had been brutal.

Maybe my depraved sister had slipped some acid into my lunch. My turkey sandwich had tasted a little off.

Maybe I'd been studying too hard. After all, keeping up a 4.0 GPA was draining. Or, maybe—

You are neither ill nor suffering from head injuries, Ellie, the lady's voice said, her tone still amused.

I couldn't believe I was going to respond to this, but, hey, it seemed my life wasn't weird enough already. Even if replying put me into the Potentially Insane category, I needed to know who this woman was and what she was doing in my head.

So I asked, in silence this time, *Who are you?*

I heard the twittery laughter again, but not one of my classmates had uttered a sound.

Why, I am Miss Austen, of course, the voice replied. *But you may call me Jane.*

As you can well imagine, Jane's manifestation in my life created some complications for me at school.

Since I was reasonably sure I'd be sent off to a psych ward if I didn't figure out what was going on, I ignored Mrs. Leverson's structured reading assignments and inhaled the whole novel in two days, snatching moments to polish off a chapter or two between classes, at lunch or late into the night. I was a girl obsessed.

Jane's voice in my head, instead of lessening, grew stronger with every page turned. While she insisted it was too early to explain why or how she'd chosen to inhabit my mind instead of, say, Sam's, Tanya's or Mrs. Leverson's, she sure was right about that Mr. Wickham character. What a prick he turned out to be.

And—fine, call me crazy—I went along with it all. I asked her endless questions, of course, about her sudden appearance in my previously silent mental world. I responded skeptically, sure, to her reticent but ever-proper replies that there was "a good reason" for her being with me (one I was frustratingly unable to pry out of her ghostly lips). But I was an egocentric teenager. I expected to be Special. I expected the Universe to have a Grand Plan for me. And I supposed this Jane thing was part of it.

Or, maybe, I was just really lonely.

Regardless, I got used to Jane being there, real fast. I rejoiced in the secretiveness of our conversations and started to enjoy the company. To count upon it.

As for Jane, she chatted, not constantly, but pointedly. She had her figurative index finger aimed in full accusation at human folly. According to her, there was plenty to criticize about her nineteenth-century era and homeland, and she didn't exactly spare me her sarcastic opinions of my time period.

Take gym class, for instance.

Young ladies engaged in sport with the gentlemen? Jane said that first day, her tone incredulous. *How barbaric.*

I stretched in my assigned spot, wishing I were anywhere else.

"Barbaric" is the word. It's downright gladiator-like. Gym is an endurance test to see how much humiliation you can tolerate before you die.

I see, she replied, but I didn't think she had any idea. Gym was my daily nightmare. Having Jane with me, though, made those forty-two minutes of hell pass far more quickly.

On her second day, she turned her dry wit to the world of academia. And, more specifically, to my place in it.

Our history teacher asked, "Who can name the three-word motto the people of France chanted during the French Revolution?"

I'd read the chapter and could answer this, but I didn't want to be the one to raise my hand. Sam, who was sitting across the aisle from me and knew the answers to everything, ignored the teacher completely and played with the Velcro on his Trapper Keeper. Our teacher, however, shot us pleading looks, and, to me, it felt cruel to refuse to offer him some kind of lifeline. So, I made brief eye contact. Big mistake.

After another twenty seconds of silence, the teacher sighed and said, "Okay, Miss Barnett. Why don't you tell us? We all know *you* know the answer."

The class snickered as I murmured my now obligatory *"liberté, égalité, fraternité,"* and some smart-jock buddy of Sam's whispered, "She can remember *that,* but she can't remember to 'bump, set, spike' in volleyball?"

Sam laughed loudly at that one, as did most of the class, and I vowed then and there never to bail out our history teacher again. But Jane, at least, came to my defense.

Do not be embarrassed, Ellie. Let them enjoy their amusement now. For what do we live, but to make sport for our neighbours, and laugh at them in our turn?

Her confidence grounded me and helped me remember not to take myself so seriously. It was a reminder I desperately needed throughout high school.

And then there was Stacy Daschell, the girl I despised most in our entire sophomore class. On day three, while changing back into our regular clothes after gym, an item Stacy wore beneath her red-and-gold cheerleader's sweater snagged Jane's attention.

Pray, what is that? Jane inquired, her voice horrified.

I didn't own such an item myself, but I'd heard about Stacy's purchase ad nauseam that week. *It's a lavender Victoria's Secret demi bra. Heavily padded*, I answered silently.

The slender, pointy-nosed Stacy, who'd recently returned from a trip to San Francisco where she'd encountered the first of these soon-to-be-famous stores, swept a cascade of blond curls off her shoulder, giggled seductively at her mirror image across the room and showed off her orthodontically perfect incisors right along with her enhanced cleavage. "It's called the 'Emma,'" Stacy informed her friends. "Pretty cool, huh?"

Jane sniffed. *Strumpet.*

My good friend Terrie, in an independent assessment at her locker next to mine, used the modern American equivalent. "Slut."

I laughed at their comments and, consequently, was rewarded with an extra-nasty sneer from Stacy.

Then she, with her Victoria's Secret uplift and her cheerleader's outfit snugly back on, adjusted her leg warmers, slipped on her gold-glittered Nikes and blotted her hot-pink lipstick with a tissue as she tracked my far-less-fashionable footsteps down the hallway toward algebra.

Unfortunately, coming from the opposite direction strode my *other* worst nightmare.

A gaggle of senior girls materialized like a firewall, blocking our path. There were four of them—all big hair, big boobs, big attitude. The leader crossed her arms over a thin, low-cut sweater, which emphasized her abundant chest, and nudged one of the other girls to speak.

A leggy blonde—more specifically, Stacy's older sister—turned to Stacy. "Where do you think *you're* off to?"

"Math," Stacy said with a weary flip of her hair. She tossed a disgusted look in my direction. And, though she was failing algebra, she added, "Anything's better than gym class with losers."

The seniors cackled and broke the human wall open just wide enough to let Stacy pass through.

"Well?" another girl said, expecting me to defend myself.

I kept my mouth shut. There was no way to win this kind of battle. I could only wait it out.

Their leader finally stepped forward, shaking her head so the long ash-brown strands brushed her shoulders. Her squinty eyes glittered with general malevolence, her expression pure scorn.

"Ellie, Ellie, Ellie Barnett," she said. "What exactly is your problem? How is it that you're so *competent* with classroom shit, so very *responsible* in your stupid little academic life, but such a fuck-up in everything else?"

Jane chose this inopportune moment to chime in. *This young woman hardly seems a paragon of virtue. What manner of conduct is this?*

I clutched my algebra notebook and pencil a little tighter, but I didn't answer either of their questions.

"You're becoming quite a legend at school," the leader said with her trademark mockery. She scanned me up and down, rolled her eyes and burst out laughing. "Just look at you! Scraggly hair. Dressed like a geek. No makeup. Digging yourself into a hole of permanent unpopularity. Sometimes I can't stand to be in the same hallway with you. Make an attempt to get with it or I'll make you sorry. You know I can."

Oh, yeah. I knew.

The two-minute bell rang and, with a taunting shove to my shoulder, an "accidental" treading upon my left toes and an intimidating parting glare, the leader and her gang finally let me go. I hobbled the rest of the way down the hall.

How deplorable, Jane whispered, and I could envision her pursing her thin lips with disdain. *Who is this individual?*

Oh, she would be last year's Homecoming Queen and this year's titleholder for Most Likely to Get Laid on a First Date, I said. The leader had been away for two days on a college scouting trip and Jane hadn't encountered her before. I envied Jane that, inhaled deeply and tried my hardest to laugh off the incident.

But, even this early on, Jane had developed an unnerving habit of persistence. *By what proper name is that young lady called?*

Ah, well, if you must know, most people call her Di, but her full name is

Diana Lynn Barnett. I paused for dramatic effect. *Otherwise known as my big sister.*

Just then, I saw Sam on the other side of the hallway eyeing me strangely before breaking into one of his smirkiest grins. With his index and middle fingers, he made a V for victory, which he held above his head, since his team had just annihilated mine in volleyball. Again. Then he switched the fingers around—index and thumb—to form an L for loser, which he directed at me.

God! Why did I still like that guy? He was too competitive, too arrogant, too intense for me, or so I tried to tell my bruised ego. He added too many distractions to my already complicated life but, stupidly, I couldn't quite let go of my fantasies about him.

At the same moment, this other guy, a hotshot basketball player named Jason Bertignoli, walked by, too. He'd been on my losing volleyball team, but he didn't blame me or mock me or ignore me. He turned around and said, "Don't worry about the game, Ellie. We'll get 'em next time."

I smiled. Jocky Jason was nice. Then again, he was new to the school and still being nice to everybody.

Sam saw Jason talking to me, and he sent us the evil eye, which did not go unnoticed by either Jason or by Jane.

Wickham, Jane said.

"Asshole," Jason muttered, glaring at Sam as he walked away.

As for me, I sent Sam the evil eye right back before he disappeared down the hall.

Little did I know, as my irrational heart trailed after him, that I'd just embarked on the Odyssey-like saga that would set the course of my romantic journey for the next two decades. . . .

🔹 1 🔹

There is meanness in *all* the arts which
ladies sometimes condescend to employ for
captivation. Whatever bears affinity to
cunning is despicable.

—*Pride and Prejudice*

Almost seven years after Jane first spoke to me, the August late-afternoon sun beat down on my head as I bolted from the Glen Forest Public Library. We'd been short-staffed again, with two people out on vacation and one last-minute sick call. And, while I loved my summer job—well, most of the time—my day hadn't been the greatest, and I yearned for a calm, relaxing evening.

Dominic, my boyfriend of eight whole weeks, had other plans.

"Can we take your car tonight?" he asked when he came to pick me up. "I'm running kinda low on gas and—" He glared at his beat-up Pontiac. "I don't trust the transmission."

I shrugged. "Fine," I said, though it wasn't really fine. We were going into Chicago—*again*—because he just had to meet with his loud, pseudo-radical friends who liked to think of themselves as "mavericks."

"We'll only stay at the bar for an hour," he promised when I told him I had a massive headache and wanted a quiet night. "Then we'll grab a couple slices of pizza at the restaurant next door. Just you and me."

I wanted to believe him, but the reality was he couldn't get enough of his discussion group. Once they started yakking, one hour had a way of turning into four. I wasn't in the mood this time.

Not that I wanted to deprive him of his friends and make him cling only to me. He'd explained that this group was his lifeline, particularly during the summer months, since he was away from his nonconformist college buddies and living with his parents a couple of suburbs over. Unlike me, though, he'd get to see his university friends again in the fall. At nearly twenty-two, I'd just graduated. Dominic, already twenty-three, was on the five- or six-year plan.

"But what about the guys at work?" I'd asked him a month before when we were at my sister's wedding to her punk-rocker/bank-manager boyfriend Alex Evans (i.e., irrefutable proof that there was a psycho out there for everyone). "I thought you all got along really well, especially since your neighbor and his cousin got you the job. Don't you ever want to do things with them?"

"Nah. Besides, I quit on Tuesday."

My eyes flew open at this news. "You quit the deli?" He'd only been working there a few weeks, but his hourly salary had been higher than mine at the library. "I thought you liked it there."

"The work wasn't that challenging." He wrinkled his nose. "I'd rather do something where I can use my mind, not just slice up salami or provolone, you know? I'll get some other position in a week or two."

But he hadn't and, therefore, he claimed he especially needed the outlet of meeting his friends after a stressful day of dealing with his nagging parents and their demands that he "grow up."

So we went to Chicago.

"Can you spot me a five for a beer?" Dominic asked when we got to The Bitter Tap. "It doesn't look real sociable if I don't have one in my hand, too."

I sighed, but I bought him a beer and got myself a Long Island Iced Tea. Then I sat at the edge of the table, had a private conversation with Jane about the merits of combining multiple liquors in a single mixed drink, and listened to snatches of Dominic's latest discussion. Something about the ethics of genetic engineering. One of the guys pulled out a pack of cigarettes and offered them to us.

"No, thanks," I said, but Dominic reached for one and lit it expertly. He waved it as he made each point, his face aglow with that feverish excitement I'd found so intriguing when first I spotted him in my final college semester's Films & Lit class.

He'd always hop on his soapbox, saying things like: "We're privileged to be part of society's free thinkers. We need to help others shape their understanding of our world while keeping it a positive, affirmative kind of activism. And it's all here, you know. The change." He'd jab his thumb at his chest. "Here is where we need to make our decisions about the way we organize our culture. Not from pure intellect. Not from our pocketbook. Not from the restricted mores of our narrow-minded predecessors who call us 'radicals'—like it's a bad thing." He'd roll his eyes at the absurdity. "It's only through a continuous dialogue about our creative and cultural life that we can achieve the kind of human connection we all seek."

It was still mesmerizing to watch him get into a debate, like a televangelist preaching the Word of God.

He smoked five more cigarettes and mooched another beer off someone else before the first hour was up. I checked my watch and made polite conversation. An hour and fifteen minutes. An hour and a half. Still no sign of him wrapping things up. Time for a nudge.

"Dominic." I tapped my wrist.

He nodded at me, held up his index finger in the Just-One-More-Minute position and resumed talking. For another half hour.

Granted, I was tired, I was cranky and, now, I was hungry, too. I may not have been in the cheeriest of moods starting off, but that didn't mean he could worm out of a promise, so I said, "Dominic, it's been two hours."

"Okay, okay. Just five more minutes. Please. Let me finish this thought."

I picked up my purse, waved goodbye to the guys and walked out the door.

I heard a "Shit!" from inside the bar and, a moment later, Dominic was by my side looking furious.

"Dammit, Ellie, that was so fucking rude!"

"You said one hour. I waited twice that long. I've had enough now, and I'm going home. Come. Don't come." I shrugged. "It's your choice."

"I—" Dominic looked between me and the door to The Bitter Tap, clearly considering. "Look, sorry. I just . . . I just really love being in that environment, and I'm . . . surprised, I guess, that you don't, too." He gave me a hurt look. "Those guys are my best friends."

I nodded. "Well, perhaps one of them can give you a lift home." I turned and walked toward my car.

"Ellie. Wait." He ran up behind me and put his hand on my shoulder, caressing it with his fingertips. "Let's get a slice of pizza for the road. It's just right here." He pointed to the Italian carryout joint next door. "I know you've gotta be starving."

Not wanting to make a huge scene on the sidewalk, I agreed and, of course, I knew that also meant I had to spring for the food. It may have taken me almost two months of dating this cretin, but I was starting to see a pattern here.

When I got home I watched the taillights of Dominic's Pontiac fade away into the distance, and I thought about our deteriorating relationship. Who I was. Who he was. Where we were going. Or not going. I'd almost broken up with him an hour before, but I'd held on. Why, why, why?

Perhaps it is because you feel lonely? Jane suggested.

Yeah.

And because you are about to embark on something unknown next month—your graduate studies at a new university—and you crave the familiar?

Yeah. That, too.

And, additionally, because you will be two-and-twenty next week and wish to celebrate it with someone dear to you?

I didn't speak, but I nodded. I should've known Jane would figure it out. She'd been my constant companion, my most secret friend for years. She knew me as no one else could . . . or wanted to.

All will turn out right, Ellie, she said softly. *Trust in yourself and in your instincts. You have a strong intuition about the honour and character of others. It is stronger, perhaps, than you realize, and it gains further strength with time and experience. Do not despair.*

Thanks, Jane, I whispered, fighting back the despair that curled in my stomach nevertheless.

So, a week later, when I found myself sitting at that same Chicago bar, after being promised a romantic birthday dinner we were already thirty minutes late for, I took a good long look around me:

I was in a place I didn't want to be, with people who talked about big change but did nothing.

I was dating a man who, while attractive and reasonably intelligent, didn't appreciate me, and who was also part leech.

I was exactly twenty-two (as of 8:28 that morning), unmarried, inhaling secondhand smoke, bored, frustrated and hungry.

The evening couldn't get any worse.

I grabbed my second white wine at the bar and took a turn about the room—sipping my drink, chitchatting idly with Jane, glancing at the framed autographs hanging crookedly on the walls and contemplating Dominic's untimely death.

The driving beat of a Def Leppard song came on, competing with the ambient noise, and I felt a gust of hot summer wind next to me as the front door swung open. The woman who walked through it was about my age and height, only really stunning. Her hair was a long, soft auburn that curled at the ends like some L'Oréal hair-color model. She seemed as gleeful walking into The Bitter Tap as I'd be if I could walk out of it. A tall, dark-haired man followed her inside, and I looked away.

Then I looked back.

Holy shit.

There'd been times since high school ended, times over the past four years—indeed, a great *many* times—when I'd wondered what I'd say or do if I ever ran into the loathsome Sam Blaine again.

I imagined myself holding my head high and carrying on with whatever I was doing without acknowledging his presence.

Or, I thought I might lift an elegant eyebrow in greeting and say with perfect indifference, "Is that you, Sam? I hardly recognized you. You look shorter."

Or, maybe, I'd be in the midst of laughing over something hysterically funny when someone else would break in and introduce us. I'd shake his hand and pretend not to remember him until he insisted we'd gone to kindergarten and all twelve grades of school together. And that we'd spent one really memorable night in each other's arms . . . a night that had inexorably shaped my view of love. Then I'd reply with an amused "Oh, yeah. *Sam*. That's right. Sorry, your name slipped my mind."

That night, in sad reality, I stood utterly still and gaped at him.

He moved toward me and, as recognition dawned, his handsome features contorted into a look of pure horror.

My God. I must've looked pitiful.

Turn away, Jane commanded. *You need not speak to him.*

But I couldn't make myself turn away.

"Ellie?" he said.

"Sam." His name came out of my open mouth with a veritable squeak.

He cleared his throat. "I'm surprised to see you. I almost didn't recognize you."

I laughed aloud, and Sam shot me an odd look. Yeah. Irony was a bitch.

"Same here," I said, though we both knew better. I pointed to the auburn-haired chick, who'd been watching our exchange curiously. "Your girlfriend?"

He nodded and introduced me to Camryn, a fellow future med student with sharp, assessing green eyes in addition to all that TV-commercial-worthy hair.

Dominic, of all people, chose this particular instant to stride up to us and lay his hand on my shoulder. "Hey, darlin'," he said to me, but he fixed his gaze on Sam and Camryn. "We'll be outta here in just a couple of minutes. Mick's trying to find an article for me in his bag."

He pointed in his buddies' direction, where Mick alternately puffed on a cigarette and dug through a rumpled backpack. I knew this task would take another half hour at least.

"We've gotta get you to your birthday dinner," Dominic continued, punctuating his bald-faced lie with a possessive squeeze.

I forced a grin at the jerk. "Take your time, um, sweetie."

Dominic looked back at me, his eyes widening in surprise. "Uh, thanks." He nodded to the couple in front of us. "Hi. I'm Dominic, Ellie's boyfriend. You guys old friends?"

Camryn started to shake her head, but Sam said, "Yeah," before she or I could reply. "Very old," he added.

"Yep. Ancient-history old." I smiled toothily at the other three and took a long swig of my wimpy wine. Crap. I wanted a margarita *now*, heavy on the Jose Cuervo Gold. If ever there was a time for strong drinks, this was it.

Do whatever you must, Jane said, with hot fury in her voice, *but get away from that despicable man.*

I wanted to listen to her. I really did. But my feet were rooted to the spot for the duration.

Camryn's gaze ping-ponged between her boyfriend's face and mine. Her green eyes narrowed. "Pleasure meeting you both," she said to Dominic and me, her gritted teeth indicating her definitive lack of enthusiasm. "But I've been waiting all day for a daiquiri, so, we'll see you later. Enjoy your birthday . . . Emmy."

"It's Ellie," Sam said, beating me to it.

Camryn cast him a lethal look and began to walk away.

Hmm. So that was how it was.

Sam opened his mouth but then closed it again. He lifted his arm up in a half wave and followed his girlfriend to the bar.

Dominic squinted after them, turned back to me and shot me a puzzled look before rejoining his fellow mavericks.

Jane, who'd begun ranting with fervor since Sam appeared on the scene, scarcely paused for a breath between words. *That rake! That rogue! The nerve of him to cross your path again after what he did. How insupportable!*

I let her continue her tirade of antiquated English insults a while longer, but the combination of seeing Sam again and Jane's marked displeasure had given me the headache from hell. Swift action was required. With a sigh, I told Jane to *please* calm down and gulped the rest of my drink. It was going to take an act of God to stop me from getting one very necessary and immediate jumbo birthday margarita. For medicinal purposes.

I sized up the people sitting at the bar, scanning for a good spot to squeeze in. Sam and Camryn were up there, and they'd just ordered their drinks. I watched the bartender hand Camryn a pink daiquiri with a cutesy umbrella. He passed a foamy beer to Sam.

I hoped they'd sit down. At a dark table. Preferably in some other bar. Like one in downtown Pittsburgh. (Too close?) Then I could get a jigger of fortifying tequila in peace. But they seemed ensconced where they were, leaning up against the padded side of the bar, facing each other. And I was getting desperate.

I pushed the smoky air out of my lungs, edged up to the corner of the bar's counter and tried to blend in with the other patrons.

"What'll you have, Ellie?" the bartender boomed in a jovial voice.

I gave him my margarita order, attempting to concentrate only on the task at hand. I studied the bartender who, after a dozen of my visits, had spent more time talking to me at The Bitter Tap than my own boyfriend. He was a nice guy. About thirty. Slightly overweight. Smooth, cocoa-colored skin. Always wore a gold chain around his neck and a warm smile. I worked hard to keep my attention focused on his friendly face.

But the ever-obsessed psycho in me wouldn't take the hint.

My gaze kept drifting to Sam's beer glass, the way he held it and brought it to his lips. I hadn't forgotten a single detail about Sam's mouth, his hands. My cheeks warmed at the memory of those inquisitive fingers touching my body that long-ago night, then they burned as I remembered the shame and hurt that followed.

I got my drink and licked the salt off half the rim before taking my first swallow. The sting of tequila short-circuited my senses for, maybe, thirteen seconds. Not long enough.

I glanced at Dominic, who'd returned to pontificating about some post–Cold War, Baltic-immigration policy that apparently had international significance, then over at Sam again, who was staring right at me, his jaw tense.

I looked away.

Can't say I was proud to admit this, but I was still really mad at Sam.

Well, no. That would be a prime example of my ability to utilize subtlety and massive understatement, which had proved helpful in my university lit courses. Long live English majors.

More accurately, I was insanely, unrelentingly furious over the way he'd let things end between us. I wasn't over it, like I should've been. I hadn't moved on, like a true adult would have.

In fact, four years after that particularly painful one-night stand, I'd go so far as to claim I felt *more* pissed off there in the bar than I'd been back then. And that was saying something.

Clearly, these thoughts didn't reflect well upon my maturity level. I knew I should've grown up, walked away, traveled on, let it all go—or, at least, chosen to go into denial or therapy. But, see, a Zen-like acceptance of my fate just wasn't my reality.

As I watched Sam steal glances at me while lounging at the bar with Camryn, I had only one prevailing thought—I wanted to get bloody even with him. A few related thoughts followed:

I wanted to extract some serious revenge in return for the emotional damages I'd suffered that last week of senior year in high school.

I wanted him to endure, if only for one day, a fraction as much hurt as I'd felt.

I wanted to make his life such a living hell that night that he'd wake up in the morning clutching his ribs, feeling agonizing stabs of pain where his heart should've been.

I wanted his whole body to ache from the emotional torment. Just like mine had.

I was a really nice person, huh?

I shrugged to myself. Having once come so close to loving Sam, no degree of hatred seemed too extreme or even remotely unjustified.

However, before I could work out my best strategy for dismembering his life piece by piece, I decided I needed another gulp of my drink. When I lowered the glass from my lips, Camryn was standing right in front of me.

"Look," she said, her voice chilly, "Sam's in the bathroom. I've only got a minute, so I'll say this fast. He's taken." She paused, leveling those green eyes at me with utter gravity. "I saw the looks that passed between you two. I don't know your history with him but, whatever it was, it's over now and he's with me."

A granule of salt must've caught in my throat because I had to cough a few times before I could laugh. "Camryn," I said between cough-laugh spasms, "I am *so* not after him. He's *all* yours, and I sincerely wish you the best of luck because, honey, you're gonna need it." I took another sip.

Her eyes narrowed. "Why do you say that?"

A glimmer of a strategy started to coagulate at the fringes of my mind. A devious one, true, but both drinking to excess and being around Sam had a way of bringing out the worst in me.

Again, I told Jane to calm down. (She wasn't letting up on the ranting.) I assured her I was doing all right and had the situation under control. Really.

Then I smiled sweetly at Camryn. "You each got into med school, right?"

"Right," Camryn said.

"The *same* med school?"

"No."

"The same *city*, at least?"

She shook her head and the gorgeous dark red tresses swayed like weeping willows. "But he'll be in New York, and I'll be in Philadelphia. They're not that far apart. We may be busy, but we'll see each other on some weekends and—"

"When do you leave?"

She pressed her lips together and her grip on her daiquiri tightened. "The end of the month. Why?"

"He'll break things off before then," I told her, my voice projecting a certainty I didn't feel in truth, but I made sure I sounded believable.

She tried to shrug it off. "Just because you couldn't hold on to him doesn't mean I—"

"Has he told you he loves you?"

"I don't have to answer that," she shot back.

"Fine, don't answer. Just think. Has he made you any promises? Or, when you bring up the future, does he deflect your questions?" I stopped for a long swallow of margarita.

Camryn remained silent, a cloud of uncertainty darkening her eyes.

I pressed on. "How about this—does he hide his feelings behind a façade of arrogance and cleverness, so you never really know what he's thinking? Does he enjoy the sex, but always keep a barrier between you? I'm talking emotional, not prophylactic," I clarified, although Camryn was, I gathered, a smart enough cookie to figure it out.

The slight pallor of her complexion let me know I'd hit a nerve. This should've made me feel guilty. But, guess what? It didn't.

"You seem like a very intelligent person," I told her with measured condescension, "but even clever girls make mistakes in judgment sometimes. No one would blame you if you got taken in by him. Temporarily. Although, knowing the truth, one has to wonder why you'd put up with it for—"

"What the hell *is* this?" a furious male voice demanded.

Sam.

Camryn and I swiveled toward him. "Back so soon?" I said.

Sam's eyes sparked with blue fire. Guess he'd overheard some of our conversation. Oops.

He speared me with a glare, then turned to his girlfriend. "Seems Ellie has become a bitter, spiteful person who never forgets the stupid things that happened in the past, and she can't see beyond her own issues and biases. Oh, *and*—" he said and glowered at me again, "she has a history of lusting after loser guys like Jason Bertignoli, for God's sake, so her judgment is questionable."

Every syllable leaving his mouth jabbed me like a stiletto to the heart. He thought our night together was a "stupid thing." God damn him. But, yeah, he was right about my judgment being bad. After all, I'd practically fallen in love with him.

He returned his gaze to Camryn. "So, regardless of what she's told you, just because she and I had no way of working things out four fucking *years* ago—" He paused to frown at me. "It doesn't mean it'll be the same with us." He reached for Camryn's arm.

She snatched her arm away. "What went wrong?" she asked him.

"What?"

"'Four fucking *years* ago,' Sam. What went wrong? How did it end?"

"Yeah, Sam," I chimed in. "Tell her. Please. And, while you're at it, I'd appreciate an illuminated recap because I was kind of deprived of your high-level reasoning back then." I drained my drink, set the glass on the counter and crossed my arms to keep them from trembling. "Whenever you're ready."

Sam looked between us, an expression of incredulousness on his handsome face. "I can't believe this," he muttered. "I am *not* doing this. Here. Now. With either of you."

"So, she wasn't lying then," Camryn said, her voice turning several degrees colder. "You really did something to warrant her anger and total bitchiness."

Total bitchiness? "Hey," I said. "I'm not being—"

She pointed a well-manicured fingernail at me. "You shut up. You've caused enough trouble."

Then she scowled at Sam. "Were you planning to break up with me this month? Is that why, no matter how many times I asked you about Labor Day plans or whose house we'd meet at for Thanksgiving, you kept putting me off? Is that why you couldn't commit to going to my brother's wedding in October? Why you kept saying, 'We'll see, Camryn,' every time I brought it up?"

Sam stared at her. So did I.

"Answer me, dammit!" she shrieked.

He exhaled long and hard. "Camryn, please. Let's go somewhere else and discuss this rationally. I don't want—"

"No! I want to know *now*. I don't want you trying to weasel out of it again."

Sam shrugged, but his shoulders looked so stiff I thought they'd crack from the motion.

"Okay, fine," he told her. "The thing is, I don't know about the wedding. I don't have a clue what our schedules are going to look like then. We'll both probably be up to our ears in work. You know as well as I do that's what med school is all about."

"We're talking about two national holidays, Sam, and one once-in-a-lifetime event. Three lousy days out of four months." She twisted her fingers together into a warped steeple. "I told my *family* all about you. They wanted to meet you. I told them you might be someone they'd be glad they got to know. Someone I might have in my life . . ." A few tears dropped from her eyes, making the green even brighter. She swiped them away viciously and bit her lower lip.

I took a step away from the two of them. I didn't belong in the middle of this and, I'll admit, I was beginning to feel a few pinches of remorse for my—how did Camryn put it? Oh, yes. My anger and total bitchiness.

I took another step back but, in a flash, I was pulled nose-to-nose with Sam.

"Don't. You. Dare. Leave," he said in a low, very dangerous voice, his clenched fist full of my pink light-knit shirt. "If we're having a public confession session, you're damn well going to be a part of it, Ellie Barnett."

I swallowed and looked into his enraged face. He hadn't changed much, really, in the years since I'd last seen him this close up. His skin was a little tauter now, perhaps. His bone structure a bit more defined. His hair a fraction shorter. His muscles a tad firmer. His eyes were the same cool blue, though, with maybe a hint more malice.

Jane cried out, *Make him release you. Insufferable man!*

"Let go of my shirt, Sam," I managed to say in what I hoped was a composed and level voice. Inside, though, every part of me quivered, and I couldn't figure out the reason. Fear? Shame? Anger? Jane's unaltered disdain? All of the above or something else entirely?

Sam released me, but his eyes didn't let me go. They trained on me with a wrath I hadn't been the recipient of since, well, since high school.

Camryn's response to this little scene bespoke a different reaction altogether. She no longer looked infuriated, just deflated. Disappointed. Sad and kind of hurt. "You don't love me, Sam. And you're not going to, are you?" She didn't wait for his answer. "I'll take a cab home."

"Aw, Camryn, c'mon." Sam tried to touch her again and, again, she pulled away.

"No," she said.

"Can't we at least talk? Can I call you tonight? Tomorrow?"

She gave a short, humorless laugh. "We'll see, Sam." She turned and marched out of the bar.

Sam stared after her in stunned silence.

I should've shut up, but I was slightly toasted. So, I said, "Well? Get going. Aren't you gonna run after her? Aren't you gonna tell her you love her and that you really *do* want to go with her to her brother's stupid wedding?"

My hands shook. To stop them, I squeezed my fists so hard my fingernails dug deep into my palms. I looked at them and saw those familiar crescent-shaped welts. Visible signs of a habit I'd never broken.

"I don't love her."

"What?" I glanced up from my hands to study Sam's face, now shuttered against all emotion.

"I'm not going to run after her because I don't love her. But"—he gave me a frozen glare—"I really did *like* her. She's bright, funny, a little high-maintenance, maybe, but a good person underneath the cool exterior. And you had no business at all doing what you did. That was heartless, Ellie."

My breath caught in my esophagus. "*I'm* heartless? Me? Screw you, Sam—"

He raised a brow. "So, your relationship with that Dominic dude is real wonderful, eh?" he said, implying with a tilt of his head that he didn't think so. "You two have got it all together? You're *happy*?"

"It—it's pretty good," I lied.

His eyes traveled down my body and then back up again. "How good?"

Intolerable rudeness, Jane muttered, along with a few other choice phrases.

I mentally turned down the volume on her complaints and swallowed. "Don't be an ass," I said to Sam.

"Don't sidestep the question," Sam shot back.

"It's better than it was with you," I retorted before I lost my nerve. No doubt I'd burn in hell for all the lies I'd been telling, but I couldn't let Sam know the truth. He already had too much dirt on the real me.

Sam pressed his lips together until they were nearly colorless. He then focused the intensity of his gaze on Dominic, whom we spotted chugging the last of his beer and bumming a smoke off of Mick.

"Hey, Dominic!" Mick called out, too loudly because he was, as usual, thoroughly smashed. "Maybe you can score some more cash off your girlfriend and get us another coupla beers." He blindly looked around. "Where is Miss Moneybags anyway? She didn't take off on you again, did she?"

I sucked in some air and hoped, no, prayed that Dominic would take offense at Mick's words. That he'd say, even if only for appearances' sake, that he appreciated lots of qualities in me, not just my willingness to share my paycheck.

But Dominic said, also too loudly, "By the bar, I think. I'll go ask her in a sec."

As their voices floated back to Sam and me, I closed my eyes. I had to block out Sam's steady gaze. I didn't want to see that look of his, be it retribution or pity.

"So, that's how it is," Sam whispered, not unkindly, just very matter-of-fact.

My injured pride made me want to lash out at someone. At Sam. At Dominic. At anyone who crossed my path. Being that Sam was my only choice at present, I started with him.

"You know," I said in the iciest tone I could produce, "it's amazingly hypocritical of you, doing the medicine thing. I mean, I always thought doctors had to take an oath—'First, do no harm,' or something like that." I shook my head. "That's gonna be a tough one for you, considering your tremendous skill in hurting people."

I glanced at him once to see if I'd hit my target. I had. His face colored red and his jaw turned even more rigid. At first I thought he merely looked angry, but then I looked again. The expression in his blue eyes exposed as much worry as it did offense. I guessed I'd found a way to blister one of his insecurities while meting out my revenge.

Unfortunately, it didn't make me feel any better.

"When did you turn into this, this . . . person, Ellie?" he asked softly. "You're not who I remember. God, this can't all be because of me or what happened between us. Because I hurt you once, can it?"

I forced myself to stand up straighter. "Hey, you were the one who called what happened between us a 'stupid thing' from the past. What makes you think it'd affect me or that I'd care about it now?"

"Jesus, Ellie." His expression turned to one of pure pain. "I meant my idiotic reaction in school *after* what happened. *That* was the stupid thing you wouldn't forget . . ."

Sam's words still dangled in the air between us as Dominic jogged up ten seconds later. "Hey, darlin'," he said. "Seeing as how you're having a deep discussion of your own right now, maybe we could hang out here a little longer?"

My mind, reeling from Sam's revelation and the consequent reinterpretation of those end-of-high-school memories, couldn't shift gears so quickly. I knew Dominic wanted something, as usual, but I was in no mood to offer a light, agreeable response. I just stared at him.

Dominic glanced between Sam and me, but received only silence back from us. "Hmm. Are you getting hungry?" He studied his watch. "We've kinda missed our dinner reservation, but I'll order us up some nachos at the bar. Maybe a few beers, too."

"Thanks," I said flatly. After all these weeks he still didn't remember that I detested beer.

"But, uh—"

"Yeah?" I wanted to hear him ask for it this time. I wasn't just going to hand him another twenty.

Dominic turned to Sam. "Could you excuse us a minute? I need to talk to Ellie privately."

Sam raised both eyebrows and folded his arms across his broad chest. He didn't budge from his spot.

I silently blessed him for this, and even Jane, to my shock, murmured, *Correctly done, Mr. Blaine. For once.*

Dominic squinted at him and said, "Okaaaay" under his breath. Then he tugged on my arm. "Can we go over there for a sec—"

"I don't think so," I told him.

Dominic looked confused. "What? You don't think you can talk to me alone for a minute?"

"That's right." I sighed. It was crash-and-burn time for Type #4 (yes, I had categories for the men I dated), but a woman had to know when she couldn't fake it anymore. Since Sam had already guessed the truth, I'd been defeated on all fronts. No use pretending.

Dominic sputtered out a few incoherent syllables, but he finally managed to say, "What the hell?"

I let out a long, slow breath—one I'd been holding for about four years. "I'm sorry, Sam," I said.

Sam's eyes met mine. He half nodded and whispered, "Me, too. Really."

I then returned my attention to Dominic, who was staring at me like I'd just sprouted horns and was brandishing a sharp-'n'-shiny pitchfork.

"I'm not your chauffeur, your mommy or your meal ticket," I told him. "Get yourself a job and buy your own damn beer. And, in case there's any doubt, no, I'm not driving you home and, yes, this is goodbye. Have a nice life."

"Wait! Is this because I didn't buy you a birthday gift?" Dominic demanded. "Ellie, I *told* you I'd take you out to dinner. We were just running a little late tonight. It's not like we won't go sometime soon—"

I lifted my hand in a parting wave to Sam, who returned it. Then I gave Dominic the finger.

"Happy birthday to me," I said to myself as the bar doors swung shut behind me. I inhaled the warm Chicago night air and escaped into my car, planning to drive only a block or two so Dominic couldn't find me. I needed to sit somewhere for an hour and let everything wear off.

Happy birthday, Ellie, Jane's voice echoed in my mind. *And good for you. Your life is just beginning.*

Yes, it was. Finally.

I blinked back a tear, hummed a few bars of Boston's "Don't Look Back" and hit the gas pedal.

❧ 2 ❧

There is nothing like dancing after
all . . . one of the first refinements of
polished societies.

—*Pride and Prejudice*

To know what, exactly, I *wasn't* looking back on and to understand the intricacies of my relationships with my sister Diana,
my brother Gregory and my cousin Angelique, you'd need a detailed chronicle of our family dynamics. I don't have the patience
(or the lifespan) to be that comprehensive.

Let's just say, though, that while Jane's appearance added a new
zing to my home/school existence and bestowed upon me an
amazing best friend, it made life instantly tougher for me, too.

The weekend after Jane's arrival, I was awakened early by a
jostling—or, more accurately, a violent shaking—of my rib cage.

"Get up, geek," Di said, moving away from my body to flick up
the window shade and flood my room with unwelcome sunlight.
"Aunt Candice, Uncle Craig and our freak-show cousins are coming, remember? Get your butt outta bed."

I groaned. Yes, because Di's method of rousing lacked finesse,
but also because any amount of time spent with our Indiana
cousins was, and always had been, a trial of the highest order.

I tossed on some clean sweats and stumbled into the family
room. My mother, already coiffed and lipsticked, raced between the
kitchen and every other room in the house issuing commands.
"Girls, get rid of this clutter on the kitchen table. Now! Throw

that garbage out. And, for God's sake, Gregory, put away that stupid Rubik's Cube! They're going to be here in twenty minutes."

We, thus, began a frantic attempt at picking up our stuff. As we worked, my brother warbled a version of *The Music Man*'s "Gary, Indiana" under his breath followed by a few choruses of "Pick-a-Little, Talk-a-Little." The former was a depiction of my aunt's hometown, the latter, her conversational style.

Di countered his thirteen-year-old notion of musical coolness with her own seventeen-year-old version: Madonna's "Like a Virgin." Normally, I would've tried to zone out, but Jane's newfound residence inside my head made that an impossibility.

Jane, ever the witty conversationalist, remarked, *Transcendent talent is not so rare as was once believed. Apparently, everyone these days has been blessed by the muses.*

Yeah, I'm feeling real inspired right now, I said to her.

She laughed. *Oh, do not judge them too harshly, Ellie. They would have been great proficients . . .*

. . . if ever they'd learnt, we finished together in a sentence reminiscent of one of Jane's more obnoxious book characters.

I giggled aloud. Unfortunately, I was within Di's earshot.

She elbowed me. "Don't laugh at me, geek."

"Diana, try not to call your sister names," our mom bellowed from the kitchen.

"But she *is* a geek," Gregory offered. "She's so damn boring, no guys like her."

"Gregory, honey, it's not polite to swear."

Need I mention that in both instances of sibling abuse Mom neglected to demand an apology on my behalf or discount the Geek label? Didn't think so. Being the middle child (most ignored, least liked) was chock-full of touching family moments like these.

"Your sister's not a geek," Dad broke in, stuffing a box of snow hats and gloves into the closet and safely out of sight.

Ah, thank goodness for dear old Dad.

"She's just an intellectual," he added. "It takes awhile, sometimes years, for guys to learn to like that in a girl."

Terrific.

Such stunning words in your defense, Jane mused, *the likes of which I have heard but rarely.*

Well, they're commonplace enough around here, I told her.

"'Course, she's nothing like Angelique," Mom said.

"No one's like Angelique," Dad admitted.

My cousin, Angelique Lawson, is a Genius, I explained to Jane. *And my Dad's posh sister, Aunt Candice, never tires of telling us so.*

How delightful, Jane said. *There is nothing like geniuses when a party is in want of enlivening.*

Angelique's sixteen but already a junior because she skipped a grade. And very musical. She takes her cello with her everywhere and will probably play it for us today, I added. *And she'll never pass up an opportunity to speak French.*

Ah, très bien. I consider myself well warned, Jane countered.

Mere seconds later, the Lawsons' distinctive canary-yellow Cadillac pulled into our driveway. Angelique breezed cheerily into our house. On her heels was her mother, who swept inside like an empress inspecting the servant quarters.

"Bonjour!" Angelique declared at the earliest possible moment. She flicked her long tawny-blond ponytail behind her and beamed a pretty grin at us so bright I had to squeeze my eyes shut.

"Oh, fuck," Di murmured next to me.

"I'm so *glad* to see you all," our cousin exclaimed. "We have so much *news!*"

"Aw, crap," Gregory whispered.

Di and I actually laughed at the same time to the same thing.

"Be nice," Mom hissed. So I clenched my jaw and steeled myself for all the fun I knew was coming. "Where's Craig? And Aaron and Andy?" Mom asked Aunt Candice, referring to our uncle and the five-year-old Twin Terrors.

"The flu claimed them," our aunt replied. She sniffed to indicate poor health was something she considered an inexcusable offense. "Angelique and I are on our own today."

"But they're on the mend, so please don't worry," Angelique hastened to assure us in that sweet, mature voice our genius cousin was known for.

Di rolled her eyes, and I, admittedly, was grateful not to have to deal with the little demons. Aunt Candice presented work enough just by herself, and Angelique, well, she was sweet but . . . draining.

"Let's sit down," Mom offered, ushering us all into the now clutter-free family room and serving lemonades all around.

I perched at the edge of the sofa with my drink and tried to blend into the décor. But, despite my best attempt at camouflage, Angelique chose me to cozy up to. My aunt scanned me speculatively but not with anything resembling loving kinship. It was, I guess, too much to hope I'd be ignored by these relatives, too.

"Our news is so *magnifique!*" Angelique exclaimed, seemingly unable to contain her enthusiasm. "We're moving."

Mom's eyebrows shot up in alarm. "Where?" She and my aunt had a strange but undeniable form of friendship.

Our aunt displayed her razor-sharp teeth. "To Illinois and—"

Her genius daughter burst in, "And it's so near you! We'll only be about twenty minutes away instead of three hours. *C'est absolument excellent, n'est-ce pas?* I mean—" She glanced between me, Di and Gregory. "Just think of the things we can all do together!"

Oh, *nooooo.*

Mom clasped her hands together in unadulterated delight. Dad blanched. Di and Gregory appeared to be beyond speech.

"Wow," I managed. "That's unexpected, isn't it?"

"No, not really," Angelique said. "I've been accepted at Pierson's Academy. I was on their waiting list, but someone flunked out this semester, so I got in. *Un jour joyeux!* So, I'll start there right after winter break."

"You're going to a private girls' prep school?" Di asked.

"Well, um, yeah. I'll be able to study there for a year and a half before I start college, which should really help me—"

"Get into Harvard, Yale or Princeton," Aunt Candice interjected. "Stanford at the very least."

"Maybe you'd be able to show me around the area a bit after we move?" Angelique asked, biting her lip and gazing at us hopefully.

Gregory downed his drink in one long chug and left the room.

"Um, yeah, sure, we could probably do that . . . sometime," I said to our cousin. Di maintained a death silence.

"Diana, sweetie," Mom said, "maybe you could take Angelique to a few socials at the high school."

"*Socials?*" Di said, choking on the word. "We don't have socials. Just a few lame dances and pep rallies. I think, though," she added as she shot me a demonic look, "Ellie really gets into crap—I mean, school events like that. She and Angelique could have an *awesome* time."

Mom, ignoring Di's wicked expression and my pleading one, said, "That's great. When's the next one?"

"This coming Friday." Di grinned. "Big school dance after the basketball game. I won't be going of course, but Ellie will, won't you?" She didn't call me a geek aloud, but it was implied.

"We're coming up here again to house hunt next week," Aunt Candice stated. "We'll make sure to drop off Angelique by seven or seven-thirty."

"Oh, make it six," our mother said. "Then she can have a nice dinner with us. Maybe pizza?"

Angelique looked thrilled, Di victorious.

Jane whispered, *Une tragédie, n'est-ce pas?*

I sighed. *You're not kidding.*

"Angelique, play us something on your cello," Aunt Candice commanded. "Mozart or Beethoven or one of those dead Viennese guys."

Une idée terrible, Jane commented.

Enough already with the French, I said.

My cousin retrieved her instrument from the car, readied it and glowed her warmest grin at us. "Mozart's '*Eine kleine Nachtmusik.'* A Little Night Music,'" she translated primly. "In G major."

Her fingers flew impressively across the neck of the cello. Her bow danced. For me, painful memories intruded.

I thought of the flute I'd failed miserably to master in seventh-grade band. The piano lessons I didn't have the aptitude for, even at fifteen. The time I broke two strings on Terrie's guitar when she tried to show me how to tune it. Despite my passionate love of music, my playing was horrible enough to deafen the ears of small animals.

So, I envied Angelique her musical gift, resented her for having her life together, but mostly I was ticked off because I couldn't hate her. She might be on the intense side and, yeah, more than a little annoying, but she was so damned *nice* to me.

I sighed.

Why was it that *I* couldn't be loved despite my flaws? Why couldn't *I* be "quirky" in a "cute" way? Why couldn't *I* excel at anything? Okay, correction: Why couldn't I excel at anything anyone *valued?*

No one can be really esteemed accomplished who does not greatly surpass what is usually met with, Jane remarked. *Your cousin, though, is rather accomplished,* she added, which only made me feel worse.

Yeah, I know.

Of course, your abilities are equally . . . well, perhaps even more desirable.

I saw my dad squinting at a black, Rorschach-like smudge on the otherwise pristine family-room wall. It looked like a frantic butterfly, trapped in its 2-D prison. I longed to set it free. *Sure they are, Jane.*

Pray, do I detect disbelief?

Now you're thinking, Sherlock.

There was a long moment of silence. Then she asked, *Who?*

Never mind, I said as Angelique continued on to the second movement. *Just tell me what you mean. How could my abilities, such as they are, be considered desirable? And before you say it, getting good grades doesn't count. No one cares.*

Without an instant of hesitation, Jane answered, *You are more imaginative than any of them. Your cousin. Your siblings. Even your schoolmates. They have talents, to be sure, but beyond an intelligent mind there must be a creative spirit. It is not enough to absorb mere facts. True invention is in the application of vision. This you have in grand measure, far beyond your years and experience.*

I don't know what came over me. Tears sprung to my eyes at her kind words. My aunt, misinterpreting as always, whispered proudly to my mother, "See how touched Ellie is by Angelique's performance. My daughter is a musical prodigy."

Mom bestowed a sage nod upon her. "It's as we always say, Angelique is a genius."

Jane said, *Ignore them, Ellie. Your turn will come. They will all appreciate you someday.*

I seriously doubted this, but hope was a powerful thing. For a moment, it trumped skepticism, and it buoyed my spirits in spite of myself. And I loved that Jane could do that for me. I loved that her wisdom, so evident in her most famous novel, seemed to shine through and illuminate the character of each person I met and, most impressively, of the people I knew best.

She single-handedly made me feel less like a loner. She made me believe it was okay that I was nothing like my Bad Girl Sister, my Dismissive Brother or my Genius Cousin. With Jane in my head and in my life, I could just be *me*, and this gift helped me deal with the worst of my adolescent high school existence.

The day of the game, however, I stood at my open locker, counting down the seconds until Angelique arrived and the solidification of my total lack of coolness was complete. I jammed my books into my straining backpack while, two lockers to my right, Jason Bertignoli stuffed his backpack with similar items.

Barnett.

Bertignoli.

Which left—guess who?

Blaine.

Three lockers down from Jason stood Sam, of course. (And can I tell you how much I *hated* alphabetical order?) He leaned against the gray metal and sent me an indecipherable look. He seemed about to speak, but then Jason waved and said a jovial "Hi, Ellie!"

I said "Hi" back.

Sam's neutral glance turned to one of exasperation. I figured this was because he and Jason had just finished the last day of their villainous volleyball rivalry and Sam, who did not take defeat graciously, lost in the final match.

I expected him to walk away, but he didn't. He just stood there, arms crossed, watching us.

Jason, proudly wearing his basketball jersey and looking very hot in it, said to me, "So, are you going to the game tonight?"

I nodded.

He grinned. "That's totally rad. I'll be starting."

I returned the grin. I already knew this. "Are you? Well, good luck. I'll be cheering for you."

"Cool."

Jason, whose back was still to Sam, didn't see the gagging motions Sam made behind him.

"Well, I guess I'll see you tonight then," I said to Jason.

"Yeah. You going to the dance?"

"Yep."

"Will you save one for me?" he asked.

I shot him a sharp look to see if he was kidding. He wasn't.

I nodded, my heart thudding at a frantic pace. Oh, my God! Jason Bertignoli asked *me* to save him a *dance!* Then, just in case he missed my meaning, I shrugged and said, "Sure."

"Great." Jason shut his locker. "I hope the music doesn't suck."

Sam's jaw dropped and he flipped Jason the bird behind his back. Ever the music lover, Sam led the student council committee that chose the tunes the DJ would spin at the dance. I knew this. Jason, evidently, did not. He'd unknowingly made an enemy for life.

I laughed. "We'll see, I guess." Then I waved goodbye to Jason, who walked away, still oblivious to Sam's fury.

"That new guy is an asshole," Sam spit out the minute Jason rounded the corner.

"Funny, he said the same thing about you." I paused, pretending to think. "Hmm. Who should I believe?"

"Screw you, Ellie."

"Not in your wildest dreams, Sam."

I don't know why I said this exactly, other than that it was the standard teen reply. I didn't consider it a particularly nasty retort nor did I suspect blatant foreshadowing.

But Jane said, *You are being unpardonably coquettish.*

And Sam looked taken aback, almost hurt.

For a long moment he and I scowled at each other, our eyes locked in a stare-down. The latest in our battle of wills, and one I presumed was indicative of why I needed to avoid him, despite my hormones telling me otherwise. He'd fight me on this, or on anything, not because I mattered to him, but just to win. Sam seemed to like me best as an opponent.

Finally, he stalked off. And I left.

Three hours later, though, Angelique arrived on my doorstep and, after dinner, Di dropped us off at the gym entrance for the basketball game and dance.

"Hope the *social* is fun," Di said with feigned sweetness.

"Thanks," our cousin said brightly.

Di rolled her eyes at me. "I'll pick you both up at eleven. Don't do anything stupid, geek."

The tires screeched as she zipped out of the parking lot and went to do whatever High School Bad Girls did on Friday nights in November. Angelique and I walked into the school, and she eyed the two thousand students in the stands with amazement. *"C'est formidable,"* she murmured behind me.

I swiveled around and stopped her right then and there. "Listen," I told her in my most patient voice. "Your French is great. Really. But here, in this gym, it's not a good idea to use it interchangeably with English. Okay?"

"Why not?"

"Well . . ." There were so many reasons, I didn't know where to begin. Because it was annoying? Because I already had enough problems? Because French was such a freaking pretentious language? Take your pick. But I said, "Because the goal of this evening is to be social, right?"

"Right."

"So, people can't socialize with you if they have *no clue* what you're saying."

She thought this over for a second. "Oh. Okay."

I felt a surge of relief. "Okay. Now, let's find a seat."

We met Terrie at my favorite spot in the bleachers, admired Jason's perfect free-throw form and watched our team get soundly crushed by the visitors. And, though Angelique totally got into the game, even she knew the real event was yet to come.

Terrie said, "Well, we lost, but at least we had the game's best scorer on our side. Number forty-five. That new Jason guy."

I grinned. "Yeah. He was good, huh?"

My friend squinted at me. "What's that smile mean, Ellie? You don't like him or anything, do you?"

Always, always deny.

I made a face. "No, of course not. But this afternoon he asked me to save him a dance tonight."

Terrie's eyebrows rocketed upward, and Angelique looked at me as if I'd just recited a flawless, accent-free verse by Sartre.

"It's no big deal. He probably already forgot about it."

My friend whooped and grabbed my hands. "C'mon, Ellie! We've got to get you ready before the dance starts. I have makeup with me." She tugged at me until I stood. "You, too, Angelique. Let's pretend we're hot girls on the town tonight, okay?"

Angelique answered with an enthusiastic, "Okay!"

A half hour later, with faces adequately freshened, we entered the second gym, the one we lowly underclassmen used daily for PE.

I felt the usual pit-of-my-stomach nausea just walking through those doors but, I'll acknowledge, the place had been transformed. Where there'd been floor mats and tubs of volleyballs, now stood a DJ with giant stereophonic speakers, two turntables and four boxes of LPs and cassettes. Where nets had been, there were now snacks, streamers and colored lights. The gym looked almost inviting.

The dance started in the usual way: Kids milling around trying not to meet anyone's glance as they plunged their hands into bowls of pretzel sticks or corn chips. The lights flashed and the music blared frantically, pushing me into a state of fuzzy sensory overload. The moment I saw Jason strolling toward us, though, my attention became laser-focused.

"Hi," he said.

"Hi," I said.

"Hi," Terrie and Angelique said together.

"Great game," I said. "You scored a lot." Then, when his smile brightened, I wanted to shoot myself.

But Jason wasn't Sam. He didn't fire back a rude retort like *Yeah, but I'd like to score some more.* Jason only said, "Thanks." Then he turned to Angelique. "Are you new to the school, too?"

She shook her head. "I'm Ellie's cousin."

He nodded once. "Cool."

And that was our complete, unabridged conversation.

As my heartbeat raced in time to The Cars, we munched on Doritos. The DJ played Blondie, Styx, Asia, REO Speedwagon. We drank Dixie cups of Pepsi. The tempo slowed to a moderately paced Elton John song. Terrie nabbed four stale brownies and passed them out to us on little cornucopia napkins.

None of us looked each other in the eye. Not once.

I noticed Jason surreptitiously checking out Angelique, and I could tell he approved. In his defense, my cousin was not—objectively speaking—unattractive. She just had a bad habit of saying screwy things. In French. My new fear was that, though Jason wanted to start the night with me, he might decide he wanted to end it with her.

I glimpsed Sam and one of his buddies across the room, conferring with the DJ about the tunes. I couldn't hear a word of their exchange, but lots of hand-waving and head-nodding resulted.

A couple of guys from the basketball team greeted Jason with a wave. He returned the friendly gesture. A Journey ballad began to play, and Jason's teammates pulled two girls onto the dance floor to get the ball rolling. I sighed.

"How 'bout that dance now?" Jason asked.

I waited a second to make sure he was talking to me and not to my cousin. "Okay," I said.

He grinned and reached for my hand. It was just so, to use a Jane word, *chivalrous.*

Jason held me loosely as we danced. We grazed against each other in a stream of bodies that soon grew to be a sea of teens. He tightened his grip, and the other people—like the popular guys, the cliquish girls and even Sam—faded into the backdrop.

When the song ended, he leaned in as though he might kiss me, but he didn't. "Thanks," he whispered. "I really liked that."

I looked up at him, mute, and nodded.

He squeezed my arms and went off to join the other basketball jocks. Then all three guys promptly disappeared into the night.

I didn't mind their departure, though. One nice dance was all I'd been hoping for, and I hadn't yet learned to demand more from men. But, despite my low expectations, what happened next blindsided me.

As I walked back toward Angelique and Terrie, foolishly meditating on how satisfying the evening had turned out to be, something slammed into me. Hard. Sam Blaine.

"What now?" I said, surprised, as always, by the magnetism he projected at close range.

"Nothing." He glanced at Jason's retreating form and his blue eyes iced over. "Let's dance."

Before I could argue against it or come up with a good excuse not to, Sam pulled me back onto the floor.

I pleaded to Jane with silent insistence for help. *What should I say to him? What should I do?*

Let him lead you in both the dance and the conversation, Jane instructed. *He will reveal his intentions presently.*

"So, what do you think of the music?" Sam said, his tone proving this was no casual inquiry.

I listened as Don Henley lamented "The End of the Innocence," my fingers tingling and nearly shaking from the contact with Sam's hand and his muscular shoulder. "It seems good."

"It better be," he replied sharply, but I wasn't sure if he was directing this warning at me or at the DJ.

I swayed ungracefully in his grasp and both of us lapsed into silence. I appealed to Jane again. *Can't you do some kind of Cyrano thing? Make me sound sophisticated for a change?*

She tsked. *This is an awkward phase you are in, Ellie, but it will pass with time. As others learn to see you more clearly, so you will learn to see yourself. You are lovelier than you think and have admirers already. Albeit inappropriate ones.*

Who? Jason? I asked her. *He's friendly to everybody.*

Perhaps, but there is also Mr. Blaine. Though I urge you to discourage his attentions.

I studied the insolent teen staring down at me, his lips rigid, his eyes forbidding. Much as I wished otherwise, I was sure he was up to no good. *Sam? That's ridiculous,* I told her.

It ought to be so, replied Jane, *but I fear it is not. He appears to be capable of very little of value, but he did manage to detect your intelligence and kindheartedness. He seems drawn to these qualities in you.*

I considered this and, for an instant, I was flattered. But Sam being sincere in his admiration struck me as preposterous, and I said so. *The guy only likes to fight with me.*

Jane sighed. *You have much to learn about human nature, Ellie.*

Sam puffed out some air. "Are you bored or something?"

"What? No," I said to him.

"You look like you're really out of it. Or lovesick over that loser Jason. Or maybe high," he added, as if issuing a challenge.

"Well, I'm not any of those."

He rolled his eyes and his grip on my hand and waist tightened. "Heard you brought your cousin along tonight." He nodded in the direction of my companions. "She's kinda hot."

My throat seized up.

"Maybe I should ask her to dance later," he threatened.

"Maybe you should," I snapped back, although, like a brainless twit, the thought made me irrationally jealous.

"Well, that's why I asked *you* to dance. Figured you could give me a proper introduction." He shot me an audacious smirk.

Ouch.

To Jane I said, *What did I tell you?*

To Sam I said, "Fine." I pulled out of his grasp, crossed my arms and glared at him, hoping to God I hid my emotions well enough. Sam could never be trusted with the truth about my feelings for him. He'd pounce on any display of weakness.

He stared at me in frigid silence before pivoting on his sneaker sole and ambling toward Angelique.

I took a deep breath and followed him.

"Hey," he said to her. "I'm Sam and you're . . . cute."

Gag me, I thought, because it was, you know, still the '80s.

But Angelique grinned at the lame line. "Hi, Sam," she said.

Terrie, who stood watching this train wreck from a mere two feet away, murmured, "Watch it, Blaine."

Sam shrugged, then turned his highest-wattage smile on my cousin. "What's your name?"

Angelique glanced between the three of us and looked confused. "Angelique?" she said, her voice uncertain.

"Yes," I said, trying to help her out because, no matter how displeased I might've been about her tagging along with me that night, everything about Sam's recent hot-cold, fake-flirting, wacko behavior displeased me more. "Sam Blaine, this is Angelique Lawson. She's here visiting. Try to be polite for a change."

Sam acted as if I were invisible. He said to Angelique, "Too bad you're not planning to stay for good. We could use a few new faces here, especially pretty ones like yours." He grinned at her and my insides twisted. "Can I talk you into hanging around?"

Angelique blushed. She looked so flustered I worried she might break into nervous French at any moment.

He didn't wait for her to answer. "Ah, Angelique. Well, I'm glad we met. Maybe I'll see you later tonight?" He reached out and patted her arm.

"*Peut-être,*" she murmured. "I mean, perhaps."

Sam's eyebrows shot up and he became even more debonair. "Oh, you speak French? *J'aime le français.*" He bowed slightly and gave her another of his winning grins.

Jane declared, *I abhor this boy,* her tone startling in its vehemence.

I gulped back my own displeasure. Since when did Sam Blaine speak French? He'd taken only Spanish classes since sixth grade.

My cousin stammered out a timid "*O-Oui.*"

"*Fantastique,*" Sam said, glancing over at me. Finally. "Well, we've got Spandau Ballet coming up soon, and there's somewhere else I need to be for it." He arched a victorious eyebrow in my direction, then turned back toward Angelique. "*Au revoir, ma chérie,*" he told her.

Then, very deliberately, he eyed a sophomore female I recognized all too well. The girl stood along the wall with a small troupe of friends nearby, and Sam made sure I knew who he was looking at before striding toward her.

With Terrie glaring at his back and my cousin staring at him with an expression of pure astonishment, I told myself I was glad to see Sam walk away. I just wished he'd have walked toward almost anyone else.

Ellie, stop this, Jane ordered. *Feel no regret in his departure. You are right to be rid of him.*

Yeah, probably, I said as I watched him sidle up to Stacy Daschell and grin at her in that charming, charismatic way that came so naturally to him.

Jane's disdainful sniff echoed in my mind. *He would have brought trouble upon you, and you know too well he meant only ill will to your cousin.*

I know. Then the voices outside my head began debating and I was forced to pay attention to the females I could see.

"He's an, um, interesting guy," Angelique said.

"He's a little snot," Terrie replied. She made a fist, punched it into her opposite palm and caught my eye.

I blinked but tried to keep my expression impassive. Jane was right, of course. Sam's intentions toward my cousin were hardly, as she would say, "honourable." Especially not now when he had his arm around Stacy's shoulders. Damn him.

Angelique saw where I was looking and frowned. "Um, Ellie, is something going on that I should know about? Should I not be talking to him?" Her forehead creased and she squinted at me with a look I interpreted as total bewilderment. "There was an odd . . . oh, *je ne sais quoi,* I guess, between you two. Sorry about the French." She nibbled on her lip.

I almost laughed. "Yeah, I don't know what it is either, but total *hate* has to come pretty close." I shrugged at her, trying to keep the hurt from showing. "Talk with him, if you want. I don't care."

Terrie's gaze flicked toward the ceiling and back, but she refrained from saying the "Yeah, right . . ." that I knew she was thinking. Terrie had, after all, caught me writing "Ellie Blaine" on a piece of scratch paper back in September.

As we watched Sam pull Stacy away from her friends and toward a darkened corner, Terrie motioned us closer. "Stacy's totally wasted," she said, the voice of authority on school gossip. "And she just got dumped, you know."

"Really?" I didn't know. I didn't think anybody ever dared to cross Stacy, not even her upperclassman, wrestling-champion, now ex-boyfriend. And he dumped her! Huh. Wonders never ceased.

"You mean that blond girl, right?" Angelique jabbed her finger in Sam and Stacy's direction. "The tall, snooty-looking one with the really pointy nose?"

In spite of myself, I did laugh this time. Sometimes it was easy to appreciate my genius cousin. "The very one."

Do not look, Jane told me.

Why not? I looked anyway.

Across the gym, Sam whispered something in Stacy's ear, which made her crack a smile. Then she leaned against him and touched her pointy nose to his straight one. He grinned at her again, extra brightly.

I swallowed.

Terrie grabbed a few more brownies from the refreshment table. "Here," she said, thrusting the dried-out chocolate squares at my cousin and me. Repulsive, but eating them gave us something to do.

When I stepped away to toss out my napkin and scavenge around for another Dixie cup of soda, I saw a couple of guys from Terrie's biology class talking to her and Angelique. All four of them spontaneously laughed about something.

I downed my thimble of Pepsi and took a step back toward them just as that Spandau Ballet song came on. It was "True."

Do not look, Jane said again.

But I ignored her and glanced over at Sam, who had his lips on Stacy's neck. Stacy, meanwhile, threw her head back and put her hands on Sam's ass.

Aw, no.

I saw my friend and my cousin being led to the dance floor by the two bio guys. All of them looked like they were having more fun than actors in a *Love Boat* episode.

Do NOT look, Jane warned for the third time.

But did I listen? No. You'd think I'd learn.

Now Sam's mouth covered Stacy's. He was in the process of devouring her whole, and she was letting him. Right there. In full view of everyone. To the sounds of Spandau Ballet.

I winced.

Then the worst of it happened.

As he traced patterns on her back and dipped his fingers to her waistband to skim the top of her jeans, he caught my gaze and held it. He lifted one corner of his lips in acknowledgement and projected his most conquering stare right back. He all but shouted across the gym, "See what you're missing, Ellie Barnett? See how I don't need you to have a good time. I could have anyone I want, and I don't want *you*."

And at that moment, when his triumphant blue eyes turned away from mine and fixed on Stacy's unnaturally perky chest, I vowed I wouldn't want him either, not even in secret. Jane was right about him being a big jerk like Wickham. And I knew with absolute certainty that I'd *never* let myself get seduced into liking Sam Blaine again, no matter what.

Let me repeat: NEVER.

Which just goes to show how wishy-washy I turned out to be. Because, as the years went by, look at what I did. Not only did I let myself get seduced into *liking* Sam Blaine and into taking some consequent action (but just once, okay, and we used a condom), in no way was I able to keep secret the private heartache that resulted.

Sam knew.

Jane knew.

Hell, *Camryn* knew, and even that bastard Dominic might've guessed.

All these years later and I was *still* being driven to battle Sam— and my inappropriate feelings for him—by forces that seemed beyond my control. So, I decided my only hope for the dream relationship I longed for rested in finding a man who was the Anti-Sam. The Anyone-But-Him Hero of My Heart. I still didn't know where, precisely, to hunt for such a mortal, but I was open to possibilities and more than willing to stalk a little, if necessary.

And I was just optimistic (and, well, desperate) enough to think I'd succeed in capturing a guy like that. One who'd be my Sam-Antidote and heal the hurt Sam had inflicted.

❧ 3 ❧

Women fancy admiration means more than it
does . . . And men take care that they should.

—*Pride and Prejudice*

In the weeks that followed Sam and me running into each other
at that bar, my life began the last stage of a drastic surface meta-
morphosis.

In one sense, I knew I was finally becoming the monarch I'd
dreamed of. I'd emerged from my cocoon of adolescence, transi-
tioned into young adulthood and was incredibly close to being able
to float around the world of grown-ups in my butterfly costume.
Inside, however, I remained much the confused caterpillar I'd always been.

The problem, of course, was that the people around me, with
the exception of Jane, rarely looked beneath the surface so, to them,
I appeared fine. Or, at least, as fine as they figured I *should* be. And
this forced me to keep up the charade of fineness at home.

Case in point: we had a family dinner the night before I drove
off to grad school. Mom made her famous chicken potpie, which I
usually loved, but in the wake of having so recently seen Sam
again and having just broken up with Dominic, I didn't have much
of an appetite. So I picked at my food while my family discussed
me in their typical, ever-tactful manner.

My dad, smiling at the steaming potpie, said, "Our Ellie, off to
do more studying. Hmm. I hope you like it." He sounded slightly

mystified. Dad was a pretty bright guy, but he let me know on multiple occasions how, when *he* was in school, he couldn't wait to get out of college and get his first real job. "Two more years, right?"

I nodded. Two more years of going full time and I'd have dual master's degrees: MA (Master of Arts in English Lit) and MLS (Master of Library Science).

"Well, good," he said. "We know you'll do well at that."

Di snickered and hissed under her breath, "Yes. It's the *one* thing 'Our Ellie' knows how to do well."

I glanced at her mutely and sighed. Becoming Mrs. Evans had not improved my sister's temperament one whit. Name change or no, she remained the same nasty Diana Lynn Barnett who'd hated me since toddlerhood.

My brother, Gregory, however, in a rare gust of goodwill, said to Di's new husband, Alex, "Ellie was always the best student in the family. She got more A's in one year than I got in all of high school."

"That's cool," Alex said, his dangly silver earring swinging freely between strands of his long, dark hair as he nodded politely and dug into his dinner.

I shot Gregory a brief and grateful grin, but then Mom burst in. "Well, no. I think Angelique got more A's than anyone in the family. She's at Stanford now, you know."

Mom said this for Alex's benefit, but I was, indeed, *well* aware of my cousin's whereabouts. Aunt Candice, whose move to Illinois those years ago had afforded her easy weekly visits to my parents' house, proved herself incapable of speaking a multi-syllabic sentence without referencing her daughter's battle against "those uncouth Californians."

"Angelique is, of course, going to Stanford for *her* graduate studies," my aunt often commented. "They overlooked her after high school, put her on a waiting list for undergrad entry—the nerve of them! But, they sure realized their mistake later. I told her, I said, 'Angelique, darling, you should just forget about Stanford. Make them suffer. Give the Ivies another try, or keep living at home and continuing on at Northwestern.' But—" Aunt Candice sighed. "She insisted on moving out West and joining all those surfing and

Rollerblading Californians." She grimaced. "They're going to get skin cancer, the lot of them. I keep sending her bottles of sunscreen, but I'm not sure it's enough."

Since I was staying safely in the frigid Midwest, I didn't require nearly as much sunscreen as my genius cousin, but Mom tucked a bottle into my bag anyway. And the next morning I left home and soon found myself on my new campus in my new life, three hours south of Glen Forest, registered as an official grad student.

Unlike my undergraduate years, I wasn't forced to take any sucky PE courses, pointless mathematics classes or boring humanities prerequisites. I could focus exclusively on literature with my side order of library science.

But, just like my undergrad years, and my high school years before them, it turned out that academic issues weren't destined to be my problem—guys were. And just like my coursework increased in difficulty from the undergrad to grad level, so did the degree of conniving I encountered from the male members of the species. Brent Sullivan headed the 400-level class on Problematic Men.

"Check the list," Brent said to me one early winter night during my first semester. "I dare you."

The curly-haired, future MBA grad leaned across Wilder Hall's front desk, where I was working the eight-to-ten p.m. shift. (I needed the money and wanted a job nearby. I lived on the third floor of Wilder, the only all-grad student dorm on campus, so it took me thirty-two seconds to get to work.)

Brent pointed to the reservation book. The saucy twist to his lips only grew more pronounced as he edged nearer to me.

I flipped open the book and, sure enough, his name was penciled in. Sauna key. Ten o'clock. That very night. In my best barbed tone, I said, "So, what then? Are you issuing a general invitation?"

He laughed and brought his nose a mere two inches from mine. "No. A very specific one. To you."

"I see." I pretended to be like a fine English lady I knew, and I forced my excitement and my anxiety under control. The sauna was our university's equivalent to something like Make Out Point, a locale visited for the purpose of getting personal with someone of the opposite sex. A private invitation to the sauna was right up there with the come-on "My roommate's gone. Wanna come up and see my beer-can collection?"

"Do you, Ellie? Do you see?" Brent asked me.

I stared at Brent but didn't answer. He loved the chase and, having been his prey for a month now, I knew better than to give in too quickly. In studying his face for so long, though, I noticed that only a couple of small blemishes marred his smooth, golden complexion. His pores, though large, were somehow intriguing, especially up close like this. It made me laugh. That was my test to see if I had a bad case of lust—when even a guy's pores looked sexy.

"What's so funny?" he said, seeming surprised by my reaction and, for once, a little vulnerable. It was the vulnerability that finally got to me.

He pulled back a few inches, and I realized this was the moment of truth. The time when I needed to choose whether to follow up or not.

"You are," I told him. I glanced down at my Poetry 417 notes, riffled through them until I found the Henry Vaughan page, and began quoting from a complicated seventeenth-century poem called "Corruption."

I finished reading and Brent grinned carefully at me. "I have no freakin' idea what that means."

"I'll give you a hint," I said, pointing to the title.

His grin broadened. "Ah. So that's what you see."

"Exactly," I said dryly, but I added a smile and a wink so he knew I was stepping into the game. "The verse is actually about death, but Vaughan named it 'Cor—"

He reached out and snagged my sweatshirt collar with his finger, tugging me toward him. He planted a kiss on my lips. A long, hot one. No doubt at all about his sexual orientation. (Given my vast history of mistakes, I didn't want to misinterpret a guy's intentions again. I'd already made that error as an undergrad.)

"I'll be back at ten, then," he informed me. And he strode away, the picture of fearlessness and unquestioned masculinity. The sauciness back in place. The vulnerability a well-used, now discarded tool.

The desk phone rang.

"Wilder Hall," I said, my lips still smoldering from Brent's kiss, my mind racing with the possibilities of where this relationship might be headed.

"Hi, Ellie! How are you?" The relentlessly cheerful voice of my cousin came across the line loud and clear.

"Angelique. What's up?" I asked this although I already had a sneaking suspicion. She'd been calling me from Stanford with goofy questions about sex and dating all semester. California guys were, presumably, a new breed of male, and any prior advice about Midwestern men didn't apply.

"I've got a question for you." She paused to add suspense. "What do you wear to a bar mitzvah?"

"What?"

"A bar mitzvah. You know, that Jewish ceremony thingy where the boys—"

"I know what it *is*, Angelique. But what are you doing going to one?"

"Oh, well, my boyfriend's Jewish," she said breezily, as if the knowledge of this wouldn't give her mother—and half the members of our extended WASPy family—a coronary. "His nephew is having his next weekend, and Leo invited me."

"Leo? That guy you thought was so cute in your Renaissance Music class?"

"Yeah." She sighed happily. "I think I'm going to marry him, Ellie."

"Wow. That's . . . wow. And, um, about Aunt Candice . . . you've maybe mentioned this possibility to her?"

"Nope. Not yet. But she's going to *love* him. Dad and the twins will, too, I just know it. Leo's so smart and funny, and his parents are the nicest, most laid-back people ever. *Très gentils.* His sister, Lily, kind of reminds me of you, actually. Really into books. It's her son who's having the bar mitzvah."

"Got it," I said. "Well, I've never been to one, but I hear they're kind of like weddings as far as formal attire goes. You should dress up."

"See, that's what I thought, but Leo likes to joke around so much. He said I could wear whatever I wanted. That he'd like me best in a toga." She laughed. "But then, he's a fan of the Roman period." When I didn't laugh along, she added, "He's getting his PhD in Italian history."

"Ah," I said. "That explains it."

"Anyway, thanks for your help! I'm going to make dinner now," she informed me, which made sense since it was only six-thirty Pacific Time. "What do you think? Egg salad sandwich and soup or a veggie-and-cheese omelet?"

"The omelet, and let me know how the bar mitzvah goes, will you?"

She blew me a kiss over the phone line. "I will. Thanks, Ellie. Love you!"

"You, too," I said, but she'd already hung up.

Whoa. Marriage.

Again.

My first seriously close encounter with it had been my sister's wedding to Alex, of course, but that hardly counted, since Di kept me completely out of the loop as far as her matrimonial affairs went. Kim, my good friend and undergrad roomie, was getting hitched soon to her longtime boyfriend Tom, and I was going to be in that wedding. But Kim and Tom lived hours away in central Wisconsin. I wouldn't see any of their post-marital stuff close up.

But now—Angelique?

I couldn't help but wonder: Would *I* ever meet a guy I could marry? A guy who'd propose to me? One I could take home and introduce to my parents as my fiancé?

Maybe Brent will be the one, I suggested to Jane, trying out the idea. True, I didn't know him that well—yet—but he was manly enough. A macho man, actually. The only type of male I'd endeavored to date since Mark Williams (a genuinely wonderful guy who was the greatest boyfriend ever during college . . . until he "came out" to me). *But Brent also has something of Sam in him, with that love of bantering and his natural . . . oh—*

Impertinence? Jane supplied.

Well, yeah.

She sniffed, making it clear she didn't endorse Brent as a marital prospect.

Your sister is a married woman now, perhaps she can offer you some beneficial advice?

I laughed aloud. *Not likely, Jane. You know how I feel about trying to talk with her. You know it's futile.*

I know no such thing, Jane retorted. *You are such a stubborn young being, Ellie. I only mention this because a time will come when you may wish to cherish your sisterly relationsh—*

"Can I have change for a five?" a second-floor resident asked me, interrupting Jane's latest lecture.

"Sure," I said, pulling out the cash box and contemplating doing something reckless with Brent Sullivan.

I decided I didn't want to think about marriage. I didn't want to imagine Angelique getting wild-'n'-wacky at a bar mitzvah with her Stanford boyfriend. I didn't want to patch up my relationship with my malicious sister. In fact, I didn't want to have the voices of Reason and Maturity in my head at all that night.

Instead, I just wanted to think about Brent. About being young and free and potentially in love. About my own life and what I wanted from it: Some respect from my immediate family. A career I enjoyed and was good at. One man who cared about me and whom I cared about in return.

How bad could it be to, for once, go after exactly what I needed, even if the method wasn't wholly and completely honorable?

What are you devising, Ellie? Jane said in her Warning tone.

Nothing.

Nonsense. Tell me. I implore you not to do anything regrettable.

But because I'd momentarily forgotten the tremendous pain I'd endured at the hands of men when I'd ignored Jane in the past, I shut my eyes and shut Jane out of my mind for the night.

While this skill was something I'd learned to do as I'd grown older (one I'd often had reasonable grounds for exercising, particularly when boys and bedrooms were involved), and while Jane herself elected to shut *me* out on occasion as well . . . this time it was a mistake on my part. No question about it.

* * *

Brent led me by the hand through the door of the now unlocked sauna room. Then he locked it behind us.

"Alone at last," he said with his trademark spider-to-the-fly smirk.

"Yep," I replied, eloquent as always.

I wondered what his lead-in line would be. How long it would take before he began to kiss me. If I could give off the appearance of cool until I knew where he was headed. And, mostly, if our month of verbal foreplay meant anything when it came down to lip-to-lip action.

I took a couple of deep breaths and surreptitiously studied Brent's attractive physique. My fingers itched from wanting to run them through his dark curly hair, but I clasped them together instead.

I wasn't quite subtle enough. He caught me staring and looked at me as if he knew what I was thinking.

"I brought along a deck of cards." He punctuated this statement by pulling them out of his back pocket and waving them in the air. "Thought, maybe, we could play a game or two of Go Fish."

Not the opening line I'd expected. "Here?" I said, unsure how to respond. "In the sauna?"

"Well, yeah. Every time I have to fish for another card, I also get to fish for an item of clothing." He grinned. "One of yours."

My heart, which had been pounding frantically, stopped. Then restarted. "Oh. Uh, Brent—"

"Now before you go disagreeing with me, just think of how fun it'll be. I bet no one's done that in here yet. We could be total originals."

"I—I'm not sure I want to make my mark as a trendsetter in quite that way." Not that I was opposed to seeing more of him, but I'd expected at least an attempt at hugging or kissing before we started discarding clothes. I had to laugh, though, and eye his body one more time. Who else would've thought of Strip Go Fish?

Unfortunately, when he caught my admiring stare, Brent had his way in, and he knew it.

"Ellie," he said, his voice low and seductive. "Remember, if you have to go fish, you get to make a clothing selection, too." He held my hands and pressed them up against his hard chest. "Aren't you even a little curious?"

This was the dangerous line women had to walk. Curiosity versus consequences.

"Of course," I whispered. "But we haven't known each other for very long and—"

"That's not true," he said, adamant. "We've been friends for ages, and I know you're nice and friendly, cute and smart, into poetry and English and stuff. I *know* you, Ellie. I just wanna get to know you better."

I was being an idiot. Exhibit A: Even *thinking* of considering a Very Lame Line like that. Exhibit B: Going ahead and considering it anyway. However, this was a case where curiosity bested consequences. In my defense, I did make a brief plea for responsibility.

"Let's get to know each other then," I whispered. "But, please, let's take things slow. I'm not ready to go too far, not just yet. Okay?"

He nodded, looking gleeful, and I realized I'd just given him the female equivalent of a Very Lame Line.

Brent turned on the switch to start the sauna. Within moments the room began heating up. At this rate, we might have to begin removing clothing before the card game began. I unbuttoned the top of my shirt and pushed up my sleeves. Brent untucked his jersey and plopped down on the floor.

He shuffled the deck like a Vegas dealer. The cards buzzed in his palms, smacking into each other and falling neatly into place. Then he dealt us seven cards each, placing the remainder in the middle.

He studied his hand and rearranged a few. "You can go first," he said with a gallant smile.

I fanned out my cards. Two eights, a four, a three, a ten, a king and an ace. I removed my pair of eights and laid them on the warm tile.

Brent looked impressed by my early match and winked at me. "Way to go."

"Thanks. Okay, I'd like a four please."

He scanned his cards and his grin broadened. "Sorry, don't have it. Go fish."

What to do?

I selected a card from the pile. A six of spades. I added it to my hand and stared at him.

"What else will you take?" he asked, pointing to his torso with his open palm.

"Your, um, left shoe."

He raised his eyebrows and slowly untied his sneaker. He pulled it off and handed it to me. "Hope it's not too stinky for you."

I shook my head. "Your turn."

"A jack, any suit."

Damn. I didn't have it. I swallowed hard and said, "Go fish."

Brent grinned as he reached for a card. "And I'll take your shirt, too."

"My shirt? Already?"

"Yep. Off with it." He motioned for me to pass it over to him.

So, he was going to play hardball, was he? I unbuttoned my blouse and slowly tugged it off, glad my bra was full coverage and freshly washed.

He eyed me with an appreciation far more licentious than reverential. "Thanks. Back to you."

"A three," I said.

He raised a cocky brow and plucked one out of his hand. "Here you go."

"Thank you." Then I winced. Since we'd agreed not to have double turns, even if we got a matched card from our opponent, it was already his turn again.

"Ten," he said.

I exhaled and handed my ten of hearts over. "Okay, Brent, give me a king."

"No king. Sorry, sugarplum." He shook his head with feigned sadness. "Go fish."

I blindly grabbed a card, then pointed my index finger at him. "And I want the jeans, too."

A laugh erupted from him. "Okay. Now you're getting into the spirit of things." Then he very deliberately unfastened his belt, his eyes never leaving my face, and he slid them off, taking the right sneaker with them. He tossed the jeans over to me and retied his remaining sneaker as I watched. The distorted shape of his white briefs boasted full arousal.

I felt the room temperature spike. Boy, that sauna was really working.

"My turn, Ellie." His voice was even lower now and even more seductive. I felt a chill of excitement despite the heat. "Do you have a five for me?"

"No," I whispered.

He paused, waiting.

"Go fish," I said finally.

He grabbed a card from the pile and winked. "Bra."

My jaw dropped. "I—uh—"

"Don't back out on me now."

"Umm . . ." Oh, what the hell. I shrugged and unhooked the back clasp. So much for full coverage.

"I'll take that," he whispered.

I handed the bra to him and crossed my arms.

"No fair."

"Tough," I said.

"Your turn," he reminded me.

"Yeah. That's right. And I want an ace." The kind of ace that would get him back good.

He shook his head. "No ace, baby doll. You know what to do." His grinned dared me. "Go fish."

I drew a card, leaned toward him and said, "Your briefs, please. Now."

His look was jubilant, not embarrassed. Brent knew what he was doing. He pulled the briefs off and dangled them on his finger. I, of course, wasn't really focused on the underwear. Brent had been fortunate in the endowment department, and it was a pleasure to observe the length and firmness of him. So much so that I'd forgotten to keep my arms crossed.

"Finish the game?" he asked, his tone amused.

"S-Sure."

"A nine, then."

I didn't bother looking down at my hand. I knew I didn't have it. "Go fish."

He put his cards on the tile floor. "I want the rest of your clothing."

"Okay," I heard myself say. "Likewise."

We shucked whatever we were still wearing, and Brent swept the cards aside. He pressed his body against mine and his lips swooped in to taste my mouth. To consume it.

I felt like a kid sneaking chocolate bars on Halloween night. How after a busy evening of trick-or-treating, when we'd already eaten our allotment of sweets, I'd tiptoe out of bed and into the kitchen, find my stash and secretly devour another Snickers or Milky Way. It was bad for me. I knew I didn't need it. It kind of made my stomach roil. But the temptation was too strong for me to ignore. Brent Sullivan was just like that candy.

"I want you," he whispered. "I'm crazy about you. Be my girlfriend, Ellie."

I nodded and hoped, rather than believed, he was sincere in his intentions.

He didn't waste time trying to convince me further with words after that. He just used his hands and his mouth and his hips and his . . . well, let's just say that Brent had come prepared for safe sex, and what followed wasn't at all mediocre. My body was euphoric. My heart less so.

Brent nibbled on my neck in that rare, tranquil moment of afterglow. "We've gotta return the key by midnight," he said between nips. "That gives us only another fifteen, twenty minutes. Anything special you wanna do?"

"Can we just talk?"

He shrugged and withdrew his teeth from my neck. "Sure. What do you want to talk about?"

"Our relationship."

His eyes grew wide, but he glanced away—to keep me from reading his expression, I figured.

I sat up.

"Yeah?" he said.

I picked through the clothes until I found my bra and panties. I slipped those back on, fast. "So, when you said you wanted me to be your girlfriend, did you mean just for tonight? Or were you thinking longer term? Like that we'd be, you know, exclusively dating now?"

He met my eye and beamed a bright smile at me. "The second option, Ellie."

Thank God.

"Oh, fine," I said, trying to sound nonchalant. "I was just checking."

"I don't hide out in the sauna with just *anyone*. I really, really like you." He paused and his look turned serious. "You feel that way about me, too, right? You're not just using me to get your jollies, are you, El?"

"Of course not. You're smart and funny and very, very sexy. I really like you, too."

He exhaled heavily. "Well, that's a relief. I don't wanna play those kind of games. You know, where one person is in it only for the sex. Somebody always gets hurt then."

I nodded, seeing new depths in this guy that I'd missed during our bantering sessions at the front desk. My heart started to relax a little and marriage, suddenly, didn't seem quite so much of a long shot. I mean, there we were—both twenty-two—legal and nearly self-supporting adults. Within a year and a half we'd be all set to live responsible, grown-up lives. We could realistically get married within a few weeks of grad school graduation. In a matter of seconds, I had our lives planned out until retirement.

Brent gave me an affectionate peck on the cheek. "Yeah, let's be exclusive," he said, almost to himself. Then, apparently deciding to go commando, he zipped up his jeans and expertly tucked his white briefs into his waistband. He covered it up with his jersey and slipped on his sneakers. "I'm ready to get outta here whenever you are."

I finished getting dressed and we left the sauna holding hands and grinning at each other.

I thought it was the start of a beautiful relationship.

As usual, I thought wrong.

With the exception of enjoying a couple blissful months of hot sex, life went on much as it always had.

In the light of day, and with my full conscious mind open to her again, Jane, of course, tried to advise me.

She cautioned, *There is, in every disposition a tendency to some particular evil, a natural defect, which not even the best education can overcome.*

She counseled, *Every impulse of feeling should be guided by reason.*

She said, hopefully, *You are too sensible a girl to fall in love merely because you are warned against it.*

But I wasn't sensible. I was a fool. And I let her words of wisdom float in and out of my lust-crazed brain, until one afternoon when I went to visit my friend Erica in another dorm.

Erica was an undergrad, a senior, but only a year younger than me and in one of the lit classes that could be taken by both grads and undergrads.

Like me, she was an English geek.

Unlike me, she'd set her sights on a somewhat more illustrious career path than that of a high-school librarian. She wanted to become a famous poet and—for income until the fame kicked in—a professor at a Big Ten university. When we got together we liked to talk Classics.

That day, with the help of passages from a variety of mournful poets, we were discussing her feelings toward her high-school boyfriend Dylan, who died in a tragic car accident back then.

"I don't think it's wrong for those memories to dim, Erica. I doubt Dylan would want you to stop living. To still be thinking only of him."

"I know he wouldn't. But I feel odd about letting go completely. It's as though I'm losing a sensitivity I'd had. I'm afraid if I really put my love for Dylan in the past, then I'm not *feeling* enough somehow. That a *real* poet would never recover. Do you know what I mean?" She squinted at me.

I squinted back and nodded. "I think so. That someone else might think you don't have the heart of a poet or that you're incapable of really *getting* literature if you move on from this tragedy that shaped your youth."

"Yes!" She paced the dorm-room floor. "And that's a stupid, selfish motive, I know." She paused. "Do you think I'm repressing things?"

At this I laughed. "Nobody I know dissects thoughts and emotions like you do. If you're suddenly repressing your grief, you'd need someone a whole lot more skilled in psychotherapy than I am to figure it out. I think maybe you're just finally healing."

"But so soon?"

"Soon? It's been six years."

She wrinkled her nose. "Yeah."

As my friend took this in, I thought about what I'd lost in high school. True, not a literal death, but the demise of an innocence, a hopefulness. And, yeah, my virginity, too, but who was counting?

Okay, so it was clichéd.

All of it.

I wasn't a completely unaware idiot despite this latest lapse into melodrama. But—I had to say it—being with Brent, despite Jane's disapproval, was bringing me back to life.

"Did you ever read—" Erica said as she riffled through one of her lit texts. Most of our conversations began with that phrase. "Oh. Here it is. This passage by Elizabeth Barrett Browning?" She handed me the book, and I'd just begun skimming the lines she pointed to, when Erica's door banged open and her roommate waltzed in.

Disappointment surged through me. "Hey, Rochelle, how are you?" I said, striving for friendly but detached. I hoped the dopey senior would grab a granola bar and leave again, but she dropped down beside us and exhaled breathily.

Conversations were always reduced to the lowest common denominator and, in this case, I knew we'd turn from Classic Poetry to Campus Gossip in a matter of nanoseconds. Rochelle didn't prove me wrong.

"Lord, did I ever hear the stupidest thing today!" she said, shaking her shoulder-length hair and getting comfortable on Erica's bed. "Some boys are *soooo* obvious. Trish's boyfriend is here again."

Erica groaned. "That guy has to be such a sleaze. I've never met him, but she talks constantly about what they do together. It's nauseating."

Rochelle twisted a lock of her streaked hair and sent us a smirk.

"Well, now he's gotten her into stripping during card games. She was jabbering about it before he showed up. Then they disappeared into the sauna."

I felt a blush begin at the base of my neck and knew it was creeping its way upward. "The sauna? Really?"

"Yeah, because Trish's roommate studies a lot in their room and Trish's boyfriend isn't from this dorm. He's a *grad* student," Rochelle explained with a roll of her eyes. "But he hangs out here often enough. Like practically every afternoon for *hours*. I try to avoid him."

"Oh," I said. "Um, what's his name?"

Rochelle bit her lower lip. "Brad—"

I felt a tiny swell of relief.

"—or maybe it's Brett. I don't remember exactly, but it's something like that. Anyway, he told her they were going to play Strip Go Fish today. Can you believe it?" Rochelle rolled her eyes again.

I closed mine and tried to rein in the tears fighting to escape.

Duped again.

An idiot after all.

How much more proof did I need?

I heard Jane sigh deep inside my mind, but she didn't berate me. She had to know my days of being naively trusting of men were over.

OVER.

"You okay?" Erica asked me, tilting her head to one side and studying my face.

"Yep." I blinked and began gathering my things. "But I need to get to the library to finish a project for one of my MLS classes." I forced a bright smile at both of them. "Good talking to you two. See you in lit, Erica."

I waved and walked out the door fast, still grinning like the mentally deficient person I was.

And, of course I didn't go to the library.

I clomped down four flights of stairs and camped out in their dorm's basement, in the little study right across from their sauna room. Clearly, I was a glutton for humiliation, but I needed to be absolutely, positively certain.

After all, it wasn't *impossible* that some other guy could use the same sex-getting tactics as Brent.

There might actually *be* a Brad or a Brett.

Maybe there was a *group* of grad-school guys who strategized together—as part of some morally decrepit team or something—and they'd come up with foolproof lines to use on their unsuspecting girlfriends.

It didn't mean Brent cheated on me. Not for sure. Not yet.

I pretended to read one of my MLS books. *The Dewey Decimal System: Selected Readings in Theory, Organization and Application.* Second edition. Written by Someone Very Pretentious, PhD, and penned with all the humor and insight of a text on dental flossing techniques.

An hour and seventeen minutes dragged on. Then the door to the sauna swung open. I heard female giggling first, followed by a male laugh.

Brent.

So, all hope for our Happily Ever After ended right there.

The pain of betrayal burned down my throat as I swallowed, but I didn't plug my ears or close my eyes. I didn't run and hide. I listened. I watched.

I had my book open, its spine cracking, and I peered over its creased pages as Brent and a blonde I figured must be Trish walked out of the steamy room and into the hall. He was framed through both doorways, The Other Woman by his side. What a picture. What a con.

His gaze met mine, initially friendly, not comprehending. And then the eyes grew wide as recognition dawned. Four seconds, at most, split into subdivisions of time like an atom in a nuclear reactor, and equally explosive. Melodramatic emotions detonated in my brain.

"I—I gotta talk to someone," I heard him say to Trish as he bid her a quick farewell. But not before she kissed him hard on the lips and grinned at him. He smiled tightly at her. His next glance in my direction was sheepish and utterly vulnerable.

That was when I closed my eyes.

When Trish was safely out of sight, he bolted into the study and stood by me, looking hurt and, unbelievably, like *he* was the one who'd been wronged.

"What are you doing *here*, Ellie?" He shifted his weight between his feet a time or two, then ended up leaning against the back of one of the chairs. "I mean, this dorm . . . it's, um . . . I didn't think you ever came here. Is it something you do often?"

I looked at the seven other people studying in the room, their gazes ranging from seemingly absorbed by their own stuff to obviously irritated by our distracting conversation.

I sighed. "If I didn't already know the answer, Brent, I'd ask you the same." I got up and pushed my way past him to get to the door.

He chased after me. Down the hallway, up the stairs, through the first floor corridor to the dorm's back exit (I couldn't fathom walking through the crowded lobby) and outside into the winter chill.

As I stepped onto the wet sidewalk, avoiding the clumps of snow clinging to the pavement, he called, "Please, Ellie. Stop. I'm sorry."

I stopped.

I swiveled toward him, my heart and my fingers already numb, and I realized with a clarity I'd never before experienced that I had no idea what I was doing.

I didn't know who I was.

I didn't know who I wanted to be with. Hell, after the past couple of hours, maybe nobody.

I didn't know where I was going in life or even where I was walking to in the next few minutes.

I didn't know anything other than I wanted the day's nightmare to end. And that somehow, somewhere there had to be an easier way to meet a good man, and I desperately wanted to know the secret.

"It just happened once or twice," Brent explained, as if fewer than five indiscretions didn't count. "And I like you better than her. I—I really, uh, kind of love you." He paused. "C'mon, Ellie. Say something."

I studied his handsome face, so flushed with embarrassment—

real or contrived—then turned my attention toward the quad, where scores of students milled around and chatted daily, regardless of the weather. About twenty yards away a lively assembly of females had gathered and several delighted giggles rose above the pack.

I pointed at the group and said to Brent, "Go fish."

❧ 4 ❧

They who are good-natured when children,
are good-natured when they grow up.

—*Pride and Prejudice*

The rest of that year wasn't much of an improvement as far as how things played out in my dating life. I saw the occasional date movie or action flick with a guy here or there and went out for a few uninspiring dinner dates at off-campus restaurants, but no man really captured my interest long term, nor I his. Can't say I fared much better during the second year of grad school either.

So, a couple of months short of graduating, I ventured home for spring break and spent several lazy days ruminating on my single status and overdosing on pricey, caffeinated beverages.

Maybe, I projected, things would get better once I was officially in the workforce.

Maybe I simply needed to move across the country to find my man. Angelique, whose funny phone calls always seemed to brighten my day, kept telling me that California guys were the way to go, and she was getting increasingly serious about "her Leo."

Or maybe making my brain move faster by drinking more coffee would provide me with the answer I sought.

I grabbed a windbreaker and bolted out of the house to test the latter theory. The day was sunny, though, so I left my jacket unzipped and inhaled deeply. The scents of late March pervaded the air of neighborhood Glen Forest. Crabapple blossoms. Wet grass.

The distinctive odor of worms out for a squiggle after the morning's rain. And I was walking the sidewalks like a tourist. Weird.

About two blocks from my parents' house stood my favorite corner coffee shop, Brew Masters. I entered to the piped-in, vintage sounds of Echo & The Bunnymen. Appropriate enough, I supposed, for early spring.

Jane and I chitchatted silently about the differing musical styles of our eras (Beethoven versus the Beastie Boys—who proved more rebellious? Discuss . . .) as I ordered a cappuccino and wandered over to the condiments counter. I was deeply involved in the delicate process of flavoring my drink with cinnamon when I heard a voice from the past.

"Ellie? Is that you?"

I swung around to see none other than Jason Bertignoli (Oh, my God! We were both *twenty-three*. How did we get so old?!), sitting alone at a tiny table, reading a newspaper and sipping a small coffee.

Jane groaned and said, *Oh, heavens*. But I waved and walked over to him.

"Hi," I said, trying to keep the surprise from my voice. It'd been more than two years since I'd seen him in town. "What's up? I haven't run into you in ages."

"You either." He stood and gave me an awkward hug. "Finished grad school yet?"

I nodded. "Well, nearly. Two more months. You?"

"Not exactly." He pointed to the paper. "I've been job hunting this semester and have a bunch of interviews lined up for April." He grinned. "A lot's happened this year, Ellie."

We sat down and I took a cautious sip of my drink before asking the obvious. "Like what?"

He laughed. "Um . . ." He laughed again, but I clearly wasn't in on the joke. "I think maybe we oughta work up to it. Start with small talk or something."

I set down my cappuccino. "Okay. Well, I'm fine. My family's fine, except for my sister Diana, who's as much of a pain as ever." I rolled my eyes and Jason laughed. Even though he and my sister hadn't interacted much during high school, *everyone* knew Di back then. She'd had, to put it euphemistically, a "big personality."

"She's been married for almost two years, though, so she's her husband's problem now," I added. "But, otherwise, I'll just be finishing up my classwork and starting the job hunt for a librarian position this summer." I paused to consider what passed for Big News in my world. I came to the rapid conclusion that my life was boring as hell. (Well, except for the Jane-Austen-voice-in-my-head thing, but there was no way I was telling Jason about *that*.) "There ends my small talk. Your turn." I smiled at him.

He gave me an endearing grin, looking very cute in a significantly more grown-up way than I remembered. But still, even now, I couldn't see his face without thinking of going with him to our senior prom and the whole drunken debacle that followed. It was a memory that saved me from feeling something like sentimental over him.

Just for good measure, though, Jane murmured, *He seems as much the affable lackwit as before.*

I inwardly rolled my eyes at Jane and outwardly nudged Jason. "C'mon. You can tell me."

"Okaaaay," he said, dragging out the word. "I'm fine. My family's fine, except for my mother, who's a little worried. My girlfriend's pregnant and we're getting married this Sunday." He paused and watched my expression, which I'm certain must've been one of shock, then said, "Oh, and I had to drop out of grad school. I'd only taken three classes last year but, anyway, I might go back sometime. At least I've got my bachelor's in marketing now because, you know, having a degree will make supporting the family easier."

He stopped talking and waited for me to speak. After a full fifteen seconds I was finally able to.

"That's actually a lot of news, Jason."

He nodded. "Yep."

"Are you okay? I mean, how are you and your girlfriend doing with all of this?"

He glanced out the window, then looked back at me, his eyes serious. "Look, I know it's not ideal timing. It'd be better if this all would've happened another year from now and we were a little more settled in our careers and everything, but—" He shrugged and kind of grinned. "Anyway, I love her, so we'd have gotten here eventually."

About ten different emotions battled it out in my gut, not the least of which was envy. Envy of Jason's girlfriend/fiancée at having someone love her like that, stick by her, be loyal to her. I didn't covet Jason—both God and Jane knew *that* wasn't the case—but I'd been in enough bad relationships to yearn for a man who cared about *me* as deeply. The kind of man that, say, Brent or Dominic or Sam had never been.

"She's lucky," I whispered, not realizing until I heard my voice that I'd said the words aloud.

Jason dipped his head. "No. I'm the lucky one," he said, his tone quiet but fortified with conviction. Then he picked up his coffee cup and drained it in one gulp. "I need to get going now, but it was great seeing you again. You take care of yourself, okay?"

"Thanks, Jason. You, too."

A minute later he was out the door, and I was left with a budding hope in man's faithfulness, a renewal that both buoyed and haunted me throughout the next several months.

Unfortunately, that hopefulness did not last forever.

By the time I'd received both master's degrees, gotten a full-time librarian job with the Meadowview High School District (about a half hour west of Glen Forest) and worked for a couple of years, I was on the verge of giving up the whole depressing dating scene altogether.

I had friends, of course, who never tired of trying to set me up with random single men. And then, naturally, there was my overly romantic and highly delusional cousin. Who happened to be in town one New Year's Eve. Husband of three years—and young child—in tow.

Angelique grabbed her daughter's elastic waistband and yanked the toddler away from the hot curling iron on the bathroom counter. "No! Not a toy. Go play with LEGOs."

Lyssa looked up at her mommy with big brown eyes. "Toy? Me

have toy." She reached out a chunky hand and took a big step forward.

"No." Angelique yanked her back again and jabbed a parental finger at the hair-styling tool. "Icky. Hot. Bad." Then she pointed toward the hallway of my parents' house. "Toys there. Go."

When the little girl finally waddled away toward her LEGO collection, my cousin sighed and sent me an exhausted smile. "This mommy stuff really changes your life. I haven't spoken a complex sentence in twenty-one months." She grimaced at her reflection in the mirror. "And just look at my hair!"

I grinned and helped her brush out a few snarls. "But Lyssa's a sweetie, and she's grown so much just since the summer. I could hardly believe it when I saw you guys at the airport. She's got to astonish you every day."

"Yes." Angelique kissed my cheek and squeezed my shoulder before returning her attention to her tangles. "But today she's astonishing me by how insane she can make me. I'll never be ready for tonight. Three measly hours isn't enough time to make myself look like a woman again."

"Leo thinks you're as gorgeous as ever, and you know it. You don't have to try so hard."

"But we don't get many dates together, El. That makes tonight special." The lines at the corners of her mouth tightened. "Thanks for watching Lyssa for us and for being so welcoming. You don't know how—"

She stopped, and I saw her flick an errant teardrop away.

"Hey, it's nothing," I said. "I'm crazy about her. So are Mom, Dad, Gregory, even Di and Alex. And Aunt Candice is starting to come around about Leo. No one can resist your little girl—"

We heard a delighted shriek from the hallway and the crash of LEGOs.

"—even if she *is* kind of loud," I added, chuckling.

Angelique's amusement was fleeting. "My mom'll never really forgive me," she whispered. "You know that, right? No matter what front she puts on in public."

"Is falling in love with a man who's smart and kind something anyone should have to forgive?"

She shook her head. "But, in Mom's opinion, marrying him was going that little step too far. And even getting a granddaughter out of it hasn't been compensation enough."

I thought about this. Aunt Candice didn't cast quite the welcoming eye on Angelique and Leo's engagement that my cousin had hoped. In fact, my aunt's reaction to their subsequent elopement (when I was still in grad school) was even less congenial. To date, the best spin she'd managed to put on her daughter's marriage was—*once*—when she called the relationship "surprising."

"Do you have any regrets about marrying Leo, other than your mom's disapproval?" I asked.

"None," she said without hesitation. "Not a single damn one. He's the best, and I hope you'll find somebody equally as amazing. You deserve someone great."

At this point, I suspected finding someone moderately tolerable would've been big news, but I said, "Thanks."

My cousin curled a section of her hair into a springy ringlet and looked pleased with the result. "You know," she said, twisting a new strand of hair around the curling iron, "Leo has a ton of friends. Most live near us in California, of course, but he's got a few pals here in Chicago, too. We could hook you up with somebody *vraiment fantastique*." She winked.

I rolled my eyes. "Thanks, but no thanks. I've vowed never to go on another blind date again."

To solidify my point, I spent the next ten minutes recounting in extensive detail some of the torturous dates I'd suffered through during the past year alone. "Besides," I told her, "it wouldn't matter. You could present me with forty such men, all as wonderful as Leo, and it wouldn't work out."

"Why the heck not?"

I looked over my sweet, warmhearted cousin from her now curly head to her sock-footed toe. "Because I'm not cute and nice and funny like you. I don't have the kind of disposition that attracts really thoughtful men or the temperament to keep one if I did. I'm a louse magnet."

"That's absurd!" Angelique set down the curling iron and stared at me. "What kind of God-awful guys have you been dating to make yourself believe such a thing?"

"My point exactly. But not *all* of them could've been weirdos or imbeciles, though I thought so at the time. I must've misjudged at least one or two. I mean, statistically, it has to be impossible to have a string of duds like that."

Angelique laughed. "You *are* funny, El, cute and very nice, too. And, for the record, I think your theory is totally bogus. You're just insulated in your high-school-librarian world. You don't meet a wide enough assortment of men."

Okay. She might be onto something there. The school-district staff I worked with consisted of lots of balding, married men who taught subjects like government or mechanics, but who really dreamed of coaching varsity football or basketball. Most of the un-married guys also wanted to coach some sport but, if they didn't, they spent their free evenings hopping the clubs downtown. Not a poet in the bunch.

"I'll see what I can do to expand my social circle," I said, lean-ing against the doorframe, "but I'm starting to think there's got to be an element of magic involved somewhere. I'm not saying you and Leo don't work at your marriage, but you two didn't work that hard when you first met. You spotted him in that Renaissance Music class of yours, thought he was cute, talked to him. He saw you and thought, 'Oh, she's hot and a brainiac to boot. We could have beautiful genius kids together.' Then he asked you out and you got to know each other. It was a natural thing. It progressed to the next stage without being forced or manipulated. Without strat-egy. That's what I want this time."

Angelique fashioned a few more ringlets and took in my words. "It's always more work than you think, Ellie. Even in the most compatible of relationships there's still strategy—on both sides. And things can change between two people in an instant. There are never guarantees." She shrugged. "But knowing that doesn't help you much, does it?"

"Nope." I blew her a kiss. "Thanks for the words of wisdom, though. I appreciate them. But no blind dates. Got it, Angelique?"

"Fine, fine. Have it your way." She paused. "But if you ever change your mind, there's this really gorgeous professor of Gaelic studies who—"

I slammed the bathroom door on my goofy cousin and went in search of her daughter. Lyssa's conversation might be limited, but at least I didn't have to defend my pathetically single status to her.

Problem was, I'd totally lied to Angelique. I didn't require magic. I was willing to work at a halfway-decent relationship until I turned a shade of toxic green. I would've even gone on yet another blind date if I thought it'd do any good.

Why?

Because the fringes of desperation danced through my bloodstream every time I met a new man or even spotted one walking down the sidewalk.

Because I'd look into his eyes as we passed each other and ask myself, "Is that My Guy? Could he be The One?"

Because I was so worried True Love would never happen for me that I was willing to expend huge amounts of energy trying to maneuver a compatible match into place.

Because I knew the clock was ticking on finding someone, and soon all the good ones would be taken.

Because I was twenty-six and so lonely. Still.

But my optimism, which I used to think had been my birthright, had faded, or at least gone into deep hiding. And that was my biggest lie to my cousin: The inherent implication that the happily-ever-after thing was really possible.

Truth was, except for an occasional spasm of something resembling hope, I'd stopped believing.

Work resumed a few days later and, as the students struggled to re-assimilate into the school-day structure, the staff was abuzz with post-holiday gossip.

While I checked back in books the high schoolers had checked out over winter break, my friend and colleague, Sarah, leaned against the library desk and appraised me.

"You ought to give The Dragon's Lair a try," she told me, raising a dark eyebrow that all but twitched from the possibility of near-future matchmaking. "That's where my roommate said she went over vacation. And she found herself a new man."

"You know I'm not a club-hopping type." I checked in a copy of Twain's *The Mysterious Stranger* with the scanner and put it on the to-be-shelved cart.

"Technically, there's no *hopping* involved. You just go to that one club, you stay there, scope out guys for a few hours, take down a few phone numbers and go home. It's really a very simple process, Ellie."

She smirked, of course, as she said this. I narrowed my eyes at her.

"I'll go with you," she volunteered cheerfully. "Liam won't mind." She paused. "Well, he won't know about it."

I reached for Clarke's *Childhood's End*, grimaced at the novel, which I remembered reading myself in Mrs. Leverson's English class, and scanned it back in. "One of the things I love about you," I told Sarah, "is your unabashed ability to lie to your boyfriend for the sake of the greater good."

She grinned. "So true. Although, technically, it's not a *lie* if—"

"It's a lie by omission. But it won't be required of you regard-less."

Her enthusiasm dimmed. "Aw, c'mon. You won't even consider going? I hear it's a real fun place."

The next book I reached for turned out to be Austen's *Persuasion*. I rolled my eyes heavenward, even if it wasn't a sign from Jane. "Okay. I'll consider it," I said aloud. "But I refuse to make any promises now."

"Good enough. Oh! I almost forgot to tell you." She leaned closer, in full rumor-divulging mode. "Did you hear about Coach Rooney and Frau Weiss?"

I shook my head. The newly divorced ice hockey coach and the spinster German teacher had been making eyes at each other since September, but this wasn't news.

Sarah lowered her voice. "Caught by the janitor—*in flagrante delicto*—in the copy room over Christmas break."

"WHAT?"

She nodded. Then she added sagely, "See. Everyone else is having hot sex, Ellie. Get with the program."

I almost threw *Persuasion* at her, but she laughed and ran out of the school library.

The fact that she was right did not please me, which was my only defense for what happened next.

I was sitting on the floor of my one-bedroom apartment a week later, three scented candles lit and my favorite Survivor CD playing, when the phone rang. Mom.

"Diana's back home."

"Okay," I said. All three of us kids lived within forty-five minutes of my parents' house, so this wasn't really an occurrence of unusual significance.

"No. Permanently." My mom's voice sounded strained. "She left Alex."

"Oh, God." Although my sister and I had avoided each other like a viral infection in recent years and were no closer now than we'd been in high school, my heart went out to her. She must've felt so down, so depressed, so confused—

"She's driving me crazy," Mom said, "and I need your help. You need to do something with her. Take her somewhere and talk some sense into her. She says she wants to *meet* people."

"Already?" I sputtered. "How long has she been back at home?"

"Since yesterday. She says she wants to start *dating* again."

"She must be in denial, Mom. Or in shock. What happened with Alex?"

"She said they've grown apart. That they never belonged together, and now it's over." My mother sighed. "Do you think she's serious?"

"Um, well, I—huh." I exhaled. How the hell was I supposed to know? But I said, "Has Alex called or stopped by to talk to her? Do you get the sense that he, at least, wants to try to work things out?"

"He called once, but I didn't hear either side of their conversation. Could you speak to her? Maybe she'll confide in you."

This, I decided, was my mother at her most Pollyannaish. But it wasn't as though I could refuse. "Sure. Is she there now?"

"No. She went to the store to buy shampoo, moisturizer and Ho Hos, I think." Mom sounded baffled by the combination. "But tomorrow's Saturday. You don't have any weekend plans, do you?"

"No," I said, regretting not only that this was the truth but that I had to admit it.

"Then come by for dinner. Maybe you two can talk or do something together in the evening."

Di and me. Out on the town. Together.

Those were three phrases that had never been used jointly in over a quarter of a century.

"Yeah, all right," I told my mother, then I hung up. I lit another candle, raised the volume on my stereo and, since I'd given up heavy drinking, devoured three Twinkies in rapid succession.

For courage.

To better illuminate my adult relationship with my sister, I refer you to one of our typical conversations (along with Jane's inevitable commentary), which took place about a month before Di and her then-fiancé tied the knot:

"Alex and I are engaged!" Di informed me, sticking her ring in my face and speaking with a degree of liveliness unusual in one so typically bad-tempered.

I confess to staring, somewhat rudely, at the rock. "It's, um . . . orange," I said, noting its similarity in hue to the kitchen wall tiles near my parents' sink. Their décor could be best described as "circa 1976."

Di cackled. "It's sardonyx, you idiot. Mine's from Uruguay." She pulled her hand back and shot me an irritated look. "It's one of the birthstones of August—*your* birth month, geek. I'm surprised you don't recognize it."

My whole life Di had called me a geek, yet *she* was the one conversant on birthstones. Go figure. But it fit with the latest New-Age incarnation she'd been trying to project and, besides, there was never any point in arguing with her.

"I didn't know that," I said. "Well, congratulations. When's the big day?"

"Next month. And, no, I'm not pregnant," she said, anticipating my unspoken question. "We just didn't want to wait and do that long-engagement shit. Don't worry, though. I already asked Kendra Daschell to be my maid of honor. You remember Stacy's older sister, right?" Di looked smug. "She'll be my *only* attendant."

I felt a strong pang of something. Hurt, I supposed, both at her choice of attendant and at this offhanded dismissal of me from the wedding party. True, I didn't want to be in it, not exactly, but, for the millionth time, I wished my sister and I could've had that kind of relationship. The kind where we were able to confide our secrets in each other, call each other first when big moments in our lives arose, insist on getting married only with the other by our side for support.

This was *so* not our reality.

"I'm sure it'll be great," I murmured.

Di shot me a strange look. "You can bring whoever you want to it, you know. Even that dork you've been dating." (I was still with Dominic then.) "You can relax and not have to do any work or anything. I thought you'd like that."

I managed a semi smile. "Thanks."

She shrugged. "Well, all right. I'm going out now. See you later." She stomped away and I sighed.

Expend more effort next time, Jane suggested. *She was getting closer to trusting you.*

Yeah. I'm sure that's where all those insults were leading. I closed my eyes, buried my face in my palms and just rested. Interacting with my sister had a way of draining the lifeblood out of me. Every single time.

You know, Ellie, it surprises me that you have neglected to discuss courtship issues with Diana. She might prove to have valuable insights.

Di? I scoffed. *Not hardly.*

Do not be so hasty in your dismissal. She is on the verge of matrimony, after all. Perhaps she is maturing and shedding the capricious irresponsibility of her youth. You have not spent much time in her company as of late.

True enough, I replied. *But that would be because she hasn't yet shed the mean streak of her youth.*

Ellie, I am simply suggesting you ponder the possibility that your sister may now have something to offer you—

Besides criticism?

Yes, Jane said. *And, indeed, you might consider offering her the same.*

This felt like a slap. I had never, not even remotely, been as nasty to Di as she'd been to me. I was really pissed off at Jane. How dare she get all parental and reprimand *me* for thinking critical thoughts. *I haven't been—*

Your attitude does not reflect favorably upon you, Jane murmured. *That is merely my point. And you may be missing what goodness is present in your relationship with your sister because of your determination to find fault.*

I couldn't think up an immediate rebuttal, so I pushed my chair away from the kitchen table and got up to walk off the anger and claustrophobia.

I know I spent my college years dating a confederacy of dunces. It's not that I don't need the relationship advice, I told Jane finally. *It's just that Di and I are too different to EVER find common ground. Period.*

With a sniff, Jane let the topic drop. But Jane and I had spent years talking and arguing things out, albeit mentally. Di and I had no such precedent.

So, when I walked into my parents' living room the day after my mom's frantic phone call about Di and Alex's separation, my expectations for deep conversation weren't high. But I was determined to be brave and, hey, judging from my first glance at Di, we were at least united in our partiality for sweet snack-cakes.

My sister, feet planted firmly on the coffee table, had the TV remote in one hand, a big Hostess box in the other and a Ho Ho half-stuffed in her mouth.

"Wann wrun?" Di said, chewing.

"What?"

She swallowed and held out the box. "Want one?"

"Oh. Okay. Thanks." I reached for a Ho Ho and smiled at Di. See, I could do this. Sisterly bonding in action. "So, what's going on?"

She shrugged. "Didn't Mom tell you? I thought she'd blabbed to all the family and most of the neighborhood by now." Di snapped off another half of a Ho Ho with her teeth and chewed hard, which was when I noticed the conspicuous absence of the gold band from her left ring finger. "I left that bastard Alex," Di continued. "We're separating and soon I'll be free of the fucker."

"Uh, yeah. Mom did mention that." I nibbled on my treat. "She phrased it somewhat differently, though."

Di laughed and shoved the rest of her chocolaty dessert into her mouth. "Snanns."

"What?"

She swallowed and put the Ho Ho box down. "I said, thanks. Thanks for making me laugh and for coming to see me. It's . . . nice of you."

My knees nearly buckled. In all my life, I don't think Di had ever said anything to me so sincerely appreciative. "I—well, you're welcome."

"So, I haven't really talked to my friends about this separation shit. I know they'd wanna get me drunk or something, but I just feel like doing totally different things. Being with people who don't know me."

Which would include me, I gathered. "Yeah."

"Mom said you or Gregory would probably know a few good places to hang out. Like downtown, maybe." She forced the dessert-box flap closed, dropped it on the coffee table and glared at the Ho Hos as if they were chocolate miniatures of Alex. "I wanna pick up a guy tonight."

My breath caught. "Di, listen, I know you must be really hurting right now, but—"

"*You* listen, geek. I don't need a lecture. I need the name of a hot club. It's not like I'm asking you to go along with me or anything. But if you won't help, that's fine. Gregory might know something, or I'll find someone else who will." She jumped up and took a few purposeful strides toward the door.

"Just wait, Di. Wait."

She swiveled around and stared at me.

"I heard about this new place in Chicago. The Dragon's Lair. It's supposed to be great, but I haven't been there yet. I'd really, really love to see it, though." My latest in a long string of falsehoods. "Maybe we can go there tonight."

"Why?"

"What do you mean, 'why'? You just asked me for the name of a club."

"I meant why would you offer to come, too? You and I never hang out together."

"Well, it—it's probably a good time to give it a shot," I said. Then I shrugged, incapable of pretending any longer that we had a normal sibling relationship. "I don't know, Di. It seems like if you ever needed a sister, it'd be now. I'm sorry you're stuck with me, but I'm trying, okay?"

For a long moment she didn't say anything. She just stood there, motionless.

"You're not *that* bad," she muttered finally. Then she marched back across the room and grabbed the box of Ho Hos. "For the road," she said, pushing her feet into her black leather boots and snatching her winter jacket. She tapped her foot against the ceramic hall tiles. "Let's go already."

❧ 5 ❧

From all I can collect by your manner
of talking, you must be two of the
silliest girls in the country.

—*Pride and Prejudice*

Instead of dining on our mom's meat loaf and mashed potatoes, as originally planned, Di and I stopped for dinner at a burger dive en route to the city.

I began to order their tamest menu option—a fire-grilled chicken salad with lite vinaigrette dressing—when Di interrupted.

"Two double cheeseburgers," she said to the waitress, "with fries and milk shakes." She slanted me a proud grin. "My treat, geek. What flavor shake do you want?"

I went with chocolate, of course, and my sister, nodding with rare approval, ordered the same.

The waitress left.

"Cool," she said, bouncing a little on the cushy red vinyl. "This is the kind of crap I missed most when I was married."

"How do you mean?"

She waved her palm in an arc, taking in the place with a sweep of her hand. "See all these people? None of them are looking at me. None of them are gonna stay up all night wondering where I am if I don't call to check in with them. And I don't have to worry or wonder about any of them either. Because—" She raised her voice. "I don't care! We're strangers and we're also grown-ups, so we can do whatever the hell we want without answering to anybody."

I thought of my apartment, empty of anyone who'd miss me if I disappeared for a day . . . or for forever, and my heart clenched. "That's what you liked best about being single? Not having someone around who cares about your well-being?"

"Hell, yeah." She paused. "Well, kind of. I mean, there are no more restrictions. No expectations. Nobody else's standards that I have to deal with every goddamn day. I'm free."

I squinted at her. "What did Alex do to you, Di?"

She looked at me, startled, then looked away. "Nothing. He was just an idiot."

"C'mon," I said. "Tell me the truth. This all didn't come out of nowhere, did it?"

The waitress returned with our food: thick shakes, platters heaped with greasy fries and burgers that would've toppled over if not for the gooey cheese gluing them to the bun.

Di doused her plate with half a bottle of ketchup and slurped on her chocolate milk shake. "Mmm," she said, ignoring my question.

I decided to let it go. It was a bloody miracle the two of us were even sitting in a restaurant having what would appear to anyone on the outside as a cordial meal together. She didn't want me psychoanalyzing her and, hell, I'm sure nothing I came up with would've even been close.

Jane, of course, had her own theories.

Ask your sister if her husband was in any way an abusive man, Jane urged.

Uh, no. There were few things I knew with certainty about my sister, but one was that she'd break the bones of any guy who'd try to hit her. Even our brother, as a toddler, knew better than to raise his hand at Di.

"Want my onions?" I asked Di instead, picking mine off the burger.

"Nope," she said. "I plan to be making out with some hot-blooded man before midnight." She wrinkled her nose. "Not an early-to-bed wimp like Alex." She mumbled something about men who'd lost touch with their dreams and didn't believe in having fun anymore.

Perhaps Mr. Evans was unfaithful, Jane proposed. *That would be most intolerable.*

Boy, I doubt he was, I told Jane. *I never got the sense that Alex would—*

Ask her, Jane insisted.

I sighed. "Was there someone else in the picture?" I said aloud. "For either of you?"

Di attacked a couple of ketchup-covered fries and snorted. "Not hardly."

Might it be possible, then, Jane said, *that she is with child and afraid?*

I choked on a mouthful of milk shake.

"You okay?" Di asked, shooting me a strange look.

"Um, yeah," I said, wiping my lips with a paper napkin. "I just swallowed too fast."

She shrugged. "Look, I appreciate your concern and everything, but it's not like there was any one thing that caused this. Alex and I are just different people now than we were four or five years ago. He's been acting like a fucking control freak for the past few months, but it's not like he screwed around on me. I'd have killed him." She took a huge bite out of her burger and the juices dripped down her chin.

"So, you already tried working things out with him? Talking about it?"

"Oh, yeah, we talked about it all right. I told him last week if he didn't give me some goddamn space, I'd walk. And he didn't give me any space."

Ah, Jane said in her Appraising voice. *Mr. Evans may have been attempting to compel your sister, and rightly so, to act in a more ladylike manner and—*

Di belched. "Sorry," she said. "Anyway, it's time for me to meet someone new. The four-and-a-half-year itch and all."

"So, you're really serious about replacing him?" I said. "You're really ready to move on?"

"Yep," Di replied. "But I'm not looking for a new husband. I just want to get laid."

I nodded. Jane didn't offer further suggestions.

An hour later we walked into the club.

The Dragon's Lair thrummed with energy and loud dance-mix tunes. Colored lights flashed around us like comet streaks, and I could feel the compulsive beat of rhythm all the way to the tips of my boots.

We found a free spot near the bar, and Di went to grab us a couple drinks. "Jack Daniel's straight up for me. Fruity wine cooler for you." She rolled her eyes. "Boring, but then again, you're driving us home."

I accepted my bottle. "Thanks. Next round is on me."

She waved her hand as if dismissing the idea. "Don't worry about it. I've actually got a lot of money saved, and I'm getting another raise in three weeks."

Di had been working at Fashion Plate, a suburban clothing store, for close to a decade. I'd never thought about it before, but she must've been pretty good at her job to be at it that long and to get so many promotions. She was now a senior manager.

"Congratulations," I said.

She grinned at me. "Thanks. You done paying off grad school yet?"

"Yeah. I'm finally beginning to build up my savings account."

"Good. You do that. You can't trust a guy to provide for you. Even marriage isn't a guarantee."

I raised my eyebrows, wanting to ask her more about Alex, but she gave me a Don't-Go-There look and so I took a long drink instead.

Still, this conversation had my head reeling, and it was clearly uncharted territory for both of us.

Di and I, discussing our finances.

It felt so bizarrely *adult*. And it kept forcing me to look at my sister in ways I'd never before considered.

"Are you thinking of going back to school?" I asked her. She'd squeaked through college and gotten a four-year general business degree, which was impressive given her lack of study habits in high school, but she'd vowed never to do the grad-school thing.

"Nah, I don't think so. I'm pretty happy where I am. Well, with my career and all."

"Gregory seems to like his job, too," I said. "All those computer-techno thingies he does."

"Yeah, but—" She made a face. "He and Nadia are getting too

serious, too fast. Those guys are practically living together, you know."

I didn't know, although I'd suspected. Gregory couldn't keep his hands off his latest and most curvaceous girlfriend, not even in front of our parents, to Mom's eternal agitation.

"Did you talk with him about it directly?" I asked. "Did he tell you his plans?"

"Yep. Get engaged before the end of the year. Get married next year. Move to Colorado, if they can swing it, because the skiing is really great there. Squeeze out a couple of kids sometime after that." Di raised up her second shot of Jack. "Here's to them."

I lifted my bottle also and clinked with her, aware we weren't merely talking theory. When Gregory set his mind to doing something, it pretty much went down that way. In a flash I saw the rest of my brother's life whizzing before my eyes like so many of the colored lights at the club.

Di turned her attention to the guys in the room, not being remotely subtle about it. She stared, mouth agape, at one hunky specimen who passed by our table.

"How old is he, do you think?" she asked me. "Twenty-nine? Thirty?"

"Yeah, probably. Why?"

"Because he looks experienced enough. I think I'll sleep with him."

"*Di!*"

"What?"

"You don't just look at a guy and decide to proposition him. He could be married or here with his fiancée or . . . his boyfriend." Although, from the predatory way the man moved, he certainly seemed well suited to the hetero set.

My sister considered my words. "He's not gay," she said dismissively, "and he's sitting at the bar with a group of five very naughty-looking men. No adoring woman on his sleeve, though. No gold ring on his finger."

Not exactly proof of singlehood, since Di was still technically married and didn't have a ring on her finger either. But I had to admit to being impressed with Di's powers of observation. She took in quite a lot on first glance.

I, too, studied the guy in question. He was tall, muscular, Slavic-looking. His longish, dark blond hair swayed against the back of his neck as he walked or, rather, prowled. He had the natural gait of a panther.

"Help me pick him up," Di said.

"No," I whispered, not so much because I didn't want to help her but because the man kind of frightened me. "Are you sure he's your type? What about one of them?"

I pointed toward a couple of harmless-looking accountant types on the dance floor, and Di snickered. "What are you, blind? If you think those guys are hot prospects, you need to get laid more than I do."

"Look, Di, this whole idea is—"

"Shut up. I just caught his eye."

Cripes. I stole another glance at Slavic Man and his Bad-Boy Posse. He looked right back at us, his light eyes bright with growing interest. My psyche plummeted back in time, to high school and to what it felt like to gaze at a group of guys across a crowded dance floor. Everyone eyeing each other, nobody talking.

I remembered Jason Bertignoli.

And Sam Blaine, of course.

I closed my eyes. I was getting too damned old for this.

"Ladies," a deep, accented voice said. "May we treat you to another drink?"

I opened my eyes to the vision of Slavic Man leaning on the table, his ruddy lips curved into a wicked smile, his gaze boring through me like Superman's X-ray vision. I managed to glance at Di, whose eyes were fixed on the attractive black-haired, brown-eyed man standing just behind him. A few yards away, the now smaller group of Bad Boys looked on with fat grins.

Finally recalling that an answer would be expected of us, I said, "That's very kind of you, but we're—"

"We'd love another drink," Di blurted.

The guys nodded briefly at their gang (obviously acknowledging they'd all but scored with these ditzy American chicks) and then pulled up two chairs beside us.

"You are from Chicago, yes?" the dark-haired guy asked us in broken English.

"Yeah," Di said. "But you two aren't, are you?" She grinned at them and laughed her flirtatious laugh. She'd been a pro at that laugh since high school. Both men turned appreciative eyes upon her.

"We are Russian," Slavic Man said. Oh, shocker. "This is my friend Mikhail." He pointed to the dark-haired guy. "And I am Andrei. Andrei Sergiov."

In spite of myself, I smiled. The way he said his name reminded me of James Bond, only Andrei was more like one of the evil guys 007 battled. He was all Slavic suave and loads of untamed passion. My head filled immediately with Pushkin's verses of Russian Romanticism.

East versus West colliding yet again.

But, in one of Pushkin's most famous poems, "Eugene Onegin," it was Western intellectualism and decadence that supposedly contaminated Eastern virtues. That night, though, I wasn't sure just who was going to be tainting whom.

Di, meanwhile, introduced us to the guys. She seemed mesmerized by both men, unable to decide which would make a better one-night stand. Her gaze darted between them and, a few times, she looked over at me, mystified.

After her third questioning glance, I gave her a slight shrug and mouthed, "Take your pick." I sure wasn't about to make the decision for her.

The Russians ordered drinks all around. Even though I was driving, I agreed to another wine cooler. I got the sense from the way these two guys settled into their chairs that we'd be there for several more hours. Long enough for me to regain a clear head and pull my sister away from certain disaster before hitting the road.

Besides, I needed something to occupy my hands. The urge to run them through Andrei's wavy hair had become uncomfortably tempting.

Mikhail leaned in and said, "You are beautiful sisters." He licked his lips in a manner so lascivious I almost laughed. Was he being serious or was he mocking the whole hooking-up-with-a-stranger-at-a-bar convention?

I shot a look at the original Slavic Man. Andrei raised an eyebrow in his buddy's direction, and his lips twisted into a perplexed grimace. Perhaps he and I were wondering the same thing.

As if in confirmation of this, he turned his magnetic gaze on me. The change in his expression was so subtle as to be unnoticed by the other two, but I could read it clearly. He wanted me to know he was better at this game than Mikhail, and I ought not to forget it.

No freaking chance of that. I hoped for the first time that night that my sister would set her sights on the attractive but moronic dark-haired stud and leave The Panther to me.

As miracles would have it, she did.

Di slid her chair closer to Mikhail and nodded once in my direction. In response, I moved my drink a few inches nearer to Andrei's. The teams were decided.

The boys sized up the situation remarkably fast and relaxed into their roles.

Mikhail soon began whispering jokey comments into my sister's ear. She laughed uproariously, although I feared the real comedy-inducer was the one-two punch of good ole Jack D. combined with being on the verge of achieving her evening's objective.

On my side of the court, Andrei rested a large, warm hand on the back of my chair and, against all reason, my heart swelled with delight at this territorial gesture.

"Ellie," he said to me, his accent making my name sound erotic and exotic simultaneously. "I wish to hear of your work during daytime hours."

I smiled at his phrasing. If he'd been an American, his words might've implied something darker, as if my nighttime activities were somehow nefarious compared to whatever occupied my time during the day. But I knew he meant only to ask about my job, so I told him about being a high-school librarian.

Unlike 99 percent of the American men I'd met since I started my career, Andrei, to my shock, did not consider my occupation to be bland and unexciting.

"So, you are knowing much about great literature!" he said, bringing up a few of the Russian greats: Chekhov, Pushkin, Tolstoy and Dostoevsky, of course.

"'I am a sick man . . . I am a spiteful man,'" he quoted with frightening believability before he broke into a charming grin. "You know this, yes?"

I nodded, awestruck. It wasn't every day a girl met a hunky guy who could spontaneously recite lines from Dostoevsky's *Notes from Underground* while sitting in a nightclub drinking imported beer.

"I work, during daytime, as house painter and maintenance man. I have work visa and good job here in States. Someday I will be citizen, too, but my true heart"—he brought his palm to his solid-looking chest—"is with poets."

Is he a writer? Jane asked, suddenly paying attention.

I asked him if he was.

"Yes. Of words. Lyrics," he clarified. "I am playing my music now, my guitar, for beyond twenty years."

Ah, a musician with poetic tendencies. Jane declared this to be an interesting development, but Di overheard him and shot me a troubled look. Her soon-to-be-ex-husband's instrument of choice was a Fender Telecaster electric guitar.

"I'd like to hear you play sometime," I told him, partially to be polite and make conversation, yes, but primarily because he'd aroused my curiosity. And a few of my other parts. "Are you currently with a band?"

He radiated pride and waved his hand in the direction of Mikhail and their other buddies still near the bar. "We are Red Square Warning."

"You're what?"

"Our band. We have name—Red Square Warning. We are all here this night."

I sent a look back across the table at Di, whose brown eyes were now open wide with an expression of general alarm. "Mikhail's in the band, too?" I said.

"Yes." Andrei raised his beer bottle to his friend.

Mikhail pointed to himself and boasted, "I am drummer. Like Ringo."

"Oh, hell," Di muttered.

"Oh, well—how interesting!" I said, trying to cover for her. "What kind of music do you play?"

"We are like Russian U2," Mikhail said. "Except Andrei's voice is too, too . . . *pree-yat-nee*."

I didn't know what that Russian word meant but, whatever it was, Andrei didn't appreciate it. I glanced over at him for a translation, but he was too busy slugging his friend in the bicep.

"He is liar," Andrei insisted, although he shot a grin at Mikhail.

"You sing for them," Mikhail said. "Let beautiful sisters hear." He turned to Di and devoured her with seductive eyes. "You will comprehend then. He sounds like sweet angel, not like rock star. Very, very . . . pretty."

Andrei snorted and shook his head, but the three of us looked at him expectantly, and Jane said, *I wonder at his level of accomplishment.*

"I cannot sing here in noisy bar." Andrei glanced around. "Maybe you both come to my place?"

I envisioned the look of horror etched on our mother's face when she and our dad would be called in to identify the dead bodies of their foolish daughters. "What were they doing in this foreign man's apartment?" Mom would say to the officer at the crime scene. "What were they thinking?"

So, to Andrei, I said, "No, thank you, we can't—"

"Not a good idea," Di interrupted, agreeing with me on something for a change.

Andrei nodded, understanding. "Okay. Maybe then we go to upstairs level." He pointed toward the marginally quieter second floor, which was loft-like and reassuringly open, but away from the largest of the speakers and the majority of the patrons. "I will call others to join us. We sing you one good song all together. Very safe then."

He smiled at me, a winning grin that sent my resolve melting to my toes. I'd follow him alone down a dark Chicago alley if he kept looking at me like that.

I glanced at Di. She inclined her head in a gesture of assent, so we trailed the two guys up the metal stairs. With the flick of Andrei's index finger, their four remaining friends jumped up to join us.

After conferring briefly in rapid-fire Russian, one of the men bolted out of the club and returned three minutes later with two small instruments from his car. One was something kind of mandolin-like. The other was a shoebox-sized accordion.

Mikhail pulled a couple of drumsticks out of his coat pocket, and another guy produced a harmonica and some jingling hand bells.

Instant band. Just add audience.

"Sit, please," Andrei instructed Di and me, pointing to a couple of chairs in the corner farthest from the flashing lights and hip-hop sounds below. "We play you music—from our souls to yours."

Up until now, I knew how to identify all the males I'd encountered in my life. Male Types #1 through #5 could be spotted from a striking distance of several yards and, thus, avoided. My system was developed—and numbers assigned—based upon my personal relationship chronology. To elaborate:

Type #1 = Absolute bastards like Sam Blaine, however good-looking they may be. Arrogant, heartless pricks with too much intelligence and too little sensitivity.

Type #2 = The Jason Bertignolis of the world. Nice, overall. Fairly cute. Not as bright or as mean-spirited as Type #1 but, for a number of reasons, not as alluring either.

Type #3 = Fun-loving, sappily romantic, not-quite-one-hundred-percent-all-American males, namely, guys like my college boyfriend Mark Williams and his Gay Band of Brothers (who finally decide to embrace their true sexual orientation after stringing along naïve girls like me). Nothing wrong with their lifestyle, but it puts a serious crimp in a woman's fantasies of hot, kinky sex.

Type #4 = Attractive, masculine and definitely in favor of hot, kinky sex. Very verbal guys who possess an artistic flair but have some unfortunate authority issues, an inclination toward procrastination and a decided lack of a work ethic. In a nutshell, Dominic Reyes-Jones and user guys like him.

Type #5 = The macho bad boys, the cheaters-cheaters-pumpkin-eaters of the dating universe whose only regrets come when they get caught, i.e., Brent "Strip Go Fish" Sullivan.

But Andrei presented something altogether different. He formed a new category all by himself, and I was, I confess, smitten with what I designated on the spot to be the rare Type #6: A man who was talented, straightforward, virile and utterly unique.

Di and I sat awkwardly in our new seats as the men readied themselves. Mikhail flipped a chair around and began drumming a rhythmic riff on the back of it. One guy tuned the mandolin thing and strummed a couple of practice chords, and all of the men hummed a few notes in some kind of vocal warm-up.

Then everything stopped abruptly.

A few seconds later, a haunting accordion melody rose above The Dragon's Lair dance mix. The mandolin and the other instruments joined in.

And Andrei began to sing.

A lady's imagination is very rapid;
it jumps from admiration to love,
from love to matrimony, in a moment.

—*Pride and Prejudice*

Andrei's voice pierced my soul with its lyricism and bathed me in an experience not unlike spirituality.

Yes, without a doubt, there was something otherworldly about Slavic Man when he sang, but the celestial cadences struck me as more phantasmal than angelic. I felt myself slip inside an aural dream sequence and wouldn't have been surprised if little bits of my being were spirited away on the wings of each musical note.

The men's voices merged for the first chorus. Although this was a song I didn't know, the words were familiar, English. They'd been grafted, however, with husky Russian pronunciation and elongated by the silken melody. So much so that the tune might well have been a completely foreign one.

Then, Andrei sang alone once more.

He sang of freedom and passion. He sang of discovery and a call to one's personal journey. He sang to me, directly, and the rest of the world faded into the void.

Amazing.

Some guys really understood foreplay.

When they were finished, Di and I clapped, as did a few other people who'd been listening in on the Russians' second-floor performance.

"Dudes! Awesome song," one drunk guy exclaimed.

"You were great, man," said the drunk guy's friend, who was also wasted.

They were, however, completely in earnest and, in my opinion, right on target. Andrei and his buddies appeared pleased with the positive reception.

The drunk guy's Southern-belle girlfriend, who was, by contrast, as sober as a Sunday-school teacher, turned to me and whispered, "That looker of a lead singer must think you're hotter than a porch swing in August. He didn't take his eyes off you the whole time he sang, so, either you're sleeping together already or he's got *plans* for you."

I felt my face flush. "We just met an hour ago," I told her.

She raised both eyebrows and tossed me a saucy grin. "You better watch out, girl."

Di cast me an odd look the moment the woman walked away. "She's right, you know." Then Mikhail appeared at her side, presumably to claim a kiss for his part in the concert, and her attention was diverted.

"Did you like it?" Andrei asked me tenderly, as if he hadn't already guessed.

"Yeah." I took a step closer to him. "You have a remarkable voice."

"But it is not 'pretty.' Say no." He gave me a forbidding headshake.

I laughed. "No, it's not pretty. But it *is* a gift. People must be in awe every time they hear you."

He shrugged. "It is not always possible to sing from my soul, Ellie. I am saving such moments up for special people. For people like you."

He seared me with one of his intense gazes, and I could feel the sexual heat between us nudging me closer to him while, at the same time, nipping me with its tiny burns.

I took a step back and tried to deflect the flames.

I did a quick check on Di's location, only to see her in full liplock with Mikhail. Drummer Boy had both his hands covering her butt and had pulled her against his chest. Didn't look like water could separate them.

I squinted at the new couple until I felt a calloused finger touch my chin.

"Look at me, lovely lady." Andrei stared into my eyes with another of his commanding gazes, his light gray irises compelling me to gawk at him. "We see each other again, yes? We go out together sometime, you and me?"

He drew his arm around my waist and tugged me near. When my body brushed against his, it ignited.

I considered it an achievement that I managed a nod in response.

"Good," he said, smiling down at me from a very intimate distance. Then he brought his lips slowly and deliberately to mine.

This was no typical first kiss.

This was no sweet union of mouths.

This was a consuming, mystifying, intoxicating combustion of beings.

This was what people meant when they referred to "physical chemistry." Two different elements that, when combined, were transformed into an entirely unique entity. So unique, in fact, that I no longer recognized myself.

Andrei snatched a few gulps of air. "Maybe we go out *now?*" he suggested.

I didn't answer, but I leaned into him and again pulled his mouth down to mine.

Everything about this should've been wrong.

He had smoker's breath and still tasted of beer, neither of which I liked.

He was built large and imposing, both of which made me feel insecure.

He could've had reprehensible motives, the possibility of which had me worried because, for all I knew, he could be merely trolling for an American wife to make green-card acquisition easier.

But, somehow, when our lips met, every reasonable fear washed away. I floated on the waves of a passion I didn't have much experience with, my body being spoken to in a language it didn't understand. All of this rightness despite all odds could not, I figured, be without purpose. This could only be part of some Divine Grand Plan.

Do not be so certain, Ellie, though he IS so very handsome and accomplished, Jane said dryly. Then again, she'd witnessed me falling in love before to disastrous results. I could hardly blame her skepticism.

But, this time, it really *was* different.

"You will come to my place tonight?" Andrei smacked his pelvis into mine in such a scandalously sensual way that my legs weakened under me to the point of near collapse.

I held him tight for balance and said a very eloquent, "Mmmm."

He took this to mean yes.

A few vague thoughts skittered through my lust-fogged brain, the predominant one being: Where was Di?

As Andrei dug into his coat pocket for car keys, I spotted my sister standing apart from us, her face pale, Mikhail by her side whispering something in her ear.

My mind cleared long enough to catch her eye, and that was when I saw it. Tears. Di's tears, streaming down her face in silent grief. God. What did that Mikhail idiot say to her? I was going to kill him.

"What happened?" I demanded, striding over to them, glaring at Drummer Boy and putting a protective arm around my sister's shoulders. "What'd he do?"

Di looked at me with a grateful glance I'd never seen her direct my way before, but then she shook her head. "Nothing, El. It's me, not him."

"You sure?"

"Yeah," Di said as Mikhail edged away from us. "I'm sure. I just want to get outta here. But—" She paused and gave me a sad half smile.

"But what?"

"I know you probably want to stay or . . . or go somewhere else with him." She pointed at Andrei, and I marveled at my new man. Then I marveled even more at how quickly I'd begun thinking of him as My New Man.

"Well—" I skimmed my gaze over the Slavic hunk again, who had a pretty decent mastery of smoldering from a distance. But this was one case where sisterly bonding had to take precedence over sex hormones, despite my body's rebellion. "Nah. We can leave. Let me just say goodbye, okay?"

"Okay," Di said. "Thanks."

I returned to Andrei, every blood cell threatening mutiny if I actually left him for the night, but I made myself explain aloud that my sister and I had to go.

He said he understood, and he scribbled his phone number down. I took it. I then gave him mine, and he put the slip of paper carefully into his shirt pocket, the one above his heart. He reached for my hand and pressed both of our palms against that pocket.

"I will call you," he said. "I mean this. Please do not forget me."

I assured him that would be impossible and, after one parting kiss, Di and I were out the door.

"I've never seen you like that," she admitted on the drive back to Glen Forest.

"Like what?"

"Like, you know, in the throes of passion." She gave me a look that was part grin, part grimace. "Something other than your geeky side."

"Gee, that's heartening."

I thought she was laughing, but then I caught a few tears clinging to the corners of her eyes.

"What happened back there, Di?" I asked her as gently as I could. I wanted to know but, truth be told, it was also freaking me out. My hard-ass sister never cried.

She swallowed. "I thought I was ready to move on." She paused. "I'm not ready."

"Well, no. Of course not. You need to give yourself more than forty-eight hours to recover from a nearly five-year marriage. Most people would take at least a week."

She snickered and looked at me strangely.

"What?" I said.

"When did you grow a sense of humor? You were never funny when we were kids."

"You never talked to me when we were kids, except for the occasional threat."

"That's not tru—" She stopped. Thought. "Well, okay. Maybe it is."

Vindicated, I looked at her askance. She was again crying a stream of silent tears. "Di, c'mon. Talk to me now. What's going on? What happened with Alex?"

"It's the whole musician thing. That really got to me tonight, you know?"

I totally didn't know, but I said, "Yeah."

"I miss that side of Alex. I've missed it for a long time. He got all respectable and everything, and that's fine, but instead of just polishing up the rougher edges, he got rid of his whole wild side. He doesn't play his Fender much anymore, and when he does, he doesn't do it with the drive he used to have. He's all into working at the bank now and being responsible, and those are good things, but—" She grabbed a tissue, blew her nose and shrugged.

"But you miss the guy you married?"

"Yeah. A fucking lot. He had *dreams* once. Things he wanted to do. I wish he'd have held on to a few of them. They kept him fun and young, and I felt that way, too, back then. Now," her voice turned hard, "he tries to say that I'm, like, *reckless* or *immature* for wanting to have a little fun sometimes. For wanting us to go out with friends. Such a total load of crap. So I told him, fine! He doesn't have to come along. I work hard all week, too. I look managerial enough at the store every day. I handle all kinds of goddamn crises. It's not like it's a crime to want to blow off some steam on Friday or Saturday night. Is it?" She turned to me with a demanding glare.

"Um, no—" I began.

"See! But does that bastard listen to reason? No. He goes off and calls me *irresponsible*. Says I should be home at a *reasonable* hour, like fucking ten o'clock on a weekend! And the sad thing is, I didn't even care much about going out. I just wanted us to laugh again and have fun and talk about something other than work and retirement funds and old-people crap like that. I thought when you got married to someone they'd sort of stay recognizable."

"But they don't, huh?"

"Hell, no. At least Alex didn't," she murmured. "You think you know someone, but a few years go by and nothing's predictable anymore."

I tried to wrap my mind around this and apply it to my life. What would happen if Andrei and I got serious? We probably wouldn't, but what if? Would that phenomenal chemistry between us fizzle out within a couple of years? Would we eventually tire of talking about Russian writers? Would his singing someday cease to amaze me?

Di seemed to sense where my mind was headed. She sniffled a time or two and said, "Watch out for musicians, El. I mean, he might be your guy, The One for you, I don't know. But most of the time you're either second place to their rock'n'roll ambitions or they get realistic, give up their dreams and become soulless dweebs. Like Alex."

"I'll be careful," I told her.

Di nodded at me in approval and, in my head, Jane applauded as well.

"Tell me every detail, Ellie," my old college buddy/boyfriend Mark said over the phone a few weeks later, "starting with whether or not the man can dance."

I smirked into the receiver. "Andrei's a singer and a guitarist. He has a great sense of rhythm. He can dance."

"But can he dance *well?*"

"I know what you want me to say, so, yeah. Okay. You win. He can dance, but not as well as you, Mark 'Jitterbug King' Williams." Mark had a God-given talent for intricate footwork and shone like Fred Astaire on the dance floor. (And, boy, could he lead. He'd led me on for three months.)

I heard a heavy faux sigh on the line. "That's a relief. I couldn't stand to be outdone by a straight guy. And a foreigner to boot. He's really *Russian?*"

"Yes."

"Huh. Well, you'd better bring him in May. I want to check him out."

"Bring him to Toronto? To a gay union?" I said, laughing. "That's *so* not going to happen."

"Why not? You ashamed of us?" Mark's voice sounded light, as though he were still joking, but I heard the catch in it that signified hurt.

"Absolutely not," I told him truthfully. "I just have no idea where he stands on stuff like gay marriage."

"What, you two don't talk when you're together? You don't discuss issues?"

I thought of the things Andrei and I had been doing together and, well, "discussing the issues" wasn't the main one.

"It's only been about a month," I said to Mark, evading a bit. "There are lots of topics we haven't covered yet."

"Hmm, yeah. Like how freaky it was when you found out one of your ex-boyfriends was dating your old roommate's husband's old roommate?"

Admittedly, convoluted as it was trying to explain it to anyone else, yes, Mark and Seth together did blow my mind at first, but I got over it. So did Kim and Tom.

Kim, my friend and favorite undergrad roommate, had eventually married Tom in a beautiful (and lengthy) Roman Catholic wedding the summer after my first year of grad school. Tom's roomie for one of our undergrad years had been a football-playing, Army Reserve guy named Seth—who had, incidentally, gone to high school with my then-in-the-closet gay boyfriend Mark (whom I dated that year after we met in Ballroom Dancing 102, which, let me tell you, is the most fabulous way *ever* to satisfy the college PE requirement).

Kim, Tom, Mark and I went on a few double dates but, after Mark finally came out, he started hanging around Tom and Seth's room . . . and, well . . .

"It wouldn't have been such a shock to all of us if Seth hadn't been Mr. ROTC Dude," I said to Mark, thinking of Seth's stocky build and buzz haircut, and how different he was in style and temperament from the lean, suave, near-preppy Mark. Kind of like *Top Gun* versus *Top Hat*.

"Just goes to show, people shouldn't stereotype."

"Very smug of you. I hope that means, if I do bring Andrei in May, you're going to keep an open mind about him. No anti–Bolshoi

Ballet slurs or criticisms of Moscow's purportedly inferior wine. You'll behave?"

"If I must." Mark paused. "Hey, is this guy treating you well, Ellie?"

"Yeah," I said, feeling the smile grow on my face. "He's thoughtful and sweet. He gave me the most romantic Valentine's Day I've had since the one with you."

"Only, you two actually slept together at the end of the evening, right?"

"I don't have to answer that," I said, but I giggled, giving it away. It'd only been two days since the candy-heart-filled holiday, but the dreamy images from that night continued to make me euphoric.

"Oh, gawd," Mark said, groaning. "You're still in *that* stage."

"Mmm-hmm."

"Well, forget I asked about details, then. I don't want to know." I grinned into the phone.

"Snap out of it, El, I'm serious! We've got my ceremony to discuss, and you need to help me decide which poems should be read."

But as Mark dithered between the Khalil Gibran, the Goethe and the W. H. Auden, my mind wandered into the land of romantic fantasy it'd inhabited since Andrei entered my life.

For the first day in ages, I felt as though everything might just work out. That I'd get my happily-ever-after ending after all.

It sure as hell was about time.

A couple of Saturdays later, at Andrei's apartment, I pulled a can of tuna and a jar of pasta sauce from his grocery bag and handed them to him. He shelved them in the cupboard and reached behind him, palm open, for me to give him the next item. I dug into the bag again, this time retrieving a box of stuffing and a bottle of ketchup, and I had to fight the urge to laugh.

"You know, we're acting like an old married couple," I told him. "Grocery shopping together. Stocking the pantry." I didn't add that I loved it. *Loved* it.

He smiled at me. "This is not bad thing."

"No," I said, my heart soaring at this display of confidence and commitment-readiness. "It's not."

I could feel us moving toward that elusive Next Stage every time we spent more than a few hours in each other's company. Like that morning. Hunting for the cereal he'd tasted at Mikhail's but couldn't remember the name of. (Turned out to be Cocoa Puffs.) Laughing over which soups to buy. Racing to load the items we'd chosen, all of which he insisted on paying for, on the conveyor belt at checkout. Leaving the store hand in hand.

Women who were used to such intimacies might take them for granted, but I didn't. Mundane chores—car washes, laundry, cooking—all were better, or even kind of fun, when I did them with Andrei.

So when we finished putting away the groceries, I said, "I have a wedding to go to in three months, and I can bring a guest along."

He put his arms around me. "I am being invited?"

"Yeah. If you want to go." I waited to hear him say something like "It's still a long time from now" or "We'll see when things get closer," but he didn't.

He nodded and pulled me to him, kissing my forehead. "I go with you."

I snuggled into his chest and squeezed. "There are a few things you should know first. The ceremony's going to be in Canada."

"This is not problem. Work visa lets me go short time out of country. I have all papers in order."

"And it won't be difficult to take off work for three or four days?"

"Not if I am knowing from now." He moved his kiss down my nose, lingered for a moment on my lips and headed lower still to my neck.

Before I allowed myself to rip off his clothes and throw myself at his heavenly body, I figured I'd better tell him the rest. "There's, um, just one other thing. The couple getting married is gay."

He pulled back and raised an eyebrow. "You are meaning two women?" He looked interested.

I shook my head. "Two men."

He shrugged. "Oh. Less exciting, but also okay." He returned his full attention to my neck, and I felt a switch flip on inside of me.

This was love. It had to be. I was in love with him. I may have been for a week or two already. Maybe. In some form or other. Possibly even since the night we met. Love at first sight can happen. (Can't it?) But that day I recognized it for *sure*. That day I just *knew* my feelings were for real.

I yanked his cotton shirt out of the waistband of his jeans and ran my fingers in the space between the fabric and his back. It was a study in contrasts—the soft, downy material against my knuckles and his hard, knotted muscles against my palms. I tried to massage away the tension.

"I need more than back rub, Ellie," he said, his voice half laughter, half whisper.

"And I need more than kisses," I replied, which was all I knew I had to say to get what I wanted. Even so, I added, "I need you inside me."

Andrei didn't answer. He just began peeling off our clothing until there were no obstructions.

We collapsed onto his double bed, on the coverlet, which was a thin blue spread he'd picked up from Wal-Mart. I brushed the pads of my fingers against it, caressing it like I might his skin. He'd gotten it the first time we went out shopping together, and now I was becoming sentimental over it.

He opened the bedside drawer for a condom and slipped it on in a motion so smooth, so practiced that I'd been worried the first time I saw him do it. But Andrei had made it very clear he was a one-woman man, and nothing he'd said or done in the past month or so indicated otherwise.

"Are you ready for me?" he asked, running his tongue from my neck to my tummy, pausing to kiss my belly button and then continuing down to my upper thighs and the space in between them.

"Yes," I managed to gasp out as he flicked his tongue over and around the sensitive skin and inside the folds a time or two, making me even wetter.

He moved up on me, his larger body flush with mine, and he pulled our hips together. He held my thighs apart and pushed into me with a force that would've been brutal if I'd been a smaller woman. As it was, the fit was so tight, so intense and so incredibly erotic that every time we had sex I screamed. Every single time.

He covered my mouth with his to stifle my cry and began a slow thrust that would exponentially increase in speed and power as my body adjusted to his.

While relationships might bring with them, as Di suggested, a whole lot of unpredictability, the uncanny sexual chemistry between Andrei and me didn't fit into that category. We could count on it without reserve. It had become the most steadfast element in my life, and I knew he was bowled over by it, too.

"Come for me," he whispered in my ear, pumping harder now. He said this more for the effect of being a little naughty rather than because he had any fear of it not happening. It always happened with him.

"I'm almost there." I cupped his bare ass in my palms and strained against him, my body floating closer to completion with every labored breath.

He groaned and I wrenched away just far enough to watch the passion build on his face. To see the heightened color of his complexion and the light of his eyes spike darker with the growing fervor between us.

A guttural moan came from deep within him. His gaze met mine as the swell inside him rose further, crested and then broke in climax.

"God, Ellie. Come."

He stayed with me and surged over and over for the final few seconds until I could join him.

I did. And, again, I screamed.

But what was different about this time was that, though I wanted the release, I didn't need it. The attachment I'd begun to feel had more to do with an emotion that defied physicality, however pleasurable.

Love?

Love.

It scared the shit out of me. No way could I utter it aloud.

"Unbelievable," Andrei whispered. "It is always so with you."

I smiled and kissed his shoulder, clutching him to me for a moment before he had to pull away.

He removed the condom, perched on an elbow and looked down at me, his expression serious. "This is strange attraction. I am not ever experiencing such a thing before."

"Me either."

Only my one-night stand with Sam had approached this level of intensity. But, while the emotions may have been equally potent at the time, Sam proved to me that any fantasies of love were pure delusion.

Was I being delusional now?

"Andrei," I began. "What would happen if the sex part between us were more, um, normal? Not always this spectacular? Would you still want us to be together?"

He cast me an odd look. "You are not liking that things work this way?"

I laughed. "No. I mean, *yes*, of course I like it. It's amazing. But I was wondering if you'd still want to see me so much if we just had average sex."

He flopped down on his back and put his head on the pillow next to mine. "Do all American women ask these crazy questions?" He nudged my leg with his foot and trailed his fingertips over my naked breasts.

We weren't quite ready to do it again, but I could feel faint stirrings of arousal already and my breath quickened. The fact that Andrei was trying to change the subject kind of pissed me off, though, so I replied, "Only American women who are crazy enough to be sleeping with Russian men."

This answer did not faze him.

He circled my nipples with his index finger and licked his lips, so I knew what was coming. "I am Russian man wanting to explore all parts of you. It is great bonus we can join our bodies in sex this way, but you are lovely woman. You are kind person. For now, it is working to be with you and also to be fucking. I am not seeing problem."

No, he wouldn't, would he?

I decided to try again. "Look. All I'm saying is that I hope you're not with me *only* because of how good things are between us in bed. I've had men cheat on me before, and I won't let that ever happen again." I looked him straight in the eye so he'd know I meant every syllable.

He nodded, taking it in.

"So," I continued, "if you someday find yourself liking the sex, but not liking me as much, it'd be better for me if we broke things off instead of trying to stay together. I don't want you being with me for physical things but wishing you were talking with someone else."

He put his wet lips to my nipple and sucked on it hard. The delicious tugging made my heart fillip. "I am not wanting to talk to or have sex with someone else, Ellie."

Not quite a declaration of everlasting love, but it was hopeful. And I needed that kind of hope.

Less than a half hour of suckling and licking and stroking later, I screamed again.

His name, this time.

The week before Easter I took a personal day off work to go shopping. The wedding/union was still six weeks away, but I needed to find a really great dress since Mark and Seth had asked me to be one of their readers. Plus, I needed to buy a few other things, and I wanted to shop for them without Andrei knowing.

I went to the mall alone, which is to say, Jane went with me.

Why do you linger in this section? Jane asked as I wandered around the lingerie department of Marshall Field's, admiring the many lacy, silky fabrics.

No reason. But I made a note to visit Victoria's Secret later.

She sniffed. *There seems no need for special undergarments. You and Mr. Sergiov appear to require very little by way of intimacy inducements.*

I grinned. *True.* I always mentally locked Jane out of the bedroom, but she knew what went on nevertheless. The heat between Andrei and me had only risen, and I wanted to keep stoking that fire. I figured a sheer teddy might do the trick.

Jane said, *Were you two married, I could not imagine a couple more inclined to take their connubial responsibilities seriously. There is surely no need for much more . . . kindling of flames.*

But we're not married. And it's the dawning of the twenty-first century. No matter what, I don't want him to lose interest. Because I— I hesitated, then went ahead and told her the rest since she could deduce it anyway. *Because I want him to marry me. I want him to WANT to.*

There was a long pause.

I realize marriage in your era is not quite as intractable a situation as it was in mine. But, Ellie, are you most certain you wish this foreign gentleman to be your husband forevermore?

Andrei's foreignness scarcely registered anymore, and I adored his accent, so I scoffed at this.

Jane sighed. *Aside from your shared passion, are you truly in love with this man? Is he really the person you wish to cleave to? Whose name you would welcome as your own? Do you desire to link your ancestry with his through the connection of parenthood?*

I thought of having Andrei's babies and smiled. They'd be so cute, a combination of features and ethnicities, like Angelique and Leo's daughter, Lyssa.

Mmm-hmm, I replied.

You are not merely feeling the tug of motherhood since you have grown old?

Old?

My apologies. It would have been considered old in my day. Rather, I mean since you have grown up.

That's better. I couldn't deny that being a mom had become increasingly appealing recently, but I had lots of time left for that stuff. (Right?) I didn't have a ticking biological clock. I really didn't.

It's not just about having babies, Jane. I'm getting ready to settle down, be with one person. I'd always heard that when you were truly ready for something in life, it would happen for you. Well, I'm there now.

And you can be certain of this? You can be fully assured of God's will?

It's not like the Big Guy told me his plans, no, but I can feel it. This is the right time. My relationship with Andrei is going strong. We have great chemistry together. It's got to be a sign that he's The One.

Jane did not immediately answer.

What? I said.

She coughed. *I do not wish to dampen your enthusiasm, Ellie, but I believe in no such signs.*

My reaction was, I'll confess, a bit on the defensive side. *And how would YOU know? Can you see into the mind of God? Can you recognize a divine message when one appears in the world?*

I waited for her to respond and, when she didn't, I lashed out. *I know our relationship—yours and mine—is kind of odd. I don't know anyone else who talks to ghosts of famous authors and, to be honest, it's frequently more of an inconvenience than a delight. But in the past, oh, almost twelve years, although I've learned a lot from you, I've also learned you have limits. This is one of those things you can't possibly know—*

You are worried, are you not? Jane asked quietly, ignoring my tantrum. *You fear he does not love you in the same way you love him.*

I snatched at a light blue negligee, ripping it off its plastic hanger. *No,* I told her. I held the flimsy thing up to my body and glared at my reflection in the store mirror. It looked dreadful. I didn't look so great either.

Why do you fear this, Ellie?

I don't fear anything, I insisted. *The time is right. HE'S right. I'm done talking about this.* I shoved the ugly negligee back on the rack and marched toward the dress section.

Very well, Jane whispered.

And that was the first time I could remember her conceding an argument. Even then, I more than suspected I shouldn't have received quite so much satisfaction from this.

&ep; 7 &ep;

Vanity and pride are different things . . .
A person may be proud without being vain.
Pride relates more to our opinion
of ourselves, vanity to what
we would have others think of us.

—Pride and Prejudice

Jane and I had, of course, tangled before, over both shopping and
men. There were times—*many* times—when we disagreed about
some fundamental issue. In high school, for instance, regarding
Jason Bertignoli and my need to do some very specific shopping
for a very specific occasion.

Up until then, I thought I'd had a good handle on my emotions
or, at least, that I was believable in my pretense. Turned out this
wasn't quite true, although for the rest of my sophomore year, all of
my junior year and up until spring of my senior year I kept the vow
I'd made to myself after that horrid school dance: I did *not* like
Sam. I did not like Sam in the rain, I did not like Sam on a train, I
did not like him in trigonometry, he was such an S.O.B. (Sam "the
Obnoxious" Blaine), you see.

Even Jane, who'd easily grown to be my closest friend and most
trusted confidant—though, much to my disappointment, she con-
tinually denied any blood relationship between us—did not need
to remind me of Sam's malevolence. But sometimes she did
anyway.

She'd spout phrases like: *He is an insufferable fool.* Or, *He is a
disgraceful presence in your neighbourhood.* Or simply, *He is such a
Wickham.*

And I had to agree. Seeing him with Stacy Daschell that night of the dance, and for two whole weeks afterward—until she dumped him for "Rockhead," the toughest quarterback in the class above ours—really did a number on me. He couldn't have chosen anyone worse. And, like an elephant, I had a long, *long* memory.

But an event loomed before me in late April of our senior year that had the power to weaken the resolve of most teen girls. A social affair that made even the normally sane, obedient ones forget their mothers' sage advice and their fathers' dire warnings.

Senior Prom.

I'd just heard Sam Blaine would be taking a pretty junior I barely knew, Amanda Roberts, to the big dance. I, myself, was currently unattached and had spent much of the early spring wallowing in a puddle of self-pity over this fact. So, when Jason Bertignoli leaned against my locker one afternoon and asked me to go with him to prom "as friends," I jumped at the chance.

Now, it's a truth universally acknowledged that a young woman in possession of an important date must be in want of a hot outfit. In the Marshall Field's fitting rooms that weekend, with my mom waiting for me just beyond the curtain, Jane studied my apparel possibilities.

Pray, Ellie, you are not wearing THAT, are you? she said, her voice laced with her peculiar brand of British horror.

I held up the slinky, deep-purple dress that reached no lower than mid-thigh and had a lot of nifty black fringes. *This?* I asked innocently, though I knew it was the cause of her shock. *I think I'd look great in it.*

It is scandalous. You would not dare.

What makes you so sure? I asked her, but I had the answer already. She knew me too well. We were the most intimate of companions, and conversations with her were nearly like talking to myself. Psychologists might've gone so far as to label my relationship with Jane "benign schizophrenia," but I, of course, attributed it to something else entirely: to the power of an author's mind to transcend time and space. A kind of literary *Twilight Zone* thing.

Or so I told myself.

On such days as those, however, when Jane argued vehemently back, I had to remind my confused psyche that consorting with the paranormal didn't automatically make me crazy.

It would be deplorable, and you know it, Jane said, still fixating on the dress.

Yeah, I know it, but I just wanted an excuse to try it on, I informed her.

Oh, well, if that is all, Jane murmured sarcastically.

I slipped the dress over my head and let the silky fabric fall against my skin.

Jane gasped.

Truly, and without a shred of modesty, I looked stunning.

It is lovely on you, she admitted as I admired my reflection in the three-way mirror. *But now is not the time for such a garment. You have not yet the maturity . . . or the nerve.*

I wanted to disagree with her—at least about the maturity bit—but, unfortunately, she was right. I didn't have the nerve. I wanted to be one of those women who made men's jaws drop in amazement. The kind of woman who'd turn male heads 270 degrees and make their testosterone levels skyrocket.

But I had a reputation to maintain: Bland, boring, brainy Barnett. I knew full well that while I was still in high school I wasn't allowed to change it, and I didn't dare try. Even if I waltzed into prom looking like a total knockout, I'd still be seen as the same old fish in the same old pond come Monday.

I sighed and opted, instead, for a traditional ankle-length, white gown with small pearl flowers. It was pretty. It was on sale. It was something Mom sanctioned. And, yeah, okay, it was as close to a wedding dress as I'd get for eons.

That is nice, Jane said, a hint of disappointment in her tone when I tried the white gown on for the third time.

Yep. I frowned. I looked nice, not beautiful.

You must stop this incessant worrying, Ellie. Truly. The day will come when life will embrace you as you embrace it. The day when you have learned to fully express yourself. Then you will not have to be as stringently proper as, indeed, you must be now.

Ah, yes. Cryptic projections about my future and the lessons I was bound to learn someday. All part of Jane's never-ending lecture series on Adulthood 101.

Jane continued, *And you will not have to concern yourself so rigorously with others' perceptions once the pressure to marry has passed.*

She always spewed crap like this and, after a while, I had to say, it really pissed me off. *I WANT to get married someday, Jane.*

Hmmph.

I DO. And, for the eight-thousandth time, there's no "pressure to marry" while I'm still in high school. Trust me. It's discouraged.

Officially, perhaps, she said stiffly. *But that is not the truth as I have observed it.*

Look, just because YOU ultimately chose to stay single and to live in isolation with your sister rather than succumb to the rule of a man and the burden of bearing babies, doesn't mean I have to decide between similar fates. Women these days have as much power in a relationship as men do—

Jane snickered. Loudly.

Oh, c'mon. It's . . . mostly true. Plus, we have birth control, so yearly pregnancies are optional, and we don't even have to sign any paperwork to live together. We can just move in. I stopped a moment to catch my breath. *But, Jane, I'm seventeen and still a virgin. I'm going away to college in the fall. It's not like I'll let myself get emotionally attached to anyone. And as for Jason, he and I are friends, not lovers. Believe me, I won't get tricked into marriage.*

There was a long pause.

Jane?

Perhaps not, she said finally. *Perhaps marriage itself will not be foisted upon you just yet, but beware, Ellie. I more than suspect you will be made to feel incomplete without it. The seeds of such societal artfulness are planted early and, if not tempered by the greatest and truest of loves, can be dangerous, too. You will cease to work on your natural talents, and you will have the passions of others set before you in place of your own. I fear this fate for you.*

I swallowed. I decided she was being a combination of mulish and nineteenth-centuryish (she could get like that sometimes), and she was making this whole prom thing out to be far more symbolic than it was. I told myself it was just a fancy dance, that I wasn't getting set up for anything, that I'd become my own person in time without any undue pressure to bend to the whims of men and society. That the fact that she'd been disappointed in love during her lifetime had influenced her perceptions of romance too much.

But as Mom and I paid for my pricey purchase, I had to wonder if maybe Jane hadn't amassed a bit more wisdom about human nature than I had. I wondered further where her prejudices ended and the universal truth about a woman's experience began.

"Heard you're going with that loser Bertignoli," Sam said to me at the start of our chemistry II class about a week before the big event. "Still have a crush on him after all these years?"

Sam's lab partner raised a very blond eyebrow at Sam. "You're talking about *Jason?* Jason Bertignoli? But he isn't a los—"

Sam elbowed him.

I'd be damned if I'd tell Sam Blaine, who'd been bragging about having the Hottest Prom Date in Town, that I was going to prom with anyone Just As Friends. So I said, "Jason's great. And he's hot. Really hot."

Sam's lab partner grinned.

Terrie, my lab partner, nodded helpfully.

Sam gave me a long, blank stare.

The bell rang and all conversation ended. As we left class three-quarters of an hour later, though, carrying our last week's quiz on molecular elements (I got 94 percent, Sam got 97 percent and, yes, I *did* keep track), Sam brushed up against me.

"Look," he said, "you know I hate that guy but—"

"If you're talking about Jason, yeah, I know you can't stand him. And I also know your hatred is totally immature."

Sam shrugged. "Whatever. I just wanted to say to . . . to be careful because, uh, sometimes guys like that aren't what they seem." He shrugged again. "Okay?"

My heart started pounding for no good reason. Sam must know something about Jason's motives that I didn't. I opened my mouth to question him but closed it again. What, exactly, would I ask? It would be humiliating and embarrassing and—

Jane scoffed at this. *Ellie, I dare say you ought not to give credence to the opinion of one such as this Wickham.*

Before I could answer either of them, Sam said, "Later." He bolted down the hall.

Good riddance, Jane hissed.

But what if he's right? I said. *What if Jason has ulterior motives for wanting to go to prom with me? Maybe he's trying to make another girl jealous and Sam knows about it.*

This was actually the only reason I could think of, besides that Jason really, truly liked me. I'd plunk down money that all the guys in my class knew I was a virgin, so I was confident I didn't have the reputation of being an easy lay.

If Mr. Bertignoli is a young man of little honour, Jane said, *you shall soon be sensible of it. I, however, would think him a better suitor—if indeed you must have one—than Mr. Blaine. Thankfully, the latter seems well occupied with others.*

But maybe Sam's not entirely wrong—

Nonsense. Jane's response was swift and dismissive. *Your Jason may be of simple mind, but his manners are consistently pleasant and attentive, despite his limitations.*

Of "simple mind," you say? His "limitations"? Be nice, Jane.

Jane laughed as I raced toward my locker. *It is hardly a secret that Mr. Bertignoli lacks wit—*

Hey, Jason gets good grades in calc, which is more than I can say for most of the senior class. Stacy Daschell, for instance, couldn't even get in to calculus or chemistry II, which blissfully meant I hadn't seen much of her since sophomore year.

He receives passing marks in mathematics. He is far from your intellectual equal, however, Jane retorted.

I threw my chem II book in my backpack and fished out my Shakespeare notebook. Lit class started in four minutes. Jane really liked lit class.

If you're basing your view of who I ought to spend time with on the intelligence factor alone, how do you account for Sam? I asked her. *He's a stellar science student. He routinely outscores me. And, though we're in different periods for calc, I know he does exceptionally well in there, too.*

There was a pause. *It is true, of course, that intellect is not everything. One must also take character into consideration when drawing conclusions about a man's nature.*

Uh-huh.

You are too, too generous to trifle with young men such as these. Either of them, she added. *Your willingness to overlook their faults would be better suited to a saint. I have little patience for saints.*

Perhaps it's YOU who is too generous to trifle with ME. I slammed my locker door shut. *I wonder—frequently, in fact—why you do it.*

She gave a girlish laugh. *Do not allow your imagination to get the better of your sense. The exalted beings of heaven have a logic all their own, and their infinite wisdom will surely be revealed to you. In time.*

I arched an eyebrow at the pervasive spirit of Jane Austen, knowing even if she didn't see me directly that she surely intuited my every emotion. *Don't try to tell me you're my guardian angel, Jane. I'd have a real hard time believing that one.* Especially now that I'd grown well accustomed to her mischievous streak.

I make no such claim. But, Ellie, there is a purpose behind everything.

And yet, your part in being in my life remains a mystery. Why won't you tell me what you know? Why do you keep me guessing?

Because, she said, *what I know will not satisfy you.*

Try me.

There are lessons, Ellie, that we both must learn.

I stifled a sigh. Again with the lessons. Like I didn't get enough education at school.

These are lessons we must learn from each other, she added. *And I fear they will not be mastered quickly.*

Really? I said, delighted by the idea of getting to instruct Jane on something for once, and praying I'd finally convinced her to answer one of my most pressing questions. *What are they?*

But she changed the subject. *It is at last time for "Hamlet."*

I sighed. *I wish you'd just be open with me and stop treating me like a child.*

If the shoe fits . . . Jane murmured.

It doesn't. And while you're at it, you can damn well leave off the Cinderella references.

So, prom night came.

"Whoa. You look sweet," Jason said when he picked me up, dressed in his black tuxedo with tails and carrying a red-rose corsage for me. He briefly eyed my traditional white dress and sent me an absentminded nod of approval.

I handed him his boutonniere and said, "Thanks. You look great, too," but I thought, *Sweet?* Even as a synonym for lovely, I didn't want to look sweet. That word had such overtones of *nice.* I wanted to summon to a man's mind something more memorable, something like spicy. Sweet was nice, but you *remembered* spicy.

I continued to mull over this distinction as we muddled our way through the Mocktail Hour, the first of several pre-prom events. Held at prom-court member "Princess" Amy's house, this affair (complete with fake piña coladas, olives-n-wienies on toothpicks, annoying "royalty" and endless small talk) was about as much fun as sticking my hand in a meat grinder.

It was followed by dinner at Chez Alexander's with Terrie and her boyfriend Matt; Jason's buddy Steve and his giggly girlfriend Krista; Terrie's kid sister Sabrina, a junior, and her date Nate, a nice but intensely quiet senior. While I had no complaints about my chicken Kiev, my wedge of key lime pie or even my watered-down iced tea, the event itself was worse than the mocktails.

Why?

Well, because Jason—although unfailingly friendly toward me in the manner befitting a date who was "just a friend"—seemed awestruck by the cleavage of every other girl in attendance, from the tiara-wearing Princess Amy to the incurably ditsy Krista to the envy-inspiring Amanda Roberts.

And while on the subject of Amanda, I kept running into her. Every-fucking-where. At the mocktail hour. At the dinner. With Sam trailing her heels and gazing at her as if she were the only female in the entire state of Illinois. She wore some sleek and dazzling outfit, of course. And though it wasn't as short or as slinky as the purple dress with the fringes that I'd loved, it was, painfully, the same color. Naturally, Amanda looked amazing in it.

I *tried* to relax and have fun. I *tried* to catch the prom-night spirit. I *tried* to at least appear as though I were enjoying myself, especially when I'd spot Sam, Amanda and their friends having a rollicking good time. I wanted Romance and True Love so much that night I could've cried. And I thought maybe, if I acted the part, it would happen for me.

It didn't take long to realize I'd need decades to master any such social charade. My heart wasn't in it, and all the fake grins and fake drinks in the world wouldn't convince my soul otherwise.

By the time we slid into the white limo to go to the dance, I could feel myself beginning to lose it. The dejection, discouragement and frustration had built up, leaving me seething with an anger I couldn't justify or control.

On the road, Jason grabbed for my fingers. The other couples were all holding hands, so I didn't pull away when his hand covered mine. But I did curl my fingers into a fist and, a few times during the drive, I squeezed it tight, letting my nails bite into my palm. Marking it the way I'd once marked Sam Blaine's wrist.

You are not thinking of coming to blows with someone, are you, Ellie? Jane whispered, her humored voice rising above the roaring in my head. *It is most unladylike to consider striking another person. However well deserved.*

I clenched my fist tighter. *If I could decide who to punch out first, you might have something to worry about,* I told her in my snottiest silent voice. *But as it stands, I'm mad at too many people to single out only one of them.*

Ah, she said. *So the list has lengthened beyond the irredeemable Sam and his lady friend, the inattentive Jason, the Princess Amy, the frivolous Krista, the dreary Nate and the irksome Steve? You have had much to occupy your thoughts, I see.*

I grimaced. She knew very well that would've been plenty, but I was also mad at myself. While self-loathing was never pretty, it wasn't the only emotion I felt. Sadness, anxiety and resentment kept playing musical chairs inside of me, making it impossible to decide when I was feeling lonely versus furious. And of course, as usual, Jane wasn't making matters easier.

Just imagine, Jane told me, *all the sparkling moments ahead for you at this ball. The dancing and the—*

Prom. It's called PROM.

Ball. Prom. Similar events, Jane replied. I could almost feel her shrug. *Regardless, there will be much to experience and observe, Ellie. Keep your fists at your side and your eyes open.*

I squeezed my fist even tighter and pressed my eyelids closed.

My, you are a defiant one, are you not? Jane said, her parting words to me before I slipped out of the limo and entered the glittering "ballroom" of our high school.

As Jason and I danced, I was rocketed back in time to sophomore year, seeing him as I had that long-ago night. Seeing the possibility of a relationship between us. Maybe. Someday.

Then, just like that night, I saw Sam. Only this time he was watching us over Amanda's shoulder. Our gazes collided seconds before the DJ shouted "Switch Dance!" into his microphone.

A gleeful shout went up. Chaos swirled around me, a flurry of pastel taffeta and ivory lace. Sam and Amanda stood toe-to-toe with us.

"Wanna switch?" Amanda asked me cheerily. Then she grinned at Jason.

"Um," I said.

Jason said, "Yeah!" at the same time, staring with obvious appreciation at Amanda's low-scooping neckline. He dropped my hand and reached for hers.

Sam remained silent, but he held out his palm toward me in an unlikely invitation. Freaky déjà vu.

How unfortunate, Jane murmured.

I reluctantly put my hand in his and, for the first time, I decided Jane might've had a point with her "ball" references. This must've been how Elizabeth Bennet felt at the Netherfield Ball, dancing with an aloof, impassive Mr. Darcy.

Sam wound one arm around my waist. I shivered at his touch. Wait! What was I thinking? Sam was a Wickham type, not a Darcy.

Wickham wasn't even *at* that ball. Remember that, I told myself. And remember those were *book characters*. This was real life.

Nevertheless, in his tux, it was impossible not to notice how gorgeous Sam looked. Unfair, because it reminded me I wasn't exactly indifferent to him. Although, God knew, I'd tried to be.

As we swayed together, something recognizable sparked between us, but it wasn't love or even lust. It was awkwardness. For a split second, Sam seemed as uneasy and uncomfortable as I was, which must've been a first in Glen Forest history.

"Having fun?" I managed to murmur.

"Yep," he answered, not quite believably, as the music changed to "Sister Christian" by Night Ranger.

"Um, well . . . good," I said, not knowing what else to say.

Comment on the weather or on the number of couples, Jane instructed helpfully.

I smiled.

"What's so funny?" Sam asked, his eyes lighting up a bit, as if the prospect of a joke made dancing with me more bearable.

"Nothing much."

"So," he said as he shot a look in Jason and Amanda's direction, "is Bertignoli behaving himself?"

"Yeah." I stared into those mocking blue eyes. "Are *you* behaving yourself?"

He raised an eyebrow. "Sure. So far." Then he did something he'd never done. He winked at me. "But the night's still young."

"What? Planning Amanda's deflowering later?"

A dangerous grin played at the corners of his lips. "Been there, done that, no T-shirts necessary."

"Great," I said, noticing the predatory way he looked at me.

He laughed. "Don't worry, Ellie. There's plenty of sin and debauchery to go around."

I considered this. I probably shouldn't have said anything, but my inquisitive nature and the strangeness of being in Sam's arms again made me bold. "Guys don't really want that, though, do they? They want to at least have the illusion of being the pursuer. They don't want a girl who'll give in too easily, right?"

He looked at me, startled, then narrowed his eyes at Jason's dancing form with surprising animosity. "Depends on the guy." He returned his gaze to my face. "And on the girl."

I didn't answer this time.

Jane *tsked* loudly and muttered a series of comments that included the phrases "appalling behaviour" and "unpardonable lout."

Sam's grip tightened around my waist. The weight of his fingertips pressed into me—a sensuous, seductive touch—and I felt the smooth glide of his thumb over my knuckles.

He stepped two inches closer as we moved to the melody, and I inhaled his scent. Pure masculinity. And probably his father's cologne. Or, did he buy his own now? The possibility made him seem so grown up. He pulled me closer still, and my heart began to thump. When did the arrogant Sam Blaine turn into someone other than the Brainiac Bad Boy I thought I knew? When did he begin to change into a man?

"Switch dance!" the DJ bellowed.

I stepped back so abruptly I made Terrie's sister, Sabrina, who was dancing near us, jump. Her partner-of-the-moment tripped.

"Sorry," I said.

He regained his footing, though, and asked, "Wanna switch?"

"N-Not this time. Thanks." Walking backward, I skittered away from them, my eyes still trained on Sam's face. "I need to get some water," I called out. "But, uh, you guys have fun."

Sabrina's partner shrugged and turned toward another couple. Sabrina slanted me an odd look. Sam just raised a brow and the corresponding corner of his lips. I ran off the dance floor, the newest INXS song—"Need You Tonight"—nipping at the heels of my white pumps. Then I hyperventilated in the hall. Alone.

Two minutes later, a familiar male voice whispered in my ear, "Are you okay, Ellie?"

I looked deep into Jason's warm, brown eyes and found the comfort I'd been seeking. I nodded, and he walked me back into the gym, his arm tenderly draped over my shoulder.

Jason was my *friend*. Okay, so he didn't fill me with wanton lust, but his less-demanding nature took the edge off my loneliness and off the haunting desperation I couldn't seem to let go of.

"When's the crowning of the king and queen?" I glanced at my watch, which read a depressingly early 9:23.

"In an hour. Once that's over we can blow outta here."

I infused high-voltage warmth into my grin and radiated it at him. "Sounds like a plan. Maybe we can liven things up then."

A perilous glint of interest—curiosity, I gathered, mixed with something I couldn't deduce—sparked in his eye. "You can count on it," he said.

Later that night, at the city's finest hotel, the Glen Forest Four Seasons, our gang was "Locked In" for the evening. With the limos gone and parent chaperones at the ready to guard exits, confiscate alcohol and prohibit lustful behavior, we were effectively trapped until morning.

Terrie, Sabrina, Krista and I parted company with the guys, agreeing to meet them soon for the Post-Prom Party. We then hopped into an elevator heading toward the girls' floor. With the coast clear, Terrie and Sabrina began whispering about which cover story to tell their parents and how the logistics of the evening ought to play out. It was decided that Terrie and Krista would sneak onto the guys' floor for the night while Sabrina and I would stay in our assigned rooms . . . but with our dates.

Thirty minutes later we were on the down elevator, and then in the dimly lit Winnebago Room. A strobe light illuminated the parquet floor with dappled streaks of color, and the piped-in strains of "(I've Had) The Time of My Life" from the *Dirty Dancing* soundtrack floated above us. The guys spotted us right away and marched in our direction, plastic glasses of punch in their hands.

Jason handed me one and winked. "I just fixed it for you."

I took a sip of the bright red drink and my tongue burned with the distinctive sting of cheap vodka. "Mmm," I managed to say before coughing. "Thanks."

He grinned. "You're welcome." He lowered his voice and added, "Don't worry. I got enough left to doctor everyone's second glass, too. Then we can break into Matt's Everclear."

"Super," I murmured, forcing myself to take another sip before scanning the room. Couples littered every corner, the watchful eyes of the chaperones darting between them.

I eyed the couples I was with. I didn't know Sabrina and Nate's intimacy status, but Krista and Steve had obviously done it before, as had Terrie and Matt. For the first time ever, I had to admit being a virgin was starting to become more of a liability than an asset. My reputation might be snowy, but was it worth the price of not feeling close to anyone?

A few couples left the room and my field of vision opened up to include Sam and Amanda in the panorama. She nuzzled against him and his hand stroked her swaying dark hair with a gentleness I could detect even from a distance. As I watched them, I felt Jason's strong fingers grasp my hand. He tugged me toward him, and I let him hold me as we stood there, marking time, seeing our friends and the other teens float in and out of the Winnebago Room. Foreigner's "I Wanna Know What Love Is" came on.

Jason groaned.

"What? You don't like this song?" I asked him.

He blinked and pulled me closer. "I like it. I just—" He downed the rest of his punch.

"You just what?"

He sighed. "Is there anywhere we could go to talk, Ellie? It's kinda loud in here."

I shrugged. "Sure."

We told the others we were leaving for a bit. Terrie's grin brightened. I rolled my eyes at her. Steve winked knowingly at us, and I felt Jason's grip on my hand tighten.

We found a secluded spot off the lobby, a gingham-covered loveseat across from two potted ferns. Very relaxing ambiance, or it would've been if I hadn't been aware that some Momentous Occurrence might well be on the horizon.

"So, what's up?" I said, my palms beginning to sweat. I let go of Jason's hand.

He glanced around us, then balanced his empty punch glass between his legs and poured most of the remaining vodka into it. "Want any more?" he asked me.

I shook my head. He dumped the rest of the alcohol into his glass and returned the empty bottle to his tux pocket. He took a long, slow drink and smacked his lips. "Mmm."

"Are you okay?" I said, noting the way his lips kept twitching and how he seemed to be unable to look me in the eye.

"Oh, yeah." He guzzled about half the vodka, which made *me* cringe even if he didn't. I took a deep breath and was about to make some inane comment about the hotel's décor when he blurted, "Can I kiss you, Ellie?"

I swallowed and kind of nodded. He brought his lips down on mine in one smooth swoop. They were a little rough, but warm. The taste of pure vodka lingered on them, a flavor that blended together with the natural tang of Jason's lips.

He slipped his tongue into my mouth and my lust hormones surprised me by kicking in. My pulse thrummed with the wanting I'd tried so stubbornly to ignore as his fingers skated along the fabric of my dress, inching ever higher. He ran the pad of his thumb against the side of my left breast and, suddenly, hard curiosity squashed all thoughts of romantic theory.

Yeah, I wanted to know what love was. But did I want Jason to show me?

As if realizing this was his audition for the part of First Lover, Jason murmured, "I really, really like you . . . and I think I could make you really happy tonight."

This was, without a doubt, an amazingly lame line, but he had a decent follow-up: "I'm not going to make stuff up to get you to go to bed with me, Ellie. I know you're not stupid. I know you have a good reputation and maybe you wanna save sex for marriage. If you do, I'd understand that, although I really want you."

I blinked. "You do?"

"Definitely." He let out a low chuckle, paused to finish his drink, then kissed my neck. "I want you to be my first."

I gaped at him. "What?" Did that mean he'd never—

"I think you heard me."

"So, you haven't . . . um, yet . . . either?"

"Nope." He nibbled on my ear. "Although I'd appreciate you kind of not mentioning that to your friends. Or to mine."

I covered my ear to stop the sensual assault. "Well, no, of course not, but I would've thought you—"

He sat back and sighed. "It's like this, Ellie. You and me—we're friends, right?"

"Right."

"Well, to be close to someone like that, close enough to have sex with them, you've gotta feel like it'll be okay the next day. You know, that the other person really likes you for you. Do you get what I mean?"

I assured him that, yes, I did.

"It's not always that way with other girls in our school. With you, I think we could do it and still be friends. I mean, I'm attracted to you, but it's not a *crazy* kind of attraction. It's not something that makes me lose control." He gave me a serious once-over. "And I don't think I have that effect on you either."

Fog rolled around in my head as I tried to grasp what he was saying. "So, you think we should have sex because then we can do it and it won't make us all insane and irrational."

He exhaled, sounding relieved. "Yeah, exactly. We can do this together, help each other out on our first time and, because we're friends, everything'll be cool tomorrow. 'Cuz college is coming up, and it'd be a lot easier for both of us, I think, if we got this whole rite of passage thing out of the way before then."

I looked Jason in the eye. Finally, I understood his motives for asking me to prom, and I knew I should've been angry about it. Or indignant. Or something. But I couldn't work up the emotion to feel anything but drained. In an odd way, his logic made sense to me. Sure, he was trying to use me. Then again, he was also being completely honest about it and inviting me to use him, too.

It all came down to how desperate I felt for a romantic connection. How much, for once, I craved being a totally reckless teen like my sister instead of The Responsible One. How I knew I could never pull off a Bad Girl image for long—either in high school or in college—and that Jason wasn't asking me to pretend I knew more than I did. We could get our experience together and, later, release each other without all the hurt.

Maybe it was the spiked punch or maybe it was Jason's hot kisses or maybe it was spotting Sam out of the corner of my eye, walking with his arm around Amanda, but I whispered, "Okay."

ELLIE! What, pray tell, do you think you are doing? Jane screamed in my head. I jerked back in surprise only to see Jason's smiling face.

"Great," he said.

No! Jane, who'd made only serene comments for much of the evening, yelled. *It is not intended to happen this way.*

I willfully ignored her.

"Are we on fourth or seventh?" he asked, standing up and pulling me to my feet.

Return at once to the Winnebago Room, Jane commanded.

"The seventh," I told Jason. "With Nate and Sabrina."

He nodded. "I think Nate's got whiskey upstairs, if you're interested. Otherwise, if you want something a little lighter, Steve brought Bacardi. I could get some for—"

"That's okay," I said. "I don't want any more to drink."

He kissed the top of my head very gently and tugged me toward the elevator.

Within minutes we'd retrieved a few "necessary items" from Jason's room and were safely locked in mine.

Ellie Barnett, I forbid you to remain alone in a bedchamber with this boy, Jane squealed, as Jason dragged the zipper down the back of my dress and nudged me onto the mattress so we lay face-to-face, both of our heads on the same pillow.

He rubbed the small of my back, making little circles like widening waves against my skin. I sighed and curled in toward him. He must've taken this move as permission to speed right along because his hand dipped lower, beneath the elastic of my panties.

"I've got lots of protection," he whispered, "so whenever you wanna start . . ."

I, however, was anything but ready to start. Hadn't Jason Bertignoli ever heard of foreplay?

"I—um, well, there's got to be a few things we should do before then." I tapped the black bow around his neck with my index finger. "Like getting undressed, maybe?"

He grinned. "I was working up to that." He wrenched my dress off one shoulder then the other before yanking at my bra clasp. "You gotta get this thing undone for me or I'm gonna rip it off."

I unfastened the back clasp, my fingers shaking, my stomach quivering and Jane howling with rage in my brain.

This is all WRONG, Jane pleaded. *You must comprehend that. Please do not take this severe breach of reason one step further.*

I let Jason push away the creamy fabric of the bra and heard him suck in a gulp of air as his hand squeezed my breast. "God, you're so sweet," he said, dipping his mouth to taste my nipples.

I swallowed and reached for his belt. How did a woman unfasten it gracefully?

Jane's familiar voice blurted, *I will keep trying to stop you, Ellie, by any way I am able.* But I was beyond heeding her threats.

A moment later, we heard the telltale scratching of the hotel room's door lock and the hushed giggles of Nate and Sabrina. Oh, hell. Now what?

See? Jane said, all but gloating. For a split second I wondered at the extent of her powers here on earth. Could she have been responsible for compelling Nate and Sabrina back to the room?

Didn't matter, I decided, as Jason sat upright in panic. I had a plan. I grabbed two pillows off the bed and motioned for him to follow me. Into the closet.

"Quick thinking," he said appreciatively. He pulled on the door until it was almost closed.

"Uh, Ellie? Are you here?" Sabrina's voice called out.

I took a deep breath. "Yep."

We heard Nate chuckle. "Jason around anywhere?" he asked. "Or did you ditch him downstairs?"

"Present," Jason said, his tone sharp.

Nate laughed a bit louder. "Alrighty then. So, are we, uh, all *locked in* for the night?"

I looked at Jason. He nodded. "Yeah," I said. "You two?"

There was a pause then Sabrina answered, "Yes."

"Goodnight, then," Jason said. "And, Nate, stay the hell out of here." He tugged on the doorknob until the closet door clicked in emphasis.

Jason and I didn't move for a few long moments. We stood next to each other, the odor of vodka pervading my senses and the cool air dancing against my bare chest.

As my eyes adjusted to the dark, I saw Jason's shadowy figure stirring. He removed his tux jacket and dress shirt and pulled a bunch of small squares out of his pocket. "Trojans," he whispered.

I nodded and hoped he could see me because, suddenly, my throat was too parched for speech.

Jane tried one more time to reason with me. *Ellie, you can still stop this—*

I know, I told her. Then I locked her out of my conscious mind. Before that night I'd never wanted to block her from my thoughts, but if ever there was a time to do it, this was it.

Jason dug into his jacket pocket and then pressed a plastic soda bottle into my hands. "I also brought us this."

I squinted to read the writing. "7Up?" I rasped out.

"Um, no," he said.

I unscrewed the cap and a new alcoholic aroma wafted up to me.

"Some of Matt's Everclear," he said. "I know you said you didn't want any more to drink, but in case you changed your mind and *did* want some."

I already had the bottle to my lips and was in the midst of a long swig. Yeah, I'd changed my mind all right. Fire burned down my throat, but at least I could speak freely again.

"Thanks," I said as I dabbed my mouth with the back of my wrist and returned the bottle to him.

Jason leaned in to kiss my forehead before guzzling several swallows of the stuff. Amazing the guy was still conscious after all the liquor he'd consumed in the past few hours. I'd had only a fraction as much, but I could sure feel it taking effect.

We heard Nate and Sabrina's moans on the other side of the door. The closet afforded only so much privacy.

After listening for a sec, Jason shoved his belongings to one side and positioned the pillows on the floor. We'd spotted an extra blanket stashed in the closet, so he put that on the carpet, too, patted it and whispered, "C'mere, Ellie."

I peeled off the rest of my dress, kicked off my pumps and joined him on the floor. He slid his palm down my body, a slow glide starting at the curve of my shoulders and snaking past my waist to my hips. His fingers came to rest on my thigh.

"You feel really great," he said, his voice a hoarse whisper in the darkness. He pushed his body next to mine, squeezing me to him in a straightjacket hold. His belt buckle stabbed my stomach, and I had to pull away.

"Can you get rid of that?" I whispered, tugging on his belt.

Jason, obviously interpreting this request as my uncontrolled eagerness, kissed me hard and said with enthusiasm, "Totally!"

He shed the rest of his clothes, placed his fingers on top of mine and slid my hand right to the hard part. "Here," he said, stroking upward. He moved my fingers over him, and I felt his penis jump. "Like that."

So I did it again.

"Oh, baby, yes."

And again, about ten more times, marveling all the while at my control over him.

Jason became increasingly less coherent. He mumbled some words I couldn't catch, pumped his hips toward me and, finally, shoved my hand away, breathing hard. In one stunningly swift movement, he tore off his briefs and grabbed at the Trojan squares.

"You-your p-p-panties," he said in my ear.

"What about them?" I watched him, in an oddly detached way, as he fumbled with a condom.

"Off."

But before I could do that, he'd gotten the Trojan on and had both hands squeezing the edges of my lace-trimmed panties. With absolutely no attempt at finesse, he dragged them down my legs and whipped them off. A second later, he had me on my back with his hands between my thighs and his tall body poised above me.

"Oh, God," he groaned, pushing my legs further apart and sticking a couple of fingers into the sensitive area between them. I was dry, so let's just say this was less than comfortable. "I'll make it good for you, Ellie."

He poked and prodded at the soft flesh there, reminding me of the unpleasantness of that gynecological exam Mom made Di and me go to once. I swallowed and tried to relax. In no way did that work.

I felt the sharp jab of a fingernail against my inner wall and gasped. Jason increased his poking until the discomfort was too much for me to take.

"Stop," I whispered, batting at his hand.

"Too intense for you, too?" he said, grinning. "I know. I can't wait anymore either."

Without giving me a chance to correct his latest misperception, he shackled my wrists above my head with his hands, constricting my circulation. His mouth latched onto mine and the force of his body plunged on top of me.

I writhed beneath him, trying to loosen his grip. His hands relaxed a fraction, but his hips crushed mine and his erection pressed tight against my opening.

"Jason," I managed to say. "Slow down—" I was feeling a little warmer at my core now that he'd removed his fingers, but I was nowhere close to catching up with him.

"I'm so hot for you." He pumped his hips again, the tip of his penis sliding just barely inside me.

Then a peculiar thing happened. Jason's face contorted strangely, and he arched his back and pushed, moaning all the while. Only, his erection popped out of my body and, instead of bursting through my virginal wall, it slithered between my legs. I suspected he didn't notice.

After a few additional moans, he collapsed against me and hugged me tight. "You're so amazing, Ellie," he mumbled in my ear before falling to the blanket with a thump.

"Um, thanks."

I paused, waiting for him to acknowledge that what he'd *planned* on happening didn't, in fact, happen. But there was nothing. Not a sound out of him.

I nudged his shoulder. "Jason?"

"Mmm?" He swiveled slightly toward me and glanced at my face with a sleepy, half-glazed-over smile. "So sweet," he murmured.

"Do you need to do anything else?" I hinted.

"Hmm," he sighed. "Don't think so." There was a pause. "Go to the bathroom, maybe." He looked down at his limp condom and tugged it off. "But I'm too tired."

"Oh."

"Thanks, Ellie. You were great." Thirty seconds later he was snoring softly.

I shut my eyes and, if my soul hadn't ached so much, I would've laughed. I remembered something Jane once said: "The power of doing anything with quickness is always much prized by the possessor, and often without any attention to the imperfection of the performance." Truer words.

Please, I thought, tell me all guys aren't this stupid. Or this incompetent. Are they? Without thinking, I opened my mind up to Jane again and asked her this same question.

After a few huffs, she answered tartly, *I would like to think not. You, however, have been remarkably foolish. Get dressed.*

For once I didn't argue with her. I slipped my clothes back on and positioned myself on my pillow, my head five inches from Jason's. I didn't touch him, though.

Nate and Sabrina were still going at it on the other side of the closet door, having a more mutually good time. I felt a pang of envy and brushed away a tear that wouldn't go away on its own.

This couldn't possibly count as my first time, could it? If so, sex really sucked. I hugged myself and tried to keep from clenching my jaw.

Take care, Ellie, Jane whispered in the moments before I finally fell asleep, her tone the comforting voice of a caring elder. *A mistake was made this one time, but you need not reproach yourself forever. You shall recover from this hurt,* she promised me. *I shall help you.*

The next morning I awoke, in the closet, amidst a sea of scattered belongings: high-heeled shoes, hairclips, Jason's discarded clothing, the empty 7Up bottle still reeking of Everclear, used and unused Trojans, my ruined reputation . . . you know, the usual post-prom wreckage.

I brushed myself off, tried to stretch the kink out of my neck and opened the closet door to slip into the bathroom just as Terrie and Krista snuck into our room.

"Morning," I whispered, since the others were still asleep.

Krista gave me a good once-over and giggled. Terrie grinned and said, "Congrats, El! The first time's really exciting, huh?"

I caught my reflection in the room mirror and gasped before I could stop myself. I looked flushed. Tousled. Like I should've been auditioning for the role of Streetwalker/Chorus Girl in Pat Benatar's "Love Is A Battlefield" video. I opened my mouth to explain, but just then Jason emerged from the depths of the closet.

"Mornin', ladies," he said, kissing the top of my matted hair. "You look sweet today, El," he whispered to me before sauntering into the bathroom with a blanket wrapped around his waist, a saucy smile on his lips and a prideful gleam in his eye.

Terrie winked knowingly. "Wow, you got yourself a gentleman."

Appearances can be QUITE deceiving, Jane inserted.

"Uh, yeah," I murmured, more to Jane than to my friend.

"Glad you two had fun," Terrie said before waking up Sabrina.

And so the day began.

A little over an hour later, we entered the restaurant for the Morning-After Breakfast. Jason slung that proprietary arm around my shoulders and, again, pecked the top of my head with a kiss. He caressed my arm slowly with a fingertip and, I swear, gave off some kind of I-Just-Had-Sex-With-A-Virgin pheromone.

Heads turned. The overt signs of our familiarity were not lost on anyone. Peers, who'd been too self-absorbed to care during Prom—Day One, now watched us with real scrutiny.

I was tempted to give Jason a good hard shove and announce to the crowd that Jason Bertignoli didn't know how to satisfy a woman, or even know what he'd done (or hadn't done) the night before. But, of course, a Good Girl wouldn't blow the charade, so I didn't.

Amanda was whispering something to Sam as we walked passed the long table where they sat. He nodded at her, but he turned his eyes toward Jason and me. An expression, somewhere between a glower and a grimace, flashed across his face. A moment later it was gone, and so were we. The waitress seated us in another room.

As we waited for our food, the guys debated the instruments they wanted to "play" for the upcoming Air Band Bash. Matt proposed they take on a Guns N' Roses song, and Nate said, "Hey, the girls could be back-up singers and—"

"For GNR?" Steve laughed. "Nah, man, I don't think so."

"What if we did Robert Palmer's new one, 'Addicted to Love'?" Jason suggested. "Our girls could dress up in short skirts, wear shiny red lipstick and pretend to play guitars behind us."

"Awesome!" Matt said.

Nate nodded.

Steve smirked and said, "Now that's an image I like."

I thought, *Our* girls? Shoot me now.

Jason gave me a warm, lingering look, which should've brought a feeling of relief after our embarrassing night in the closet. Maybe I was the only one who was embarrassed, though. Jason, by contrast, looked exultant, and the other three couples seemed closer this morning. More relaxed with each other.

I felt strangely disconnected from all of them and more exposed in jeans and a tucked-in T-shirt than I had that morning in my crinkled, half-on/half-off prom dress.

I forced a smile and said, "Thanks for my share of the invitation, but I'm not into performing onstage."

Merely into acting everywhere else, Jane chimed in.

I took a long, slow sip of ice water, hoping it wouldn't add to the chill running through my veins.

Terrie and Sabrina begged off the project, too, but Krista really got into it. She giggled and announced, "I have lots of short skirts." Steve raised an eyebrow at that and began giving her air-band pointers.

As Terrie and her sister worked on getting their stories straight for the upcoming parental inquisition, I sat back, watching it all with a painful vulnerability churning in my stomach that I wanted and needed to squelch. Soon. And with a lack of sexual satisfaction too intense to verbalize, even to Jane. (Although, certainly, she'd guessed.) And with a sheer determination never, ever to feel this indifferent toward making love again.

I gritted my teeth and stabbed at my French toast.

Next time, I promised myself, I'd get it right because *next time* I'd choose the guy, not let him choose me.

❧ 8 ❧

Everything nourishes what is strong
already.

—*Pride and Prejudice*

I'd choose the guy next time.
What a vow to make. But, oh, how right it had seemed then in
theory. How admirable I thought it was in principle. How very
wrong the reality turned out to be.

Funny how the passage of time lets you see your youthful decisions with more clarity. Hindsight being 20/20, and all that. Especially when, as a grown-up, you find yourself surrounded by angsty
teens. All day long. And, at times, even in the midst of the dreaded
prom season.

One late-April morning, a few weeks after my Easter shopping
excursion with Jane and about a month before the big wedding/
union in Toronto, I was in the school library filling out order forms
for the latest Hot Teen-Reads. I'd be damned if Meadowview
High didn't keep the most current award-winning authors on the
shelves right alongside the young-adult classics, so I had a stack of
requests in front of me and I was silently working my way through
them.

Two senior girls sat at a small, round table a few yards to my left.
They were not working—silently or otherwise. They were com-
paring notes on their prom, which was coming up that weekend.

After some chatter on the subject of dresses, the one I knew to
be Simona said to her friend Karyn, "Jenni told me that Mike told

her brother that he asked Liz to prom after he heard that Scott asked you."

Karyn inhaled sharply and said in a voice too loud for the library, "That's *so* not true! He's just saying that to screw with me. To start a rumor or something." She glanced wildly around her, saw me staring at them and lowered the volume (but not enough so I couldn't still hear her). "He's a loser," she whispered.

Simona crossed her arms and raised her eyebrows. "That's *not* what you thought when you hooked up with him at Jenni's party."

"That was *weeks* ago, and anyway—" Karyn inhaled again. "Oh, my God, shhh! There he is."

Simona tried to swivel around in her chair in a nonchalant manner, but she couldn't pull it off. She was as obvious in her actions as Karyn and, it turned out, as lacking in subtlety as the lanky, dark-haired boy I recognized to be Mike. A boy who loitered near the teen magazine rack, skimming the titles and shooting glances at the girls—at Karyn in particular—in between his every breath.

There was something in the intensity of his gaze that made me think, Ah, so Mike really *does* like her. Even though he'd asked someone else to prom, Karyn was the one he wanted.

Had it been that way between Sam and me? Had our game of teen attraction-repulsion been so apparent that any adult observing us, even fleetingly, could've guessed where we were headed?

Yes, Jane replied shortly.

I sighed. As I said, 20/20 hindsight.

A somewhat similar sense of improved vision happened for me in regards to weddings. I'd attended a number of them in my lifetime, a few especially memorable. However, up until I drove with Andrei to Mark and Seth's Canadian union, the pièce de résistance had been the June afternoon Di and Alex joined their lives together. Forever. Or so we'd all hoped back then.

I went to *that* big event with Dominic and, although Reverend Jacobs officially presided, it was Jane who actually narrated the ceremony.

Those gowns are deplorable, Jane told me with indignation, as if they were a personal affront. *I have rarely been witness to an occasion where the natural female form was marred so profoundly by lack of taste.*

I appraised Di's wedding gown, such that it was, as she sauntered down the aisle to the sounds of "Here Comes the Bride," the alternative-rock version. The light orange sheen of the clinging silk was pretty but, admittedly, an unusual choice given the occasion. Her pointy-nosed maid of honor wore a dark pink wraparound, which made the color scheme of the four-person wedding party a bit discordant. As for the cut of the dresses—well, let's just say Di's stance on wedding attire could most politely be defined as "minimalist."

Alex, however, stared at Di with a half-lidded gaze of sheer lust, so I guess he'd been a fan of the dress, even if most of the congregation (and especially Jane) found it appalling.

"Dearly beloved," the reverend mumbled, "we are gathered here today to celebrate the union of Diana Lynn Barnett and Alexander Sinjin Evans—"

Sinjin? Jane repeated with surprise. *How odd a choice for a Colonial man.*

I stared from my pew up at my sister's almost-husband. Alex's dark hair was spiked in the front, longish in the back. His dangling silver earring caught the light through the stained glass. It seemed a genuine accessory, while the navy-colored suit he'd chosen, eschewing the traditional tux, fit well enough but appeared awkward on him somehow.

Yeah. I had to agree with Jane. There was nothing remotely Sinjin-like about him. Except, of course, that—like many of us—he'd had English ancestors in some prior century.

Colonial times ended two hundred years ago, I told her. *You might not want to set your expectations too high for finding look-alikes from your era.*

True. There was a pause. *But faces really do not change, Ellie. At least, I had thought not.* She directed my attention to Di's maid of honor, the elder Daschell sister. *Notice her features. Very Germanic, do you not think? My family entertained visitors from the Continent who had similar face shapes and colouring.*

But, Jane, remember that Kendra and Stacy are first-generation Americans. Their parents are both German. In general, there's been a lot more mingling of blood in the centuries since Europeans came to the New World. You saw kids in my high school and college who had blended ethnicities.

Perhaps, but families still encourage their children to marry within certain boundaries.

I laughed. *But they don't always listen. Just think about Angelique and Leo. Not only are they different religions, but his background is mostly Hungarian, while she's a UK mutt like me—part English, Irish, Scottish, Welsh—with another nationality or two thrown in from her dad's side. Their kids are going to have a real mix of features, and if any one of those kids marries someone Asian or Hispanic or Black—*

Yes, I understand your reasoning, yet how commonplace is such a thing?

Look around, I told her. I pointed out Alex's best man—a black-haired, Cuban-born guy—and his blond, fourth-generation Tennessee-born wife. She sat across the aisle from me and gazed at her husband with pride. *They've been married for a year.*

I nodded toward some of the other racially mixed couples in the congregation, some married, some engaged, and I reminded Jane of the guys I'd dated in college whose ethnicities and religions were different from mine, including Dominic, who was half Latino.

I would agree you were often willing to take a chance on a gentleman regardless of his background, she said magnanimously, although it may well have been veiled criticism. *But while the search for true love in your time has the potential to expose you to a multitude of possible partners, it brings an equal abundance of heartbreaks.*

I rolled my eyes, not at all shocked by this latest pearl of Regency wisdom, but one didn't tell the formidable Jane Austen "Duh."

Before I could respond more appropriately, however, Jane added, *It is also a rather repetitive, cyclical process, it seems, as the same individuals, or those representing the varying types of male, keep reappearing.*

She was right about this, of course. I hadn't spent time compiling a list of male categories for no reason.

She began quizzing me about my then-burgeoning relationship with Dominic. *Tell me about Mr. Reyes-Jones,* she said.

I like him, I admitted. *I'm attracted to him. I want to believe in him. But I don't know, Jane. Will it work?* I inhaled as much air as I could take in. *What do you think?*

She considered. *What is it that most draws you to him?*

His passion, I said without hesitation. *The wild enthusiasm he has. He's not cold and cowardly or unintelligent or remotely effeminate or—*

Like any of the gentlemen you have thus encountered, she finished for me.

Right. But, I mean, what do I know? He could be as stupidly self-centered as Jason. Or he could completely betray me like Sam. At what point do I take the risk? And, even if I decide to go for it, what if HE doesn't? What if I'm just another person he wants to have deep philosophical discussions with?

Jane thought about this as the Reverend droned on. "Diana, do you take this man . . ." and blah, blah, blah.

What I hated to admit, even to myself, was how much I'd been hurt by bad boyfriends in the past. How cynical they'd made me. How I doubted I'd ever find the soul mate I'd fantasized about. How I feared the thoughtful, romantic man who loved to dance with me and make me dinner and hold me was a myth. Someone who only existed in fiction through a writer's sleight of hand.

Well? I finally asked Jane, eyeing a somewhat smug-looking Dominic, who sat next to me, alternately flipping through the hymnal and staring idly around the church.

Indeed, he does seem comfortable with himself at present, Jane commented. *But his words and his actions are, in truth, occasionally at odds. I have suspicions I am quite unable to substantiate.*

I stopped listening to Reverend Jacobs altogether. *So, wait—you don't KNOW? You're as clueless about his character as I am? And all this time I thought you were supposed to be wiser than me.*

Neither of us is a perfect being, Jane said, with no trace of venom. Then, less benignly, *I, of course, am not the one with a history of such lamentable suitors.*

I almost laughed aloud. *You forget, I've read your biography. Plenty of "history," as you say, was hinted at for you, dear Jane. Just because the intimate details of your romances weren't recorded for posterity doesn't mean they didn't exist.*

A moment of stone-cold silence followed. *My history lacked the outrageous drama of yours*, she retorted.

Well, she had me there.

Yet, at Mark and Seth's union, five years later in Toronto, I felt sure I was not in the midst of some new romantic melodrama. I felt sure I'd matured greatly. And I felt sure that what I was now experiencing with Andrei was merely a part of the relationship process—the next step, if you will, on my own road to eventual holy matrimony.

That bright, late-May afternoon, with Andrei as a member of our merry crowd, I scanned the congregation from my place at the podium, under a billowing white canopy, and read into the microphone a selection from Gibran's *The Prophet*.

> *"When love beckons to you,*
> *follow it . . .*
> *And when its wings enfold you,*
> *yield to it . . .*
> *And when it speaks to you,*
> *believe in it . . .*
> *Think not that you can direct the course of love,*
> *for love,*
> *if it finds you worthy,*
> *directs your course."*

I looked into Mark and Seth's eyes, aglow with what I'd undoubtedly call love, and I smiled at them both. Then I stepped down from my perch of honor and wound my way back to my seat next to my Slavic boyfriend. He spread his palm over my bare knee and shot me a wink.

My old roommate Kim, who was sitting on the other side of me and struggling to keep her three little ones from whining or crawling under the seats, nudged me once and said, "Nice job." Then she hissed at her husband, "Grab Jordan! Don't let him eat the grass!"

Tom, who was the parental bookend further down the row,

snatched up their nine-month-old son, pried the fistful of crabgrass from his little hand and stuck an arrowroot cracker in the kid's mouth.

Kim and I laughed. Tom grinned at us. Andrei's hand slid a few millimeters up my thigh. Jordan gummed the cracker and gurgled while Mark and Seth exchanged rings.

It was a near-perfect moment, and I could feel in my nerve fibers that I should be next. That I should get to have this crew all around me again—a year from now, perhaps—only Andrei and I would be the ones up in front of the crowd, pledging our vows and our intention for a shared future.

I impulsively turned to Andrei and planted a wet kiss on his cheek. He responded by slipping his fingers under the hem of my tasteful rose-colored dress.

"Not here," I whispered in panic.

"Where then?" he countered.

"Nowhere *now!* This is a wedding—"

"Then afterward. At big reception." He squeezed my thigh for emphasis before releasing me, and I tried to block out an unwelcome wave of dread.

Mostly, I loved sex with Andrei but, lately, it'd been getting wilder. Louder. Kinkier. And increasingly less discreet. We did it once in the employees' bathroom at the Shop-N-Save. We did it with handcuffs. Twice. He insisted we try it blindfolded, under the stars, at the park, before midnight one Tuesday. Thank God we didn't get caught.

But here I glanced around us, almost frantic. Where could we go so he could get his fix? And that was exactly what it felt like—a kind of addiction—especially when we were trapped in not-very-sexually-conducive moments like these, and I was stuck trying to arrange something to tide him over for a few hours. I wanted to be able to socialize for at least part of the reception. I didn't want to be biting my lip in a dark closet somewhere to keep the other guests from hearing my screams of rapture.

However, since this was an outdoor wedding, our options were limited.

"I'm not doing it in the port-o-potty," I informed him. "And our hotel is a half-hour's drive away."

He nodded. "How about car?" Then he paused to reconsider. "No, too easy."

"Too *easy?*" I imagined the logistics of getting in a position even remotely comfortable in that tiny car. And his Volkswagen had a stick shift.

"Too easy for people to see us," he explained. "Maybe there is good place on other side, by workers?"

There was a small building, not far from where the reception garden was, where the caterers could organize their trays before bringing them out. However, service people swarmed that area and everything else was pretty much open air. We had tents or canopies covering us but, since the day was cool yet very clear, there were few hiding places.

"I guess we can look," I said, wanting to please him but not knowing if it'd be possible. "I doubt we'll find anything really private, though."

He shrugged and a grin tugged at the corners of his lips. "I know we find something."

A cheer went up around us, and I realized that our negotiating had distracted me. I'd missed the announcement of Mark and Seth's permanent couplehood.

I stopped whispering with Andrei and joined in the clapping. I saw a line forming to greet and congratulate the new pair.

"Let me talk to Mark and Seth for a few minutes, and then we'll figure out a place, okay?"

He studied me with those intense gray eyes, his expression one of assessment rather than of passion. "Okay," he said just before I turned away to shake hands with the grooms.

Seth gave me a jolly hug and Mark kissed my cheeks, both sides, when I offered them my congratulations.

Mark leaned in. "You caught yourself one hunky Russian dude, babe. I couldn't help but stare at him when the two of you got here."

I grinned. "Yeah. I'll introduce you to him later when we have more time to chat."

Mark raised his blond eyebrows. "I'll hold you to that, Ellie."

"But remember," I told him. "You're a married man now. No flirting."

He shot a look at Andrei, who seemed to be people-watching from his chair. "Oh, don't worry about *me*. You'd better keep a tight rein on him, though. The flock thinks he's delicious."

I followed Mark's gaze and saw immediately that he wasn't kidding. There was a small tribe of single women—Canadian, I think, none of whom I knew—who kept eyeing Andrei and sending flashes of carnal interest his way. To Andrei's credit and to my heart's relief, he smiled at the women, but conversed with no one.

I walked back to Andrei and sat down next to him again. "Alrighty. We're clear for a while. Did you figure out a good spot?"

To my surprise, he shook his head and said, "Maybe now is not best time. We can wait for after dinner."

Grateful, I reached for his hand and squeezed it. "Thanks. Yeah, we'll be better able to slip away unnoticed then."

"Yes."

Although Jane chatted constantly throughout the dinner—commenting on the meal, on the variety of outfits, on the reception guests and on Canadians in general—Andrei, by contrast, was unusually silent. He'd send an occasional heated look my way, though, and he seemed to be enjoying the spirited conversation Kim, Tom and their brood of antsy young ones brought to our table, so I figured the long drive and active weekend had begun to take their toll.

"Callie, put the fork down. Down!" Kim cried. "Do not stab your brother with it." She motioned to her husband across the table. "Tom. Stop her."

Tom, who'd been picking rice-cereal clumps out of little Jordan's hair, reached around Callie's quieter twin, Zack, and grabbed the offending utensil. Two-and-a-half-year-old Callie gave him a demonic glare and snatched up her spoon. She aimed it menacingly at her baby brother. Baby Jordan responded with a shriek and soon the whole table was in an uproar.

"Remind us to get a sitter next time," Tom said to Andrei and me with a sheepish grin.

We laughed, and I couldn't help but wonder yet again what it would be like to be parents with Andrei. I could see him holding our baby, cradling the infant in his large arms ever so gently. I was nearly moved to tears by the image. I caught his eye and tried to convey my devotion with a glance. His look telegraphed tenderness. I hoped that was what he felt. I hoped, in fact, he felt the dawning of commitment.

This is a rather romantic setting, is it not? Jane observed. *In spite of the bevy of youngsters.*

They say there's nothing like a wedding to bring a couple together, I replied.

Jane laughed. *"They" say a great many things better left unspoken. Think for yourself, Ellie. Do not rely on the professed wisdom of others.*

I rely on YOUR wisdom, Jane. Would you suggest I start ignoring you, too?

She sniffed. *I believe you already do that routinely.*

Well, that shut me up.

A few minutes later, the cake was brought out. Andrei nudged me with his knee. "I have idea."

I watched in anticipation as Mark and Seth cut their cake—complete with two grooms atop it—and the photographer's camera flashed to document the occasion. The caterers began passing out slices, and we were one of the first tables to be served.

Andrei stood up and snagged both our plates of cake while Kim and Tom tried to keep their children from smearing the frosting on each other and themselves. "Excuse us," he said. My preoccupied parent friends scarcely noticed our departure.

"This way," Andrei whispered to me. And, little sheep that I was, I followed him without a second thought.

He led me back toward where the catering trucks were, and he pointed to a small one. "That is one big cake came in," he informed me. "Workers are too busy now cutting pieces and serving. Truck is empty."

"Oh," I said, but I was thinking, How *resourceful* of him.

"Come."

The back doors flapped open in the breeze, so he lifted me inside and locked them shut behind us. With the doors closed, it was pitch black.

"Take off pretty dress, Ellie."

My eyes hadn't adjusted to the dark, but I glanced around, trying to see the inside of the truck anyway. "Here?"

One of his hands groped my breast. "Yes. Here."

I was only just beginning to detect shadows and could now perceive Andrei's silhouette in front of me. He was still holding the cake plates, both in his right hand while his left continued to caress me.

I unzipped the scoop-necked dress, shivered and stepped out of it. Then I placed it carefully on a box or a crate or a something, away from us. When I stood near Andrei again, he dipped his finger into the frosting and smeared it on my chest.

"Yummy," he said as I gasped. "This is how I want to eat cake." Then, as his fingertips decorated my body with white cake and frosting, he began to sing to me, low and slow, half in broken English and half in Russian, in between licking off his designs.

I locked Jane out of my mind (best for all concerned) and what followed was raunchy, wild, highly erotic and unbelievably weird.

Every second that ticked by I wondered if someone would swing open those doors. I wondered how I'd keep pace with Andrei when we were married and together every night. And I wondered how my body could respond with such explosiveness whenever we touched.

What began as a fog of confusion, though, cleared into sky-blue certainty: This must be special. A rare connection. A *sign*.

And Andrei's lyrics in the midst of his sexual fervor brought E. M. Forster unwittingly to mind. " 'Only connect the prose and the passion, and both will be exalted, and human love will be seen at its height,' " I quoted to myself, giggling at the juxtaposition.

"What is funny?" Andrei asked me.

I kissed him hard. "I'm just happy. You make me happy." And I meant it. As offbeat as our relationship had been, I could feel the completion of my life just beyond my grasp. This time, I'd reach it, and I'd "live in fragments no longer."

He returned the kiss, nipping a bit more, too, but he said nothing until we heard voices outside.

"Who is here?" he whispered.

"Oh, shit!" I jumped away to slide again into my dress, and Andrei hastily re-zipped his pants.

The truck's back doors jerked, but didn't open.

"It's locked," a male voice said. "You got the key?"

"Nope. Where's Val? She should have one," a lady answered. "You wanna wait here while I get it?"

In the dark, Andrei shook his head, as if telling the man to say no, but even in deep shadow I could make out the broad grin on his face. My heart pounded in my chest like we were tangoing on landmines, but he was enjoying this. No, *loving* this. I held my breath. We were such different people, Andrei and I. But opposites attracted, right?

The guy outside answered, "Nah. I'll go with you. I can grab a few more trays then." I heard their voices grow softer as they walked away.

We managed to slip out of the truck unnoticed, but on our way back to the table Mark materialized, a blond Adonis in a black tuxedo.

"Well, here you two are. I've been looking all over for you. Been wanting to meet you." He held out his palm toward Andrei, and the men shook hands.

I spoke too fast, I knew, explaining with wild hand gestures how we'd been out taking a walk . . . because, um . . . it was such a lovely area and the weather was so mild. Mark shot me a sharp look and Andrei glanced around as if searching for an escape route. I pressed on anyway, eventually making the official introductions.

Andrei spoke up then. "This is very nice ceremony and dinner."

"Thanks. We've been looking forward to this day for ages." Mark sniffed the air. "Hey, did you guys get any cake? God, I'm smelling it everywhere." He paused and looked around. "Hmm. Anyway, I think they've got a few pieces left on the table if you missed out."

We assured him we'd tried it.

"Good," Mark said. "So, Andrei—" He got the devilish glint in his eye that I remembered so well from our college days. "Tell me, what are your intentions with our young Ellie? Should Seth and I have reason to expect a cake-filled celebration for you two anytime soon?"

Andrei looked momentarily confused, no doubt trying to reconcile the way we'd conducted ourselves over the past half hour in regards to "cake" with what Mark had really been asking. "We see in time," he said finally.

Mark cocked a brow. "Well, just keep us posted, will you?" Then he shook hands with Andrei again and leaned in to plant more kisses on my cheeks. "You smell tasty, El," he whispered in my ear. "Hope it was fun."

My eyes widened at this, and I tried to look innocent, but from the expression on my friend's face, he wasn't buying it. He winked at me, waved to Andrei and strode off grinning.

"He knows," I said, closing my eyes. "I don't know how, but he figured it out."

Andrei shrugged.

Then I looked down at my dress. It was on correctly, but a streak of white frosting marked my chest like an insignia, just above the plunging neckline. "Oh," I said.

Andrei rested his hand on my shoulder and patted me. "I missed a spot."

"Guess so." I tried to fight the embarrassment as I brushed away the smudge with the tissue he handed me, but it was a losing battle. Andrei was unconcerned, probably even proud of his sexual exploits. I was still a geek at heart.

But I had a great lover now. One who'd stand by me. I had a reason to change.

I took a deep breath, determined to be cool for once in my life. The words that emerged from my mouth, however, were anything but.

"So, about what Mark said—" I began. "We haven't really talked much about the future . . ." I trailed off, hoping he'd take the hint and finish the thought.

He said nothing.

"Um, well, do you have some kind of a plan in mind? A sort of time frame for getting more involved, you know?"

He gave me a blank stare.

I waited him out this time.

"It is wedding now for other people," he said. "We talk more when we go home."

In an odd way, I took this as symbolically encouraging. He didn't want to mix up our own wedding plans with those of others. He wanted our marriage to be distinct from the events around us. Something just the two of us would construct.

Throughout the dance that night, I watched him carefully. Everything I thought and felt, he confirmed by his actions. He sat back and relaxed, allowing me to chat with friends as he absorbed the atmosphere in reflective silence. We danced together several times, but on the few occasions when some other woman approached him, undoubtedly to beg for a waltz or a two-step, he always politely turned her down.

I considered this proof he was mine.

Twenty-four hours later, on the eleven-hour drive back to Chicago, I napped in the passenger seat while Andrei sped us home. I was exhausted from the busy weekend, pleased to have seen my old college friends again and relieved Andrei didn't suggest stopping at a roadside 7-Eleven for a quickie. One happy girl.

"I am caring deeply about you, Ellie," Andrei said after I woke up.

I grinned at him. "I feel the same way about you. You know that."

He nodded. "Yes. But here is problem. I want to be with other women."

I blinked, aware the Michigan landscape was going by far too fast and maybe I'd missed something in the blur. "Sorry, um, what?"

"I am wanting to be with other women. You know. Talking? Dating? Fucking?"

Something inside my chest turned to lead. *"What?"*

He sighed. "I know you are not wanting to hear this, but I care about you. I remember what you said long time ago. If I am wanting to cheat, you say, I should break up with you." He looked me in the eye, which wasn't a real bright idea given his driving speed. "I am doing this. I must break up with you now. It is your wish."

"No!" I ground out. "It's *not* my wish. I don't want our relationship to end. Andrei, I—I love you."

There. I'd finally said it. I'd finally gotten those words out to him, and I was sure . . . well, pretty sure I meant them. He *had* to feel the same way. My God, after everything we'd done together, he had to love me back. Or at least be close to it.

He nodded some more and stepped harder on the accelerator. "I am caring for you, Ellie, but is not deep love. I am sorry. I quickly am—what is right word? Finding boredom? I need our sex to be more exciting and, after while with same person, this is not so possible. Even when we try new things." He paused to catch his breath and shift gears. "It is not good idea to stay in relationship. I will be having other women soon."

"Please don't do this. *Please.*" My voice sounded pitiful.

He looked at me as if he'd known all along I'd react like this. As if this were the reason he'd waited to broach the topic. He sensed I'd dissolve into a blubbering, begging mess, and he didn't want it witnessed by anyone.

"I am feeling sorry to make you sad. But this is truth, Ellie."

"Well, I don't *want* the fucking truth right now," I shouted. And for the next three hours at least, I meant every word.

I wanted my fantasy, dammit.

I wanted my goddamn happily ever after, complete with cute babies and an adoring husband.

And, despite being given every reason to hate the guy, I still wanted Andrei.

He'd been honorable enough to face me. To break things off before cheating on me. To let me sniffle like a lost toddler for hours in his car. How could he like me, respect me, make love to me as only he had done, and not want to be with me forever?

Over the next couple of weeks, I tried every Get-Him-Back ploy in the book. I did all those embarrassing things that desperate women do:

Calling him at odd hours then hanging up the phone when he answered.

Writing him long, plaintive letters—complete with the

world's worst poetry—some of which I sent, many of which I thankfully didn't.

Stalking his apartment complex like a drive-by shooter might, fantasizing about pitching soggy tissues at him if ever I saw him in passing. I never did see him.

Meeting him for a few of those awful, post-breakup tête-à-têtes where the breakup-er suffers through an hour of memory rehashing and the breakup-ee pleads their relationship's hopeless case.

None of it worked and, despite Jane's attempts at comforting me, I wrapped up the school year in a haze of wretchedness.

My sister, now legally separated from Alex and waiting out the last month until their divorce was finalized, said after another week of my moping, "I know it sucks, El, but move on."

This was one situation where I knew I couldn't say, "What do you know, Di?" because it was clear she did know. Her big brown eyes showed surprising compassion.

So, I said, "I'll try."

Of course I really didn't try. It was too hard. I missed Andrei— our companionship, our in-jokes, our incredible sexual chemistry, even our dangerous liaisons in public places. And too many things reminded me of him.

I'd gotten a summer job at the Glen Forest Book Shoppe for the extra cash and the employee discount, but everywhere I looked there were books or CDs that screamed out Andrei's name to me.

Immigration in America.

Chicago Nightlife—The Hot Spots.

U2's Greatest Hits.

And, of course, anything by Dostoevsky.

I once had to restock the "World Music" CDs, and I almost broke down when I got to the Russian section. It was bad.

One late-June afternoon, as I was working the cashier station, a voice I'd never forgotten said, "Hi, Ellie."

I looked up. Sam Blaine.

I looked down and sighed. The man had a gift. He had a knack for showing up at the worst possible times in my life. Why should this time be any different?

Oh, good Lord! Jane exclaimed. *Not HIM again.*

I looked back up and mustered my courage. "Sam. This is a surprise. You're back in Illinois?"

"Just for a few weeks." He plopped down a stack of Harry Potter books and pulled out his MasterCard. "Belated birthday presents for my nephews," he explained.

"Mmm-hmm." I rang up his purchases and stuffed them in a large plastic bag. "Would you like your receipt kept separate or shall I put it in with the books?"

He took the slip of paper from me, his fingers brushing mine in the process and causing their usual spark, damn him.

"I've got it," he said.

"Okay, well, that's . . . good. Nice to see you again, and have a lovely day."

He grabbed the plastic bag I'd pushed toward him and laughed. "Oh, c'mon, Ellie. Surely after all this time we can have a civilized conversation, can't we?"

I sucked in some air and stared at his still-handsome face. Like a 1987 Bordeaux, Sam Blaine aged well.

"I thought we were being exceptionally civilized." I forced a bright smile. "Really. It's been *great* seeing you again, but I'm in the middle of work." I paused and added the customary, "Thanks for shopping with us. We appreciate your business."

I turned my attention to the line of customers waiting to check out. Unfortunately, there was no one else there. Even more unfortunately, Sam noticed this.

He stepped closer to the counter and said, "It's been almost five years since we ran into each other at that bar—and that time, well, you remember what happened."

Of course I remembered what happened. Personal moments of mortification were hard to forget. I nodded.

"When are you done with your shift?"

"I—I just started, so not until late. Very late."

"Okay. When do you get a break? Do you have time for coffee?"

Tell him no, Jane advised, her voice chilly.

"I—" I began to shake my head, but something in Sam's blue eyes stopped me. "Four o'clock," I blurted. "I can take up to a half hour then."

Jane huffed. *Foolish girl.*

"And you're willing to spend that whole half hour with me?" Sam asked.

I opened my mouth to reply, but he held up his hand. "No, no, don't answer that." He chuckled. "I know I'm strong-arming you into this, but I do want to talk to you again. I'll see you at four." He pointed to the café section of the bookstore. "I'll wait for you over there."

"All right."

As he left, I cursed my lifelong weakness for those eyes and, in punishment, was required to listen to Jane's rants of displeasure for a full hour.

❧ 9 ❧

Heaven forbid!—*That* would be
the greatest misfortune of
all!—To find a man agreeable
whom one is determined to hate!

—*Pride and Prejudice*

I'd had bad weeks in my life, both before and after the week that began with Air Band. But that last week of my senior year of high school turned out to be my Number One, Hands-Down, Worst Week *Ever*.

It did not, of course, start that way. Actually, I stupidly thought after prom night there was nowhere down left to go, nowhere further to drop. But, as had often been the case when it came to guys (Sam Blaine in particular) and me, I was wrong. Really wrong.

I'd spent the majority of that bright Saturday morning studying for the chemistry II final I was going to have on Monday and the entirety of that afternoon staring into space, daydreaming about college dating while chatting with Jane.

When evening finally came, I dressed in jeans and a pink T-shirt, draped a white sweatshirt around my shoulders, and drove to the school to watch Steve, Matt, Jason, Nate and, yes, Krista air jam to "Patience," a power ballad of Guns N' Roses.

The stage, such that it was, was a platform in the middle of our otherwise dark football field. A few of the senior male electronics geeks were in charge of sound, blasting the records over the speakers that littered the edge of the stage. Students crowded the track and the bleachers, watching and listening. Colored lights illuminated the performers and, for a few minutes, those who'd dreamed of rock stardom had a taste of it.

As Steve writhed onstage in uncanny imitation of lead singer Axl Rose, Matt played to his one groupie (Terrie) and Jason dove into his role as bass guitarist. I sat at the edge of a bleacher row and surveyed the field beyond the band. Alone on the track and heading straight in my direction walked the inimitable Sam Blaine.

Our gazes converged.

I blinked and looked away. Glancing far down my row, I spotted Amanda Roberts sitting on the lap of a cute blond guy and laughing. Ah. Now I knew why Sam was looking up here.

I figured Sam, who'd studiously avoided exchanging with me even his usual trite harassments since prom night, must have a broken heart. His relationship with Amanda reportedly fizzled out in the same amicable manner that Jason's and mine had, only I wasn't harboring any secret disappointment about the breakup. As I returned my gaze to Sam, I caught a forlornness in his expression as he scrutinized our row. Clearly, he wasn't over Amanda yet.

Steve, Jason and the gang abandoned the stage to wild applause. A girl band quickly replaced them, and soon I recognized the opening strains of Roxette's big hit, "Listen to Your Heart."

I closed my eyes and let the night swirl around me, the music a pulsing I could feel under my skin. May had a scent. A tipsy, dancing spearmint, full of tantalizing promise. I inhaled its flutterings and felt, far too briefly, my spirit taking flight.

"Hey, Ellie. What's up?"

I forced open my eyes. Sam stood in front of me, staring at me strangely.

"Oh. Hi, Sam."

He squinted, appearing to want to ask a question. Then he shrugged, as if dismissing the idea. He pointed to a spot to my right. "You saving that for someone?"

"No."

"No? Really?"

"Did I stutter?" I said, exasperated. Then I moved my legs closer to the bench so he could get in.

He slid next to me without saying anything else.

The song played on and we watched the group go through their motions of passion and anguish onstage. I closed my eyes again but, this time, I couldn't recapture that feeling of elation and freedom I'd had only a few minutes before. I sighed.

Sam nudged me. "You okay?"

"Yes, of course." It came out more sharply than I'd intended.

"Sorry, it's just—I just—well, you looked sort of weird for a second."

"Gee, thanks." Then I remembered Jane's common complaint that I "too frequently employed sarcasm in conversation" and I laughed.

"What?"

"Nothing." I sighed again. "Look, Sam, I know why you're sitting up here. You can keep a better eye on Amanda this way. I get that. But you don't have to pretend to talk to me. Actually, I'd rather you'd just pester someone else."

His forehead wrinkled and his mouth dropped open. "Amanda?" His tone was heavy on the disdain. His eyes darted around until he saw her. He turned back to me with a look of fake surprise. "Hey, I'm not here to spy on anyone. I just wanted to sit down."

"Yeah, right. Whatever you say."

"Ellie—" His voice came out so oddly I had to look him in the eye. We stared at each other for a minute until I crossed my arms and pressed my lips together. Then he said, "You know what? Never mind." And he stood up and stalked away.

"Fine," I muttered to myself.

"What's fine?" Terrie asked, appearing from behind me with Matt's fingers latched to the back pocket of her jeans.

"Oh, hey, nice to see you," I said, not answering her question, of course. "Great performance, Matt."

He grinned. "Thanks. It was cool."

I scooched over. "You two want to sit down?"

"No, thanks, we're gonna get a jump-start on Chad's party just as soon as they announce the winner for Best Air Band." Terrie glanced at her watch. "There's only a song or two left, so we thought we'd catch them from the track." The Roxette girls cleared the stage and a few new guys came on. "You're coming to Chad's, right?" Terrie asked.

"Sure," I said. Chad Dennahey's parents were in the Bahamas, so he was hosting the biggest bash of the weekend. Why not go? After all, I didn't have anything else to do that night.

"Great," she said. "See you there." Then she and Matt walked down the steps and melted into the crowd on the track.

Over by the stage platform, I saw Sam again. This time he was chatting it up with the electronics-sound geeks. Gone was that lost, lonely look. Standing there, he seemed as self-assured and downright cocky as always. What a freaking irritating quality.

I saw him turn and glance up at the bleachers. My row, to be precise. I looked to my right. Amanda and her new boyfriend had left. Ah-ha. He'd just have to hunt for her somewhere else now. But when I looked back at Sam, he wasn't there either. So I directed my attention to the new band and did a literal double take. Just guess who was front and center?

Sam Blaine—smart, intense, arrogant—looked nothing like any rock 'n' roll star I knew, despite his addiction to Top 40, but the air of haughty confidence he displayed onstage made him almost believable.

The familiar, soul-stirring bass of the intro preceded Eric Carmen's voice through the speakers as Sam and his buddies began their lip-synched version of "Make Me Lose Control." Sam's body swayed to the rhythm, and I watched him, mesmerized.

What was it about music that always made my blood race? The entwining of poetry with tune? In spite of myself, I began to sway, too. My toes tapped the bleacher floor. My lips hummed along. I closed my eyes and the fragrance of May flooded back to me, a warm, whirling symphony of minty lightness.

When I dared to look at the stage again, Sam had begun mouthing the lyrics, his eyes trained on me. Our hearts beating to the same rhythmic patter.

Only, my hammering pulse soon began to outstrip the melody, galloping through it as though the record had been set to the wrong speed.

I jumped up off the bench and dashed down the bleachers' stairs. I sprinted across the track, then beyond the football field and into the parking lot. To my car.

Safe.

But safe from what?

Whatever this feeling was, it was ridiculous. Whatever I'd imagined had happened, hadn't.

I shook my head hard. Sam and I didn't make sense together. Ever. I'd decided that long ago, and some truths remained truths no matter what the soundtrack.

A wise decision, Jane said as I sped through the clear, tree-lined streets of Glen Forest to Chad's parent-free house.

I know, I whispered back. *I know.*

And, in the fall, there will be mature college men, she reminded me.

That's right. And I'll be free! Free of everything here but you, dear Jane.

You wish to be free of me as well?

Of course not. It's just the opposite. I paused at a stoplight, taking a few deep breaths. *Say you'll come with me, Jane. Say you won't suddenly disappear from my life. That you'll be there for me to talk to next year, no matter what . . . please?*

Certainly. If you wish it.

I do wish it. I need you. I don't know how I'd have made it through high school without you. I asked again the question I'd asked her a thousand times before. *Are you SURE we're not related?*

I am quite sure, Ellie.

Then I asked the other question that'd needled me for years. *Jane, why do you think Sam's always gotten to me? Why do I still—*

Think no more of Mr. Blaine. His antics haunt you only because he revels in pursuing ignoble games. The winning of the game is his aspiration, not the prize itself.

What could I say to that? I'd always thought so myself. And Sam had a history of arrogance, of competitiveness, of generally dishonorable juvenile behavior. Only that day, for the first time, it felt like a totally different game somehow. *This is diff—*

It is not different, Ellie, Jane insisted with some annoyance. *He has not changed. Although, perhaps, you have.*

How so?

Merely that you are becoming a woman. Your expectations are higher, more sophisticated. You project similar depths and desires upon others where none exist.

I grinned into the darkness, the road winding in serpentine patterns now that I'd reached the outskirts of town. *Yeah, that must be it. I'm the epitome of maturity.*

That, Jane retorted with a sniff, *I would NOT be inclined to say.*

I stepped out of the car, slammed the door and marched toward Chad's expansive backyard—if that was what you'd call two-plus acres of rolling land. Laughter and loud music emanated across the night with an occasional howl to break up the redundancy.

"Hey, El!" a few drunk senior girls yelled. I waved to them.

"Grab a beer," someone else shouted, pointing to the fat keg on the patio.

I meandered over to it and filled a plastic cup half full of the flat, vile-tasting stuff. I took a single sip, so I could have its smell on my breath, and I tried not to shudder. I didn't like beer. I never had. But it was necessary to carry one around in order to appear appropriately sociable.

Over the next hour, more and more Glen Forest seniors filtered in to the party. Stacy Daschell stumbled into the yard, guzzling beer like a trout slurps water and, when she was sure she had an audience, started groping her best friend's older brother, who was home from college. I rolled my eyes and gossiped about her with Jane. Then Terrie arrived, along with Matt of course, and for a while the three of us chatted about nothing. Steve and Krista showed up, too, and so did Jason . . . on the arm of Princess Amy.

Terrie stared at them, then squinted at me. "Well, now, that's a new development."

"Good for him," I said back, almost meaning it. Sure, he could've and should've chosen someone with a smidgen of character, but he had Amy as his "sweet" date now, and she could keep him.

While Terrie and Matt refilled their beers, in between making out, and Amy was off babbling with a few other girls, Jason approached me.

"Hi, Ellie," he said.

"How are you doing?"

"Good, really good. Thanks. How are *you?*"

"Oh, great."

He glanced around. "Are you meeting anyone here?"

"Just my friends," I said, pointing in Terrie's direction.

"Lots of guys are coming here later, you know."

"Oh, that doesn't surprise me." I smiled at him. "Events with beer and without chaperones are traditionally popular."

"Yeah, but you—you're such a friendly person. You meet people easily, especially when there're lots of people to meet."

I didn't exactly agree with this but, since Di had left to go to college, social interactions at school had become less torturous. "Thanks," I told Jason.

"And Glen Forest's a real friendly place, too. I've always thought so, haven't you?"

He was losing me with his thought progression, but I was in the mood to be agreeable, so I said, "Sure."

"So many nice people in one spot," he added, then he studied his cuticles for a second. "Um, Ellie, about that—are you okay with me being here with Amy? I know we said we were just friends and could date whoever we wanted, but I don't want you to feel—"

"I'm fine with it, Jason. Really." I plastered an absolutely delighted grin on my face.

He exhaled hard and heavy. "Oh, good. I was a little worried, but you're really cool, you know that?"

I just nodded and kept grinning.

He leaned down and kissed me on the cheek. A peck that hardly registered. "I'll never, ever forget prom night," he said with a seriousness that bordered on the comical.

"Me either," I assured him.

He flashed one last bright smile at me before bounding off to find his princess. Nice guy, despite his memory impairment and complete lack of lovemaking skills. Jane often likened him to her affable, albeit simplistic book character, Mr. Bingley, which, I supposed, wasn't too far off.

But where, oh, where was my hero? My Mr. Darcy? Not here, to be sure. Glancing around Chad's backyard, I spotted a handful of other Bingley types, the scary Mr. Collins replicas, and a bunch of pure bad-guy Wickhams but—

"Are you still grumpy?" the voice of the Mr. Wickham I knew best said behind me.

"I am never grumpy, Sam. Although, occasionally, I'm rather irritated."

He elbowed my ribs as he came to stand beside me. "What's with the snooty language? 'I'm rather irritated . . .'" he mimicked. "Been reading all those highbrow British novels again?"

That boy is detestable, Jane remarked.

He, apparently, doesn't think too highly of you either, I replied to her. *And your highbrow language is rubbing off on me.*

Nonsense! she said.

"Nonsense." I slipped and said this aloud in imitation of her. Sam quirked a disbelieving eyebrow.

"Yeah, you have been," he said. "You really get into all that English lit crap, don't you? But, hey, that's okay by me. It keeps you from being my competition."

"What do you mean?"

"I'm planning on med school," he said, pride and a hint of worry in his voice. "So don't suddenly give up the English and decide to pursue science." He grinned a little. "I'm hoping my classmates will be a bunch of morons."

I chose to overlook the backhanded compliment and focus on Sam's professed career goals instead. I'd suspected his interest in medicine, but I hadn't gotten confirmation of it before that night. Certainly, his fascination with human anatomy was clear.

"So, that's what you're going to study?" I asked, knowing my love of literature would, indeed, keep me away from the sciences. "You're *that* sure you'll like it?"

"I'm *that* sure." He shrugged. "I still need to get through four years of undergrad bio stuff before applying but, yeah. There were a few things in life I knew right away. That was one of 'em."

Distracted by him, I took a sip of my beer before I realized it, then grimaced at its unrelenting bitterness. "Blah. I can't stand this stuff."

He gave me a speculative glance. "Well, I've got something else in my car."

"What?"

"C'mon." He tugged on my arm. "I'll show you."

I stood firm. "Sam Blaine, I won't be dragged into your car and plied with alcohol, never to be seen or heard from again."

He looked offended. "The hell with you, Ellie. It's not like I'd drug you, attack you and then toss your body into a swamp. Get over yourself." He took several angry steps away from me.

"I—I—" I began. I didn't know why he always brought out this combative side of me but, this time at least, he didn't deserve an accusation like that. "Sorry," I said finally. "I didn't mean it that way."

He shot me a look, unsmiling. "That's okay. Listen, I have rum and Coke. Come have some with me if you want. Skip it if you don't." He took another few steps away, but then he paused and turned back toward me. Waiting.

Ellie . . . Jane said, her tone heavy with warning.

I followed him.

Unlike my car, which was parked pretty much right outside Chad's front door, Sam's was a good block away from the house and from most of the other cars. But, with four minutes of brisk walking, we got to it fast.

As we slid into his parents' Oldsmobile, I couldn't get over the weirdness of the whole thing. Me and Sam. Sitting in a car. Drinking. Talking about our college plans. It was like a scene from a John Hughes teen flick. I glanced around but didn't see anybody filming.

"Give me your beer," Sam commanded.

I handed it over and watched as he dumped the disgusting liquid out the window. He flipped open a Coke can and poured half of the soda into my plastic cup. Then he pulled out a small bottle of rum and added a generous amount to both my glass and into his half-full Coke can. He handed the cup back to me.

"Cheers," he said. "Here's to finally graduating."

"If we survive finals next week," I added, clinking beverages with him.

We both drank. The sweet, syrupiness of the mixture was heaven after the beer, but beneath the sugared swirl of caffeine, an alcoholic bite lay in wait nonetheless.

After several swigs, I blurted, "You were really great onstage tonight. I didn't know you were planning to enter Air Band."

He shrugged but couldn't hide a grin. "A bunch of us decided to do it last week. We were fooling around but it was kinda fun."

"Oh. Well, nice job. I—I didn't see the very end, but I heard that the guys doing the Scorpions won it."

"Yep. They closed the show. They were awesome." Sam paused, his blue eyes burning into me. "Why'd you leave early?"

I gulped some air. "To get a good parking space here, of course."

He nodded, but he didn't look like he believed me. And, since it was a total lie, he had good reason not to. I was reminded of something Jane told me once: "If a woman is partial to a man, and does not endeavor to conceal it, he must find it out." I knew I'd let my guard down too much with Sam. That I was being too obvious. So I tried to relax, pull back, be cool.

He pointed to my almost-empty cup. "Want some more?"

"Sure."

He opened a new can of Coke and fixed both of our drinks stronger this time. A half hour went by. Maybe an hour. I don't know how long we sat there, sipping, talking and eventually laughing. I felt lightheaded to the point of giddiness, but it wasn't from the rum.

Jane said, for probably the tenth time, *You should leave.*

But I shrugged her off and, instead, found myself talking with Sam about the chemistry II exam we had coming up on Monday.

"Stop worrying, Ellie. You're gonna ace it. You always do." He slanted a devious look my way. "And you can bet I will, too."

I smirked, feeling full of myself and of the confidence that alcoholic consumption brings. "If I were a betting girl, I wouldn't waste my time on such an easy wager."

His brows rose slowly and he leaned in close. "Really? And what would be one worth your time?"

I looked deep into his eyes. His pupils had dilated to huge dark orbs ringed by blue. He must be pretty buzzed if not actually drunk. I sighed and figured Jane was right and I should leave.

"I said *if* I were a betting girl, but I'm not one." My confidence slipped a notch. "Not by a long shot."

The edges of his lips curved upward. "Well, I'm a betting guy. And I've got a wager for you."

I blinked. Curiosity made me ask, "Really?"

"Really," Sam said.

Really foolish, Jane chimed in. *It is long past time to return to the party, Ellie. This instant would be preferable. Say goodnight to the conniving Mr. Blaine.*

No, Jane. I want to know.

As the saying goes, Jane began coolly, *curiosity killed the—*

"Tell me, Sam," I said. "What would you bet?"

He gave me a long, hard stare. "Put the cup down, Ellie."

I put it down.

"Slide a little closer to me," he said.

I slid.

I saw him put his Coke can on the floor. He swallowed. "I bet," he whispered, "we can't stay this close for two minutes before one of us makes a move."

I swallowed this time. "A *move?* You mean, on each other?"

He nodded.

"So, um, one hundred and twenty seconds." I glanced at my watch for emphasis. It had a second hand, but I couldn't read it. My entire arm was trembling.

He reached over and grabbed my wrist, twisting it a bit so he could check the time. It didn't hurt, but his very grasp made my skin tingle. "It's been thirty seconds," he said.

"What counts as a move, in your opinion?" The longer he held my arm, the less bold I felt. Breathing became a challenge, and my heart raced so fast I could no longer distinguish the beats.

"A touch that would be considered inappropriate in public." He eyed me archly. "Or a kiss, of course."

"Of course."

I could almost taste his rum-soaked lips on mine, and a thought that would've been inconceivable two hours ago hit me like a slap: I really wanted him. I wanted Sam Blaine.

In an instant I dismissed my old vow to avoid him and remembered in its place a different promise to myself. That this time I got to choose a lover. And I was going to choose *him*.

Dear heavens, no! Jane cried.

Sam bent my wrist again to read the watch. "Fifty seconds. You're really holding out, Barnett."

"You expected me to be overcome by your charm?" I gave a breezy laugh, a shallow, flirtatious trick for garnering male attention, but effective.

He blinked and put his mouth against my ear. "Yes."

I held still, but the tiny hairs covering my body jerked to attention.

"One minute, ten seconds," I said calmly, although I had no idea if this were true.

I felt his breath on my skin—first my earlobe, then my neck, then my cheek.

"How many more seconds?" he rasped out. "Are we there yet?"

He was too near me, I couldn't think. I couldn't even fake it. "I don't know," I admitted.

"Close enough." He tilted his head and brought his lips down on mine.

Sam's kiss was long and slow and utterly inquisitive. His hands roamed my shoulders, giving off a penetrating heat that singed my skin beneath my clothing. He pulled off the sweatshirt I had draped around me and untucked my T-shirt with a single tug. I felt his fingers walk up my spine and burn delicious tiny tracks on my back. A moan escaped me.

"Oh, God, Ellie," he murmured as my own hands grasped the taut skin that rose just above the waistband of his Levi's.

He lunged against me, chest-to-chest, his tongue entering my mouth more forcefully now. I couldn't help it. I welcomed the invasion and craved more.

The back of my head pressed hard against the passenger-side window. I felt the jab of the door lock in my left shoulder blade.

My legs twisted awkwardly to the right, and I was getting a cramp in one foot, but I didn't complain. I didn't want Sam to stop.

He did anyway.

He pulled back and gave me an almost tender look. "That can't be comfortable."

I shook my head.

He kissed my nose. "Doyouwannamovetothebackseat?" he whispered, a sentence spoken so hurriedly it might've been one slurred word instead of seven.

I nodded.

He lifted himself off of me and clumsily climbed between the two front seats and into the back. This inelegance, in a guy who so often radiated cool self-assurance, was more endearing than a love note. He held his hand out for me and helped me make the awkward journey as well.

We sat for a long moment, facing each other on the smooth vinyl cushion, until Sam, with a very deliberate gesture, wrapped his arms around me and brought me to him again. His expression had a seriousness etched into it, a combination of intensity and vulnerability I'd never before seen in him. His pupils looked more dilated than ever, a sure sign of inebriation, and I felt an acute stab of disappointment that he was only here, only with me this way, because he'd been drinking.

"Look, Sam," I began, "I'm not drunk and—"

"I'm not drunk either."

"But your eyes are dilated, and we did have all this rum—"

His lips formed a lopsided grin. "Your eyes are dilated, too, and you drank just as much rum." He shrugged. "Hey, I'm not kissing you because I'm wasted," he said, somehow able to read my mind. "Pupils can dilate not just from being high on something. It happens in dim light. It also happens when you like somebody."

I put my arms around him now. "Is this the future doctor speaking?"

He shook his head. "This is the guy who's wanted to kiss you like this since sophomore year speaking."

"Oh."

He licked his lower lip and tugged on me until my hips slid along the seat. Until I was lying down and he was above me, his face millimeters from mine. "Yeah, Ellie. 'Oh.'"

Then he kissed me again, holding nothing back.

While the Oldsmobile's backseat could hardly be considered spacious, I was impressed by the degree of maneuverability we achieved. In the course of less than five minutes, he'd wedged off my T-shirt and bra and managed to unsnap and unzip my jeans.

In another five minutes, I'd divested him of his shirt and wrestled his Levi's to the floor. He jerked my jeans down the rest of the way until there was nothing between us but my panties and his boxers. Yes, he was a boxers guy.

With a groan, he pressed his hard erection against me and my breath got stuck in my larynx. I labored for air.

He kissed my mouth with a wanting that made my nipples peak, then he broke away and kissed my nipples. His tongue swirled over them, suckled them, very gently loved them. I wanted to melt into him as our bodies moved together. He put his cheek against mine and thrust his hips hard again. Desire shot through me, and I had to smother an overwhelming urge to shout out.

"Please, Ellie. Say yes to the question I'm about to ask."

"Yes."

I heard him gulp some air. "But you don't know the question, and I don't want you to—"

"Sure I do," I said, my voice breathy. "Make love to me, Sam. Please. Right here. Right now." Because I've chosen you, I added silently.

There was a long, heated pause in which I heard Jane screaming Exclamations Of Horror in my head. I'd ignored her rising levels of aggravation for the past hour, but it was time to lock her out. *Sorry, Jane,* I said as I did it. Then I waited for Sam's reply.

"You really are incredibly smart," he said into my ear at last. "You guessed my question."

"Yes, I'm brilliant," I replied, not that it took a PhD in neurochemistry to figure out a teen male's backseat intentions. "Look, Sam, if you hadn't asked me, I'd have asked *you.*"

He chuckled with what sounded like incredulity. "I had no idea you'd developed this wild side, Ellie Barnett." He grabbed for his jeans, pulling a thin wallet out of the back pocket. "But I've never not liked anything about you."

The double negatives gave my slightly rum-addled brain a second's pause but, once I'd determined his words were intended as praise, I let it go. For one of the few times in my life, I let everything go and just allowed myself to fall into the moment.

He drew out a condom and ripped the foil. Instead of rushing to put it on, though, he set the opened packet on the ledge by the rear window and returned to kissing me. Something in that simple gesture made my heart leap.

His fingers slid down my hips and over—then under—the fabric of my panties. He rubbed his thumb pad against the sensitive folds of skin between my legs and up to the aching nub. He lifted his fingers off me and shifted just enough to move his hands more easily. Then, in one fluid motion, he skimmed the panties off my body and placed his thumb back where it had been before.

He slipped one long finger inside of me and pulled it out. He repeated this, his thumb rubbing and arousing the whole time. A wet stickiness began to flow freely from deep within me, and I wanted to call out to him to stop because I couldn't control it. My nerves took part in a frenzied dance just beneath the surface of my skin. The rest of my system was pure chaos.

He thrust the long finger in again, farther this time, pulled it out and brought it back, now joined by another. The pressure inside me was harder, more intense. I couldn't help it, I moaned and, in response, he moaned, too. I lifted my hips up to meet his fingers.

"What can I do to get you closer?" he asked.

I didn't speak, but our eyes met and, silently, I tried to express that he was already doing everything right.

So he kept probing, his strokes smooth and sensual, until my remaining control almost fractured from the agony of wanting him.

In desperation, I snatched at the foil packet and pressed it to his chest. When he withdrew his fingers from my body to grasp it, I jerked his boxers down. He winced.

"Sorry," I said.

"No, it's okay. I just—my body's a little touchy right now. It's not a bad thing." He glanced out of the car window and into the depth of the night, inky-black except for the thin beam of illumination from a lone streetlamp. Then he looked down at me and broke into a grin. "If anyone interrupts us, I will kill them with my bare hands."

I laughed.

He got the condom on within a few seconds and tossed the packet to the floor. With the best of our ability we angled ourselves so everything that needed to connect would be aligned . . . but this proved trickier than I'd thought. Jason Bertignoli hadn't managed to maneuver it right and hadn't noticed. But Sam Blaine—well, he knew the difference.

Sensing the depth of his extensive past experience filled me with my first real bolt of apprehension that night. How many girls had he had already? How could I possibly measure up?

But Sam refused to allow time for second-guessing. He puffed out a couple breaths then said in my ear, "Guide me."

"What?"

He exhaled another few times. "Reach up, between your legs, and guide me. I don't wanna hurt you."

I swallowed, nodded, did as he asked. The thin plastic of the condom slipped against my palm. His penis jumped in my hand—just like Jason's, I remembered. But, unlike Jason, Sam was a near master at nuance and control for a teenage boy.

I helped Sam slide an inch or two inside of me. Then I released him. I got the feeling he wouldn't need more help than that.

He didn't.

He filled me with himself with one quick thrust, breaking through my physical and emotional barriers in an instant. I cried out, and he caressed me, whispering, "I'm sorry . . . I did that too fast. I'll go slower now, Ellie. I promise."

True to his word, he began moving his hips in a slow, sinewy fashion, creating in me a longing for him so strong I had no idea where it came from or how I could possibly bear it. He thrust in and pulled out again, and again, and again. Every time we joined closer together, we leaped higher toward a place of unrecognizable origin. Maybe where our souls mingled before we were born.

"Sam, I can't—can't believe this—"

He moaned. "I know." Then he looked right into my eyes, and what I saw there rooted me more firmly to the backseat than anything else could have. His expression was one of pure powerlessness against this energy between us. It was disbelief combined with adoration and merged with undisguised terror.

"It's okay," I told him, straining upward to lightly kiss his cheek.

I heard what sounded almost like a whimper coming from deep within him. It may have even been a sob, but he buried his face in between my breasts to muffle it. Then his fingertips grasped the backs of my thighs, and he brought his mouth to mine, covering it as if to stifle a scream.

The tilted angle changed the way our hips pressed together, and my very flesh began to quake. Sam's motions quickened, and he slipped one hand between us, touching me just above the union of our bodies. It sparked pure combustion and engulfed me in fire.

A moment later, Sam came apart in my arms as the flame that lit me ignited him as well. He cried out my name and then pressed me to him.

He held me and nuzzled his chin against my neck. "That was incredible," he murmured.

"Yeah."

After a few minutes, he kissed my nose and heaved himself off me, reaching for a tissue box under the driver's seat. When he removed the condom, I heard a sharp gasp.

"Jesus, Ellie. There's blood on the tissue." He stared at me, horrified. "I thought—I mean, everybody thought you and Bertignoli did it. I didn't know . . ." He gulped. "God, you could've said something—"

I sat up. "*Everybody* thought that? So, that's why y-you figured it'd be okay to sleep with me? Here? Tonight?" I asked, my face heating up and my stomach twisting into an entity my body didn't recognize.

"NO! No, it's not that. I'm just—it's just—" He stopped and looked at me hard. "Are you okay?"

"Yeah," I said. And physically I was. Emotionally, not so much.

He touched my shoulder gingerly, as if it were breakable now. As if it weren't one of the body parts he'd been squeezing with such vigor just a few moments ago. "You sure?"

"Yeah, really," I told him. "Don't worry about it." But it looked like he was doing more than worrying. Panicking seemed closer to the truth. Did I ruin it? Were we going to be okay?

The two of us drew our clothes on in silence and my heart waited in limbo. I wanted him to be affectionate toward me again. To look me in the eye as he had only a few minutes before.

Finally, he glanced around the car—the backseat littered with evidence of prophylactic usage and the front seat with proof of underage drinking—and he said, "Looks like I'm gonna have to really clean up here before I give the keys back to my dad, huh?"

I sort of laughed and, a second later, he joined me. He put an unsteady hand over mine. "You'll be all right getting home? I mean, I could drive you if you think—"

"I'll be fine. The rum wore off a long time ago."

He nodded. "Then I'll walk you to your car." There was nothing optional about this statement. Sam seemed determined to play the gentleman until the very end. This eased my mind. Gave me hope. Convinced me things between us would turn out fine.

Hand in hand we strolled down the block, the music at Chad's house growing louder as we neared it, but no one—thankfully—lingered out front. Everyone had stayed in the backyard where the booze and the action were supposed to be. Everyone except us.

"Good night, Ellie," Sam said, kissing me breathless against my car door. "Thanks for an amazing evening. I hope it was, um—"

"Good for me, too?" I supplied.

He shot me a sheepish glance and chuckled. "Uh-huh, yeah."

"You couldn't tell?"

He closed his eyes and tilted his chin upward, as if remembering. Then he faced me. "Guess I'd give it a thumbs-up."

"And you'd be right," I said. "See you Monday, Sam."

A troubled expression crossed his face. "Yeah, well . . . okay. Drive, uh, safely."

I got in the car and pulled it into the street, Sam's reflection in my rearview mirror showed him standing still as a marble sculpture, watching me leave. He cared about me. Sam *cared!*

I floated home on the wings of newfound love.

The next morning, as I awakened into my bright bedroom, the world aglow with recollections of intimacy and evening delights, I remembered Jane. Finally.

Morning, Jane, I said, opening the door of consciousness wide enough to let her in again.

No answer.

Jane, c'mon. Don't be pissed off. I told you things would be okay, and they are. Sam was wonderful. So amazingly wonderful! He's not a nasty Mr. Wickham after all. You believe me, right?

No answer.

I laughed. Everything in the Grand Universe seemed magnificent on this electrifying Sunday. *Okay, fine. I know you're just being stubborn and don't want to admit you were wrong about him. I'm sorry I didn't listen to all of your advice last night, but I think I made the right decision after all.* I paused. *Do you think this is what love feels like?*

No answer.

I sighed. *Have it your way. I'm feeling too good to let you spoil it.*

By the next morning, however, some of my giddiness had worn off. It wasn't as though I'd seriously expected Sam to stop by or call me at home . . . not exactly. He'd never done either before. But if he'd *wanted* to, he *could* have. Our phone number was listed. He knew which street we lived on. His house was within easy walking distance. And no one would've given him a hard time for visiting because no one (but a silent Jane) knew what'd happened between us.

I was certain, though, that things would be great in school that day. Our only scheduled final exam was in chem II, and there was no way he'd miss that. I counted the Monday-morning minutes until I could get to class.

With a grin on my face that I couldn't hide, I marched into the chemistry room ten minutes early and looked around. Sam's lab partner sat at their table poring over his notes, and Terrie waited for me at ours, but Sam wasn't in the room yet.

I did the usual chitchat thing with Terrie, who thought I'd left Chad's party early because I had a headache. Then I pretended to review a few formulas, all the time keeping one eye on the door.

Terrie said, "You're looking way too cheerful for test day."

"I'm just glad this is our last week," I told her. "We can't get to summer and freedom without the finals, right?"

She warily agreed. "Still, that's no reason to look so thrilled. Someone'll think you have crib notes."

I shrugged off her irritability. Nothing was going to put me in a bad mood that day. Nothing.

Then, with a minute to spare, Sam slipped into the room.

I looked up and smiled at him. A really big and probably very geeky smile, but I was ecstatic to see him again after thirty-four eternity-long hours apart.

He met my gaze and gave me a tight smile in return. Mine dimmed a little and my heart's fluttering turned to a painful quiver.

Once he'd had a chance to sit down at his lab table, I swiveled around and said to both him and his lab partner, "So, are you guys ready?"

His partner answered in the negative with one worried shake of his head then turned his attention back to his notebook.

Sam shrugged and pulled out his pencil. "I think we'll all do all right." His voice was bland. Unemotional. Almost robotic. In the past, he'd used virtually every vocal tone on me—sarcastic, cold, infuriated, moderately friendly on rare occasion and, most recently, passionate—but he'd never sounded like this. He'd never been so believably indifferent.

I tried to swallow back the hurt and blink away an intense sadness I felt rising behind my eyes. I stared at Sam, and waited for some clue, some indication that he was behaving this way for a logical reason. Or, at least, for a reason that wasn't going to break my heart.

"Put away your notebooks," our teacher commanded, slamming the door and waving the exam booklets in the air. "Test time."

I reluctantly turned away from Sam, my mind still racing to solve a puzzle that couldn't be unraveled with proven mathematical equations or valid scientific theory.

Somehow I muddled my way through the exam. If I hadn't crammed so much before Chad's party, I might've flunked it. As it was, it seemed I was capable of passing every test but the one that mattered to me most: My First Real Morning After.

Sam finished his final before any of us, and he flew out of the room. Despite my difficulty concentrating, I finished third and hoped he might be in the hall waiting for me. I turned in my exam booklet, collected my things and left.

The hall was deserted.

For a full two minutes I just stood there, breathing. My body's involuntary functions were all I could handle. My heart pumped blood. My lungs took in and expelled oxygen. My stomach fought to digest the buttered toast I'd blissfully nibbled on at breakfast, a time that now seemed like generations ago.

My world had become littered with the irreparable shards of what was left of my happiness.

I ran into the bathroom, hid in a stall and sobbed as noiselessly as I could.

After three days of numbness and misery, my path and Sam's crossed in the hallway.

"Hey," he said, by way of pathetic greeting.

I couldn't bring myself to answer. I ducked my head and bolted for my locker. But, to my astonishment, fifteen seconds later he stood half a foot away, waiting for me to acknowledge him.

"What?" I made my voice icy, forbidding. I refused to look at him and vowed to God Almighty that no matter what other things in my life I screwed up, this particular confrontation wouldn't be one of them. Sam Blaine would *not* see me crying over him. The fucking bastard.

"Look, Ellie—" He sighed. "I guess we never talked about that night at Chad's . . ."

I shrugged and busied myself with cleaning out the remains of my locker. I crumpled up an old calculus worksheet, ripped down a magazine photo of Bon Jovi I'd taped up back in September (yeah, Sam gave love a bad name), dumped everything else on the tile floor by my backpack and slammed the locker door shut. "What about it?"

"Uh, you know, how afterward we didn't really have a chance to discuss anything, and—"

I finally looked at him. "There's nothing to discuss, Sam. It was fun. Now it's over. We're both going off to college in a few months, and I'll probably never see you again." I paused long enough to get in a good glare. "Well, at least not until our ten-year reunion. Although I might skip that one and hold out until the twentieth. I'm sure you'll be balding and getting kind of chunky by then. The perfect 'doctor' look."

"Okay, you're mad. I get it. I'm—" He stopped talking.

"You're what?" I said, expecting at least a measly apology.

"I—I guess there's no other way to say this." His face took on the pasty cast of someone about to walk into a confessional. "I'll be working constantly this summer to make money for school, and I know you'll be busy, too. Then, like you said, we'll be going to different colleges and won't run into each other much. The timing's really bad now. Things just wouldn't work out long term . . . right?"

I picked up the last of my books and papers, and I removed my school lock. "Congratulations, Sam. You've officially made me regret every second of Saturday night. You're a coward and an idiot and I'm glad to be rid of you." Then, dramatically, I slung my backpack over my shoulder and walked away. He didn't follow me this time.

I told myself I'd survive seeing him the coming weekend at our graduation, but I prayed I'd never have to lay eyes on him after that. I didn't want to put up a front like this ever again.

Jane, I whispered, *I'm really sorry. Really. Sorry. You were right about him, I was wrong. I'll never ignore your advice again. I swear.*

But, as had been the case all week, she didn't answer, and I realized I was truly alone.

I'd been abandoned by them both.

☙ 10 ☙

There are very few of us who
have heart enough to be really in
love without encouragement.

—*Pride and Prejudice*

So, nine years later, I found myself facing Sam again. This time
over the grande mochaccinos he'd ordered for us along with a
couple of chocolate-covered biscotti.

I couldn't believe we were sitting there.

Together.

The seventeen-year-old girl in me still cringed with pain at the
memories that bubbled up just from sharing the same airspace
with Sam Blaine. Even now. Even nearly a decade later.

I watched him try to get comfortable on the hard café chair. He
inhaled fully (was he remembering us as teenagers, too?), tapped
the handle of his coffee cup a few times and then opened the discussion on our past few years.

"When last we left things," he said in a somewhat forced, soap-
opera narrator's voice, "you were walking out the door of that dive
bar with your boyfriend glaring at your back. Whatever happened
to that Dominic guy?" He checked out my left hand. "I don't see a
ring on your finger."

Nothing like driving a stake through my heart.

"Dominic and I parted ways that night, as you probably guessed."

Sam raised a brow. "Breakup effective immediately?"

"Yep. Although I did receive a postcard from him about a year
later," I confessed. "He'd just gotten engaged to a cosmetics com-

pany VP, and they were in Hawaii celebrating. I think he wanted me to know he'd made it big. And almost every Christmas he sends a holiday card to me at my parents' address, but we haven't spoken again since then."

"I see." Sam fidgeted with his biscotti before snapping off a sizable bite.

"How about you and Camryn?"

"She and I lost touch," he said, chewing.

"Breakup effective immediately?" I asked.

He grinned. "Yep. I left for New York. She headed off to Philly. I do know from some mutual friends that she finished med school, though. Went somewhere warm. San Antonio, maybe."

"Are you still in New York, then?"

He shook his head. "Boston. I start the second year of my residency in a couple of weeks, but my parents have their thirty-fifth wedding anniversary next weekend and my sister's kids wanted me to be here for the Fourth of July for once. So I came home. Didn't think I'd get to see you, too."

An unfortunate coincidence, Jane grumbled.

I knew I had to tread carefully here. Jane had eventually stopped her silent treatment after the one-night stand with Sam, but this didn't happen until after college began and I was a good five-hour-drive away from Glen Forest. When she returned, she'd said it was because she was a woman of her word. Because I'd exacted that promise from her to be there with me during college, no matter what the circumstance.

I was lucky she came back.

The summer she didn't speak to me, I'd missed her like crazy, and I sure didn't want to incur her wrath again.

So, I made a conscious but very respectful request of her. *Please, Jane, can we suspend all commentary for just the next thirty minutes? I need to keep a clear head for this.*

She consented, but with a resounding huff.

I inhaled and looked sharply at Sam. I'd expected his typical sarcasm, but didn't find it. Present only was that strange light of curiosity and intensity that I hadn't seen in a man's eyes in what felt like ages.

This both frightened and saddened me.

It frightened me because Sam Blaine *was* a man. To me he'd always seemed more mature than our peers, but a nearly five-year absence since that night at The Bitter Tap (and, cripes, *nine years* since we were graduating seniors) put this growth in perspective. His adulthood was undeniable now. The next time our paths crossed, if ever they crossed again, he could be married. Or even a father. He was already a doctor, not the snotty teen I always thought of when I dredged up those old high-school hurts.

And that saddened me because Sam and I had never quite been on the same page. As teens or adults. We'd been kids together, we'd shared this intimate personal history, but that was all it could be or ever would be. He was going away again, and I was still trying to reconstruct my post-Andrei broken heart.

"What is it?" he said, his voice low, concerned.

I took a sip of my coffee and forced myself to swallow. "Nothing. Just wondering if you left any broken hearts behind in New York."

A deep crease appeared on his forehead. "Ah, well, I don't know if I'd say that. Not exactly. I had a girlfriend there my last couple of years, but I had to go to Massachusetts and she . . . she wasn't headed there."

"You mean she tried to get into the Boston residency program with you but didn't get a spot?"

He sighed. "You were always very sharp, Ellie. And, yeah. It was something like that." He eyed me again with that teasing inquisitiveness. "I don't think my leaving really broke her heart, though."

He said this with such male conviction I almost laughed. I'd bet, even a year later, his poor ex-girlfriend was still crying in her morning coffee over him. Men were so insensitive to women's emotions. I'd bet anything she didn't move on half as easily as he did when he'd abandoned her.

"I'm going to have to go soon, Sam," I told him, pointedly looking at my watch.

"What? Wait. It's only been ten minutes. You said you could take a half hour. What did I say wrong?"

ACCORDING TO JANE   179

"Nothing. You didn't say anything that wasn't true, it's just—I'm not really sure what you're trying to do here. A long-term relationship of mine ended a few weeks ago, and I can't—I just can't deal with this kind of thing right now."

"You can't deal with what thing?" he said, his face reddening a bit. "You can't sit and have a cup of coffee with an old friend?"

"Is that what this is? Is that what we are, Sam? Are we *friends?*" I looked him in the eye and saw that same excitement merged with that same fear I remembered from our one exquisite (and disastrous) night together. It was enough to bring me to my feet. I couldn't handle any more games. Not with anybody.

"We've never not been friends," he said quietly. "Look, about that day after we . . . you know, senior year . . . I knew I'd have to leave at the end of the summer. I knew I didn't have it in me to make things work between us then. Not long distance. I tried to tell you that part, but I was eighteen and really stupid, okay? I also neglected to tell you the rest."

He took a deep breath and slowly exhaled. "I really cared about you, Ellie. But you needed time and experience. You were so young. So naïve. And I needed time, too. I was looking at a decade or more of school. I didn't want to lead you on when I knew it'd be years before anything more serious could happen. Do you know what I'm saying?" He raised his gaze to meet mine.

I closed my eyes and slumped back down in my chair, tears burning behind my eyelids. "Yeah. You broke up with me for my own good."

"Yes—"

"Well, I've been hearing that a lot lately." A few hot droplets leaked out and clung to my lashes before sliding down my cheeks. "Thanks for explaining, Sam. You're exonerated." I wasn't aiming to sound caustic. I meant this. I looked into those extraordinary blue eyes again and made sure he understood my words were sincere.

"Okay," he whispered.

"Okay."

I took one last sip of my drink. Memories of Dominic and Andrei and Sam mingled in my brain, and every additional second I spent in Sam's company only made them rush through it faster. I had to clear my mind, refocus, figure out how to move on again. It'd become an odd pattern. Whenever I was around Sam I was inspired to want a fresh start. It was just something I couldn't seem to do while still in his presence.

I pushed my cup away. "It was great running into you, it really was. Thanks for the coffee and for . . . talking. But I should go." I smiled at him. "See you sometime?"

He nodded. "Our ten-year high school reunion is next summer. Planning to attend?"

"I don't think so. All of my predictions about people are bound to be wrong. Look at you," I said with a small grin. "You're neither balding nor chunky. Yet. Guess I'd better hold out until the twentieth."

He gave me a look too intense to ignore. "I've got good DNA on the hair, Ellie. My grandpa still has almost a full head of it. And I will never be chunky. I promise."

"I guess we'll have to see in a few years, then, and find out who's right." I stepped away from the café table. And from Sam.

Are you still with me, Jane? I asked her.

Yes, she whispered. *I am here.*

But Sam wasn't done with me yet. "We *will* see," he called out, as I turned to go. "You can bet on it."

❧ 11 ❧

What is the difference, in matrimonial
affairs, between the mercenary
and the prudent motive?

—*Pride and Prejudice*

It's strange how time flies. One day you're twenty-six, sitting at a
café table in the middle of a bookstore in summer, staring at
your first love over mochaccinos . . . and the next day you're thirty-
two, wandering around downtown Chicago on Christmas Eve,
wishing you were drinking mochaccinos (or *anything* hot) with your
supposedly serious boyfriend and wondering when the hell he
planned on proposing to you.

No, I know it didn't happen quite that suddenly, but it kind of
felt like it. Maybe because in the past several years—except for
taking the occasional continuing ed class or going on a mini-vacation
to break up the routine—nothing really significant had happened
to me.

Aside from dating Tim, that is. And even this wasn't truly significant until our third Christmas together.

But that frosty night, Timothy Taylor Farthington III kept yanking on my arm in a somewhat less-than-aristocratic manner, aban-
doning his thirty-three years of inbred country-club behavior in
favor of a childlike glee one might find among ten-year-olds at Dis-
ney World.

"These lights are so *cool!*" Tim said, tugging me along Chicago's
Miracle Mile inch by freezing inch. "God, I've missed Christmas
in the States."

"Yes," I told him. "I've always felt so bad for you having to suffer through a tropical December on Fiji. Must be real traumatic." I
squeezed his hand tight and he ground to a stop, his lips a tiny bit
pouty. "But I'm going to be an ice block soon if you don't get me
some coffee. How about we enjoy the nifty lights from inside Star-
bucks?" I pointed at the coffee shop kitty-corner from us, my feet
rooted to the sidewalk.

He kissed my frozen nose and broke into a reluctant grin. "Okay,
but only until you warm up. I want to walk all of Michigan Avenue
before dinner." He glanced down the famous street and exhaled,
wisps of his breath billowing around us.

He ordered us a couple mugs of some special Colombian thing
and I took a sip. Hot, thank God. "Thanks," I told him. "I think
you just saved me from being a cryogenics experiment."

He glanced heavenward, then back at me. "Sometimes I can't
believe you've been a lifelong Midwesterner, Ellie. You know, it's
about twenty-five degrees colder than this in New Hampshire
right now. You'd never survive one of our winters." He added a
sprinkle of nutmeg to his drink, tasted it and added a bit more.

"You're probably right. Good thing you're the one who relo-
cated. You're so adaptable." I made a face to ensure my mockery
was noted.

Tim wadded up one of the paper napkins and tossed it at me. It
bounced off my head and I retaliated by kicking him under the
table. Our coffee mugs wobbled and a few droplets sploshed onto
the table's surface.

He waved one of the napkins in the air. "Truce." Then, after a
few gulps, he added, "I'll get even with you later."

I laughed. Tim's idea of retribution was, at its most dangerous,
tickling. In our three years of monogamous dating, I'd never seen
him get worked into a good sweat over anything—our sex life included—so a counterattack didn't frighten me.

Not that our sex life was *bad,* per se. But, like most things with
Tim, it was refined, sophisticated, polished.

No wild-monkey sex à la Andrei Sergiov. However, for all of Andrei's explosiveness in bed, I realized later that he and I had never

made love. With him, it'd been about pure sexual impulse . . . not about being gentle, sweet or earnest, qualities I believed Tim had in abundance.

I swiped the napkin off the floor and blotted the coffee on the table with another one. "I'm going to have to have a talk with your mother about your table manners."

"Oh, crap. Bad news," he said. "I forgot to tell you. My parents left me a voice mail at work today. They added a stopover in Hong Kong, so they'll be a week late getting home. I guess Mom wanted to do some serious shopping."

My jaw dropped. "A *week* late? Tim, I'll be back at work then—"

He looked at me, apologetic. "I know. I'll change our flights. I'll go out East myself after they get back, wish them a Happy New Year for us, and you and I can do our week with them over your spring break, maybe." He put his coffee cup down and reached for my hand. "I'm sorry. I was looking forward to our trip, too, but I think Mom and Dad just got carried away. They weren't really thinking."

Well, of course they were *thinking*, I thought, feeling mean and resentful. They were thinking about themselves. As always. And they let their only child cover for them. But I said, "That's okay. It's not your fault." I sighed. "So, now that we won't be spending a cozy week in New Hampshire at your parents' place, should we go somewhere else instead?"

He raised a light brown eyebrow and looked interested. "Like where?"

"Virgin Islands, maybe. We could get our hair braided. Or—" I said, going out on a limb, "Las Vegas to elope."

His brow plunged. "Hmm. Don't know about that." The thin wrinkle brackets around his mouth deepened. "I should probably work a few of those days anyway if I'm going to have to still go back home in January. I'll need to pack in some billable hours before then."

"Oh," I said. Tim was a dedicated contract lawyer. Of course, I suspected his reticence had less to do with how seriously he took his position in the firm and more with the mention of the "E" word. He didn't sanction the elopement idea. He thought marriage ought to be undertaken with only the greatest solemnity, and he intended for us to have a big wedding ceremony someday.

Someday being the operative word.

"We could probably do a long weekend in the area, though. And something special for New Year's Eve." He drained his coffee and glanced out the window. "But tonight I want to see all the colored lights flashing and sparkling. I want to hold your hand walking down the chilly street. And I want to visit your family tomorrow for Christmas. Let's have a fun, stress-free holiday. Okay?"

This was classic Tim—dismissing the subject and putting a quiet end to any potential whining at the same time. What was I supposed to plead in my opening argument? Yeah, I embraced stress . . . No, he shouldn't do something reasonable like work when he could be doing something irresponsible like eloping with me in a place where secrets supposedly never left the city limits . . .

Only, was eloping *really* so rash and reckless?

We were, after all, mature adults who knew each other's families and, more impressively, got along with them tolerably well.

We had, after all, dated with the intent to marry.

And we did, after all, have our careers in order and jobs that supported our rather staid lifestyle.

What was wrong with us doing something kind of spontaneous if we planned to eventually do the "M" deed anyway?

I opened my mouth to ask this, but Tim cut me off. "Please, Ellie. Let's just enjoy the night."

And I gave in.

Why? Well, because of what he said next.

"I chose your Christmas present months ago." He tugged me out the door as a burst of Arctic air blew on our faces. "And I can't wait to finally give it to you tomorrow. I think you're gonna like it," he added with a wink.

If it was the gift I'd been hoping for this whole past year, I knew I'd love it.

Di, who'd been dating a string of patently unsuitable men for the past several years, showed up alone at my parents' house the next day. She had an odd cast to her complexion, part ashen, part edgy, part something else. It had me worried.

At the first opportunity, I cornered her in my childhood bedroom and closed the door. "What's going on with you?" I asked. "You look weird."

She laughed then kind of cringed. "That sounds like something I'd say."

I nodded once and waited.

She blinked at me a few times before saying, "I think I'm pregnant."

"WHAT?"

"I know you heard me, El."

"What makes you say—I mean, do you know for sure? And who's the—" I stopped the pointless rush of words. I couldn't speak any more. Hell, I could barely think.

"I don't know for sure," Di admitted. "It's not like I peed on one of those little sticks or anything. I'm kinda scared to buy a box." She sighed. "And as for the father, I don't know that for sure either."

Fuck.

"O-Oh, okay. Okay," I croaked out. "Um, what can I do to help you? Do you want me to get you a test kit? I can just run over to the—"

"It's Christmas Day, sis," she said wearily. "Everything's closed."

"Oh. Right." My mind raced. "No. There's got to be someplace that's open. The hospital pharmacy! I'll just drive there and—"

Di rested a thin hand on my shoulder. "It's all right. I can wait a day and, besides—" she shrugged, "it's not all bad news. If I am, I mean."

She was serious.

And that was when I recognized the something else in her expression. Excitement. She seemed anxious, too, of course and, yeah, she looked pretty tired. But she'd also sloughed off the apathy that'd crept into her demeanor since her divorce from Alex. There was the thrill of anticipation lurking behind those cagey brown eyes, an energy buzz I hadn't seen in her in a long time.

I gulped. "You *want* a baby?"

"Yeah." She looked at me and grinned. "Don't you?"

I nodded. I did, though I hated to admit it just then. "But what about—"

"The father?" she finished for me.

"Yeah."

"I made lots of bad choices in my life already, El. I don't want to make another one. In the past few months there've been two guys. Problem is, neither of them would make a good dad. They're not committed to me, and they don't even have half the sense that Alex had, the dweeb." She said his name almost affectionately. "And I'm just not going to settle."

I took a deep breath. "Okay."

"But you can't say anything to the folks until I know for sure. I don't need them having a conniption or anything unless there's a reason for it."

I fought back a few tears. "Of course," I assured her. But the damnable thing was that I wasn't sure why I was crying. Yeah, I was worried about my sister and nervous about how our parents would take the news, but there was a niggle of another emotion, too. If pressed, I'd have to call it envy.

Di, who in her potentially sensitive state, might have guessed this, said, "So, is Tim finally gonna make an honest woman out of you? You guys have been practically living together for a freaking eternity. You need to get married and go multiply."

I sniffled and laughed a little. "Well, he said my Christmas gift is something he picked out ages ago, and he thinks I'll like it. So maybe it'll be inside a little blue box and come with a proposal. But, Di, regardless, tomorrow we'll go get you a pregnancy test kit. Deal?"

"Deal. It'll probably take the both of us to figure out the directions anyway."

I bit my lip. "You know, there's always Gregory and Nadia. Maybe you could ask them some parenting questions." Our brother and his wife had just had their second kid. Two squalling boys in less than three years. And they'd all flown in from Colorado Springs to visit us. Next to my limited experience, those two were experts.

Di grimaced. "I'm not *that* desperate for help."

A few minutes later we rejoined the family in the living room, which included a lactating Nadia, our two young nephews and Tim, in addition to the original five of us.

"Put this on the tree," Dad instructed the elder of the boys, three-year-old Wyatt.

Wyatt snatched the candy-cane ornament and toddled over to a Christmas tree branch, already drooping from his past hour of decorating. He added this latest treasure to the collection and ran back toward Grandpa for more. Only, he neglected to notice the barrage of toys he'd scattered on the carpet, tripped over a plastic lawnmower and went sprawling.

He bawled with practiced fury, and his mom leaped up to comfort him.

"Here," Nadia said to my boyfriend, who was sitting on the sofa beside her. "Can you hold Bryce for a moment?" She dumped the squirming infant in Tim's unsuspecting lap and didn't give him a chance to answer.

Tim's eyes widened into huge blue disks, but he held the baby and kind of bounced him. His gaze never left Bryce's face, and Gregory, who should've stepped up to the plate to grab his son, stood back and just watched. Tim and Bryce were bonding.

My brother nodded slyly in my direction and Di shot me a saucy glance, although there were plenty of other emotions crossing her face as well. Mom's eyes sparkled, and even Dad grinned a bit. I could sense the swell of collective familial anticipation. Another wedding could well be on the horizon with more babies to follow. Or so they thought.

Two hours later, my fingers shook as Tim handed me my Christmas gift. The package was a little larger and a bit heavier than I'd expected, but the look on his face shone with such enthusiasm that I figured maybe he'd disguised the ring somehow. Hidden it inside a kryptonite container, maybe.

I slit the pretty red ribbon and opened the box. Underneath the tissue sat a book. An old book. *Pride and Prejudice*, in fact, with an 1894 publication date.

"I—I don't know what to say—" I began.

"Don't you love it?" Tim said. "I know what a huge Austen fan you are. It's not the original release of the novel, of course. There was no way I could find anything from that far back—1813, right?"

I nodded, and Jane whispered smugly, *My first novel was published a full two years earlier, though. Do not let Mr. Farthington forget that.*

I ignored Jane's authorial pride for the time being. I wasn't about to conduct a lecture on her books' publication dates (although, yes, *Sense and Sensibility,* the novel that launched her career, had been published in 1811).

Instead, I nodded at Tim again, fighting off a disappointment I wasn't sure I had the right to feel.

"But this one's still a collector's copy," Tim continued, running his finger down *Pride and Prejudice*'s dark green spine. "It's called a Peacock Edition because of the gold peacock etched on the cover, and the book's illustrator, Hugh Thomson, was pretty famous for his work, I guess."

"It—it's beautiful," I said, and I meant this. It was an incredibly thoughtful gesture. But, goddammit, it wasn't a marriage proposal. *Why* wasn't it a proposal?

"Oh, it's imported from London, naturally, and George Saintsbury wrote the preface. I don't know who he was, but the book dealer seemed impressed by this," Tim added. He concluded his oration by pointing to a description of the book on the inside cover flap, written in pencil above the price in British pounds.

Expensive gift, I couldn't help but notice. A few thousand dollars less than a diamond, however, not that I was ungrateful or that I even cared about the money side of it.

But *why* didn't he want to marry me?

I flipped through the first chapter, a little overwhelmed by the antique paper, which was still in surprisingly fine condition, and stared at the intricate pen-and-ink drawings that brought Elizabeth and Darcy to life on the fragile pages. The famous opening line, so familiar to me, seemed to laugh in my face as I read it again:

It is a truth universally acknowledged, that a single man in possession of a good fortune must be in want of a wife.

In Tim's case, though, I was beginning to have my doubts.

A delightful gift, Jane commented, Tim's choice undoubtedly elevating his character in her estimation.

"Thank you," I said to Tim, giving him a light peck on the cheek. "You have no idea how much sentimental value I've attached to this particular novel."

Everyone in my family nodded pleasantly at our exchange except for Di, who shot me A Very Serious Look. Then she narrowed her eyes at my longtime boyfriend with such repugnance that it almost made me chuckle. Her irreverence gave me the courage to make it through the next few hours with a thread of patience.

But, like it or not, Tim Farthington III was going to have to deal with a confrontation soon.

I wanted some answers.

That night, at my two-year-old townhouse, I poured him a glass of Chardonnay and sat next to him on the loveseat. I, by contrast, opted for bottled spring water. My plan was to loosen him up a bit, but I needed to be 100 percent sober myself.

I waited until he was three-quarters through his second glass before saying, "So, what's your plan for the next few days? Any good ideas for a nearby getaway?"

He smiled, propping his sock-covered feet on the edge of my coffee table, the very image of contentedness and relaxation as he swallowed another mouthful of vino. "Dunno. We could tell everyone we're going to Galena or Milwaukee or somewhere, but just hang out at your place for a couple days instead. Order carryout for every meal. Turn on the answering machine and turn off the cell phone. Keep each other company." He traced a pattern on my knee with his fingertip and his smile broadened.

"That sounds fun," I said, aiming for bright and amicable. This was a vocal timbre I'd honed working with teens—pleasant but not sparkling, kind but with an edge of firmness. The appropriate lead-in tone to an inquisition.

"I'm gonna have another glass of wine, can I get you something?" Tim asked, standing up.

I shook my head, waited for him to return and plotted strategy.

When he sat down beside me again, this time noticeably closer, I covered his fingers with mine and said, "I love you, Tim." Which was true. It wasn't a fiery, passionate love or the kind of love that made me hyperventilate from the sheer massiveness of the emotion, but it was a calm, gentle, appreciative love, one that felt every bit as real in a more understated way.

"Love you, too, Ellie." He kissed me lightly, his lips spiced with Chardonnay and the lingering flavor of my mom's shortbread cookies.

"I need to know something," I said to him, rubbing the pad of my thumb over his knuckles as if this were the promising start of a deep-tissue massage. "You've mentioned before that you see us getting married someday. That's still true, right?"

"Mmm-hmm." He closed his eyes as my fingers moved from his hand up his arm and across to his shoulder. I kneaded the tense muscles there and around his neck, marking time until I could ask the important follow-up question.

He moaned once. Twice. Three times. And that was my cue. "When?" I said.

"Huh?"

"When?" I repeated. "When do you see us getting married? This coming year? The year after?"

He shrugged and pointed toward a tight spot between his shoulder blades. I slid my fingers to it. "Oooh. Right there." He paused. "I'm not in a rush, El. Are you?"

"Not in a rush as in next week or next month, but I *am* thirty-two. We've been together over three years, so it's not as though we don't know each other. And if we want to try for kids, we really can't wait indefinitely on it, you know?"

He sighed.

"What's that mean?" I said, still rubbing.

"I'm not so sure about the kid thing."

My fingers stilled. "You're *not?*"

He glanced over his shoulder at me and must've read something in my expression that made him put down his wineglass, turn fully around and take both my hands in his. "No. Not really."

"But when we started dating, we talked about it! It was one of my first questions. I specifically asked you if you wanted to be a father someday, and you said, 'Sure, I do.' God, Tim, I *remember.*"

He nodded. "I remember, too. And I thought back then that by the time it'd happen, I'd really feel that way. That I'd be ready. That I'd want it."

My jaw dropped. "But wait—you're saying you *don't?* That it hasn't happened for you, this feeling of wanting to be a dad? A parent . . . with me?"

He looked down at where our hands were joined and slowly shook his head. "It's not you," he whispered. "I'm so—God, I'm so sorry, Ellie, I don't want to do it. I just don't. I look at babies, like Bryce, and I panic. They're these little alien beings and I don't get them."

I inhaled, feeling relief flood my lungs. "That's natural, though," I told him. "Almost everybody feels that way around babies. I did, too, when—"

"No, El. It's not just the babies. Wyatt, he's a cute kid and everything, but I wouldn't want to deal with that age either. And before you tell me that they all grow up so fast and they're more fun once they can really talk or once they're in school or once they learn to play varsity sports, don't. Save your breath. I've heard all these arguments before from my friends and colleagues, and I just don't believe it. I know what I feel. And it's not parental."

I let go of his fingers and collapsed into the corner of the loveseat, my brain and body having turned to pulp.

"Ellie, I'm sorry," he said again. "Maybe in another few years—"

"Stop," I commanded.

He stopped.

I could hear my voice about to crack as I said, "I want the truth now. The whole truth, Tim. Is this really about having kids?"

He began to nod vehemently, but I put a stop to that, too.

"No," I said. "I want to know everything. Is this *really* about being a dad or is it about something else? Like not wanting to settle down, maybe? Not wanting to commit? Not wanting to combine bank accounts or be tied to one woman forever or, more specifically, to me?"

"I told you, Ellie, it's not you. I know you want kids and it's not fair for me to keep you waiting. If I change my mind in five years or ten, I can still do the parenthood thing but, you're right, you probably won't be able to then. For women the window's so much shorter. I'd marry you in a heartbeat if we didn't have this difference between us but—" He looked pained. "We do, and from what you've said you want, it's not going away."

Tears dripped down my face and it hurt to even take a breath. There was one more question I had to ask, but I wasn't sure I wanted to know the answer.

I looked deep into his eyes and softly touched his cheek. "So, if I decided I didn't want kids after all, we could get married soon. This spring, maybe?"

Genuine alarm registered in those eyes before he had a chance to mask it. "Well, yeah," he said. "Of course."

Lying bastard.

I now had a ready exhibit of Male Type #7: The Commitment-Phobe. And, of course, an equally compelling example of how I'd been a blooming idiot for three years.

"Perhaps we'd better say good night." I jumped off the loveseat, the tears cascading faster now and the pain in my chest already leaving me gasping for air.

Oh, my God. It was going to be over between us. And I'd wasted all this time, energy, emotion, hope . . . I couldn't stop that thought from racing through my brain as Tim gathered up his things.

He glanced repeatedly at me in a semi-worried, semi-relieved manner. I wasn't sure what to make of that look as we stared at each other by my front door.

I was sure, though, I'd had way enough hurt in my romantic life. Every other time I'd responded by hardening my heart. Every other time when my soul felt crushed, I tied the protective shield more firmly around myself. And it was never enough.

This time, I'd try embracing the pain and letting everything go soft. Hell, it wasn't like the heartache could get much worse, right?

"Thanks for telling me, Tim." I hugged him and kissed his lips, getting teardrop splotches everywhere, but I didn't care. "I—I need a few days, but maybe we can get together later in the week and . . . I don't know, talk or something."

"Okay," he whispered. He seemed confused at having gotten off the hook so easily. "Can I call you?"

"Sure." I sniffled. "Drive safe."

He narrowed his eyes at me. "I—um, I will." He paused. "God, Ellie. Are you gonna be all right?"

I was openly sobbing. My nose was running, so I had to keep wiping it on my sleeve. My heart had broken, yes, but it had broken open. All this pain would eventually float away, and I'd come through it just fine.

Probably.

I nodded at Tim and gently shut the door.

Jane said, *Oh, Ellie. I am sorry.*

Thanks, Jane, I murmured. *But don't worry. I'll be okay.*

And—here was the really strange part—within a few minutes my tears dried up and my heart felt relief, along with a cleansing lightness I could barely recall experiencing. I vaguely remembered the sensation from long ago. From a time before my first heartache. From before high school, even.

I believe it was called innocence.

The next morning, I woke up early feeling empty, as if I'd been fasting, but I accepted the ache that came with memory, pushed past it and drove through the post-Christmas, back-to-work traffic to Di's place.

"Ready to find out?" I asked her.

She held up a pregnancy test box. "Already got the kit. Just waiting for you to get your butt over here."

I tossed my coat on a chair and marched her down to the bathroom. "You want me to come in with you, or should I just stand outside the door and twiddle my thumbs while the angels decide your fate?"

She rolled her eyes and pulled the directions out of the cardboard box. "You take these, geek, and read them to me. I can't think straight today." She pressed the brittle paper into my palm and squeezed my fingers with hers. Hard. It didn't help. Both our hands still trembled. "Just tell me what to do from out in the hall, okay?"

"Okay." I kissed her forehead, then I unfolded the paper and began scanning the tiny print.

She shut the bathroom door, listening to me as I read the instructions aloud. It wasn't exactly rocket science—pee on the stick, wait two full minutes, see if you got a blue line—but we were sweating the details as if lives were at stake.

And, well, let's face it, they were.

Di emerged from the bathroom after the proper time elapsed, holding the little plastic indicator thingy between her forefinger and her thumb. Her face was free of worry lines, but it was equally devoid of every other standard, I'm-taking-a-life-altering-pregnancy-test kind of emotion. She wore the blankest of expressions.

No apparent gut-twisting anxiety.

No praise-the-Lord elation.

No raging-at-the-world fury.

No nothing.

I couldn't take the mystery of it any longer. "Well?" I asked her.

She meekly waved the stick at me, paused for a millennium and then broke into the brightest, most genuine grin I'd ever seen on her face.

"I'm gonna be a mom," she announced.

❧ 12 ❧

It is better to know as little as
possible of the defects of the person
with whom you are to pass your life.

—*Pride and Prejudice*

Why was it that when you finally decided you really, truly
wanted something, it seemed as though everyone but you
had it already or was on the verge of getting it?

Four months later, it was April. Di was five months pregnant,
expecting a boy (or so said the ultrasound) and newly attuned to
what was happening in the Wide World of Pregnancy.

"Guess who's having triplets?" she said while we were sorting
infant clothing at her place one morning.

WXRJ's Wild Ted was spinning top hits of the 1980s, which
brought back some memories. I cranked up the volume on Journey's "Stone in Love," tossed a fuzzy blue sack-like sleeper atop
the pile of already-washed items and said, "Who?"

"You will *never* guess."

"Spit it out, Di."

She grinned. "Angelique."

"No!"

"Yep. No one's supposed to know yet because she isn't telling
Aunt Candice and Uncle Craig for another month, but she let it
slip when I was talking to her on the phone yesterday. She made
me promise to tell *only* you." Di's grin broadened. "Seems those
fertility treatments of hers finally kicked in."

Our cousin had experienced secondary infertility after Lyssa's birth so, once she and Leo reached the five-year mark, they began experimenting with more-medical, less-natural conception strategies. This latest one must've proven fruitful.

"Wow," I said. "I'm so happy for her." And I really was. She'd gone through several years of heartache and trauma for this.

"I know." Di gently rubbed her growing belly. Then she rolled her eyes. "But *triplets?* C'mon. Angelique was always such an over-achiever."

I laughed. "You never know, Di. Your son could be one of those go-getters, too. There's no way to say what combination of genes a child will inherit."

"Especially in my case," she said, a hint of defiance in her voice. Di had staunchly refused to try to determine the baby's exact paternal source and claimed to have no intention of doing so later. "All I can tell you for sure is that my kid's not gonna grow up to be some loser man. I'm gonna teach him to treat women with respect. No sex before the first date. No belching or farting on purpose in the car. No jars of anchovies for Valentine's Day."

I looked at her. "Jars of anchovies?"

"Don't ask."

"I won't." I folded an outfit with yellow footies and added it to the ready-to-wear pile, then I watched Di inspect the tiny socks and T-shirts and hats. She touched each one with reverence, her love for this unborn baby palpable. "You're going to be a terrific mom," I told her. "No chance your little guy will turn out to be anything but a great man."

She glanced up at me. "Thanks, El. He's lucky to have you for an auntie, too." She paused then said, "'Cuz you sure as hell won't be anything like Aunt Candice."

We giggled like teenagers at the thought. To this day that woman still didn't like either of us. But Di and I *had* changed how we viewed each other. And more than marginally.

Although we remained fundamentally dissimilar in personality, we'd each gained an almost grudging admiration for the other and, more recently, we'd further bonded over our various dating trials and anxieties. She'd even suggested poisoning Tim's morning latte when she heard what he'd done to me. And, though I turned her down, I appreciated the offer.

The phone rang.

Di stood and waddled over to pick it up, dancing the whole way to Duran Duran's "Hungry Like the Wolf." I fell backward laughing.

"Yeah?" she said, grinning into the black plastic receiver.

There was a long pause. I turned my gaze toward her and saw the color drain from her face and the bright smile replaced with a scowl. I flipped off the radio.

"Uh-huh," she mumbled.

Another extended pause.

"Well . . . maybe I could." This time she looked to be on the verge of a panic attack, and I started to worry. Was someone hurt? Mom? Dad? Gregory? Dear God, had someone died?

"Um, okay," Di said. "Bye." Then she stood there, the phone still in her hand, staring at the receiver as if it might bite her.

I jumped up, took the phone from her and clicked it off. "This seems bad. What happened?"

"I'm not sure."

I shook my head, my pulse racing in my veins. "What aren't you sure of, Di? Was it a family member? Is someone in the hospital?"

"It was Alex."

"Oh," I said, but I thought, Screw that jerk. He had me worried for nothing.

"He wants to 'do lunch' with me this week."

"What? After all this time? Why?"

"Because he misses me, or so he says. And he just wants to get together and talk."

I wasn't sure what emotion Di wanted me to feel at this news. Happy for her? Nervous on her behalf? But what I *did* feel was anger. Fury, in fact. What made that idiot think he could waltz back into my sister's life now, when she was finally kind of happy again, and just pick up their conversation where they'd left off? Sure, she'd been the one to leave him, but why hadn't he tried harder all those years ago? Why hadn't he fought to get her back?

"Are you going?"

"Yeah," she said, her voice betraying just how mystified she was by her own decision.

Then I remembered something. "I didn't hear you say much to him, Di, so maybe I missed it, but did you tell him you were pregnant?"

She shook her head.

"Hmm. That's probably going to surprise him. You might want to call him back and mention—"

"He already knows."

My jaw dropped and I had to instruct it to shut again. A moment later I managed to say, "He does?"

"Yeah. He saw me in the parking lot when he drove by Baby Utopia last weekend. "He—he asked me if I was okay, and he said he wants to hear all about the pregnancy and stuff when we have lunch."

"Umm . . ." I couldn't think of anything to say beyond this. What were Alex's darker motives? I didn't know. Did it have to do with some possessive, territorial thing a man channeled when he knew "his woman" had moved on?

As my sister stood still, the gears in her mind doubtless spinning faster to assimilate this late development, Jane offered her company in Di's place.

Why must Mr. Evans's motives be ominous? Jane inquired. *Might he not simply wish to enjoy the liveliness of your sister's company once more?*

I snorted—internally, of course. *He's a GUY,* I told Jane. *His motives are to get laid, to be waited on or to find some alternate entertainment in post-football season. In that order. Real life doesn't provide women with many Mr. Darcy types.*

Your Mr. Farthington III had some elements of Darcy, Jane said.

Keyword: "Elements," I retorted. Dammit. She always defended Tim to some extent, but I was pretty sure it was only because he'd gotten me that Peacock Edition of her book. *Tim had Bingley manners and a Darcy family, it's true. But he sure didn't have Darcy's strength of character or Bingley's determination to commit to a woman in marriage—*

Or your heart, Ellie. He did not have your heart either, Jane said. *You did not give your soul to that man any more than he gave his to you.*

This was not entirely untrue, but I really hadn't planned on confessing it. It may well have been the reason why my breakup with Tim, while painful, wasn't as ultimately devastating as it'd been with Andrei . . . or with Sam. *Anyway, we're not talking about Tim, we're talking about Alex,* I insisted.

Exactly, Jane said. *They are two different men. Perhaps you ought not to judge one by the faults of the other. Most particularly when some blame with the former belongs to you.*

I shrugged. *Maybe I'd been a tiny bit emotionally, oh, careful with Tim, but he still refused to make a commitment to me. And he used the I-don't-want-a-kid thing as an excuse, which was despicable.*

Might you consider that your very detachment, which you term "carefulness," may have added to young Mr. Farthington's indecision?

What? So, you're saying I should've acted more affectionately than I felt, especially at the end when I suspected he was lying to me? C'mon, Jane, I'm no Charlotte Lucas. Dammit. She was making me out to sound almost as mercenary as the *Pride and Prejudice* character who married odious Mr. Collins for a life of relative comfort. I didn't appreciate the comparison.

True. But you DID wish to secure him. And you must admit that your desire for marriage was, perhaps, stronger than your desire for the man himself.

I don't want to get married just to get married, I said, even though the loneliness was so strong sometimes and the temptation to settle overpowering. *I want to be head-over-high-heels in love.*

Then you will need to open your heart again to welcome that love, Ellie. When your relationship with Mr. Farthington ended, you opened your heart to the pain, but you have not, as yet, opened it to the possibility of joy.

I really hated it when Jane was right. "Okay," I whispered aloud.

"What's okay?" Di asked, her complexion still wan, but it looked like she'd recovered somewhat.

I'd nearly forgotten she was still standing there, but I said, "Us. We're going to be okay. And if Alex does anything to upset you or the baby, Gregory and I will hunt down the creep and dislocate every one of his fingers. Slowly."

She threw a pair of baby booties at me. "Glad to know you care, sis. And I might just take you up on that."

* * *

Di didn't share with me a detailed account of the luncheon with her ex-husband but, since she didn't seem to want him lynched, it couldn't have been too bad. If she was happy, I was happy.

Later that week I went out baby-shower shopping. And, no, not for my sister or for my cousin. It seemed every other female colleague I knew in the school district was going to have her first or third or fifth baby that summer and, since many of the showers were hosted in the school library, I was invited to them all.

As I sifted through racks filled with infant-sized sailor suits, jean skirts and sports jerseys, a voice from high school called out to me.

"Oh, my gosh—Ellie?"

I looked up, squealed and ran to give my old best friend a hug. "Terrie! What are you doing here? I thought you guys lived down in Texas now. You home for a visit?"

She grimaced and rocked the double stroller back and forth, where her four-year-old son and two-year-old daughter sat jabbering at each other. "Not exactly," she said. Then, lowering her voice, "John and I got divorced in February."

My heart clenched. "Oh, Terrie, I'm so sorry."

Matt, her high-school love, had broken up with her after a year of college, and she'd eventually married a guy she met in grad school. I remembered going to her and John's wedding—it'd been about eight years ago.

Terrie nodded. "Yeah, it sucks. Sorry I didn't tell you sooner, but it'd been awhile since we'd talked and there's only so much you can say in a Christmas card."

"You don't have to explain. It must've been a hard time."

She gazed at her two talkative children then looked at me. "Still is. There was no way we could keep the house in Dallas, so the kids and I moved in with my parents for a while, just until I can get back on my feet."

"What are you hoping to do?"

She sighed. "Don't know yet. My teaching certificate is current in Texas, but not in Illinois, and I don't know where it would be best for us to live. I do know I want to be back in the Midwest. I have full custody, so John can just fly up here when he wants to see the kids. I'm sick of being so far away from my side of the family."

"We'll have to get together then," I said, making sure I conveyed the heartfelt sincerity of the offer as I scribbled down my cell-phone number and directions to my townhouse. "I don't live that far away, Terrie, and good friendships are forever. You know that, right?"

She grinned. "Yeah. I know that."

In the midst of a harsh Illinois winter, like, oh, when my relationship with Tim had been on its last legs, it sometimes felt as if summer would never come.

But it actually did.

Every year.

A tentative spring, complete with its frigid puddles of melted mush, would finally give way to a hot, mosquito-infested June, followed by an equally oppressive July and August. And consequently, I, an autumn-lover to the bone, was left to contemplate how to spend this noisy, sticky, backyard-barbeque-laden time between school years.

That particular summer I opted for something different. A trip. Overseas.

I think I'll go to the Lakes, I told Jane, scanning the "Adventures in the United Kingdom" travel itineraries I'd downloaded off the Internet. *All I need is a passport, my Visa card and you as my personal tour guide. What do you say?*

Why do you wish to visit England? Jane inquired, using a sharp tone of voice.

Aside from an overwhelming desire to connect with my British heritage and honor my English ancestors? I laughed. *Because of you, of course. I want to see all of your old haunts. Steventon. Oxford. Bath. Southampton. London. Chawton. The whole of Hampshire. And*—I held up my local library's copy of *Guide to Great Britain*, then said, *from what I've been reading, there's even a miniature drawing of you, sketched by your sister Cassandra, no less, in London's Portrait Gallery. Gotta see that.*

Hmm.

What? You don't want to go?

I can go anytime, she replied tartly. *The matter in question is whether I wish to go with YOU.*

Oooh. Touché. I knew by now to laugh at her when she got like this. She tended to become a bit peevish if she suspected her privacy might be violated. Jane had a love-hate relationship with the whole fame thing.

And furthermore, she said, *the Lakes are in Cumbria, which is a rather hardy distance from my own Hampshire, even with modern transport. You ought to consult a map before undertaking any grand travel schemes.*

Noted, I said, reopening the guidebook. *But you still haven't answered my question. Do you want to come with me and be a part of the journey, or will you just hang around in a corner of my mind and maintain a stony silence?*

There was a long pause. *Why do you wish to go, Ellie? Apart from your newly professed interest in British culture, that is, and your surprisingly fervent curiosity about my life. What is the real reason for this venture?*

The real reason. Oh, hell.

I took a deep breath. *It's kind of like this. I'm getting the message from the Universe that I'm out of synch with things. Important things. I want a soul mate for a husband. I want a baby or two. I want a sense of contentment in my life. And those just aren't happening. So I figure, the problem is with me. That I'm missing some key component. Or, maybe, it's there, but I've misplaced it for a while, and I need to rediscover it so I'll be ready if that husband or baby ever comes along.*

But why does this self quest require a trip to foreign lands?

Oh, c'mon. You used to walk a lot in Nature and visit seaside resorts. You know what it's like to be outside, to clear your head, to see new sights. Being in a new place will give me a different perspective on my life.

Jane considered this. *Travel does afford opportunities for fresh perceptions,* she admitted.

Exactly! And you yourself are always telling me I have to learn to be openhearted again. I want to be that kind of candid, approachable woman.

Someone who's at peace with herself. Who knows her own worth despite past hurts.

A laudable ambition, she said.

*Then, if I ever run into the Perfect Guy, at McDonald's or Target or somewhere, I'll be—*I hesitated, unable to think of quite the right word.

The Perfect Lady? Jane suggested.

I shrugged. *Maybe not perfect, I doubt I could manage that, but hopefully less screwed up than I am now.* I paused. *Is that still a laudable ambition?*

She chuckled in her ever-so-slight British manner. *Perhaps. You seek to attain Wisdom, which I have always felt to be better than even Wit. In the long run, it will certainly have the laugh on its side.*

Well said, as usual. You'll join me, then?

Yes, Jane replied, her voice unusually thoughtful. *I suppose someone must chaperone and, as this involves you, it had best be me.*

❧ 13 ❧

The distance is nothing when one has a motive.

—*Pride and Prejudice*

So, we flew out of Chicago's O'Hare, en route to England, three weeks after school let out. Jane chattered on about the indignities incurred by modern travelers despite the great advancements in speed. I murmured in agreement, but mostly I studied the Mr. Collins–like guy, down my airplane row, two seats away, and watched as he pestered the woman across the aisle from him. Typical.

There were only so many kinds of men in this world. They could be grouped or regrouped, and recognition of their Male Type could make it easier to contend with their respective deceptions. I'd decided on Seven Types. Jane, too, had laid out her groupings clearly but, as in the world of *Pride and Prejudice*, she'd done it by name:

There were the Bingleys, like Jason and Tim.

The Collins types, like the obnoxious guy down the row.

Wickhams, like Brent and Sam and about half the guys I'd dated once or twice before I gained the wisdom to avoid them altogether.

Colonel Fitzwilliams, like Dominic, although I had to admit this comparison didn't entirely ring true. While the Colonel knew he had to marry for material concerns, he wasn't a blatant user of women like Dominic had been.

Which meant . . . what? That Dominic was also part Wickham? I considered this for a moment then allowed myself a pass on analyzing him further. Dominic was a strange enough guy to straddle two categories.

But then I thought about Mark. Was he a true Bingley? I cringed trying to stuff him into that box. Time proved he didn't fit any category with ease and he was, after all, still my good friend, despite the lying-to-me-about-being-gay thing. So, okay, another exception.

But what about Andrei? I sighed. Trying to pigeonhole him always gave me a headache. He wasn't any easier to classify than Dominic or Mark. Not a Bingley. Not a Wickham, except in his insatiable sex drive. Darcy-like only in bearing, which wasn't enough to qualify him there, any more than Tim's family money qualified him as a Darcy.

Damn. Where were the true Darcys? And why didn't I have one anywhere in my life?

My thoughts returned to Sam because, though he'd behaved abominably in high school, he hadn't turned out to be quite so contemptible later in life. Could I still rate him as a pure Wickham? I decided, no, I couldn't, even if Jane could . . . but where else would he fit?

I squeezed my eyes shut. This wasn't working, but maybe if I ate some airline peanuts, drank some airline orange juice and thought about it for longer, I'd puzzle it all out.

By the time we'd landed in London's Heathrow, I'd reached a point of near despair. For years I'd clutched at my well-tooled categories of men like the self-preservation tactics they were, but I was now convinced I'd have to let them go. Eight solid hours of thinking had shown me that such stereotyping was a lie that worked well enough in fiction, but it failed to capture the essence of a real man. None of those guys, upon serious reflection, could be stamped with a quick and easy label.

Jane, who'd decided somewhere over the Atlantic to join in the debate, disagreed.

Perhaps not ALL men are so simple as to be confined to merely one type of disposition, she said. *But I do believe astute observation and the em-*

ployment of rational thinking points toward categorization rather than away from it. One good viewing ought to be sufficient to draw a man's character, if one is not swayed by personal prejudice.

I considered where, exactly, my personal prejudices might have influenced my perceptions of my ex-boyfriends. *I'm not with you on this,* I told her. *Yeah, I could get a general sense of the temperaments of these men almost immediately, but I've been wrong on the details too many times for it to be a simple oversight based on presumption. Humans are complicated, Jane. Really complicated. And I've made mistakes because I've repeatedly chosen not to see that.*

She laughed. *It is more likely a result of the philosophy you persist in holding dear. Romanticism encourages an abandonment of restraint and, as you've so often wished to fall in love without regard to rationality, this invites the absurd. Your mistakes in judgment are not due to the complexity of humanity, Ellie. They are due to the lens with which you view love.*

You mean, I need to challenge the fairy tale and not the man?

Precisely, she said.

Maybe she was right—she so often was—or maybe she was gravely in the wrong. I no longer knew the truth. But I had voyaged thousands of miles to England for an adventure, and I intended to enjoy it. The time had come for me to open my eyes to new wonders, and to hope my heart would soon follow.

We started by sightseeing through London, then hopping a southwest-bound train to Hampshire county. Jane's old stomping grounds.

Lovely the way they have preserved it, Jane said of Chawton House, the seventeenth-century red-brick cottage in which she spent her final earthly years.

Yes, I said, wandering around the garden brambles out front and enjoying the sunshine and greenery. *Thank goodness for historical societies.*

She sighed. *Of course the spirit of the building is not the same, for Cassandra is not here. But, alas, she has her own pursuits in the afterlife to attend to . . . and her own lessons.*

You and your sister were really close, weren't you?

She was my greatest friend and companion, Jane said with feeling.

I nodded. *Di and I aren't quite like that, as you're well aware, but I'm glad we've become closer in recent years. Your encouragement helped.* I thought of my sister's changing body with a grin. *I can't believe she's going to be a mom in a few months.*

Yes, Jane said. *She will rely on you this fall, to be sure.*

Maybe. Unless she hooks up with another man before I get back. I laughed. *With Di there's always that possibility.*

Jane didn't comment, but I sensed she didn't believe me. She and her sister had possessed hearts more steadfast in the face of romantic adversity than Di's or mine.

I was reminded of this a week later when we were making a visit to Oxford. Two of Jane's elder brothers had been educated there and the cobblestone streets all but vibrated with the promise of history and the roar of tour buses.

After a pleasant afternoon of browsing at Blackwell's Bookshop, I strolled over a bridge, away from the city bustle, and paused to look down upon the river Thames. I was with Jane, of course, but, to the world, I knew I seemed to be just a single American woman, wandering the town alone.

Is that why you're with me, Jane? I asked her. *The reason underneath the reason? Because we are to share similar fates?*

She gave me a puzzled sniff. *You are considering becoming a lady novelist?*

I laughed. *God, no. Most writers are half crazy. I mean as far as relationships. Do you know that part of my destiny already? Will I end up being alone like you?*

Firstly, I was not alone, dear friend. I had the immense pleasure of my sister's company, the lifetime memory of a man I had loved deeply and the endless bounds of my imagination. I was neither alone nor lonely. She paused. *And secondly, SOME writers are not AT ALL crazy.*

I giggled.

You realize, Ellie, she said in her Lecturing tone, *that my childhood writing, "Volume the First," is here in Oxford University's Bodleian Library.*

Yes, I said. *And as I recall, you referred to it as "one hundred eighty-four pages of sheer nonsense." But I take back my comment about crazy writers. Or, at least, I'll exclude present company.*

Thank you, she replied, unable to disguise the amusement in her voice. *I do believe my family would have been surprised by such success. Most surprised indeed. My youthful writing here at the university. Imagine!*

I laughed with her. Millions upon millions of people had read her novels over the past two centuries and, more recently, had been glued to the movie screens to watch films based on them, yet the thing Jane found most diverting was that some of her juvenilia was housed at a major Oxford University library. No one was going to convince me that writers weren't at least a little nutty.

So, tell me more about this man you loved, I said. *I'm older now. I can be trusted with the details.* And, though I knew what she'd say (I'd asked a thousand times before with no success), I added, *I want to know this handsome clergyman's name once and for all.*

I have only ever spoken of him with Cassandra, and it is only with her that I have shared his name. Although I do know you can be trusted, Ellie, she hastened to assure me.

Yeah, sure. Where'd you meet him again? I remembered, of course— I'd pored over her biographies at my home library and memorized large chunks of them—but, though everyone knew of her youthful flirtation with Irishman Tom Lefroy, and even the much later marriage proposal of Harris Bigg-Wither, only a few scholars made note of her secret love interest in the years between. I was naturally insatiable on the subject and wanted to get her talking about The Unknown Man once more.

We met in Sidmouth, a Channel town in Devonshire, not far from Lyme, she said, *when I was five-and-twenty.*

And his brother was a doctor in town?

Yes. And Mr.— She cleared her throat. *And HE was a young clergyman who was visiting his brother for a short seaside holiday.*

And he was so wonderful even Cassandra approved of him for you, right?

She fell silent.

Jane?

This gentleman and I knew the pleasure of each other's company and conversation for but a few weeks, Ellie. And I had surely not guessed this would be my fate—to love so deeply and yet to have the object of my affec-

tion for so short a time. She paused and I could sense her measuring words, editing herself. *When I heard of his death, my sister was the one person to whom I could turn. She, unfortunately, understood the pain of such loss only too well.*

Cassandra's fiancé, Reverend Thomas Fowle, had contracted yellow fever and died before their wedding. The Austens had known Fowle since childhood, and Jane's sister had never entertained the notion of loving another after his death. It seemed Jane had chosen a similar response to the dreadful news she'd received about the love of her life.

Yet, as for knowing the truth of your fate, Ellie, I confess I do not. I do believe, however, that it is always better to have loved well—fully and purely—for once, rather than halfheartedly for always. I had hoped this advice might be of use to you, too.

I'm sure you're right, I said, but I wondered, as I always did, about whether the memory of a lasting love (even a completely mutual one) would've been enough for me.

Whom, if anyone, had I loved with complete abandon like that? And who, if anyone, had loved me back that way?

The only man whose name rose to my lips for the former question was, of all people, Sam Blaine. Though for years I'd hated to admit it, I *had* loved him. But I'd been so young and so impressionable when we'd first met that he probably didn't count. If he did, I guess it was true that we never really got over our first love.

And as for the latter question, I doubt any man had felt the way about me that Jane's unnamed Clergyman By The Sea had felt about her.

Do not worry so, Jane instructed, aware of the direction of my thoughts as usual. *Regardless of what happens in your playing at love, you will end up where you need to be. Life brings its gifts to you either way. For, though I never married nor became a mother, I felt blessed and fulfilled.*

I blinked away a sudden tear. *That may have been the case, Jane, and I'm glad of it. But you also gave back your extraordinary gifts to the world. Your presence in my life has been priceless, and I've always been grateful for the richness of spirit you brought to me.*

There was a long pause, and then she said something I hadn't expected. Something that made me feel connected to her, as a great-great niece of a beloved aunt might.

And by your kindness, your honesty and your courage in the face of love's challenges, you, dear Ellie, have brought the same to me. If I understand anything of the trials a modern woman must confront and conquer in order to find her place in the world, it is because you have opened my eyes.

❧ 14 ❧

She threw a retrospective glance over
the whole of their acquaintance,
so full of contradictions and varieties . . .

—*Pride and Prejudice*

Just a few weeks later, on August fifteenth, we celebrated my thirty-third birthday in the city of Bath, complete with high tea at the renowned Pump Room.

Rather indulgent of me, having a feast like this at a table for one, wouldn't you say? I said to Jane, taking in the full view of the open dining area from our little corner. Curious tourists strolled along the edges of the room and peered through the windows at the legendary bathing area below.

Jane made a noise that sounded suspiciously like a snort, then muttered something unintelligible.

What was that? I asked her. I raised my teacup in the air to toast myself and reached for a delicate chocolate petit four filled with custard. The jars of strawberry jam and clotted cream called to me from across the tiny table, and I was tempted to rush through my first treat so as to sample another.

I despise Bath, Jane said, louder this time. *It is a noisy, dismal place, where purported gentlemen and ladies visit for the exercise of gossiping and gazing at strangers. My opinion of it has not improved with the centuries.*

I pointed to the pyramid of sweets in front of me. *But just look at these delicious—*

Ellie, she said with a sigh. *Do you recall the emotions you experienced during your school dances? You described them as times when gentlemen and ladies stared at each other yet did not speak. And the feast items on the table did not appeal to you either. Do you remember why?*

Yeah. *They were usually dried-out, awful things we ate so we had something to do with our hands.*

Perhaps the desserts in my time had more flavour, she said, *but our intention in consuming them was for much the same reason as yours. We relied on something else to divert our attention from the matter at hand.*

The "matter" being husband- or wife-shopping?

Indeed, she said.

Okay. So you're saying spending time in Bath left a bad taste in your mouth. I laughed at my own joke and nibbled on another teacake.

Jane ignored my attempts at lightening up the conversation. *When we were living here for five years and, later, in Southampton for three, I wished only to be someplace settled. Someplace that was home. It was dreadful being on display every day and forever in transit. A short seaside holiday was a welcome change, yes. But eight years of displacement and rooming with relatives was not. I wish to depart this room and this city, Ellie. I will leave you to enjoy your desserts in the peace of your own company and shall rejoin you at a later time.*

Jane? I asked, but I received no answer. She'd left. Hidden herself in the dark unconscious of my mind, just beyond my grasp.

I popped a final pastry into my mouth and sipped on the last of my tea, mindful of my solitary state. I knew I had distant relations living in the area. Maybe I should've done some serious genealogy work before I came . . . or maybe it was better I hadn't.

Let's face it, people never knew what weird stuff they might uncover about their families when they began to dig. Truth was, I probably didn't want to know. But this left me, of course, with the downside of my reticence: There was no one I could really talk to here.

It was easy not to feel the sting of loneliness when Jane's acerbic and witty observations kept me company. In her absence, awareness of the reality flooded my mind unfiltered, and I became haunted by a homesickness I tried unsuccessfully to ignore. I, too, wanted to be back home. To be settled again in the place I belonged.

My flight back to Chicago departed in three days and, whether or not I'd gained greater maturity as a result of this six-week sojourn, the time had come for me to go back.

On a crowded 777 heading west into the sunset, I thought about my sister's soon-to-be-born baby. Di *would* need me, I reasoned. Maybe the two of us would end up like Jane and Cassandra, relying on each other when the hope of finding true love had gone.

I smiled thinking of this. Funny how life could change. Di was the one person I'd never imagined as a close friend and, yet, that was precisely what I now considered her to be. For sanity's sake, though, it would be best if we never shared a house again.

My American Airlines flight required a quick plane change at Boston's Logan Airport and, since we were an hour late departing London, "quick" meant "immediately."

"Attention passengers with connecting flights to Chicago, we are beginning to board Flight 509," I heard the gate attendant say over the loudspeaker as I wobbled my way down the plane ramp with my stuffed backpack, slogged into the airport proper and cleared the Customs line. "Flight 509 now boarding at Terminal B, Gate 17."

"Oh, damn." I was in Terminal E. "How do I get to Terminal B?" I asked the first person I could find wearing an airline uniform.

That person turned out to be a handsome, forty-something pilot (married, or so implied by his gold band) who pointed me in the direction of the shuttle bus, and off I raced. I made it to the gate just as a different attendant was saying, "Last call for Flight 509 . . ."

But it wasn't until I was struggling up this new plane ramp and away from the airport proper, that I realized where I'd been. In Boston.

Sam's city.

And though I hadn't seen him there, hadn't seen anyone who looked remotely like him even, this was where he was. Somewhere nearby. As always, almost within reach, but not quite.

I grinned to myself, for no other reason than that I knew of his continued existence. He wasn't dead, like Jane's or Cassandra's young admirers had been when the sisters were my age. No. Sam lived and breathed and was a part of my history. A history that, despite our fumbles, we'd gotten a fair amount of closure on.

And, so, I could claim the happier memories as my own. The odd camaraderie he and I shared in high school. The one amazing night we'd spent together. A night that had greatly influenced my view of love and relationships ever since. I could embrace our infrequent path-crossings in the years that followed. Sure, the recollections still held their fair share of pain, but at least I wasn't left hanging, or wondering for eternity what might've happened between us if we'd had the chance. Right?

Because, hey, if I wanted to, I could *still* reach him. I could do a Yahoo People Search when I got home and look up Sam's e-mail or his home phone number or his street address in Boston. I would've heard through our suburban gossipy grapevine if he'd moved, so he must still be somewhere in this city.

If my life were a romantic comedy, I could run right back down this ramp and look him up here and now. Take a chance he'd want to see me again. No, better yet, believe he'd fallen in *love* with me. Or, exponentially better, that he'd *always* been in love with me!

I'd call him from an airport pay phone, still breathless from my sprint past all those other gates. In violation of the laws of physics, he'd materialize almost instantly, and the two of us would pounce on each other. We'd wrinkle our previously pristine clothes and lock lips with a voraciousness only B movie stars could replicate. The flight attendants would all cheer.

Yeah.

I collapsed into my seat, 15F, and giggled at this fantastical, whimsical vision, complete with Heart's Greatest Hits as the musical score.

As if something like that could ever happen—even if I wanted it to. Which I didn't. Because I was too realistic.

Nevertheless, I daydreamed variations of this fantasy for two straight hours, amusing myself with dialogue worthy of a Mexican soap opera. Until somewhere, just above O'Hare's sacred airspace, Jane reentered my mind with a *Hello, Ellie. Enough of this nonsense, please.*

Ah. Back to my real life.

* * *

Any lingering visions of Di and me forming a Jane-and-Cassandra–like, no-men-allowed-to-come-between-us-for-the-rest-of-our-natural-lives sisterly bond were dashed the moment I spoke to Di in person.

"Alex and I are back together again," she informed me, rubbing her belly and looking large enough to be carrying twin baby Orcas. Not that I told her that.

"Really? Wow," I said, praying this was the right move for her. "And you're happy about this?"

She nodded. Happiness radiated off every part of her.

"How does he feel about the baby?"

"He, um . . . wants to assist me during the birth."

"Oh," I said, trying to mask my disappointment by sounding extra upbeat and supportive.

"I know you said you'd help me, Ellie, with the Lamaze stuff and everything. But this way you don't have to go to those classes and shit." She grimaced. "Alex took me to an information session at the hospital this week, to see what it was like and all. Man. Those leaders really try to scare the crap out of you."

"Yeah?"

"Yeah." She looked worried. "I'm not so sure I wanna do it after all."

"The Lamaze method?"

"The birth," Di said.

I put my hand on her shoulder and squeezed lightly. "You'll get through it just fine. Especially with Alex by your side." I paused. "You must still really, really love him."

She gave me a long look. "I do. And, El, he loves me, too. Neither of us ever stopped."

So, it wasn't much of a surprise when, four weeks later, my sister gave birth to a nine-pound, two-ounce baby boy she named Clifton Barnett Evans (since Di had never changed back her last name after the divorce). And, just after Clifton's APGAR scores pronounced him to be in excellent health, Alex and Di got reengaged (which made that whole last-name thing really convenient). Wedding date to be announced soon.

And it was.

Three months after that, with the fresh chill of December blowing in the door, I entered Di's new condo to find Clifton flashing his first smile and his proud mother announcing that she and Alex would get remarried early the following November.

"I wanna do it right this time," Di said, bouncing my chubby, adorable nephew in her arms twice before holding him out to me. She knew I needed to have my baby fix when I came over.

I grabbed the little guy from her and buried my face in the softness of his rounded belly before cradling him tight and rocking him to my imaginary soundtrack of '80s tunes. "You'll have a lovely wedding," I assured her. "You've put Mom on the case. Who could be more thorough?"

"I'm not worried about those kinds of details," Di said. "I meant that I want to make sure I do the important things right. Like remembering to keep my vows with Alex—in sickness and in health and all that stuff. Like not drinking tequila from my shoe at the reception—that was stupid. And like—" She shot me a look. "Having my sister be my maid of honor."

A lump formed out of nothing in my throat. I couldn't get a response out.

"Will you?" she asked me, looking as though she were holding her breath.

Tears threatened to spill down my cheeks, and I was having a devil of a time speaking. I clamped my mouth shut and nodded.

Di's eyes looked suspiciously bright, too. She nodded back at me and then leaned in to give my cheek a quick kiss. "You're such a geek," she said, but the affection in her voice gave her away.

"I love you too, sis," I said.

"Jingle Bell Rock" flooded the airwaves all that week. I remember because that was the song playing on the radio the evening I opened Terrie's Christmas card.

There were other songs, too, of course, and other cards. Actually, I'd gotten so much pre-holiday mail I'd been joking with Jane about it. That, and the fact that the date was December sixteenth, her birthday, and I'd been alternating between humming Christmas carols and "Happy Birthday to You" all day long.

We'd just finished a rousing debate over mail delivery (Early nineteenth century British versus early twenty-first century American—which was more civilized? Discuss . . .) when I'd returned with the day's postal stack from my mailbox. I tossed the bills into the Boring pile and turned right to the Newsy pile. The cards.

I'd gotten quite the assortment of newsworthy items that week already:

Tim signed his name to the bottom of a picturesque card that said only "Merry Christmas from Sunny Antigua."

Mark and Seth crowed about their new puppy in their holiday letter. Named him Spider-Man because he kept climbing all over their polished Shaker furniture.

Kim, Tom and the kids claimed to be fine in their card, but Kim was getting antsy being a stay-at-home mom. Was thinking about going back to grad school. Maybe business. Maybe art therapy. She didn't care. She just wanted to get out of the house.

Angelique and Leo, who'd had their triplets a couple months back (one girl, two boys) in California, sent a photo of their newly expanded family. They were hanging in there despite the sleepless nights, and Lyssa had proven to be a terrific older sister. "Thank God for her!" Angelique wrote. "She can change diapers like a pro." They were seriously saving for her future Stanford tuition.

And, from my annual grad-school university alumni newsletter, came this shocker: Brent "Go Fish" Sullivan had departed this earth back in July. The victim of a fatal car crash. No reported surviving widow or children, but I figured there was probably a woman somewhere. No mention of substance-related causes but, considering he loved single-malt Scotch almost as much as he loved card games, that wouldn't have surprised me either.

Regardless, I was rendered speechless when I saw his name in black ink on the "In Memoriam" page. And, to be completely honest, I was sincerely saddened.

I guess I'd hoped he'd live long enough to be redeemed. That he'd find someone he could be true to, even if he hadn't yet married her. I wished for some kind of happy ending for him in part, I supposed, because I wished it for all of us. And, yes, for me especially.

So, when I saw the two cards that came in on Jane's birthday, sure, I rolled my eyes at the first one. Dominic Reyes-Jones. But I opened up the envelope immediately. He was getting remarried, his card said. He'd had a tough start to the year—been out of work for a few months—but had gotten a new part-time job. The (latest) love of his heart and soul was taking him to the Greek Isles for their honeymoon. Life, he insisted, was fabulous.

Well, good for him. He was happily screwing someone else, literally, figuratively. That was fine by me. Hey, at least he wasn't dead.

Terrie's card I opened with much more genuine interest and anticipation. Inside I found a cute photo of her and the children, plus a handful of scented stationery sheets. She'd moved out of state again but not far, Iowa this time, following a job lead that had paid off. She'd gotten herself a place of her own and enrolled her kids in a good neighborhood school. Said she'd met a new man too. Everett. Planned to take things real slow.

I grinned at this and would've bet anyone willing to take me on that, when I invited her to Di and Alex's second wedding next fall, she'd be bringing this Everett dude along. It was something about how she wrote his name, her script so precise. Or maybe it was in the way she went on about him for a full seven pages. Kind of a giveaway.

Then, on the last page of her letter she added this postscript:

> *Oh! I thought you'd want to hear the latest gossip. My sister Sabrina told me she ran into Nate . . . and that he told her that Sam Blaine was finally getting married. Guess he's engaged to some woman in Boston. Poor girl, huh?*

The words jumped off the pretty floral pages and punched me in the stomach. Sam? Engaged? To somebody else?

Really?

I reminded myself that it wasn't as though I wanted to marry him. No. I simply liked the fantasy I'd created. It was the *possibility* I'd grown attached to . . . I told myself I didn't want to see a romantic avenue I'd imagined get closed off. That it was for this reason alone that my hands trembled and my knees shook—a bizarre reaction that had nothing to do with the man himself.

Only, I felt numb everywhere, and I knew I'd been wrong about something. When Tim and I broke up, I believed heartache couldn't get any worse. That by embracing the pain and letting everything inside me go soft, I'd recover faster.

It'd worked with Tim, but this case was different. Going soft made me feel the cruel edges of pain sooner, and they were sharper. Each sensation was more acute, more immediate, more devastating than I could've imagined, and the question barrage wouldn't stop:

Why didn't I stay longer at the bookstore café that one day?

Why didn't I really talk to Sam when I'd had the chance?

Why didn't I run back down that plane ramp in Boston and call him from the airport?

Why didn't I open up my heart more readily instead of being paralyzed by old fears until it was too late?

Why, why, why?

Goddamned story of my life.

≈ 15 ≈

If the dispositions of the parties are ever
so well known to each other or ever so
similar beforehand, it does not advance
their felicity in the least.

—*Pride and Prejudice*

Ten and a half months later, at age thirty-four, I was at my parents' house—midweek, early November, up to my eyebrows in relatives—when the doorbell rang for the first time, at noon.

"I'll get it," the bride-to-be said around her last bite of lasagna Florentine. "It's probably Alex." And Di, knowing her ex-/future-husband well, was right.

"Hey, babe," Alex said, kissing my sister and fourteen-month-old Clifton, then waving to the rest of us . . . the rest of us being me, my mom, my dad, Angelique, her husband Leo, all four of their children, my brother, his wife Nadia, their two boys and their collie, Fritz.

Various reciprocal greetings occurred, from handshakes to hugs to high fives. Mom shoved a plate of food at Alex, and Fritz contributed a friendly bark.

Dad said to Di's fiancé, "The men are gonna watch some ESPN downstairs in ten minutes. A couple college basketball teams are playing. Wanna join us?"

Alex shook his head and gave my sister an adoring glance. "Thanks, Mr. B., but Di and I need to check out a few things with the florist."

Mom shot Di a horrified look only the mother of the bride could produce with conviction. "What? Is there something wrong with the arrangements? The reception centerpieces we chose? That flower guy promised me—"

"Nah, nothing like that," Di said. "We just wanted to make sure they had the right number of corsages and boutonnieres for the ceremony Saturday."

Mom brought her palm up to her heaving chest. "Oh, good." She motioned for Alex to sit down. "Eat then. Now. We've got pecan pie and vanilla ice cream for dessert when you're done."

Alex took one look at our mother's anxious expression and, apparently, didn't dare disobey. He picked up his fork and dug in.

Mom used this opportunity to whip out her encyclopedia-sized planning calendar. "What else is left to check on today? Ellie already called about the final dress fittings. I talked with the musicians yesterday, and everything is set there. The photographer is okay. The videographer is fine, too. Di, you got ahold of the Reverend?"

"Yep," Di said. "And Ellie and I also double-checked the cake order over the weekend."

"That's right . . . the cake," Mom said. Then, "Oh, God! Ellie, the caterers! Did you—"

"Everything's under control," I told her, trying to sound reassuring. "I sampled the entire menu again on Monday, and chicken Marsala with broccoli almondine never tasted so good. The wedding dinner will be great. Don't worry."

"You can be sure it will if Ellie's in charge of it," Angelique piped up. "Remember Di's bachelorette party? The food was delicious. I'm still salivating over that scrumptious teriyaki salmon." My cousin directed her comments to my mom, but she winked at me.

"Yes, yes that *was* good," Mom admitted.

"And the mashed potatoes were super fluffy," Angelique's daughter Lyssa added, proving the ten-year-old was as sweet as she was smart.

Nadia laughed. "Forget about the food. Awesome as it was, let's not overlook the *entertainment* Ellie chose for us that night!"

This got a big laugh from the ladies present. Dad, Leo, Alex, Gregory and his sons, however, appeared less amused.

I blushed, although I'd done nothing more perverted than hire a fun-loving male dancer, whose sole job was to show us some cool moves and give us a crash course in new millennium hip-hop (while keeping on every stitch of his clothing, mind you). Even Mom got into the fun. But we'd all made a pact afterward not to tell the men what had really transpired that night, for which none of the guys had forgiven us.

Di grinned at me and said, "Yeah, that wild sister of mine really knows how to plan a party. I'm a lucky bride." Then, as I tried to shrug off her compliment, Di turned to our parents and added, "Thanks for giving me Ellie."

At this, Gregory jumped up. "Hey, what about me? Don't I count?" He tried to strike an indignant pose, but it didn't quite work.

Di said, "Oh, sorry, bro. Mom, Dad, thanks for giving Ellie to *Gregory*, too."

Our family laughter was interrupted by the doorbell ringing for the second time that Wednesday.

Mom said, "I'll get it. I'm expecting an extra package of wedding favors. That Mary-somebody said she'd FedEx over another box today."

While Mom signed for her box, Dad, Leo, Gregory and most of the males headed downstairs to watch the first basketball game, bowls of pie and ice cream in hand.

Angelique, torn between wanting to see the game and wanting to chitchat with the women, shoved one of the triplets at Leo, put Lyssa in charge of another one and chased the third one around the living room.

Alex gobbled up the rest of his lunch and, before he could pull Di out the door, was promptly handed dessert.

"Eat this," my mother said. Alex sat back down again and let Di feed him a huge spoonful of ice-cream-drenched pie.

Little Clifton toddled over to me and threw his chunky little arms around my knees. I grabbed him for a bear hug and he wriggled and giggled, making me laugh with all of his squirminess.

Over the past few months I'd tried to puzzle out which of Di's ex-boyfriends he looked liked. If pressed, I'd have to say the only male he really resembled was our brother. The Barnett side had strongly marked his young features, and Clifton seemed to know this clan was where he belonged.

Alex, however, appeared to have no recollection of Clifton not being biologically his, which pleased me to witness. When Di got up to flip through the big wedding planner, Alex waved his spoon at her son and said, "Want some ice cream, Cliffy?"

My nephew wavered between the two of us.

"Aw, c'mon, kiddo." Alex chuckled and winked in my direction. "I know no one's more fun than your Auntie El, but Daddy's got ice cream here . . ."

Clifton finally made his decision and, with a parting squeeze of those stubby, sticky fingers, waddled over to Alex, mouth open and ready.

Di caught my eye, embracing me in a glance with her heartfelt contentedness. And I could imagine her joy at being part of that happy trio, even though I'd never experience the same.

There was nothing like thinking you'd lost someone for good to put petty disagreements into perspective. Alex cast his pride aside and came running back when he thought Di might've moved on without him. Di reached true forgiveness only when she realized the love she had for Alex was much stronger than the passing fancy she'd felt toward other men.

And I'd gained a clarity of heart once I finally decided to search for myself, even though, in the process, I had to face the fact that this understanding had come too late. That I'd lost any chance of ever getting together with Sam.

Those early weeks after finding out about his engagement had been hard. So much so that I'd finally confided in Di (in person) and Angelique (via long-distance telephone) about my strange and assorted history with him. I needed advice, and Jane, who was so wise and generous in every other situation, refused to give counsel when it came to "that Wickham, Sam Blaine." Though my news surprised both my sister and my cousin, they surprised me more by being amazingly sympathetic.

"Your soul mate could not be genuinely happy without you," Angelique had said when I'd first called her about it. "If Sam has moved on, after everything you've told me about your relationship, then he was never really *your* man. You deserve someone whose eyes light up when he sees you across the room. Someone who'll rub your shoulders when they're aching just because he wants to relieve your pain. Someone whose heart never stops beating for you. And that man is out there for you, Ellie," she assured me. "It's worth taking your time to find him."

Di's advice directly contradicted this and was somewhat less poetic. "True love sucks," she'd said one day, "and there's no such thing as soul mates, no matter what Hollywood or Angelique says. It's all work and building trust and fighting for commitment, day after day after day. And both people need to want to make it happen. Bad. Otherwise, fuck it."

Months later, the memory of Angelique and Di's words of wisdom still made me grin. My philosophy on romantic love fell somewhere in the middle of their extremes, but the familial devotion and appreciation I felt flowing from my closest relatives, even from those who weren't aware of my heartache, had given me the courage to expose myself to dating again.

The results had been less than inspiring so far, but I was giving it a shot. At the start of the year, I'd written Sam a heartfelt and personally cleansing note of congratulations on his upcoming nuptials. It said:

> *Dear Sam,*
>
> *I heard the news of your engagement through the Glen Forest grapevine—congratulations. I guess there's a side of me that'll always remember our friendship as it'd been during those emotional, unforgettable high school years . . . it's hard to believe we're so grown up now. I don't think I ever told you how much those memories meant to me, though, or how glad I am that—despite everything—you were a part of my life back then.*
>
> *Anyway, I know we haven't seen each other in half a decade, and when last we did, well, it was awkward. I didn't want to leave things between us like that. So, please*

*know, I'm thinking of you fondly and wishing you and
your fiancée well as you begin your life together.*
      Best,
      Ellie

Yes, the whole message consisted of no more than six complex
sentences but, as I wrote those words and sincerely wished him
happiness with the woman he'd chosen, I also silently released
him from my mind.

It was long past time to let Sam Blaine go.

Likewise, I'd recently begun to let go of the soul-mate, fairy-
tale fantasy I'd clung to for ages while still striving to stay open to
romantic possibilities. I had to turn my attention—realistically—
toward the future.

I knew I could support myself financially and that my goofy
family would support me emotionally when I needed a boost. I
had the love of my parents, my siblings, my cousin and my friends
(including Jane), all of whom would be there for me no matter
what the circumstance.

And if the only happily-ever-after ending I would ever get in
this life would be one I had to create for myself, so be it. I was capable of making come true any dream I wanted.

If I felt the need for a large backyard and an English flower garden, I could sell my modest townhouse and buy something bigger.

If the maternal instinct got too strong, I could go to a sperm
bank and order up my own baby. I *could!*

If the will of the Universe had a destiny in mind for me, I could
wedge my heart open to it and face whatever hand I was dealt,
with the bravery of a lady warrior.

I adopted "I am woman, oh, Mighty Universe. Hear me chortle!"
as my unspoken battle cry.

Looking around the living room at the women of my family,
each busily tending to something wedding-related, I was flooded
with pride. We were strong and competent. We were making things
happen in our world. We weren't allowing ourselves to be paralyzed by old fears until it was too late. No. We could roll with any

changes that got hurled our way and positively influence our destinies.

And as for me . . . what a wonder I was. Yes, truly! How sensible I was being about all of this. How levelheaded. How unbelievably *healthy*. Damn, what a great attitude I had!

And I was in the midst of congratulating myself on these tremendous feats—and on my sense of personal power—when the doorbell rang again.

"I'll get it," I said, springing up as if buoyed by a jubilant spirit. Or, maybe, by a giant Slinky.

Jane's voice said, *Do not open it, Ellie.*

I asked her, *Why not?* but swung the front door open wide before she had a chance to reply.

And, now, here we are.

Fully in the present.

As I stare mutely into the blue eyes of the man on our doorstep.

It takes a moment of this magnitude for me to finally grasp how wrong I'd been about something important.

Because, see, until this very instant, I thought I had a shred of mastery over my life and my destiny when, clearly, the only thing I have is a theory—My Unifying Theory About the Nature of the Universe—which snaps into being, fully formed in my mind.

Simply put, my newfound theory states: The minute a person comes to the erroneous conclusion that he or she controls anything at all in this life, the Universe immediately gets even with the bloody idiot.

Let go, Ellie. Just let go of all expectation.

A voice in my head, other than Jane's, says this, and I realize, with no little shock, that it's my *own* voice.

So, miraculously, even if it's only for a second, I let go.

"Hi, Sam," I say finally, amazed by the calm flow of these words out of my mouth.

"Hi, Ellie," he says with a tight smile. He's holding a lovely bouquet of autumn-colored flowers, his knuckles white around the wrapping. "I heard there was going to be a Barnett wedding this weekend. Congratulations to . . . everyone."

He thrusts the bouquet into my hands, and I have no choice but to accept it. Then I stare at him some more.

I don't understand why he's here, and I realize I may never understand this or anything else. That I can't comprehend the Grand Plan, but I can try to handle whatever happens as it comes to me. Moment by moment.

"Why don't you invite the gentleman inside," my mom suggests, motioning for Sam to come in and yanking the flowers out of my grasp. She passes them off to Lyssa. "Put these in water, will you, dear?"

As my cousin's daughter disappears into the kitchen, I manage to step back so Sam can enter the house, but I can't quite stop gaping at him. "Everyone, this is Sam," I inform them at last, my eyes never leaving his face.

"Wait. Sam *Blaine?*" Angelique says, her voice rising up an octave, her expression so stunned she lets the triplet she's chasing slip away from her momentarily.

"I—um, yes," Sam says, looking perplexed and rather worried at the instant name recognition, but he extends his hand to her politely. "Have we met?"

Angelique laughs. "I'm Ellie and Di's cousin. And, yes. We met ages ago at a high-school dance. It's been about, hmm . . . close to twenty years now." She pauses and waits for the memory to catch up with him. "I remember you *really* well, Sam."

His brow furrows and the color slowly seeps away from his face. "Uh, Angelique, right?"

"*Exactement,*" she says in her always-impeccable French. "And have you met Alex? The groom?"

Sam swallows, shakes his head and gives Di's fiancé a dark nod.

Alex sets down his dessert bowl and offers his hand. "Nice meeting you," he says with an ice-cream-mustache grin.

Sam grasps Alex's hand briefly and, just as quickly, lets it drop. "Yeah," he says back.

A moment of morgue-like silence follows.

Then Mom begins to chatter about how wonderful it is that Angelique, Leo, Nadia, Gregory and all their kids could fly out here for the wedding and how excited everyone is about it and how there are a million last-minute details and how she and Di and I have been running around trying to take care of everything but, oh, what a joy it is to see a daughter so happily married.

Sam's expression turns, if possible, even darker and tighter than before. His gaze trains on Alex with the chill of a Siberian hailstorm.

I catch a glimpse of Di, her brown eyes round with incredulity. Then, suddenly, she laughs.

Everyone transfers their stares to her.

She strides up to Sam and whacks him on the back with what I know is intended, theoretically, to be a friendly gesture, but gentleness was never Di's forte.

"Don't know how well you remember me, Sam," she says. "I'm Diana, Ellie's older sister." Then she pauses until she's sure she has Sam's attention and mine, too. "I'm the bride."

I watch as the lightness floods back into Sam's face. His gaze darts between my sister, her fiancé, and me for a full five seconds. Then he grins. "I'm delighted to hear that."

"Thought you might be," Di whispers, her voice low enough that only Sam and I can catch the words. It's then that I realize he came here thinking *I* was the bride.

Jane gasps, but says nothing else. I think she's been stunned into silence. This, I know, won't last long.

Then Di says, louder now, "Alex and I are getting remarried."

Sam shoots a warm smile at my sister, extending it to Alex also. "That's *wonderful*."

"Isn't it?" Mom says. "Dated for two years the first time. Married for almost five. Divorced for . . . well, too long. And now soon-to-be-married again. It's so romantic!"

"Yes, it is," Sam says agreeably.

"So, you're an old friend of Ellie's?" Mom asks.

"Yeah, but I've probably chosen a bad time to visit, what with everything you've all got to do. I was just hoping to talk with her for a few minutes."

"Oh, she's free now," Mom says with a breezy wave. "We've

done everything we can do for today, and Di and Alex were about to leave anyway." She lets her gaze wash over Sam with no attempt to disguise her scrutiny. "So, what are you doing these days? Do you live in the area?"

"Not at present. I did my residency out in Boston and I'm still there, but I hope to be on staff at Chicago General soon."

"So, you're a *doctor?*" Mom says, every note in her voice also saying how impressed she is by this little tidbit of good fortune. "Dr. Sam Blaine?"

He nods.

"Well, if you're still here for the weekend, you're welcome to join us for our big celebration. The wedding is at St. Michael's on Saturday at two."

Sam glances at me.

I narrow my eyes at him. The Universe may force me to accept its machinations, but I don't have to openly invite chaos. And Sam Blaine has always equaled chaos. The sense of calm I believed I had a few moments ago decides to flee.

He begins to shake his head. "Thanks, Mrs. Barnett, but—"

Di jumps in. "Oh, yes! You must come. Please. The more the merrier." She throws a devilish smirk my way then nudges Alex. "Right, honey?"

Alex shoots me a quizzical look and, since I'm plainly trying to signal him to say *No! Not a good idea*, he's justifiably confused. But he won't go against the fervent wishes of his repeat bride. "R-Right," he tells Sam.

"Well," Sam says, "I don't know if Ellie—"

Angelique grins at me then interrupts. "Ellie's going to be the maid of honor, you know," she tells him slyly. "But she'll need a dance partner once the required reception waltzes are over. Are you still a good dancer, Sam?"

This succeeds in finally rousing me to speech. "Let's go talk, Sam. Outside. Now." I all but push him out the door.

"Bye, Sam!" I hear a chorus of female voices say from the living room as we leave. This is followed by giggling. Damn those strong women of my family. They know *way* too much.

"I, uh . . ." Sam begins.

"W-W-What's going on?" I stutter. "W-Why are you back?"

Yes, Jane agrees, recovering her tongue. *By all means, ask him this. And then suggest he depart immediately.*

I cross my arms and try to look unaffected, but he puts his hand on my shoulder and steers me down a sidewalk littered with crunchy fall leaves. My personal heat index rises.

Sam clears his throat. "Like I told your mother, I'm hoping to be working in Chicago soon."

"So, you're here for job interviews?"

"Not exactly." He scores his fingers through his hair and I notice there's no wedding band. Where's the gold band? There's supposed to be one. Isn't he married yet?

Not knowing the answer throws me. I can't analyze anything else until I can wrap my mind around his marital status. So I ask, in one long breath, "Did your fiancée fly out here with you? Are you here because you're looking for apartments to live in together? Terrie told me you were engaged . . . aren't you?"

"No," he says shortly, and my heart skips several beats. "But I was. And I got your note. It was—well, it was really nice. I read it over a bunch of times . . ." His voice trails off. Then he says, "Look, Ellie, this is gonna sound crazy. I'm not even sure how to ask you this, but I need to know something—"

"*Why* aren't you engaged anymore?"

He halts mid-step. "Does that matter?"

Yes! Jane shouts.

"Yes," I say to him, but I whisper it.

He shrugs. "We had some problems and called off the wedding."

Insist he disclose the full reason, Jane demands, adding a few barely audible remarks about egotistical doctors. *He is up to no good. As usual.*

"What kinds of problems?" I ask him.

He looks at me for a long time. A seriously long time. "The kinds of problems that happen when a man is in love with a woman other than the one he's supposed to marry."

"Oh," I say, because what do you say to something like that?

After staring at me even longer, he leans in. "Can you please an-swer just this one simple question for me?"

His baby blues have lost none of their intensity. I close my eyes then nod.

Sam runs his fingertip down the nape of my neck and murmurs in my ear, "Are you still available?"

✎ 16 ✎

My behaviour to you . . . had merited the
severest reproof. It was unpardonable.
I cannot think of it without abhorrence.

—*Pride and Prejudice*

My heartbeat skips two beats and my eyes spring open.
"WHAT?" I say.

Sam takes a step backward. "Are you dating anyone seriously?
Thinking of marrying him? I'd heard you were in England last
year. Did you meet some British bloke with an accent who was too
cute to resist? Make plans to move into his damp cottage in the
Cotswolds come spring? Anything like that?"

"No."

"A castle in the Scottish highlands, then?"

"No. Sam, stop it. What kind of game are you playing?"

"No game. I'm just very curious about you. Is there anybody,
anywhere you're in love with?"

If I don't include you, I think to myself before adding aloud,
"No, I guess I haven't met that special, marriage-ready man yet." I
shrug. "I'm keeping the possibilities open, though, and if it happens for me, great. If it doesn't, well . . ." My mature, well-rehearsed
speech on potential relationships trails off as I notice Sam's broad-
ening grin.

He exhales. "Okay."

"What's okay? Nothing about this is okay."

I say this because (a) I'm nervous, (b) I can't believe Sam is here, and (c) we're kind of having my reunion-fantasy conversation.

I have told this fantasy *Go away!* a trillion times since the day I heard about Sam's engagement. I'm not sure I can trust seeing its realization now.

"It's okay to *me*," Sam explains, "because that means things might still be possible, you know, between us. I thought you were getting married, Ellie. I was worried that, after everything, I might be too late."

NEWS FLASH: No one ever says that NOT getting what you want is easy. People tend to be sympathetic then. They know they need to send "Thinking of You" cards, bring you batches of double-fudge brownies and whisper, "Better luck next time," while engulfing you in a warm bear hug.

But when you're presented with what you've always thought you wanted, especially in a relationship, it's tricky.

You doubt yourself.

You doubt your love interest.

Other people second-guess you and harbor a belief that (a) you don't deserve this, (b) it's too good to be true, or (c) you're being downright delusional.

According to Jane, "c" is my problem.

Ellie, she tells me, *I acknowledge your opinion of Mr. Blaine has improved over the years and, perhaps in adulthood, he is less obvious in his untrustworthiness than he had once been. The man is charming, to be sure, but such charm is always just cause for suspicion. Do not let your tendency toward romanticism be the means of distorting your greater awareness, for you would be lacking in sense if you allowed Mr. Blaine to sway your understanding of his nature.*

In my haughtiest voice I reply, *I'm not easily swayed, Jane*, but of course I worry that I am.

To Sam I say, "So, let me get this straight. You heard from someone that a Barnett was getting married, and you naturally assumed it was me?"

"Yeah, well, actually—"

"So, you broke off your engagement to some poor woman in

Boston, whose affections you were merely toying with, and flew out here to try to . . . what? Stop my wedding to someone who, for all you knew, could've been the love of my life?"

His disloyalty infuriates me. After all, *I* hadn't tried to break up *his* engagement, no matter how painful it was for me. No man should do such a thing to a woman. Men who do are rotten, stinking scoundrels who ought to be strung up by their—

"Not quite," Sam says. "Yes, I needed to see you again, and I haven't been able to stop thinking of you since I got your note, but my engagement just wasn't meant to be. I called it off months ago, way back in February, because my fiancée had a little problem with fidelity."

His face pales a bit as he talks about this and, in spite of myself, I feel the stirrings of empathy. Having been wounded by an unfaithful lover before, I understand the betrayal.

"I'm sorry to hear that," I say.

He shrugs. "Trust me. It was for the best. I was angry about it and everything for a while, but I worked through most of that pretty fast. When my ex moved in with the other guy in June, I wasn't even fazed. I'd done some dating and met a couple of nice women. I was doing okay, but I decided it'd be great to get back to the Midwest. My roots are here, and Chicago will always be home. So I applied for a transfer this fall and, if all goes as planned, I'll officially start in January."

"Congratulations," I say.

"Thanks. Only, my excitement was kind of short-lived, Ellie. The following week I got this e-mail from Jason Bertignoli."

"From *Jason?*"

"Yep."

"The Jason you hated in high school? The Jason you never talked to unless you were being rude or insulting or vindictive? The Jason I made the mistake of going to senior prom with? *That* Jason?"

His eyes light up. "Ah-ha. So you *finally* admit you made a mistake going to prom with him."

I slug him in the arm. "That's not the point!"

He smiles at me. "Remember when I saw you at the bookstore

a few years back? I ran into Jason on that visit, too. He and his wife were getting ready to move to Milwaukee."

"Really?" I hadn't heard any Jason news in ages.

"Yeah. He's got a good manager job up there in a sports shop." Then he adds, shaking his head, "And *three* kids. He sends me digital photos."

I can't help but laugh at this. The mental image of Sam getting baby-picture e-mails from Jason is just too funny.

"You don't like kids?" I ask.

"I like kids a lot, but he had three before his thirtieth birthday. I'd be happy with one or two before forty."

A vision of one of Sam's kids streaks through my mind: dark hair, blue eyes, impish grin—a cute little troublemaker. With Sam's genes, one kid would probably be plenty.

"You and Jason. E-mailing. I can't get over it."

"Jason's a good guy," Sam admits. "A couple of weeks ago, though, he sends out the latest batch of kiddie photos along with news he's heard from his parents." He slants me a look. "Seems a Barnett daughter is getting married and, Jason says, since Diana's already hitched, this wedding must be yours." Sam turns toward me and takes both my hands in his. "And, Ellie, I totally panicked."

"Why?" I ask, although he's all but told me outright. I simply don't believe the answer my intuition is receiving.

Sam pulls my body up against his until I can feel the ridges of his belt against my stomach, the pulse of his heart beneath his corded sweater, the deep breaths he's blowing on my hair. "Because I love you, Ellie Barnett," he whispers before he brings those sinful lips of his down on mine.

It's as though decades melt away and time travel is a reality. Am I jumbled up and confused about this?

Yes.

Do I know how to handle this latest curve the Universe is throwing at me?

No.

Could Sam have been my Mr. Darcy all along and I was just too blind to recognize it?

I have no freaking idea.

Jane, by contrast, is not nearly so bewildered.

It is difficult, I grant you, to judge character in a world of deceptive appearances, she tells me, her voice frosty. *But Mr. Blaine's interest in you is likely as fleeting as it has always been. Please take care, Ellie,* she pleads. *For while YOU may have greatly matured, I fear he wants only temporary gratification, just as before. And just as before, he will not hesitate to hurt you. Some people may improve or change with time, but not a man with a Wickham nature. This Mr. Blaine is no Darcy.*

I break away from Sam's embrace. "I need to catch my breath," I say, not entirely lying.

He nods.

And he lets me stand there, breathing deeply, in the middle of a cracked, leaf-covered sidewalk in neighborhood Glen Forest.

"Here's the thing, Sam," I begin, not sure when I start speaking what "the thing" is, but I've given up planning and strategizing and am now just talking from my gut. "I'm not indifferent to you. But I'm also not the same person I was back in high school or at that Chicago bar or even when we had those coffees at the bookstore. What makes you think we know each other anymore?"

He strokes my arm, from my shoulder to my wrist, in one long sensual motion with his fingers. "Who you are in essentials has never changed, Ellie. Neither has who I am."

Jane doesn't waste a second jumping on this comment.

Precisely the problem, she states. *You might inquire as to why it has taken him so long to value you. You might also press him to explain why, with so little effort to win your heart, he expects you to declare your affections and faint dead away at his paltry display of passion.*

Jane, as always, has a point. It just happens to be a point my heart and my ego don't want to hear.

Sam, not being privy to Jane's criticisms, pulls me into his arms once again and sets my mouth aflame with another slow kiss. I'm flying on the wings of ecstasy and disbelief, which make a heady combination. Needless to say, I've never forgotten how good he is at the whole kissing thing—and time has only improved his skill. Even being a strong modern woman, I'm hardly unresponsive.

Plus, the pull of a traditional happily-ever-after finale to my life's story is compelling, both for its own sake, and even more so because it feels potentially within reach for the first time in eons. The only problem is that I could be completely wrong about Sam and me being right for each other.

I step back from this second kiss, my lips and heart both trembling, and stare at him.

Anyone but him, Jane urges. *Please, Ellie, promise me you will not enter into an engagement with that man. Promise me this and . . . and I shall tell you a secret.*

What kind of a secret?

One you long to know. One I have kept from you all these years. She hesitates, obviously debating, before adding, *The identity of my one true love.*

The Clergyman By The Sea? The Mystery Man? I say to her, stunned.

The possibility of this more than intrigues me, I admit, but is the knowledge worth my giving up the chance to find out what might happen next with Sam?

There is more than my love's name at stake, Ellie. It involves you directly. And your family.

I gasp and my heart pauses mid-beat. Is it as I've always hoped? *Oh, God, Jane! Am I a relative of yours after all? Was there a secret baby somewhere and now I'm—*

Dear heavens, no. You are not an Austen or a descendant of one. But in a way you are like my child, one I vowed long ago to guide and protect. There IS a reason I chose you, beyond the lessons we needed to learn. And I shall tell you what it is, but only if you leave Mr. Blaine this instant.

I breathe in. I breathe out. I twirl my hair and shuffle my feet while sneaking glances at Sam, who's staring at me strangely.

"Ellie?" he says, eyeing me as he might a psych-ward escapee.

Ellie? Jane says.

But I can't do it.

I'm sorry, Jane. I can't promise to stay away from Sam. Not even for you. Not even for a secret like that.

Because, see, as much as I want to know what Jane has to reveal, the truth is smacking me in the face today. It won't be denied, although I'd all but tramped down my own deep, dark secret and buried it: I'm an optimist.

Still.

Even though it isn't the '80s anymore. Even though I've been hurt by romantic warfare time and again. Even though I'm not a fifteen-year-old geek with my nose buried in a book who, for some mysterious reason (that I'll probably never know now), has Jane Austen as my Personal Spiritual Guide.

Hey, I waited almost twenty years for an answer to that question, what's another decade or two?

But here I am at this moment, a thirty-four-year-old geek, and against my will and against my reason (although, okay, not against my character), I still want that fucking Cinderella story for myself.

More than an amazing, no-one-else-on-the-planet-knows-this secret.

More than *anything* else.

I want that happily-ever-after ending I imagined, as a teen, I'd get someday. That daydream I held on to as my prize for surviving those sucky years of adolescence.

Dammit, I *deserve* that ending.

It's just that, if I'm truly honest with myself, I can no longer tell if it's Sam, specifically, I want or if it's the nearly two-decade-old fantasy featuring him as the heroic lead.

So, at the last second, I cop out.

"I need to think about this," I tell him. "But I'm glad you came back so we could talk." I nod ever so reassuringly and begin to back away.

He squints at me, perplexed. "But Ellie? Wait—where are you going?"

"See you at the wedding, Sam," I say. Then I turn and run back home, as though the magic were about to wear off and the naked simplicity of my desires revealed.

❧ 17 ❧

Oh! how heartily did she grieve over
every ungracious sensation she had
ever encouraged, every saucy speech
she had ever directed towards him.

—Pride and Prejudice

Three days later, at the wedding, we have forty-five minutes to go before the ceremony. . . .

Di is freaking out over some Cover Girl Orange Crème nail polish. (It matches her original sardonyx engagement ring and it looks great, but she chipped a nail, so now what's she gonna do?) Our mother is trying to calm her down.

Angelique and Nadia are in their bridesmaids' dresses, helping their respective husbands straighten their respective groomsmen ties.

Cousins Aaron and Andy show up late for their ushering duties (because the Twin Terrors may have grown taller, but they never grew up), and neither of them have their tuxes on yet. My father and my Uncle Craig are chewing them out in the dressing area.

The groom is soothing his pre-wedding jitters (with the help of his brother, Nick, and a well-concealed flask of bourbon) in the men's bathroom.

And Aunt Candice is put in charge of corralling the youngsters into the church playroom. I hear one of the triplets shriek in terror at the sound of her voice.

I grin and say under my breath, "I know the feeling, kid."

I put the finishing touches on my makeup and smooth out my

somewhat racy maid-of-honor dress. It's scandalously clingy and lusciously purple, the kind of dress I always wanted to wear but needed a tad more nerve. I have more than nerve today. I have my sister's direct orders.

"I'm the bride," Di reminded me a few months ago when we were selecting gowns. "I want you to look *hot* on my wedding day, and that's final."

A note to all wise wedding attendants: What the bride wants, the bride gets.

Thirty-two minutes before the ceremony . . .

I leave the dressing area to locate where the florist left our bouquets, corsages and boutonnieres and to make sure everything we need to have on hand is waiting for us. I find them on a table near the back of the church and count out the number of items. I compare this figure with the number of attendants, ushers, parents, etc. in need of floral adornment. Fortunately, there are roses for all.

Early-arriving guests begin to flutter in. I pause in the foyer to say hello to Terrie and her boyfriend Everett (I *knew* they were a serious couple), several friends of the family and Reverend Jacobs, who'd officiated at Di and Alex's last wedding.

"This time it'll be forever," the Reverend says to me with a hearty laugh.

I'm about to chime in with my agreement when a shrill "Oh, my God!" interrupts us.

It's my mother. She's standing three yards away, looking at her cell phone like it just mooned her.

"What's wrong, Mom?"

"They have food poisoning," she says, her voice a shocked whisper.

"Who? The caterers?" I'm seriously praying it's not the caterers.

"The band. Three out of the five members. Something about tainted shrimp at their gig last night." She covers her mouth with her hand, her chest heaving hard. I'm worried there'll be hyperventilating soon if I don't do something quick.

I snatch her cell phone. "Just relax, Mom," I say, although I'm on the verge of panicking myself. "I'll make some calls and see if we can get a last-minute replacement for the reception." But I know this'll be next to impossible. You just don't try to book a live band a few hours before they have to start playing.

Reverend Jacobs beats a hasty retreat, Mom continues to stand in place and gulp air, and the pews begin to crowd up as the well-wishers fill the church.

"What's going on?" says the most recognizable American male voice on the planet.

I swivel around to face Sam. "We're having a little problem."

Sam stares at me, but doesn't speak. He's stunning to behold in his navy suit but, then, he always did clean up nice. I watch him scan my hair, my dress, my mouth. Then he shuts his eyes and bows his head.

"What?" I say.

"Nothing. I mean, you look incredible, but we'll discuss that later." He glances up at me and grins faintly. "How can I help with the 'little problem'?"

I shake my head and glare at Mom's cell phone. "You can't." Then I turn to my mother. "I'm going to need a phone book."

Mom runs off to snitch one from the Reverend's office and almost collides with Di, who's sprinting toward us in full (albeit low-cut) ivory-and-lace bridal regalia.

"Oh, my God. Oh, my God," Di says, panting. "We're so screwed!"

"Shhh, we're in a church," I tell her. "Keep your voice down, but don't worry. I'll find another band."

"A *band?*" Sam says, his eyes widening. "For the reception? *Tonight?*"

Di gives him a fretful nod. "Can you play Billy Idol's 'White Wedding' on electric guitar?"

Sam shakes his head.

"Shit," Di mutters.

"What about Alex's musician friends?" I ask. "Could some of them pull together and do it?"

"Most of them are either out-of-state now or not speaking to each other anymore," Di says. She pauses, her cheeks flushed, her eyes feverish with alarm. "Wait. How about Andrei? He can play anything!"

"What?" I say. Then, "Absolutely not."

"Oh, c'mon, El. He'd do it for you. The guy's still in love with you, you know."

I conclude that Wedding-Day Malaria must've set in or Di would never ask this of me. I open my mouth to contradict the love thing, but Sam interrupts.

"Who's Andrei?" he says.

"Ellie's rock-star ex-boyfriend," Di explains. "He's got an incredible voice and a Top Twenty hit on Russian radio right now. He still lives in the Chicago area and *she* has access to his private cell number." My sister jabs a finger in my direction. "So, call him. For me. Pleeeeassse."

"I don't think—" I begin to say, then stop. I *do* have Andrei's number—memorized, even. I *could* call him. He'll *probably* rush right over to do this for me if he's available. But I don't want to. I don't want to use him when I know nothing will ever happen between us again.

"You were dating a . . . uh, Russian rock star?" Sam's brow scrunches up.

"We dated some years back," I explain with a shrug, "before he hit it big. But I go to watch his band perform downtown every now and then."

I don't tell Sam the rest, though. That Andrei sends me the tickets. That he's mentioned—repeatedly—us getting back together and even hinted at marriage and kids. That the certainty of seriously hot sex (in addition to the husband and child thing) makes his proposition tempting, but that emotionally I moved on a long time ago. He was great, yes, and I learned a lot about myself from being with him, but it turned out he wasn't The One after all. And I'm not settling for anything but a Forever Love now.

Still, my sister's eyes are pleading with me to do *something*, and I figure for her sake I can deal with all the awkwardness and personal discomfort later.

I sigh and say, "Okay, Di." I punch in the first couple digits of Andrei's number, but Sam's hand closes over mine. He clicks off the phone.

"Hang on," he says to me, his expression cautious but compassionate. Then, to Di, "Do you and Alex have to have a *band?* Or would a really good DJ do the trick?"

"At this point, if that DJ has a decent copy of 'White Wedding,'" Di says, "I'm fine with it."

Sam nods. "I'll see what I can do." He reaches for the cell phone just as the organist strikes the first few chords of the pre-ceremony music.

"Oh, crap!" Di says, her eyes darting wildly around the church foyer.

I glance at my watch. Eight minutes before the ceremony and counting down . . .

Mom comes rushing toward us. "I found the Chicago Yellow Pages." She thrusts the fat phone book at me. "Will this be enough?"

I glance at Sam. He squints at the phone book then holds out his open palm for it. I can tell from his determined expression that he's deep in planning mode.

"Why don't you let me take care of this?" he whispers to me, flipping rapidly through the crinkled pages of the book, looking so much like that music-loving teenage Sam that I get a vivid flashback of our sophomore-year dance. "I'll figure something out."

"No, Sam. You're here as a guest. I should be the one to—"

But Angelique races up to us and interrupts me. "Where are all the flowers, Ellie? I'll pin the boutonnieres on the guys and the corsages on the moms, but we're going to have to get started soon. The men are almost ready to walk in."

I point her toward the table of roses and tell her to grab the bridesmaid bouquets, too. She's about to leave when my dad and brother jog in, read the nervous expressions on our faces (it's hard to miss) and halt in place.

"Diana," Dad says quietly. "Is everything all right? Do you still want to do this today?"

"Get married?" my sister asks. She looks shaken from the stress, but she still manages to snort. "Hell, yeah. But it might be a freaking boring reception if we don't have any music."

"*What?*" Dad and Gregory say together.

Mom explains the problem to them while Di turns to Sam. "The dance is supposed to start at seven-thirty," my sister says. "Can you help us?"

Sam studies my family members huddled around him. I see him look at each and every one of us until, finally, his blue eyes return to me. "I promise I'll take care of it," he says, meeting my gaze. "Trust me." Then, to Di, he adds, "I've got a favor I can call in, but I'll probably have to miss most of the ceremony to do it."

"Hey, you can watch the video later if you really wanna see it." She leans in and gives him a peck on the cheek. "Thanks, Sam." Then she arches a brow at me, and I can see the familiar deviousness dancing in her eyes. "Ellie, find Sam a quiet spot to make his phone calls and then get your butt back out here. Pachelbel's Canon is gonna start any second."

Sam and I step away just as Aunt Candice emerges from the playroom.

"What do you want me to do with these smart little rugrats?" she says, unable to contain the pride in her voice, however unwillingly bestowed. "When do we release them on the public?"

I check my watch once again. Clifton and the triplets are scheduled to scatter rose petals down the aisle, shepherded by Lyssa, the official flower girl. "In three minutes," I tell her as I pull Sam away from my family.

He follows me to Reverend Jacobs's office, strides inside and points to the door. "Get out there," he tells me gently. "You've got a wedding to go to."

My heart is trying to hammer its way out of my rib cage. "Sam, this is awful. First you get a last-minute invitation to this wedding, and now you're going to spend the next hour trying to fix our mess for us. I'm so sorry we roped you into this—"

"I'm not," he says. "I'm not sorry at all." He looks deep into my eyes. "If I can't always keep from hurting someone, Ellie, I can at least try to fix a few things sometimes." He kisses my hand. "Now, get going. I'll see you soon."

And the way he says this lets me know his promise is as much a certainty as the sun shining and the earth revolving around it.

Twenty seconds before the ceremony . . .

I glance over my shoulder and see Sam grinning at me. Then I scurry back to the foyer where everybody is lined up and waiting to walk down the aisle. Here we go.

Forty-two minutes later, I'm strolling back toward the front doors on the arm of Alex's brother, Nick. Alexander Sinjin Evans has been united in holy matrimony—again—with Diana Lynn Barnett Evans, and the two of them lead us out of the church.

I catch a glimpse of Sam in the hallway as the procession heads outside. He's leaning up against a marble pillar, the cell phone still in one hand and, in the other, a stray pink rose that must've escaped one of the bouquets.

I mouth, "Well?"

He nods, raising the rose like a champagne flute in my direction, toasting me. "It's done," he mouths back.

We exchange weary smiles before Nick escorts me to my place in the receiving line. I give Di the news via a thumbs-up, and my sister whispers, "I'm thinking maybe you should marry this Sam guy. I know you said he can be a pain in the ass, but he's hot, and I kinda like him."

High praise indeed.

I laugh at her suggestion, but a tiny niggle of hope begins to tango within me, kicking at the dust in my soul and stirring up all sorts of things it probably shouldn't.

I open myself up to the feeling anyway, and I find I'm overwhelmed by a happiness I can't sweep away.

If you can overlook Mr. Blaine's endless infractions toward you merely because he rushed to your aid at long last, Jane complains, *you are ridiculously forgiving. Either that or incredibly foolish.*

And you, Jane, are unbelievably prejudiced against him, I retort, unable to contain the silly grin that's found its home on my lips. *Sam's grown up. I believe he really—*

Is unchanged, Jane interrupts. *For all your romanticism, you must realize the gentleman has done nothing worthy of note. He has not saved your family's reputation or partaken in any pursuit that requires his specialized skill or resources—*

What do you mean? He DID use his resources. He called in his contacts to get us some music for tonight.

Perhaps he may have acquired the musical entertainment for your sister's wedding dance, but this hardly indicates a grand commitment of time or effort. It fails to show an improvement in his character or his temperament or—

Sure it does. Jane, you're being absurd!

After a long, silent moment she says, *It has been my private mission to see you happily settled in this life, Ellie. Because I care about you and . . . and because you are the descendant of someone very dear to me. There. I have said it at last.* She pauses. *But I fear I have failed you.*

No, you haven't! You've been amazing. You tried to direct me away from hurt and harm even when I seemed determined to screw things up, and I— Then it hits me. *Wait, your Clergyman By The Sea? He's a relative of MINE?*

Yes. He died, of course, but his brother the doctor—an arrogant man, similar in temperament to your Mr. Blaine and an individual I confess I did not much like—DID marry and have children. You come from the last branch of that family's line.

I cover my mouth with both palms and close my eyes as I try to process this. *Oh, Jane.*

She sighs softly. *Ellie, I waited almost two centuries to find just the right one of his ancestors with whom to share what I know of human nature, what I recognize to be true about love and passion. I waited to try to connect with his one descendant that I felt shared an outlook on life most like mine, in hopes of making her life better. Perhaps it is a small gift. Perhaps it has been hopelessly ineffective, but it is the only one I have left to give to the memory of the man I loved. And to you.*

I hear her out, and my heart fills with appreciation for all she's tried to do for me since the moment I first held that paperback copy of *Pride and Prejudice*. My heart fills also with the pain of love's loss—one she's carried with her for far, far too long.

I love you, Jane, and I'm indebted to you, I tell her. *I'm so honored to be the one you chose . . . I can't tell you how much. But now you need to let me handle my own destiny. Or at least the tiny bit of it I control. I promise I'll try to make you proud.*

❧ 18 ❧

If you *will* thank me . . . let it be
for yourself alone . . . your *family*
owe me nothing. Much as I
respect them, I believe I thought only of *you*.

—*Pride and Prejudice*

F our hours later, at the reception, the Glen Forest Four Seasons
Hotel glitters with tiny white lights on the outside but, on the
inside, in Di and Alex's reception ballroom (the Manitoba Room,
not the Winnebago), the color scheme sparkles with deep violets,
smooth lavenders and accents in lilac.

The lovely dinner, complemented by good wine and humorous,
heartfelt toasts to the couple, has ended. The photogenic cake-
cutting ritual has, likewise, passed. And, at last, the dance party
begins.

"Oh, my God," Di says, pointing at Sam and the just-arriving,
hunky-looking DJ, who are busy making final adjustments to the
sound system. "You know who that is, don't you?"

I study the DJ's chiseled profile but can't recall any similarity to
anyone in our acquaintance. "No," I say.

"It's Wild Ted in the Morning!"

"Can't be."

Di grins. "Yeah, it can be. WXRJ's Wild Ted. He always does
the weekday morning show and those eighties retrospectives you
love."

"How can you be so sure that's him?"

"Seen him on a billboard out near O'Hare, *and* he was a guest
VJ on VH1 once."

"Oh, wow," I say. "I never would've guessed he looked like *that*. I mean, he sounds great on the air and everything, but DJs aren't usually so—"

"Scandalously gorgeous?" Di concludes for me. I nod. "Yeah," she says. "But he's also got one of the most famous voices in Chicago. I wonder what your Sam had to do to convince him to come here . . . and last minute like this."

"He's not *my* Sam," I say, mentally adding *not yet*, "and I don't know." But Di is right to wonder. Getting Wild Ted to work a non-celebrity wedding on one of his free Saturday nights has to be an expensive venture, even if there's some kind of favor-payback involved. "I'll go ask Sam how much we owe him."

Di nods, worrying her lip a bit.

I walk around the edge of the dance floor, approaching Sam and the DJ just as they flip on the microphone.

"Helllloooo, Barnett and Evans families! Let's give a shout out to the reunited newlyweds, Di and Alex!" The DJ pauses while everyone cheers. "Congratulations, you lovebirds, and welcome to all your friends. I'm Wild Ted—" brief pause for delighted gasps, "and I'm here to kick off this rockin' party with the first dance. By bridal request, here's Billy Idol's 'White Wedding'!"

I catch Sam's eye as the distinctive electric-guitar opening bursts through the speakers. He winks at me, and I walk to meet him at the corner of the dance floor.

"So, is this good?" he asks.

I reach for his hands, squeeze his strong fingers, feel the current flowing between us. "This is *great*, but Wild Ted . . . how on earth did you—" I shake my head. "This had to take more than a phone call, Sam. We'll pay you back, of course, but—"

"No, you won't." Sam brings my fingers to his lips and starts to sway as if we're beginning to dance. "Consider it my wedding gift to your sister."

"Quite a wedding gift."

"Quite a wedding," he replies, eyeing Di and Alex with a raised brow. "Besides, my motives were ultimately selfish. I really was only thinking of you, Ellie . . . and how much I wanted to dance with you tonight."

"Oh," I say, the crazy pounding in my chest becoming more frenzied at these words. "Well, of course we can—"

"Excuse me," Nick says behind me. I turn to look at Alex's brother. A good-looking guy, to be sure, and a nice one, but he's just not Sam. I'm coming to understand that *nobody*, no matter how smart or attractive, is Sam . . . except for Sam. An obvious concept for most people, but a real lightning-bolt realization for me.

"We're going to need to join the wedding party in a sec, El," Nick says. To Sam he explains, "The best man and maid of honor have to dance after the bride and groom."

"That's right," I whisper, shooting Sam an apologetic look.

Sam nods and points to his watch. "Okay, but I demand a rain check within the hour."

I smile at him. "You got it."

So Nick and I dance, and it's all very pleasant, effortless, un-complicated . . . and utterly bland except for the erotic vibes I'm getting from the blue-eyed doctor across the parquet floor.

Wild Ted begins working his way through Di and Alex's musical request list, featuring artists like Edie Brickell and the New Bo-hemians, Fine Young Cannibals, The Fixx and many other less-than-traditional wedding selections. When the sounds of Men Without Hats pour through the speakers, a lively cheer rises from the crowd and someone shouts, "Hey, dudes, c'mon! Let's all do the 'Safety Dance'!"

At that I leave Nick to his girlfriend and glance around for Sam. He's disappeared for the time being, so I seek out Angelique and Terrie. The three of us converge near the dessert table, chatting, nibbling on apricot-filled butter cookies and watching as Di and Alex's buddies take to the floor with spirited fortitude. It's hilarious.

"You going to force Everett out there?" I ask Terrie.

She shakes her head solemnly. "For me, it's Wang Chung or nothing."

Angelique laughs. "I'm holding out for Bananarama. How about you, Ellie?"

"It'd take a pretty phenomenal song to get me to make a fool of myself like that," I say, chuckling. "At the moment, I can't think of one that would qualify."

"Hi, ladies," Sam says, appearing at my elbow from out of nowhere. "Enjoying the music?"

"Yeah," Terrie says. She exchanges a look with Angelique and me, glances at Sam, then onto the dance floor, then back at me. It's high school all over again. "You know this is way weird."

"*Très* weird," Angelique contributes with a grin.

I nod and Sam's face reddens a bit.

"I know," he admits to us. "*Plus ça change, plus c'est la même chose.* The more things change . . ." He winks at me, clears his throat and kind of laughs. "Um, Ellie?"

"Yes?"

"I came over here to tell you something."

"What's that?" I notice my cousin and my friend aren't even pretending not to listen in.

He clears his throat a second time. "I just wanted you to know we've got Spandau Ballet coming up soon."

I emit a sound that's a cross between "Uh" and "Hmm" before feeling my face flush hot.

"I was hoping we could dance," Sam says.

And then, as if on cue (which, God knows, it probably is), Wild Ted's voice booms out to us. "Got a song my buddy Sam requested for the lovely sister of the bride. Ellie, if you're out there listening, this one's for you."

"True" begins playing.

I stand in place, rooted to the floor by my deep purple pumps and the knowledge that Sam's taken more than just tiny figurative steps today. This isn't a mere fantasy. It's not fading away. And neither is he.

"C'mon," he says. "Dance with me? Please."

So, I let him lead me to the floor and, for the first minute of the song, we're out there alone. There are no sounds, save for the music playing and the shuffling of our feet. My family and friends are watching us, protecting me in their cocoon of affection until they realize I'm fine. Okay, more than fine.

Then everyone turns their attention back to their own lives, and the dance floor fills with other couples.

Sam finally speaks. "Thank you," he says.

"For what?"

"For being you. For being a part of my life for ages. For forgiving me . . ." He eyes me as if this last part is still open to debate.

I grin at him. Truth is, I forgave Sam for everything so long ago it seems like ancient history. But I guess I'd needed the time to forgive *myself*—for squandering all those years thinking I could replace him with someone else, someone I considered less challenging.

"Boy, I'll bet Stacy Daschell would like to dance again to this song," I say, teasing him now because I know I can. "She's been married and divorced a few times already, but she's single these days. You might want to look her up."

He leans in and whispers in my ear, "You know damn well I was only trying to make you jealous that night. You drove me freakin' *insane* dancing with Jason. I chose Stacy because I was sure that'd get to you and because she was too drunk to remember much of anything. But it was you all along, Ellie. And *you*, my sweet, sexy little brainiac—" He glances down at my formfitting dress. "You *always* knew that, didn't you?"

Ah, well. Being honest with yourself is the last frontier, isn't it?

I nod, finally giving myself permission to trust my instincts. Sam draws me nearer. The song's chorus plays again, and I relax into his embrace.

Jane makes a last-ditch effort to test my resolve by applying her nearly unerring sense of logic. *Are you certain you wish to go down this path?* she asks, her voice worried. *Do you not remember your own emotions at witnessing his behaviour? Do you not recall with clarity his treatment of you? From the very first this man has abused your kindness. Long ago you called him a coward and an idiot. You said you were glad to be rid of him. Are you quite sure you can think otherwise now?*

I silently assess the messages Sam sent me this week. Three days ago he made an oral declaration of love. He spent today in action, solving our family's wedding crisis. He not only telegraphed romantic interest verbally and nonverbally in private, he had it announced by microphone tonight. At an event with two hundred people. Many of whom would dismember him if he hurt me.

Sam Blaine always had smarts. Now he's gained courage, too.

Have I?

Think, Ellie! You even made a wordplay on his initials once, Jane reminds me. *It was, as he richly deserved, a less-than-flattering association.*

I laugh at this. *That's right. S.O.B. Sam "the Obnoxious" Blaine. But, Jane—*

Precisely. You deduced the weakness of his character at a remarkably young age.

But that was the problem. I was a teen then, not much older than a child. And so was he. Don't you think I could've misinterpreted his behavior, or that maybe he changed?

*No. I do not believe—*Jane begins.

"Hey, Sam," I say aloud. "What's your middle name?"

He squints at me. "Uh, Randolph." He looks supremely embarrassed by this admission. "Why?"

"Randolph," I repeat out loud, emphasizing it for Jane's benefit. "Wouldn't have guessed that one." Then, to Jane, *And neither did you. We, neither of us, were completely fair. We didn't try to discover anything new about him. We stayed stuck in the past and—*

Oh, dear child, after he used you so ill, I could have dubbed him with a far more fitting middle name, Jane says hotly, clearly still wounded on my behalf and exhibiting her loyalty to the end. *Fiend, Devil, Brute. Any of these would suffice.*

"What did you think it was?" Sam asks me.

I shrug. "No idea, Sam. It just goes to show how many little details I still have to learn about you." To Jane, *And that's merely the tiniest of examples. He's matured. We must look at him as he is NOW.*

I dislike immensely what I see, Jane says stubbornly. *Your heart is in grave danger, and I believe you are blinded to it.*

Am I, Jane? Or, perhaps, are you the blind one this time? Tell me, have you any objection to the grown-up Sam Blaine other than your belief of my continued emotional peril when in his presence?

I confess I do worry for you, she says, though she avoids answering my question. *I suspect him to be a proud, unpleasant man, interested in no one but himself.*

I don't buy that, I tell her. *And I'm betting he'd be fascinated by YOU if I ever told him about our relationship.*

She sighs. *Again, my concern is on your behalf. I fear Mr. Blaine has never been, and is not now, worthy of you or your affection.*

Maybe. Maybe not. The point is, Jane, I don't know. And I WON'T know unless I give him a chance, as an adult.

I could not stand to witness your hurt at his hands the first time, Ellie. My months away from you then were not solely in anger. I, too, felt your injury and required some distance. So I am cautious, my friend, and I wonder how you can be certain he will not destroy your heart a second time.

I can't, I admit. *But it's a risk I'm willing to take and, for once, I'm not being childish about this, Jane. I'm not going against your wisdom out of fear, arrogance or immaturity. You're the one who's always talking about Lessons and Reasons and Purposes that must be revealed in time . . . Well, I'm convinced Sam's path and mine are meant to intersect somehow. That everything in my life has led to this moment and—*

"Ellie, where the hell are you?" Sam says.

"What?" I realize I stopped dancing and he caught me staring into space during my debate with Jane. "Oh, sorry, just thinking."

Sam shakes his head. "No. It's more than that. I swear to God, half the time I tried talking with you in high school, and even afterward, it was like you were listening to voices or something. I could never get your full attention."

He scores his fingers through his hair and scowls at me, his forehead creased, his eyes pained. "What's the deal with that? I can fight against a real opponent, and I will if you want me to, but I can't battle your memory of someone more important. Are you sure there isn't somebody else, Ellie?"

I gape at him, half impressed, half stunned. No one has ever called me on this before. No one. *See, Jane,* I say, triumphant. *In his own way, he's known about you all along. He's the only person who's paid close enough attention.*

She sighs loudly, but I can tell she's wavering a bit.

"Sam," I say to him, "I can assure you there is no other man in my life. You're the one I want. The one I've always wanted. And, yeah, there are raging arguments in my head sometimes, and there probably always will be. But I love you, Sam Blaine." I look deep into his blue eyes, his pupils so dilated that, if I didn't know better,

I'd assume he was drunk on wedding champagne. "And I have since . . . oh, the very beginning."

He exhales a long breath and bends his head to kiss me.

I pull back. "Mind you, I don't know if I'll want to *marry* you or anything. A night of wild sex every fifteen years or so is one thing—but a lifetime commitment? We'll have to wait and see on that."

Sam smiles down at me. "If you don't want to talk about marriage or kids tonight, I'm fine with it, even though that's where I'm headed." He pauses. "That was the real problem during high school, you know. Bad timing. I knew you'd make a lousy girlfriend, but I—"

"A *lousy* girlfriend!" I swat his chest with the back of my palm. "How *dare* you, Sam! Did you think I was that boring? That ugly? That inexperi—"

He laughs. "Shhh, let me finish. I didn't want you as some short-term fling, Ellie. I was certain you'd be the perfect wife for me someday, if you didn't kill me first, but I figured I'd better wait it out until we were both ready. Until I was a better man for you." He pauses again. "Sorry it took me so long."

Well, I could hardly rage at him after that. So, instead, I say, "You thought about us, about marriage . . . that early?"

"Yes. Ask me why?"

"Why?"

"Because I've always loved you, and now I want to be with you once and for all. Please, can we just see how things go between us?" He waits for me to respond, which I do with a nod. "If it doesn't work out, then I want a damn good reason why not. And, if it does, we'll cross that bridge when you're ready. You've never not been the one for me, Ellie Barnett, and I'll do what it takes to prove that to you."

Despite Sam's special ability to use confusing double negatives, I understand the sincerity of his declaration.

I grin at him. He grins back. Then he kisses my lips softly and, even with so light a touch, I can feel the electricity between us sparking. We return to dancing—our slow, body-hugging sway—

despite the fact that the music has changed and Wild Ted has put on some upbeat Modern English for the newlyweds.

Jane, I say to the wise lady inhabiting my mind, *he HAS changed. Love changed him. It's true and you know it. Sam IS my Mr. Darcy.*

She gives a short, ironic snort, but the conviction with which she'd protested earlier diminished greatly after Sam's last speech. And, hey, how could she not recognize love's power to transform?

It seems even the brilliant Jane Austen might yet have a thing or two to learn about the strength of passion through the decades . . .

Very well, she says. *You have stated your case effectively and, if you insist on trying this, I suppose I cannot stop you. Mr. Blaine may, with much good luck, turn out somewhat better than I dare hope.*

This, I know, is the closest I'll get to a concession tonight.

Thanks, Jane, I say. I realize, though, that I don't need her approval, much as I wholly respect her advice. I've finally heard the voice of my heart, and it knows when something is right.

Sam pulls me closer, I squeeze him back and we melt together. Our communication right now is silent, too, and effortless.

I appreciate your leap of faith in him, Jane, I tell her before turning my full attention over to Sam for the night. *But I hope you'll stick around and see for yourself.*

She laughs. *Ah, Ellie. You may later regret the invitation, but perhaps I shall. Your challenge gives me reason to stay.*

Please turn the page
for a very special Q&A with
Marilyn Brant.

In which author Marilyn Brant is interviewed by her main character, Ellie Barnett, on the subject of her life as a writer and why, precisely, she wrote this book.

Ellie (smiling, her pen poised studiously for note taking): Hey, there, Marilyn.

Marilyn: Hi, Ellie. How are you doing?

Ellie: Much better *now* than I was in the beginning of the book. Thanks for improving my love life, by the way. There were more than a few times I thought, "You know? This dating thing isn't going too well." So, I appreciate the upbeat, if still somewhat vague, ending.

Marilyn: Glad to hear it. I'm always at your service.

Ellie (clearing her throat): No, not *always*. That whole sex-in-the-closet scene was not good. Not good at *all*. But now isn't a time to nitpick or lament your painfully vivid authorial imagination. I have some questions here your editor wanted me to ask you, like, How did you become a writer? Was this always your hoped-for career path? Stuff like that.

Marilyn: Sure. Novelists often interview their characters, so turnabout is fair play, right? Even if, on some level, we both already know the answers.

Ellie: Stop trying to rationalize this. I asked you a question.

Marilyn: Fine. Yes, being a writer was always something I wanted. I remember announcing that intention in sixth grade, but it wasn't taken seriously by anyone around me and, at the time, I didn't take it all that seriously myself. As a teen, I thought I wanted to be a scientist or, maybe, a detective. I spent a lot of my junior high and high school years observing people and "researching" them. I even went so far as to type out little note cards about guys I was interested in, adding tidbits of information when I discovered a new fact, like his middle name, his favorite food or his professed career goals. I became compulsive about journaling, too, and I'd record snippets of conversations in my nightly entries, along with song lyrics or poems. I listened to music for hours every day and read books the rest of the time. I had kind of an obsessive streak.

Ellie: Yeah, I know. Your brother told me.

Marilyn: Very funny. I happen to have a really great relationship with him, so don't be telling tales.

Ellie: Hey, that's what you did with *my* siblings. You were making up stuff all over the place. I don't know where you came up with those things about Di . . . you don't even *have* a sister.

Marilyn: Right. Because this is FICTION. Not MEMOIR. Big difference.

Ellie (grinning): Good luck convincing people of that. Finish your story.

Marilyn: Well, my ability to fixate eventually took a scientific turn in high school biology when I learned about Mendelian genetics. I thought it was such a cool subject, and I began studying it on my own, which led quite a few people to expect me to go into medicine. It's still a point of mystification and some disappointment to my parents that I didn't.

Ellie: But blood freaks you out, you hate needles and the thought of performing surgery makes you nauseous.

Marilyn: Exactly. I'd have been a dreadful doctor, and you can feel free to remind my family of that anytime. Other people thought I had more of a leaning toward psychology, which, though true, wasn't my college major, either. Instead, I went into elementary education because I thought little kids were funny, enthusiastic, curious and very honest—characteristics I value highly—and I had an idealistic notion that I could help them hang on to those qualities for longer. Later, while I was teaching but after I'd met my wonderful husband, I got a master's degree in educational psychology, focusing on the relationship between "creativity" and "culture."

Ellie (sighing and glancing at her watch): Okay. So *then* you became a writer?

Marilyn: Um, no. Then I became a mom. And because I wanted to stay home with my son, I was determined to find a way I could do that while still making time for creative projects. This was really important to me. I felt a tremendous responsibility to my newborn to not only be a conscientious mom but a *joyful* one. To model for him the act of being fulfilled by life. In the process, I rediscovered my love of writing and wanted to do more of it. But, even though I'd always been a bookworm and had done a great deal of academic writing and some journalistic work, fiction was a different game. I started out by writing parenting essays and educational articles for magazines, branched into poetry and short stories, became a national book reviewer and, at the same time, began the process of learning how to structure and orchestrate the writing of a novel. *According to Jane* was my fifth completed manuscript.

Ellie: Do all of your books involve Jane Austen?

Marilyn: Not directly. Much like your experience, I first read Austen's *Pride and Prejudice* in high school. It immediately became my favorite novel and Jane my favorite novelist. Remember that obsessive streak? Well, I read everything she wrote and delved into her letters and her biographies, too. Her genius in depicting human character quite literally changed my perceptions of the people around me. I wished I could've had her as my guide through the hazards of teen life and beyond. Her influence on my adolescent worldview was profound and, in my opinion, priceless. So, in that way, Jane is a part of everything I write, although this book is the only one I've written so far that features her as an actual character.

Jane (strolling into the room): What a pleasing commentary. I should like to make an appearance in another of your novels sometime. Provided, of course, that it is one of my choosing.

Marilyn: Um, well . . . thanks, Jane. That's thoughtful of you. I'll have to talk to my editor, but we'll see. . . .

Ellie (scribbling a few more notes): Didn't you also formally study Jane's work and her life, you know, when you got older?

Marilyn: No need to emphasize the "when I got older" part quite so maliciously, Ellie. But, yes. I did take a class specifically on Austen. It was a fantastic course, and it happened to be taught at Oxford University. When people hear this, they'll occasionally imply that having studied Jane's work there gives me a sense of authority in discussing her writing that they don't have. The truth, though, is that I'm not a big believer in any academic institution, no matter how prestigious, bestowing legitimacy on scholarship. I really think the quality of education is directly proportional to the effort and depth of thought the student puts into it, not necessarily the building in which the class was held.

Sam (leaning against the doorway, raising an eyebrow): Kind of reverse snobbery, isn't it?

Marilyn: It is not.

Sam: Is too. You're gonna piss off the literary scholars by claiming that just anyone who *reads* a lot of Austen can tap into the small body of knowledge available on her and, if serious about studying her work, can actually *know* her as well as the academically elite claim to.

Marilyn (squinting at him): Who invited you into this converstion? Jane, tell him he's being obnoxious again. Make him leave.

Jane: Indeed, he is behaving as uncivilly as usual, but the man, insufferable as he is, may have a valid argument in his favor.

Sam: What the hell *is* it with you and the insult slinging? For the last time, I'm not *insufferable*. No one uses that term anymore anyway, and—

Ellie: Sam, don't talk to Jane like that! And, Marilyn, I've had a personal relationship with Jane for almost twenty years, and I think that level of intimacy can happen when a writer of her skill and integrity reveals her soul and her truthful observations to the reader. That's probably why millions of people around the globe feel they know her. That she's their "dear Jane"—their friend.

Sam (rolling his eyes): Some friend.

Ellie (pointing with her pen): Leave, Sam. We'll talk later.

Sam (shrugging, turns away): Whatever.

Ellie: Did you really need to make his character so defensive and difficult, Marilyn? I mean, who *is* Sam to you? Some guy from your past you were trying to get even with or something?

Marilyn: Not really. At least not entirely. Sam's character, as well as that of the other men in the book, are composites of lots of guys. Some I met in real life. And some, like Mr. Darcy, I know only from fiction. Plus, there's that whole alchemy thing that happens when writers are making up characters. It may be a cliché, but these characters tend to develop a life of their own. They have specific likes, dislikes, agendas. And sometimes they start talking to you. At really inconvenient times.

Jane (sniffing): That is utter nonsense. I could always keep my characters under control. They said or did nothing without my consent. And certainly nothing unseemly.

Marilyn: Well, Jane, that's because you're The Master. We all want to be like you.

Ellie (nodding): Yeah. You rule.

Jane: Ladies, you know how I distrust flattery and charm. And I do not tolerate such disingenuousness without mockery.

Marilyn: We know. But in this case, we're being honest and sincere. Nothing but the greatest admiration would entice an aspiring novelist to spend four years drafting and revising a story intended to honor another writer's influence. To a very large extent, you're *why* I'm a writer, Jane. This book is to thank you for sharing your astute observations and your extraordinary perceptiveness with me. For enriching my life beyond words on a page. For giving me three-dimensional characters to love for a lifetime. I can't hope to match your contribution to literature, but how else could I express my gratitude except to attempt to inspire and entertain someone else, sometime, somewhere?

Ellie (flipping to a new notebook page): Oooh, Marilyn, that's good. Let me write that down.

Marilyn: Thanks, Ellie. I'd appreciate that. . . .

ACCORDING TO JANE

Marilyn Brant

ABOUT THIS GUIDE

The suggested questions are included to
enhance your group's reading of Marilyn Brant's
According to Jane

DISCUSSION QUESTIONS

1. What are the major themes and turning points in the story? Which turning point in Ellie's thinking do you believe finally sets her on the road to greater self-understanding?

2. How is our vision of the world different as an adolescent than as an adult? Can we sometimes carry our adolescent worldview into adulthood long after we should've left it behind? Or are there some truths and beliefs about other people and/or ourselves that remain consistent through time?

3. Ellie's friendship-turned-relationship with Sam is complicated by their having met in childhood. What adolescent misperceptions about him did she persist in holding on to over the years? What does it take to see our youthful prejudices through more mature eyes?

4. Do you identify or sympathize with Ellie? Do you empathize with her relationships—be they friendships, family interactions, romances?

5. What is Ellie's "friendship" with Jane like? Do you believe a writer's work—particularly that of an author no longer alive—can be a guiding force in a reader's life? That it perhaps can even act as a form of friendship?

6. Are Ellie's romantic relationships different from one another? Or, in essentials, are they each similarly flawed? Explain.

7. Ellie delineates seven "types" of men, and Austen, too, used her characters as representatives of a group (i.e., Darcy representing the rich yet honorable "highly eligible bachelor" who is not above learning a lesson in pride; Wickham being the prototype for a "deceitful charmer" who uses his

looks and social skills for personal gain and self-indulgence; Bingley as the friendly "boy next door" who's not as sophisticated as his role in society sometimes requires, etc.). Can people be so easily categorized? Do you recognize individuals you know in either Ellie's or Jane's categorizations? Or, do you believe human behavior defies fictional stereotyping?

8. What is Di and Ellie's sisterly relationship like? How does it change over the course of the story? Is Angelique a family outsider or a symbolic sibling? What about Gregory? Could any meaningful change have taken place between these characters if the book had a shorter timeline?

9. Ellie is a middle child. Do you think she would have reacted to Sam and/or to men in general differently if she'd been the eldest or the youngest? How has birth order affected you in your relationships? Or do you think it hasn't?

10. This story chronicles Ellie's voyage of sexual discovery as well as her emotional and intellectual growth. Are these journeys interrelated? Do you believe there is any correlation between a woman's level of comfort with her sexuality and the degree of her emotional maturity or the extent of her intellectual prowess?

11. What purpose does the persistent referral to 1980s music play? Do these songs help set a scene both emotionally as well as literally? Are any of the novel's themes underscored by the unstated lyrics of the songs mentioned in the book? Do songs you hear on the radio pull you back to a certain place and time? If so, which ones? Why or why not might they be powerful tools in eliciting memories?

12. For readers familiar with Austen's *Pride and Prejudice*, what are the similarities between the characters and situations in the classic novel and those in *According to Jane*?

13. For readers familiar with Austen's letters and other biographical records, did you notice any parallels between Ellie and the real-life Jane Austen?

14. In Chapter Two, Jane tells Ellie, "You are more imaginative than any of them. Your cousin. Your siblings. Even your schoolmates. They have talents, to be sure, but beyond an intelligent mind there must be a creative spirit. It is not enough to absorb mere facts. True invention is in the application of vision." What do you think Jane means by this? Do you believe what she's saying?

15. What do you think happens to Sam and Ellie after the book ends? Do you think they'll stay together? Do you want them to? Do you believe in soul mates, like Angelique does, or do you believe, like Di, that a lasting relationship is all about hard work and commitment? And, depending on what you think happens next, what do you imagine Jane's comments on the subject would be?